Young Blood

Victoria Gemmell

Rusted Moon Press ☾

First published in 2024 as eBook and Print Edition
Text Copyright © Victoria Gemmell, 2024
https://victoriagemmell.com

Cover design © Victoria Gemmell in collaboration with Rebecca Johnstone, 2024
https://daintydora.co.uk

Cover Photography/Images by Christian Holzinger and Solen Feyissa

Poetry Quotation – *Do Not go Gentle into that Good Night*, Dylan Thomas (1947)
(Chapters 8, 11, 31, 43, 45)

All rights reserved. No part of this publication may be reproduced, stored, or transmitted in any form, or by any means electronic, mechanical or photocopying, recording or otherwise, without prior permission of the copyright owner.

Young Blood is a work of fiction. Names, characters, places and incidents are the product of the author's imagination or used fictitiously. Any resemblance to actual events, locales, or persons, living or dead, is purely co-incidental.

For two strong and special women in my family –
my late Nana Maisie (Mary) and my Aunt Irene

YOUNG BLOOD

PROLOGUE

The chorus of Happy Birthday was flat, in minor key, adding to Seb's discomfort that something was off. He watched intently as Margaret entered the hall, carrying an elaborate frosted cake towards Davey, eighteen candles dancing, flames illuminating her smile as she laid it down on the table.

There was a hush of expectation as Davey sat forward. He raised his head to survey the room, as if memorising their faces, already saying his goodbyes. Seb caught his eye and attempted a smile, but it didn't quite reach his lips.

"Make a wish." Dr Carmichael raised a glass in a toast, his sentiment void of any joy.

The liquid in the glass was blood red and Seb wasn't convinced it was wine. His arms prickled at the thought, fingers instinctively tracing the dots decorating his skin, which marked him as theirs.

Davey hesitated, before extinguishing the candles in one puff, his profile swallowed by shadows. If Seb was in Davey's seat he would wish to never return, to have the best life possible, far, far away from here. A carousel of emotions spun in Seb's gut as everyone cheered. They rushed to hug Davey, speculating about the life that awaited him, back outside in the real world.

Seb was happy for him of course and could almost taste the excitement radiating from Davey's every pore. But Seb couldn't dull the envy and sadness that washed over him in stronger waves. He was losing his one true friend in here and knew he might never see Davey again. It was six months before Seb turned eighteen, and a lot could happen in six months, no matter how many times Davey promised to get a place for them both, have a room waiting for him.

I'll break you out next week if you want, Davey said more than once. But they both knew the breakout option jeopardised their future security. *Better to wait*, Seb cautioned, caring more about mucking up Davey's new life than his own.

There was another bad feeling, deep down in Seb's core, which caused his leg to jangle, and his gaze to dart between Dr and Mrs Carmichael and the other staff, searching for clues. He was unable to shake the sensation that there was a silent communication going on tonight every time a subtle glance exchanged between them. Margaret kept wringing her hands, a sure sign of nerves. Perhaps she was just anxious about the cake, always keen for them to enjoy her food. Dr Carmichael placed what appeared to be a reassuring hand on Margaret's shoulder, inviting her to sit with him, filling her glass to the brim with the red liquid. He then stood, stretching across Davey's shoulder, picking up his empty glass and re-filling. Seb wasn't close enough to hear what was said but Davey grinned and clinked Dr Carmichael's glass, as an envelope was placed in his hand.

Twenty thousand pounds. That was the promise. One thousand in cash tonight, in stacks of notes. Then the rest deposited into a bank account set up online by the Carmichaels. Seb suspected Dr Carmichael liked to remind them of his wealth which was why he wanted to present some of the cash in person.

Tonight was all about the show. The music, the

candles illuminating the grand ballroom that they never had access to at any other time of the year. The costumes. A smile tugged at Seb's lips as he watched Phoenix twirl in her orange silk ball gown, faster and faster like a fire ball, the tattooed wings on her back dusted in glitter, her shoulder blades sparkling under the lights as she turned. Aidan bowed before her, begging her to dance. The room was alight with laughter and light. And yet none of it felt real, none of it felt like freedom. Seb loosened the top buttons of his shirt, the heat from the open fire beside the dining table adding to the sensation of being stifled.

"Have some beer, Seb." Barbara Carmichael appeared at his side, her tone more of an order than an offer.

Seb took the bottle, nodding a thanks. Alcohol was usually forbidden and he was grateful for the relaxation of this particular rule tonight.

"You'll miss your friend." Barbara nodded towards Davey.

Seb shrugged. He had learned never to give much away, always keeping his emotions in check. He knew this frustrated the Carmichaels, which encouraged him to be aloof often.

"He's going to a better place." She rested a hand on his shoulder, her fingers curling tight so that he could feel the prick of her fingernails through the thin material of his shirt. "It won't be long before you get to join him."

The bad feeling sang louder in his gut. There was a hardness to her tone that was matched by the darkness in her eyes when he looked up at her. He was relieved when Mrs Carmichael didn't linger, choosing instead to return to her usual place, by Dr Carmichael's side.

Seb watched as Davey ran a hand over the envelope, as if he was picturing how to spend his freedom. Mrs Carmichael was right of course; it wouldn't be long until Seb received his own golden ticket out of here. In the large scheme of the past year and a half, six months was nothing really. He took a long swig of beer, enjoying the warm, malty taste and tried to relax as the music and voices swirled around him.

*

As midnight struck, a red balloon tied around a pillar on the porch danced in the wind, straining to be freed. The front of the house was in darkness, silent, all echoes of happy birthday fading into deep sleeps, the kind of sleeps which had no dreams.

On first arrival to the house many believed their dreams had come true. The floorboards smelled of polish, winding along corridors furnished with beauty and wealth. Cleanliness and comfort were found around every corner, cushioned cubby holes, a den with entertainment stations, a kitchen bursting with delicious food. But nothing this good was without a price. The doors always came with keys which only the truly powerful were able to unlock.

At the very back of the house, deep in the bowels below the kitchen, a light was burning bright. A fire raged and someone kept guard, his hand steady as he sipped a mug of coffee, a smile playing on his lips. He was hesitant to let sleep claim him in case the cry of death crept into his nightmares, calling him by name.

Chapter One
Ana

School had only been back four weeks and already the dread of Monday felt like an old friend, sitting on Ana's shoulders throughout Sunday afternoon, dulling the fun of Sunday evening family film time. As she sat watching the newest Disney Animation Ana was acutely aware this was not how most sixteen-year-olds would choose to spend a substantial chunk of their weekend, but the comfort of the four of them huddled together in front of the TV, a bowl of warm popcorn balanced on her knee never failed to take the edge off the dread.

As the end credits rolled, her little sister Maisie made a face, knowing what was coming next. Ana ruffled her hair, saying goodnight, watching as dad dragged her away. Ana picked up the remote and Mum moved seating positions, wrapping her blanket around their knees. This was the best part of Sunday night family time. When dad disappeared to his play station room after Maisie settled in bed, and Ana and Mum got to watch some decent shows together.

"Gilmore Girls or Buffy?" Mum asked.

"Buffy," Ana responded, knowing this would be the preference as Mum seemed to have a newfound appreciation for Giles. Ana also secretly enjoyed listening to her reminisce about her student days, when she worked in a bar which hosted bands apparently similar to the Bronze line-ups.

The opening for the next episode was a Bronze scene, prompting Mum to jump out of her seat. "You know the old bar I always talk about still exists. We should add that to your eighteenth birthday tour list." She pulled out her notebook from the clutter under the table and Ana marvelled at the fact it was already half-full with plans, even if most of them seemed to be Mum attempting to re-live her youth.

"Remember to add in the Barcelona trip," Ana said.

Mum looked thoughtful. "Actually we should do that trip earlier. That could be a passing this year's Highers celebration."

Ana made a face. "Let's not get ahead of ourselves." The thought of having to navigate big exams along with social dramas wasn't appealing. Ana shrugged off the Sunday dread threatening to dampen the rest of the evening and allowed herself to get lost in a world of vampires and questionable nineties fashion.

By the time Ana's alarm shrieked in her ear on Monday morning she was a sluggish ball of misery. She turned to hit snooze, snuggling back under the warmth of her quilt, when she was suddenly aware of a weight at the end of the bed. Ana opened her eyes and blinked at her mum, preparing to explain she was about to get up, that it wasn't late.

"I need to ask a favour this morning," Mum talked first.

"Hmm?" Ana sat up, rubbing at her eyes.

Mum opened her mouth, then shut it again, head cocking to one side, frown lines deepening. "Did we stay up too late last night, Ana? You look so tired." She scooted closer down the bed, brushing Ana's fringe back from her eyes. Ana shrugged her off, muttering it was seven thirty, who looks awake at seven thirty?

"What's the favour?" Ana asked through a yawn, kicking off the quilt.

"I need you to walk Maisie to school. Your Dad and I have…early meetings today. I should have said last night."

Ana shrugged. "Okay. It's on my way anyway."

"Thanks, sweetheart." Mum smiled, ruffling her hair. She started to get up, then hesitated and looked at Ana with questioning eyes. "You still missing Josie?"

Ana shook her head, trying to indicate it wasn't a big deal. But it really was. She'd tried to integrate herself more into other social groups now Josie had moved away but it was so hard to feign interest in the reality TV shows she never watched, the weekend outings she wasn't a part of, and the underlying competition of who had the most interesting social media posts that day, that minute, that second.

"You just need to find your tribe." Mum smiled that knowing smile she usually hated, as it had glimmers of a superior knowledge that Ana was desperate to grasp, but knew she'd probably have many years of mistakes to entail before she was granted the wisdom.

"What does that mean exactly?" Ana grabbed around for her glasses, trying to remember where she'd left them last night before bed.

"It means there are people out there who speak your language, just waiting to have excellent conversations with you." Mum winked and exited her room, leaving Ana to hunt out her school uniform.

Ana frowned at her face in the mirror, dusting powder over the spots on her chin, trying to make them disappear. As soon as she got happy with any part of her body something new and ugly popped up.

Like spots. Or cellulite. Or weird frizzy hair that was shorter than the rest of her poker straight hair. She tugged at a strand, flattening it against her fringe. Something she *was* happy with was the bubble gum pink dye she'd washed in over the summer. It brought out the pale grey of her eyes. A little curve of blue eyeliner added the finishing effect. She started to tie her hair up in a messy ponytail just as her bedroom door slammed open, nearly knocking all the books off the top shelf of her cabinet.

"Maisie!" Ana glared at her little sister through the mirror and Maisie stood, hands on hips, looking her up and down.

"Your hair still looks dumb. I liked it brown. Like mine." Maisie sat on the bed, swinging her legs, gazing at her shoes, then at her reflection in the mirror, a satisfied little smile on her face. She was in love with her red shoes. Ana could tell she thought she looked wonderful this morning.

"You all ready for school? I'm taking you today."

Maisie nodded, buttoning up her green coat, her little face squashed in determination. Ana couldn't help but smile, feeling a tug of affection melt her heart. She often forgot Maisie was only six because she talked to them all like she was seventy. Ana sometimes wondered if that was because she was nine when Maisie was born, and desperate for them to be best friends; she talked to her like a contemporary from day one, always keeping her ahead of her years.

Ana grabbed her blue velvet coat, winding a scarf round her neck, already feeling September's wind carrying away the heat from their late summer. She shouted goodbye to Mum and Dad on their way down the stairs and turned to see the kitchen door shut, wondering why they'd not left yet if their meetings were so early.

Outside she watched as Maisie skipped down the path, waving her hands around like she was on Broadway. Ana didn't remember ever having that much energy, even when she was six. She peered in her bag, checking she had everything; phone, books, purse. As they walked along the road to Maisie's school she glanced at the other houses, stealing glimpses in to strangers' mornings. She knew some of the neighbours but not many. An old man in a dressing gown stooped down to pick up a newspaper from his porch and smiled and waved as they walked by.

"Good morning!" Maisie shouted.

"Good morning, young lady." The man's face lit up and Maisie giggled as he saluted her.

"I wonder what he eats for breakfast? Toast and marmalade I bet. Or maybe porridge." Maisie stopped dead, slapping a hand to her forehead. "Oh, no."

"What is it?" Ana looked up the street, thinking she'd seen something.

"I left my lunch box in the hall."

"Maisie," Ana chided, elongating her name in a sigh. She glanced back at the long road they'd just walked. "Can you not have the canteen lunch today?"

Maisie made a face. "It's fish on Monday and they always make it too mushy. Mum cut up my sandwiches into stars and everything. I can run back. It'll just take a minute."

"No, I'll go. Wait here. Don't move." Ana walked Maisie back a few steps, positioning her directly outside the old man's house. Knowing he'd just be a few feet away made her feel better about abandoning her sister on the street for a few minutes. Ana ran, not wanting to be late for first period. She hated having a whole class of eyes on her. She'd spent a lot of time mastering the art of disappearing into insignificance, which made people who knew Ana well, like her mum, puzzle over her decision to dye her hair such an eye-catching colour. She hadn't wanted attention; just a change, to escape her boring self, hoping it would encourage a different Ana to emerge this year.

By the time Ana clambered up the stairs and unlocked the front door her scarf was making her sweat. She pulled it off, flinging it across the banister as she grabbed Maisie's lunchbox, which was hiding under the hall table. She paused, hearing dishes clatter in the kitchen. She looked at her watch. Eight thirty. Why were Mum and Dad still at home?

She crept along the hall, feeling like a burglar in her own house as she pushed the door open a crack to hear what they were saying.

"I just can't believe I'm going back to the same clinic. It feels surreal, and like a cruel joke."

Ana's chest constricted at the tension in Mum's voice. She held her breath, waiting for dad's response.

"I know, darling. But let's not get stressed. The doctor explained it was to allow more time for them to test properly. I got the impression they wouldn't even have referred you at this stage if it wasn't for your mum."

Mum's mum? *Grandma. Clinic.* Ana backed away from the door. Her brain buzzed as she thought back through the past weeks. Mum had seemed a bit more distracted lately and she forgot to wash Maisie's gym clothes, and sent Aunt Bessie a late birthday card. But Mum had always been a bit flaky. She clutched Maisie's lunchbox tighter. Just like Maisie. They were forgetful and flighty. That was all.

Ana's head was still whirring with unwelcome thoughts as she wandered back out into the street, images of Grandma's deterioration during her last months filling her head. She squeezed her eyes shut, trying to erase them. When she opened her eyes she saw Maisie teetering along the kerb up ahead, following a small ginger tabby, trying to stroke its tail. Ana shook her head, hurrying towards her.

Maisie's name formed too late on her lips as she watched her step with the cat, out into the road. A screech of brakes and loud meow caused Maisie to jump back, her coat and shoes sprayed with mud. Ana grabbed her close, shaking, angry and terrified. She could feel Maisie's heart clamouring against hers. Maisie blinked, her blue eyes saucers of fear. Then she pushed at Ana's chest, trying to crane her head, back to the road. "Little kittie. Where are you?"

Ana kept a tight grip on her, stomach clenching as the grey car which nearly made contact rolled back towards them. The windows were blacked out, making her wonder if it was some celebrity on their way to the airport. Wouldn't that be a hilarious start to Monday? Maisie nearly flattened by Taylor Swift. Ana shivered as a window rolled down.

The driver, an immaculately dressed man, observed Ana with cool, slate eyes. His grey hair was moulded into a neat style, grey beard trimmed close to his face, his moustache curling slightly at the corners, giving him an eccentric edge.

"The girl, is she harmed?" He craned his head towards Maisie, who was now laughing and waving at the cat across the road, delighted the moggy survived.

Ana squeezed Maisie's hand tighter. "My sister's fine." She glanced at the woman in the passenger seat, grey hair wound into a glamorous bun, eyebrows in severe dark lines which were a stark contrast to her pale, powdered face. She was talking into a phone, her voice clipped and well spoken. Her accent wasn't as broad as theirs, it sounded a bit like Aunt Bessie's, 'posh Edinburgh', Dad called it.

The man's mouth set in a grim line. "Keep a tighter hold of her hand next time. Only cats have nine lives."

Ana nodded quickly, wanting to thank him, but there was something so intimidating about his stare that the words were lost in her throat.

"Yes, yes that's right," the woman's voice was becoming more animated. "Barbara Carmichael. Do you need me to spell that for you?"

Ana's attention snapped back to her face. That name… Carmichael. She frowned at the woman's coiffed hair, perfect make-up, silk jacket. It couldn't be. Ana looked back at the man. An unease washed over his face as he clocked her recognition. *Dr Carmichael*. Married to 'Batty Barb.' They used to live at the other side of Oakridge, the posh side. They had often seen Dr Carmichael running along their street late at night, frantically searching for Barb, who liked to go for a wander in her dressing gown and slippers. Dad once found her in the driveway going through their recycling bin, looking for 'her magazine'. They moved away a few years ago. Ana always presumed Barb had gone to a home, or worse, died. That surely couldn't be Barb sitting beside him?

Without warning the window slid up, leaving Ana gawking at her own reflection in the tinted glass. The car rolled in to gear, speeding off down the street. Ana stared after it, only half-aware of Maisie tugging at her hand.

"Come on, Ana. We are *so* late now."

Ana raised an eyebrow, peering down at her sister who had the audacity to scowl at her. Maisie grabbed her lunchbox and marched on ahead.

"You're welcome." Ana called after her, rolling her eyes. As they turned the corner to her primary school Maisie stepped back in line with Ana, tugging at her coat. Ana looked up from her phone, following Maisie's gaze.

Ana's heart jumped as she clocked Elliot Sanders, camera slung round his neck, reaching up to pin a poster on a lamppost.

"What's he doing?" Maisie hissed.

"I have no idea." Ana shook her head, taking in Elliot's dark floppy hair which already had streaks of grey forming if you looked closely. He got ribbed mercilessly for it in school. She thought it was kind of cool. It suited his look, long grey coat and scuffed black boots. Elliot was even quieter than Ana so the last time they'd had an actual conversation was back in second year, when they were thirteen and only on the cusp of self-conscious awkwardness. The fact he carried around a camera, snapping random pictures, was another target for the wise-cracking comedians in their year, but it was another thing Ana also found intriguing.

"Hi," Maisie shouted up at him on their way past and Elliot blinked in surprise, meeting Ana's gaze. She grinned, feeling her face heat up, pulling Maisie on before he had a chance to retort.

By the time Ana had walked Maisie to the playground and cleaned off the mud from her shoes with a crumpled bag of baby wipes she found in the bottom of her bag, it was well after nine. She was disappointed to see Elliot had already disappeared when she turned the corner. She hesitated at the lamppost, taking in the grainy photograph of a broody looking boy, the words MISSING printed in big black letters above his head. Seb Masterson. Last seen February 2018. Wearing black jeans, black jacket. If you have seen Seb please call or text Elliot. Ana whispered his number aloud, trying to memorise the digits. Not that she would ever phone him.

She studied Seb's face. She realised she'd seen this poster before, but it hadn't stayed up long last time, and she hadn't made the connection the Elliot listed was her classmate. Who was Seb? And why was Elliot posting pictures of him around the village? Over a year was a long time to be searching for someone. Ana shivered, tightening her scarf around her neck, feeling weary before Monday had even really begun.

Chapter Two
Hope

I closed the door to the attic bedroom I'd allowed myself to fall in love with. Listening to the sound of the sea every night, the waves lulling me to sleep was like a soft kiss goodnight, a reminder of a life I'd once known. Lucy and Andy, my foster carers, had been the most consistent people in my life since Mum died and the thought of leaving my sanctuary was like losing her all over again. Tears burned as I realised it was actually happening. Transfer day had arrived and it was time to leave.

I called my social worker, Ruth, a wave of emotion tumbling down the stairs with me. "I need you to come and pick me up early."

Andy had driven Lucy to the station last night and I couldn't handle being there another minute. Andy's stilted conversation was a reminder that I had become an inconvenience he wanted removed.

Ruth hesitated. "The Browns aren't expecting us for another couple of hours."

The ball of anxiety wound tighter in my chest. "Then take me out for breakfast. Please." I held my breath, hoping she would understand my desperation. Ruth relented and told me she was on her way.

Lucy's warmth and laughter still permeated every corner of the house and I pulled doors shut on my way past, not wanting any last glimpses of the life I'd let myself believe could be mine, hoping a long-term placement would mean forever. Andy was in the kitchen, unloading the dishwasher, the smell of toast wafting under the door. I rolled my case along the hall, glancing at the bubble wrapped paintings Lucy had carefully picked out for me. A spark of anger fizzed through me and I kicked one over. Lucy didn't want me and I didn't want her stupid art work.

Ruth's Mini spluttered up the drive and I slipped out the front door without saying goodbye to Andy.

I tried to erase the house from my memories as I hurried down the drive, stamping away images of the first day I arrived; the beautiful couple smiling in the doorway of their beautiful house.

When Lucy's mum got sick she dropped everything. Her job, her Pilates classes, *me*. Ruth tried to explain things like that happened sometimes. Lucy had to leave to care for her mum down in England and it could be months before she'd be home. Andy worked away a lot and when he was off shift, wanted to go down to help. They decided it was best I move on to another family. After a year and four months of allowing myself to trust and be loved by strangers it was a cruel reminder that I was not truly family, and that the word 'fostered' was synonymous with temporary.

"You okay, kid?" Ruth cranked open the passenger door, offering me a smile. Her sympathetic face made me want to cry.

I shrugged, shoving my case in the back. I was relieved when she turned up the radio, understanding I didn't want to talk.

We stopped at a quiet café and Ruth bought me orange juice and a muffin, steering the conversation onto the Browns; my new foster carers. My body relaxed at the realisation I'd be alone again, the only foster kid. I'd been dreading a similar experience to my first placement with the O'Brians.

Ruth paused when her phone rang. A look of surprise flashed across her face, then she shot me a knowing look. "Uh, sorry, Andy. She is with me." Ruth got up and wandered across the café, no doubt apologising for my rudeness. Goodbyes had the potential to unfurl too many emotions, like fear. Fear was a close acquaintance during most of my first placement.

Joe and Patty O'Brian already had a full house when I arrived, three children all under the age of twelve; one biological, and two other fostered. I had to share a room with their eleven-year-old daughter, Dana, who announced she hated me and threw my clothes out the window when I dared to claim some drawer space. She frequently slapped me awake at night, complaining I snored. I became an expert at surviving on three hours sleep.

The O'Brians displayed their 'love' through passive aggressive comments and barking orders. The kids were loud balls of energy, constantly wrecking my belongings and my nerves. Patty peered at me through a mist of cigarette smoke, leaving a trail of ash across the kitchen counters as she muttered about us kids eating her out of house and home. I ran away four times before social work placed me with Lucy and Andy.

Ruth returned to the table, not fishing for any answers. She slid another muffin my way. Chocolate chip. "We'll leave in ten minutes."

I took my time finishing breakfast. I wanted to tell her I wasn't sure I could handle starting again.

*

"We're here." Ruth nodded in the direction of my new home. I followed her gaze, noting the white rough-cast walls and cheap looking windows with frilly net curtains. Ruth pulled the handbrake on. "Now remember I told you that they're a bit older than Andy and Lucy, and quite old fashioned. They're decent people though. It will give you a quiet space to study. Just like you wanted."

I nodded. My plan was to get as many good grades as possible and then leave school, get a job, maybe an apprenticeship. Bye-bye foster families. I was turning sixteen soon and Ruth explained if I hadn't already been in the foster system I would have been taken to live in independent accommodation, and put on the housing list for my own place. I shivered. I wasn't quite ready for that yet. That would be too much quiet, alone space. I wanted the safety net of 'family' for a little bit longer, even if the term was totally illusory.

Ruth tapped the steering wheel, either coffee jitters or nicotine withdrawal. I spotted a cigarette pack peeking out from her handbag.

"Fall off the wagon again?" She followed my gaze and quickly zipped her bag shut.

"Can I have one before I go in?" I licked my lips, hands starting to sweat at the prospect of having to make small talk, getting to know new people, a new house.

"Hope." She raised an eyebrow but I could already see her relenting. "It's wrong, you know. I'm your social worker. I shouldn't be encouraging you."

"Just this once. It calms me down." It made me feel connected to Mum, who used to smoke when she thought I was asleep upstairs, the waft of nicotine revealing grown-up secrets I longed to be part of. I wanted to add that in some weird way smoking also made me feel connected to Ruth too. If I hadn't gone through a phase of shoplifting cigarettes on a weekly basis, I probably wouldn't even have a social worker. And Ruth kept me sane, even if she was a bit mental. There was a fire in her that reminded me of Mum and helped me stay strong.

She was already lighting them up before I finished my woeful plea and we sat inhaling the toxins through squinted eyes.

"You know you're going to be okay." She said it with such conviction I almost believed her. "You're one of the smartest kids I know. Use that to your advantage, okay? Keep your head down, work hard, and be nice to the Browns."

Our eyes met briefly and I puffed harder on my cigarette, scared I would cry. I often wondered where Ruth lived, what her house was like. I knew she had a cat, Sookie, and that she didn't have any children and that she wasn't very good at looking after plants or relationships, though I suspected she had a new girlfriend. She was smiling more than usual and she had new caramel highlights in her hair.

I resisted the urge to beg her to take me home with her and opened the car door, *breathing in, breathing out, breathing in.*

Entering the Browns was like stepping inside a sepia photograph; it was a landscape of beige and mauve, matching their name perfectly. The house was filled with a weird mish-mash of furniture that looked like it was from the nineteen fifties; oak bureaus and Formica tables, with electric blankets hiding under mattresses. It lacked the beauty and warmth of Lucy and Andy's, but it was safe and quiet. The air smelled faintly of cabbage and old man's cologne; nowhere ever smelled like home.

Martha gave me a tour, her manner formal, like I was a new employee she was welcoming to shared quarters. Edward smiled a quiet hello, wire glasses perched on his nose as he laid down his crossword on a footstool. He wore mauve chinos and a mustard V-neck, his grey hair thinning at the crown. Martha wore a grey smock dress, her brown hair tied in a tight bun, white streaks creating an effect like marbled cake. I couldn't quite figure out how old they were. Younger than their decoration suggested I guessed.

"I'll leave you to get yourself settled." Martha hovered at my bedroom door as I rolled my case along the brown carpet. I looked around the bare magnolia walls, took in the oak brown dresser in the corner beside a desk, a single bed with white starch quilt, chest of drawers and stand-alone wardrobe. The complete opposite to the modern furnishing and trinkets at Lucy and Andy's. "I've made some soup for lunch. I'll serve it up in an hour."

I tried to find a smile, then collapsed on the bed as soon as she shut the door.

I closed my eyes, reminding myself of Ruth's parting words: "Stick in here, kid. They'll be good to you."

I was done running. Even without Ruth's affirmation, I could tell the Browns were decent people underneath all the formality. I was happy to blend in to their beige life, to study hard and keep my focus on working towards some sort of secure future.

After lunch I escaped upstairs, using the excuse of wanting to get unpacked and ready for my first day at school tomorrow. I switched my phone on and it beeped a symphony of messages. Friends from my old school who I knew would soon forget my name.

A message from Kelly: ***Have you deleted your accounts? Or blocked us?***

I started to delete another message which popped up:

??? Where are you?

"I don't know," I whispered to my reflection in the mirror.

I glanced at the photo of Mum I'd pinned above the dresser, trying to remember her voice. Sometimes during quiet moments it was as if I could really feel her presence and it calmed me. Her photo smiled down at me, reassuring me I could do this.

I unzipped the top of my case and pulled out my familiar red velvet pouch, silver stars catching the light as I untied the string and slid out my deck of tarot cards.

Fanning out the deck across the dresser, I paused, breathing in and out, clearing my mind. Running fingers gently across the pack, focusing. My eyes scanned the rows of identical backs to the cards, the ruby red jewel in the centre of blazing suns burning bright. Mum told me Gran had been drawn to the light and colour in this deck of cards. I was too, and I knew she would be pleased I'd kept them in our line, now claiming them as my own.

I wasn't in the mood to do a full spread so I turned over the one I was most drawn to. A reassuring warmth flowed through my body as I was greeted with the familiar image of a lion with magnificent orange mane, a goddess with flowing fair hair gripping the chain wound around his neck. *Strength: You have more strength, power, and courage than you know.* I felt the tight knot of anger I'd been carrying around the past few weeks start to unravel as I remembered Mum's instruction, any time she drew this card for me, tugging on my hair which matched the fire of the lion's mane.

You are the lion AND the goddess. You remember that.

I tucked the card into my schoolbooks for a good luck charm.

Tomorrow I was going to try to be both.

Chapter Three
Ana

First period had already started by the time Ana arrived at school. Her embarrassment at walking into a silent room, with eyes staring, quickly faded when she realised full attention was on a girl she'd never seen before, standing at Mr Darwin's desk. Her mind drifted back to last week when her pastoral care teacher stopped her in the corridor. She'd been rushing to her next class and had only been half-listening. Something about a new girl starting, that she had taken a lot of the same subjects as Ana and would she look after her?

Ana took a seat at her desk and tried not to stare. The girl's hair was the most amazing wild waves of orange, red and brown, like a bonfire. Her skin startlingly pale, accentuated by burgundy lipstick and dark eyeliner. As the girl tapped a pen impatiently on the desk Ana noticed her chipped nail varnish and assortment of rings which twisted around her thumb and fingers, silver vines and emerald jewels winking under the light. She looked like a goth punk goddess. Ana immediately wanted them to be friends.

"Okay, Hope. Why don't you take a seat with Jenna and her friends?" Mr Darwin gestured towards the back of the room as Jenna pulled a chair out.

Hope frowned at the crowded table, not returning Jenna's enthusiastic smile. She looked down at her timetable, then directed her question to Mr Darwin. "Miss Clark told me I was assigned a buddy, Ana? Is she in this class?"

Ana's heart leapt. "Hi, that's me." She gave a little wave and her face flamed as everyone turned to look at her.

Hope shot Ana a small smile and Ana felt a charge of excitement. This could be a chance to make a proper friend again.

As Ana cleared a space, she noticed the empty desk parallel to them. Elliot hadn't made it in yet. She wondered again what was so important about the missing boy in his posters. She tried to think of any conversations she'd had with him over the past couple of years that would give her a clue, but realised they'd spoken so little she knew practically nothing about him. As Ana glanced around the classroom she realised she didn't know much about anyone these days, even although she'd been in classes with most of them since primary school.

As Hope slid into the seat beside her, Ana tried to see her classmates through Hope's eyes. What would she make of Jenna and friends, hair straightened and styled identically, flawless make-up and fake tans? Jenna used to be smart, probably still was, but for some reason liked to make herself appear clueless in class. Then there was her boyfriend, Gordon, and his group of friends who laughed and made farting noises, talking over each other and everyone else in class, always looking for attention.

Gordon was openly staring at Hope but she didn't appear to notice, pre-occupied with scribbling notes in her book, skimming through the exercise Mr Darwin had set. Jenna did notice. Ana could already see the cogs turning in Jenna's head: should she befriend Hope and try to power up with the pretty new girl, or would she attempt to ostracise her, take her down? It was exhausting even attempting to figure out the logic of the power dynamics in her circle.

The door creaked open and Ana's stomach gave an involuntary flip as Elliot blustered in, camera still strung around his neck. Mr Darwin raised an eyebrow. "Thanks for joining us today, Mr Sanders."

Elliot nodded his head in a greeting, or maybe an apology. As he walked to his desk he tripped over an undone shoe lace, eliciting a cascade of guffaws from Gordon's gang and giggles from some of the girls. Ana's heart clenched as he slid in to his seat, hair falling forward to hide most of his face.

"Who's he?" Hope tilted her head in his direction.

"Elliot Sanders." If it had been anyone else Ana would just have given their first name. For some reason she always liked to say Elliot's full name. Like he was worthy of that important introduction.

"What's with the camera? Is he a photographer or something?" Hope chewed on her pen as she watched him flick through his screen.

Ana shrugged. "Not like a professional. I guess he just likes taking pictures."

"It's cool. I like classic cameras. Much better than crappy phones."

"Yeah." Ana nodded in agreement. She had a hundred questions darting around her head that she wanted to ask, but was conscious of not acting too weird, or coming across too desperate to make friends, in case she scared Hope off. "Where did you move from?"

A sadness flashed in Hope's eyes, which she was quick to blink away. "A seaside town near here. I'm fostered, so I'm with a new family now, the Browns."

"Oh." This stumped Ana.

She didn't fully understand what fostered meant,

and didn't want to sound stupid or nosy by asking Hope to clarify. She was sure it was something like being adopted, but couldn't be certain. She wondered what happened to her parents. As Ana got her books and pen out of her bag she was conscious that Hope was watching her.

"I like your hair. It's cool."

Ana blushed, the compliment softening the memory of 'Marshmallow' being fired at her everywhere she walked the first week back at school.

"Thanks. I like your hair too." Ana grinned.

They sat through the rest of the class in companionable silence and it felt nice, like how things used to be with Josie. Ana was pleased to discover they were in all of the same classes up to lunch.

"So what veggie stuff is good here?" Hope screwed up her nose as they edged towards the front of the canteen queue.

Ana eyed up what looked like fish pie, cottage pie and chips. "The chips are okay. And the salad. Oh, and I think that sludge over there might be macaroni cheese?"

"Mac n cheese it is." Hope shrugged. "Beats the stuff Mrs Brown has been serving me up at home. She's a big fan of traditional roasts."

"What are your foster carers like?" Ana asked as they navigated the crowds towards the tables.

"They're okay. If they were a colour it would be brown, so their name is really fitting. They're both kind of old fashioned. Mrs B knits and bakes and Mr B tinkers around in his garage. I'm happy to have somewhere quiet to stay."

Her comment made Ana wonder again why she wasn't with family. She was on the verge of asking, when a manicured hand reached out and grabbed Hope's wrist, nearly knocking Ana's tray over. Jenna grinned up at Hope.

"Hiya. Come and sit with us." Jenna nodded to the empty chair across from her, the table crowded with her friends. Ana gripped her tray tighter, watching for Hope's reaction. There were no other seats at the table.

Hope frowned. "There's only one seat left. I'm having lunch with Ana."

Jenna's smile faltered and she blinked, as if pretending to see Ana for the first time. "Ana usually prefers to sit alone to read. But you can bring a chair over to the end of the table if you want to join us today, Ana?"

Ana's face burned. Jenna made her sound like an anti-social leper. Which in a lot of ways was true but she didn't want Hope to think she was a loser.

Hope shook her head. "A chair won't fit there. Come on, Ana." Hope didn't wait for a response, just turned and walked off. Ana followed gladly, beaming inside.

Hope glanced around the canteen looking for another space, and her face lit up in recognition. Ana followed her towards Elliot, heart hammering at the thought of approaching him. He was hunched over a plate piled with chips and baked beans, reading a comic, oblivious to his surroundings.

"Let's sit with Elliot."

Elliot looked as alarmed as Ana at Hope's choice of seat. Hope plonked her tray down beside him and his eyes were questioning as Ana sank into the chair across the table.

"Hi, I'm Hope."

Hope shook his hand and his arm flopped around

like a rag doll, brain slow to process her presence.

Elliot locked eyes with Ana and for one horrible second she wondered if she should also introduce herself, in case he'd forgotten her name.

"I saw you this morning, with your sister." Elliot pushed the hair back from his face and sat forward. Ana realised his eyes were a deep blue. She always thought they were brown. He had a dusting of freckles across his nose which made him look a bit younger than he was. His skin was ridiculously flawless for a boy, which seemed unfair when she was painfully aware of the cluster of spots trailing along her jaw down to her chin.

"I saw you too." As she heard the words spoken out loud her toes curled. What a stupid, lame response. "I mean I saw you hanging that missing poster," she mumbled, fumbling with the straw attached to her carton of juice.

Hope eyed him curiously. "Who's missing? Your cat?"

Elliot shifted uncomfortably. Ana chewed on her lip, wondering if she shouldn't have mentioned it.

"My foster brother, Seb. He left our house one day and never came back. We never heard from him again, apart from one text message telling us not to worry."

Ana's head spun. She thought back to parties she went to at Elliot's house when they were in primary school. She remembered seeing his older brother. But his name wasn't Seb. "I thought your brother was called Ben?"

The frown lines on Elliot's forehead deepened. "Ben left home a while ago for Uni. Seb was my…"

"Foster brother," Hope interrupted. "How long was he with you?"

"About a year. Then boom, gone." Elliot shook his head. "Mum and Dad were convinced he decided to set out on his own. He was sixteen when he left so no one bothered to ask many questions, but it didn't seem right. We'd been making plans to go camping up north, had mapped out our journey," Elliot's voice trailed off and he looked down at his hands, his body visibly deflating at the thought he had got it wrong.

Hope stabbed a fork into her macaroni cheese, her voice tight, "I ran away from my first foster family."

Elliot blinked in surprise. He didn't ask any questions, just waited for her to continue. Ana listened with interest too, hoping she might explain more.

"The family, the O'Brians, were my first foster placement after…Mum died. I found it really hard being part of a big family I didn't know, with loud kids. I ran away a few times."

Ana wondered why no one else in her own family took her in. Maybe she didn't have any?

"But you came back each time?" Elliot said.

Hope shrugged. "I didn't have anywhere else to go. I had just turned thirteen." Her voice wavered. Ana held her breath, wondering if she might cry. Then Hope shook her head, like she was shaking away her sadness, face hardening. "I hated that place so much. It never felt like home."

Elliot was quiet, like he was processing her words. "I'm sorry you weren't happy with your foster family but Seb was. He told me he'd never felt more settled and was looking forward to getting on with his life. It didn't make sense."

Hope looked like she might ask more but then simply said, "It's decent you're putting up posters for him. I hope you find him soon."

Ana thought back to the *missing* date and Elliot sighed.

"It's been over a year," he said. "And the posters never stay up long. I'm not sure if it's a council street cleaner or whoever taking them down, I dunno." He hesitated, then pulled out a black leather notebook from his bag and Ana waited expectantly as he flicked through the pages. "I think there might be other kids who went missing."

Elliot ran his finger across the page. "Last year, Ana, do you remember that girl, Mandy, who always got into trouble in pretty much every class for being disruptive?"

Ana tried to remember, realising Josie and her tended to cut themselves off from everyone.

"She was paired with me in Chemistry." Elliot made a face which suggested it hadn't been a pleasant experience. "She nearly set fire to my shirt and her own hair."

An image of a tall girl with a mass of spiral curls, standing with folded arms, sticking out her leg, tripping Ana on her way to music, flashed in to her head. She nodded. "I know who you mean. I thought she must have got expelled."

Elliot shrugged. "Maybe. Jenna and her friends used to whisper about her, saying she stayed in a Children's House and wore charity shop clothes. It just made me wonder."

Hope spun the notebook round to read the names. "Probably means she got moved to another house somewhere else, or maybe a secure unit if she was in real trouble."

Ana thought back to the missing poster. "Did Seb go to school here too? I didn't recognise him from his photo."

"He was a couple of years above us and did a college link thing so was hardly here," Elliot said. He looked thoughtful. "I don't think he liked school much."

"Who else is on your list?" Hope asked.

Elliot kept one hand on the book, as if protecting the contents. "A couple of names I found in local missing news stories; teenage boys who went missing from a Children's House near Edinburgh, though the journalist suggested they ran away. I couldn't find any follow up story on them."

"Maybe they were found?" Ana suggested. As soon as she saw the deflated look on Elliot's face she regretted opening her mouth. He closed the notebook and shoved it back in his bag.

Hope smiled encouragingly at him. "It's decent you're looking out for Seb. Maybe I could ask my social worker some questions? See if she's heard anything about those kids?"

Elliot's face brightened. "Thanks."

The bell rang and Elliot was the first to move. Ana glanced at Hope, curious about her mention of a social worker. She also wanted to ask Hope more about her mum, but an air of sadness crept around her as they walked to their next class and Ana didn't want it to spread, to dampen the joy of meeting a potential new friend. Ana watched Elliot's back as they turned the corner, saw him hesitate and glance round, like he was waiting for them to catch up.

Maybe two new friends.

Chapter Four
Hope

The gate squeaked as I pushed it open and a curtain twitched upstairs. I kept an eye on the front door, half expecting Martha to open it wide and start interrogating me about my day. She seemed more anxious than me that school was going okay. I turned the handle. Locked. I rolled my eyes, making a mental note to ask again for a key. It annoyed me that the Browns hadn't automatically given me one, as if I was just a visitor. *But that's all you are.* I rang the doorbell, trying to ignore the little taunting voice telling me not to get too comfortable, just in case.

I glanced across to the neighbour's house, watching as a woman unloaded her car of shopping bags, handing the smallest to her little girl, who proudly carried it up the drive, chattering happily. I turned away, squeezing my eyes shut, trying to stop the flood of memories that always threatened to catch me off guard at the most awkward of moments, a pain so powerful it left me breathless.

"Hope, are you alright? Do you have a headache?" Martha ushered me inside, her face contorted in a deep frown. Her expression softened as she glanced across the road, a flicker of understanding in her eyes.

"I'm fine." I hurried inside, not wanting sympathy. I started up the stairs, then paused as a sweet aroma circled the air. "That smells good."

Martha's face twitched with a smile. "Blueberry muffins. I've just boiled the kettle."

I took this as an invitation to follow her down the

hall to the kitchen. I laid down my bag and let the silence sink in around me, grateful for the escape from another day of new names and faces and endless instructions from teachers. As I sank into a chair at the table, Martha pottered around, pulling down mugs. I knew not to offer to help. Martha didn't like anyone interfering in the kitchen.

"How was your day?" Martha asked, stacking muffins on a plate.

I shrugged, "Okay."

Martha brought over a full tea pot, then returned with mugs and took a seat across from me. "They have a very good head teacher there, Ms Turnberry. She goes to our church."

I hoped Martha wouldn't make me go to church. Even although I sometimes pictured Mum in a sort of heaven, I wasn't on board with a God who would inflict a shitty life on me. "I had a meeting with my pastoral care teacher today, but I've not met any senior staff."

"I'm sure Ms Turnberry will make herself known soon enough. She knows you're with us, and said she would look out for you."

I swallowed a bit of muffin, not sure if that was good or bad. What if she acted like a spy, checking up on me?

"Good?" Martha raised an eyebrow as I polished off the last bit of cake.

I grinned.

She pursed her lips, clearly pleased by the approval. "I'll be making dinner soon, so I'll put the rest away for now. I thought I'd try out a new recipe tonight."

I braced myself, dreading the thought of another meat dish I'd have to pick apart.

"I picked up a new cookbook in the charity shop down the road. Who knew there was so much you could do with a cauliflower?" Her eyebrows twitched.

I blinked in surprise and before I could say thanks, Martha had cleared away our plates, already busying herself with rinsing them in the sink.

"Thanks, Martha."

She waved her hand dismissively. "I'm sure you'll have plenty of homework to be getting on with. I'll call you down when it's ready. Edward will be home at six."

With dinner served at six thirty on the dot. It would have driven Mum mad, but I was enjoying the predictable routine. It felt good to have something to rely on. I headed upstairs, reaching into the front pocket of my bag as my phone beeped. I pulled it out, seeing a message from Ana. A series of pained-face emojis popped up, with a gun, then *Maths homework.*

I hesitated, then typed back: *Come to mine after school tomorrow and I'll help? Turns out my new foster mum makes the most amazing blueberry muffins x*

Sold! Wait for me at the gates tomorrow? I hate walking in to that zoo by myself x

I hadn't planned to make friends, but Ana mentioned her best friend had moved halfway across the world, so I told myself it was me doing her a favour. And Elliot had looked kind of lonely too. It made me feel better, forming a circle to fill the gaps of aloneness.

My smile faded when I pictured Elliot's intense expression as he talked about his 'missing' theory. I didn't want it to be true, because it reminded me no one would care if I disappeared. I typed a quick message to Ruth, asking when she was next visiting.

I glanced over at the photo of Mum as I sat down at my desk, imagining her sitting beside me. "Well, that's nearly the first week over and I've survived. I think you'd like Ana. She doesn't seem to care too much about fitting in. And you'd be pleased to hear I spotted a Sylvia Plath in my English teacher's bookcase." I sighed, wondering if it was pathetic and weird, talking to her. It sometimes made me feel better, it sometimes made me feel worse.

I laid out my schoolbooks, grateful that all of the teachers had given me extra work so I could catch up on my missed weeks. I knew I'd been lucky to be placed so quickly with another family. I glanced around the sparse bedroom, wondering what other kids might have sat here, doing their homework. There was no trace of anyone young having ever slept here, and there were few photos on display in the house to give me any clues to the Browns' inner life. As I stared at the blank walls I wondered if I should have taken Lucy's paintings with me. I'd even left the jewellery they'd gifted me; expensive gems belonged to some other girl I'd dressed up as for a while.

I pulled out a Serenity incense stick from the top drawer, placing it in the open trunk of the sculpted incense tree on my windowsill, flicking my lighter. An instant sense of calm flowed through my body as the tip of the incense glowed, a spiral of smoke and woody aroma winding around me, like a magic comfort blanket. It reminded me of home. My *real* home, when I curled up on the sofa watching Mum read the neighbours' tarot.

Soon, I was lost in equations and symbols, grateful that my brain always settled back in to schoolwork without too much effort. The O'Brians always looked at me like I had two heads when I actually begged for peace and quiet to do my homework. Maths used to bore me but now the definitive answers calmed me. I liked that there was nothing left unsaid with Maths and no surprises.

I jumped at the tap on my door. I glanced at the clock. Six thirty already.

Martha popped her head round. "Edward has been delayed at work. We'll eat at seven tonight instead."

"Okay." I looked up in expectation, aware that Martha had opened the door wider. She screwed up her nose, a look of distaste spreading across her face.

"Are you smoking drugs in here?"

"You want some?" The chuckle died in my throat when I registered her anger. "It's just incense."

Her lips formed a thin line, all traces of the softening from earlier wiped from her face. "It's important that you know we don't tolerate drugs under this roof."

I blinked in disbelief, a fizz of fire sparking in my gut. "Noted."

Could she really be that insensitive, or had Ruth failed to give her the full backstory? I realised she probably had been given the full story, and Martha was jumping to conclusions about Mum, and conclusions about what influence she might have had on me.

"I'm glad we're on the same page," Martha nodded tersely. There was an uncomfortable silence then she spoke hesitantly. "The boy we had here before - he got involved in some things and it got difficult."

I tried to swallow my anger. "I'm not going to cause you bother. I just want to focus on school and get good grades." I nearly added, *and get out of here*, but in a lot of ways that wasn't true. I gestured to the incense. "And if it's good enough for priests…" I let the words trail, wondering if she would take that as an insult.

"Hmm." Martha raised an eyebrow and I was sure I saw a twitch of a smile. "Well, at least open a window. All of that smoke burling around can't be good for your lungs."

I closed my book, looking back to Mum when I was sure Martha had left. "Talk about uptight."

I traced a finger along Mum's smile, unable to stop the memories of the festival flooding my head. She always worked so hard, making sure she kept us both comfortable and safe. It was a rare trip away.

Her work friends, all younger than Mum, hated that she brought me along, on the cusp of thirteen, already well versed in teen attitude.

Mum missed the headline bands most nights, returning to curl up beside me in our tent instead. I knew her friends resented me and felt I was ruining their fun, taking her away from them. So on the last night I pretended I wanted to go back to the tent alone to video chat friends, telling her to have some fun and forget about me for a while. I could take care of myself.

It was after midnight when I wandered out to the fields to check on her. The image of her dancing unselfconsciously, arms swinging, curls cascading down her back as she laughed and spun under the moon, formed one of my worst and best memories of her. She'd never looked so young and free. She radiated pure joy and I ran to her, laughing, winding my arms round her waist. She bent down to kiss my forehead, cupping my cheek with her hand, and said, "You are such a beautiful girl. I love you."

I squeezed my eyes shut, remembering her last

words, wishing for the hundredth time that she hadn't sent me back. Or at least had come with me. If only I had been with her.

If only.

At six am I had jolted awake, a shot of panic speeding up my heart as I registered her empty sleeping bag. I grabbed my phone, a gift to ensure we would always find each other if we got separated in the festival crowds. The dial tone rang and rang with no reassuring hello on the other end.

I stumbled out of the tent, climbing over empty beer bottles, side-stepping people sleeping under coats. When Tina, Mum's friend ran towards me, I felt a wave of relief. The wave crashed when I registered the fear in her eyes and the streaks of mascara running down her blotchy face.

"Hope." She grabbed my hand. "I couldn't find your tent. It's your mum."

I shook her off, seeing an ambulance up ahead. Paramedics loaded a body onto a stretcher, and I ran towards them, feeling the world tilt and distort in front of me.

The blue emergency light rotated with no siren, picking out faces in the crowd. Mum's friends, shocked and clinging on to one another. Police officers asking questions, trying to calm hysterical tones. The light swung across the body on the stretcher and I already knew. I knew from the curve of her arm, the bracelet of hearts dangling from her wrist. I ran to her, struggled against the paramedic who tried to keep me back. Tina shouted, "It's her mum. Let her forward."

And I clung on, all the way to the hospital. Wishing, praying, pleading for her to stay with me, to breathe. But her last breath was in her final dance, I knew. Tina, riding across from me in the ambulance knew. But we kept pretending all the way to the hospital.

The conversation from paramedics was a blur, deadened by the sirens and the screams inside my head. Many weeks later, after the toxicology results, four words stayed imprinted in my mind: Ecstasy. Overhydrated. Dilated heart. A fitting description of her final hours. Now, for me, the opposite: Sorrow. Thirsty. Closed heart.

Tina was the only one who stayed with me in the hospital. She let me move in with her for a few weeks, tried to help me trace my father with the support of social services, but he had done a good job of disappearing. Mum never knew her own dad and Gran passed away a few years previously. Tina cried when she told me she'd got a job down south and couldn't take me with her. I was devastated, but it felt like an inevitability. What twenty-five-year-old would want the responsibility of taking on a twelve-year-old smart ass?

Tina reassured me Mum loved me so much, that this was the only time she had done drugs with them; it wasn't like her. I didn't need Tina to tell me it was a one-off. That's what made it all the more sickening.

The universe can be cruel, so be careful what you wish for, Mum said one day when she found me curled up with her book *The Secret*. She'd meant it as a joke, but it haunted me, that line. Because that night I understood what she wished for. She wanted to forget for a while, to be free of all responsibilities.

I jumped as I heard the front door slam. Edward called hello, keys clinking into the metal bowl by the door.

I reached up and distinguished the burning incense

stick between my finger and thumb, watching as ash crumbled onto the windowsill.

Whenever I made a silent wish, I never asked for much. I was very careful to keep it simple. I just wanted to be happy. And safe.

Chapter Five
Ana

Ana was surprised to find her mum dressed in jogging gear, doing limbering up stretches in the kitchen. The worry of an impending Maths test had prevented her from getting back to sleep, but she hadn't expected anyone else in the house to be awake.

Mum looked just as baffled to see her. "What are you doing up so early?"

"I couldn't get back to sleep." Ana flipped on the kettle. "I see your work-out gear is getting an outing at last." The impulse purchase had been made on one of their shopping trips from months ago.

Mum made a face. "I'm already going off the idea of a jog. How about you join me for a fast walk round the block instead?"

Ana hesitated, biting back the reflex 'no' to any early morning activity. She thought back to her parents' conversation in the kitchen the other morning, wondering if this could be a chance to ask about it.

"Give me a sec to get out of my PJs."

The streets were quiet, apart for a few dog walkers and cars. The first of the morning light was breaking through the clouds and Ana thought maybe morning people had the right idea. Catch the beauty of sunrises and quiet time before madness descended.

Mum smiled into the sun, swinging her arms enthusiastically, her words echoing Ana's thoughts. "We should do this more often. Make it a new morning ritual. How's school going?"

Ana told her about Hope, how she had lost her mum and was living with foster carers and that she'd invited her over to do homework after school.

"Poor soul, losing her mum so young. You should invite her over for dinner sometime."

Ana nodded, detecting a worry frown forming on Mum's face. It was subtle, but enough to make Ana think back to the kitchen conversation. She wanted to ask questions, but didn't want to ruin their walk. "So, are you on a bit of a health kick just now or what?" Ana tried to keep the tone light.

Mum smiled tightly. "A feeble attempt. Here I am, already avoiding the running part."

"Have you been feeling...okay?" Ana's chest tightened as she registered Mum's surprise, then hesitation.

"Of course, don't you be worrying about your old mum. Just trying to be more conscious of keeping fit." She threaded her arm through Ana's. "So, tell me more about this Hope girl."

Ana decided to stick with the change of topic. Maybe Mum wasn't ready to tell her about the tests yet, or maybe it had been nothing and wasn't worth mentioning. Ana relaxed at the thought. "I don't know much about her yet. Why do you think she's had to live with foster parents? Is that like getting adopted?"

"Foster carers look after kids who can't be at home with their family. Or they look after kids who don't have any family. Maybe she doesn't have any other close relatives?"

"I guess," Ana said, shivering at the thought of how lonely that would be.

Mum shook her wrist, looking at her watch. "Okay, I think my Fitbit is laughing at me for going so slow and I need to shower before work. How's about we do a fast sprint home?"

Before Ana could protest, her mum shot off down the street, leaving Ana to trail behind, laughing and clutching at a stitch as she failed to catch up.

Maisie and Dad had nearly finished breakfast by the time they'd showered and Ana worried she'd miss Hope at the gates.

"Maisie, move your stool out the way." Ana reached over her shoulder and flipped up the butter tray in the fridge, baffled when she pulled out a set of keys.

Maisie grabbed her hand and giggled. "What are those doing in there?"

Ana hesitated, recognising the diamante poodle swinging on the key chain. She turned to her mum who was glugging coffee.

"Mum?" Ana walked towards her, handing the keys over.

It took her a few seconds to focus. "My work keys. Where did you find them?"

"In the fridge!" Maisie squealed in delight, jumping down from her stool, dropping her bag of sandwiches all over the floor.

"Maisie." Mum shot forward, clearing up the mess. She glanced up at Ana, shoving the keys in her pocket without saying anything. Usually Mum would laugh when she did something silly. Ana looked over at Dad who was peering into his iPad, oblivious and deep in the world of online scrabble.

"What should we have for dinner tonight? I could pick up some veg and make a stir fry?" Mum mumbled from inside the fridge, rooting around.

Dad's head shot up. "We were going to pick up take-away this evening, Pam, remember? On the way home from Maisie's parents' night?"

Mum smacked her forehead, slamming the fridge shut and peering at the family organiser pinned on the door. "It's not on the calendar. I told you to write it on the calendar, Peter."

Dad clicked off his iPad and walked over to Mum, laying a hand on hers. "You're right, my fault. Will you be able to get away from work okay?"

Mum hesitated, then nodded. "I can flexi off early. Kick off at five?"

Dad shot her a reassuring smile and Ana noticed a subtle hand squeeze. He always offered her that gesture when she was nervous, or sad.

Maisie wriggled in between them. "If I get a good report can I have a big fish supper instead of a mini one?"

Dad rumpled her hair. "Maybe, toots."

"And the tablet ice cream. Just a small tub. But all to myself." Maisie shot Ana a look, making it clear that comment was directed at her.

"I might be home a bit later so don't bother getting me any." Ana stuck her tongue out at Maisie, hating how she brought her down to her level.

Dad turned to look at Ana in surprise.

Ana folded her arms defensively. "No need to look so shocked. I'm going over to do homework at a new friend's house."

"That boy's house? The one with the floppy hair?" Maisie pulled her ponytail forward so that it covered her forehead. Ana shot her a withering look.

"What boy?" Mum raised an eyebrow, smiling. "You never mentioned a boy would be there too."

"He's no one. And it will just be me and Hope." Ana shoved her Maths books in her bag, grabbing a banana, her cold butterless toast abandoned after the distraction of the keys.

"I'll see you later." Ana allowed her mum to kiss her on the cheek on the way past, but avoided eye contact so she didn't probe further about Elliot.

As she hurried along the road the old man who had waved at Maisie was standing at his window. He smiled as Ana passed and she nodded and smiled in return. She looked to the road, remembering the car and the couple. She made a mental note to ask her parents if they knew what had happened to the Carmichaels. Maybe the woman she'd seen was a relative of Batty Barbs. But she'd said her name. It didn't make sense.

As she approached school she spotted Hope's fiery mane and a surge of relief flowed through her. It was the first time she'd actually looked forward to going to school in ages.

"Hey." Hope grinned and waved her phone. "I messaged Elliot and told him to meet us too."

Ana's heart jolted at the thought of getting to speak to Elliot again today. She glanced at Hope's phone, wondering when they'd exchanged details.

Hope talked about a run-in she'd had with Martha, quickly adding that she was actually quite cool and had cooked an amazing meal, completely vegetarian, with a brilliant dessert to follow.

"I think she's a bit of a feeder. There's a good chance I won't fit into my uniform in a couple of weeks." Hope patted her stomach.

The roar of an engine interrupted their conversation and they both turned and watched as a sleek black car snaked into the carpark.

"Nice car. Who drives that?" Hope asked.

"Ms Turnberry." Ana jumped at Elliot's voice behind her. She smiled but he was too busy scrutinising the car to pay any attention to her. The three of them watched as Ms Turnberry manoeuvred into a space behind the wall where they stood. Ana couldn't remember ever seeing Ms Turnberry smile, and when she was angry her voice lowered into a menacing hum; much more terrifying than the shrill shrieks of the other teachers but it commanded respect from the pupils.

Something was different about her this year. Her skin had more of a youthful glow and her hair looked fuller, healthier. Ana turned to Hope to make a crack about Ms Turnberry's animal print shoes and the possibility of her having a secret boyfriend but shut her mouth when she noticed Hope shudder.

"You okay?" Ana asked.

Hope nodded, "I just got this weird feeling, like a ghoul tickled my spine."

As they headed into the main building Elliot's mind was still on the car. "I don't get how she can afford that. How much do head teachers earn?"

"How much does a car like that cost?" Ana asked.

Elliot shot her a look and she protested, "I don't have a clue about cars."

"It's a Porsche, Ana." Hope said.

"Oh." She knew enough to know that would be *a lot* of money. Maybe Ms Turnberry had won the lottery or inherited a fortune from some dead family member. That might explain her new glam look too – probably spent her summer getting Botox and hair implants.

When they walked into English, Jenna and her friends stopped talking and stared at them. Jenna whispered something to one of the girls and they all laughed. Ana's face burned. Hope rolled her eyes and linked her arms with Elliot and Ana. Ana could feel

Elliot's resistance but knew Hope's grip was strong.

"Do you think they share him?" Jenna said loud enough for everyone to hear. More giggles.

"Just ignore them," Hope whispered. She slung her bag onto the desk and moved to the one beside it, pushing it forward to join them together.

"What are you doing?" Elliot frowned.

"You should sit with us. Give them something to actually talk about." Hope shrugged, taking the end seat so that Ana was left to sit in the middle. Beside Elliot. Her palms started to sweat as she pulled out her books. She was still hungry from her lack of a proper breakfast. She prayed that her stomach wouldn't rumble uncontrollably. Really attractive.

Mr Darwin raised an eyebrow when he clocked the new seating arrangement but didn't challenge it.

"Hey Elliot," Hope craned her head towards him. "My social worker is going to visit in a few days after school. Would you be able to give me a list of the names you have? She won't be able to disclose any info she finds with me, but she was curious enough to check."

"Sure. I'll do it at lunch." Elliot's face lit up.

A hush descended as the door banged open and Ms Turnberry strode in. Her heels echoed across the floor, beady eyes scanning the room. Ana gripped her pen tighter as Ms Turnberry's attention focused on their table. She was attempting to be subtle but Ana was sure she was staring at Hope. Hope side-eyed Ana, indicating she'd noticed too. Hope scribbled in her notebook: *Seriously creepy lady giving me evil looks.*

Ms Turnberry turned her back to them, talking in hushed tones with Mr Darwin. He looked tense, but that wasn't unusual. He often looked distracted during lessons, as if thoughts were tumbling through his head that had more importance than anything in school. He'd dropped to part time hours a couple of years ago and rumours circulated that he was dying of cancer. Ana was pretty sure that was a major lie.

"I really don't like her," Hope whispered in Ana's ear. "I'm sensing a really bad energy when she's around."

It was a bit of a kooky thing to say. There was definitely a change of atmosphere whenever Ms Turnberry appeared, but it was usually because everyone knew she wouldn't stand for any nonsense. Ana jumped when Ms Turnberry's head swivelled round and her eyes locked with hers. Ana held her breath as she walked towards their desk.

"It's Hope isn't it?" Ms Turnberry's voice was loud in the silence.

"Yes," Hope said, laying her pen down, as if she was ready for a challenge.

"Welcome to Oakridge High. Martha Brown alerted me to the fact you had enrolled with us. She said you're a smart girl."

Hope smiled politely. Ana tensed, praying Ms Turnberry wouldn't focus any attention on her. Ms Turnberry looked Hope up and down and then walked on, an audible sigh of relief circulating around the room when she shut the door.

Hope made a face. "She doesn't look like the kind of teacher who appreciates smart girls." Ana realised she must have looked confused as Hope added, "You know, like she would rather have a classroom full of people who agree with every word she says. A school full of 'yes' girls."

Ana couldn't imagine ever having the courage to challenge Ms Turnberry, or any teacher really. Did that mean she was too much of a 'yes' girl? She sat up straighter, preferring the thought of rebelling a bit. Maybe Hope could be a good influence and help her achieve her mission of shaking off boring Ana. But first, she had to finish her essay.

*

"Hello, Ana. Nice to meet you."

Hope's description of Martha had been one hundred per cent accurate. She was dressed all in brown and her severe bun was definitely not a fashionable top knot. Mrs Brown radiated an air of having more important things to be bothering with than her hair. As Ana shook her bony hand there was nothing warm or reassuring about her grip, yet there was a hint of a smile in her eyes.

"We're going upstairs to do homework." As Hope skipped onto the first step, the contrast of her standing alongside Martha made Ana wonder if that's what people saw when they walked side by side down the street. Fire and Earth. But maybe her pink hair was the embers of a potential fire.

"I'll bring you up some muffins and tea. Or perhaps you'd prefer juice, Ana?"

Ana smiled at Martha's formality. "Tea is great, thanks. Lots of milk, no sugar."

As she followed Hope upstairs she took in the brown carpet and the plain magnolia walls. The house looked like it wanted to blend in, to sit quietly in a corner and not be noticed. The complete opposite of Hope. Ana was surprised the blandness extended into her space. She had pictured Hope sitting at a dressing table with mirrors, elaborate trinkets lining her shelves, with colourful bags hanging down a wall, and bright cushions stacked on her bed.

"It's...nice." Ana smiled politely.

Hope shot her an incredulous look. "No it's not. It's hideous." Ana caught her eye and they laughed. Hope gestured for her to sit on the bed and she pulled out the chair at her desk, sitting down and throwing her bag on the ground. Hope traced a hand across the top drawer, looking thoughtful. A photograph hanging above the mirror at the dresser caught Ana's eye. She walked over to get a closer look.

"Is this your mum?" She really didn't need to ask. The red waves and massive green eyes were almost a mirror vision of Hope.

"Wasn't she beautiful?" Hope unpinned the photo and handed it to Ana.

Ana nodded. "You look a lot like her. What was her name?"

"Daphne Devaney. I always told her with a name like that and those looks she should have been a film star. Sometimes I like to pretend she is. Travelling the world, too busy playing out someone else's life to be present in mine."

Ana handed the photo back and Hope looked wistful. "I wish she had been in films. Then there would always be a part of her still here, playing over and over."

The words hit Ana with a jolt. She brushed away the thoughts that kept threatening, a little voice in her head fretting about what parts of Mum might be lost if her memory was properly unravelling. "Does it upset you, to talk about her?"

"Not really. I like it. I don't have anyone to reminisce with."

Ana waited to see if Hope would say more. Hope continued, "I never knew my dad. Mum was a bit vague about it all, but I think he was a casual fling at college and didn't want to know me."

"I'm sorry." Ana's heart tightened at the thought of Dad and the way he always knew the right things to say, how he was fiercely protective of his 'girls'. She couldn't imagine him ever leaving. Or not wanting them.

Hope shrugged. "I never missed not having a dad. Mum was great. She always made sure we had lots of fun. She was close to my Gran so she stayed with us a lot. It was like having two mums."

"Could you not live with your Gran?" Ana asked quietly.

Hope shook her head. "We lost her years ago." She pinned the photo of her mum back above the mirror just as Martha knocked and entered with their snacks.

Hope seemed to welcome the interruption but Ana wanted to ask her more. How did she get fostered? Did she get to choose a family? It didn't sound like it, with the experience she'd had with the O'Brians. Ana also wanted to ask her how her mum had died. But that seemed too personal.

As Martha set the tray down on Hope's desk she asked about her day at school.

"Your friend Ms Turnberry popped into my English class and said hello."

Martha smiled. "I wouldn't say we're friends, more church acquaintances. I'm glad you've met. No doubt she'll make sure you settle in."

Hope rolled her eyes at Ana and she grinned. Ana thought back to Hope's misgivings about Ms Turnberry and the mention of church conjured up images of her in a nun outfit, locking girls in cupboards, making them repent for their sins. A shiver ran down to Ana's toes as she pictured her emotionless beady eyes.

The Browns insisted Ana stay for dinner. Martha seemed delighted that she had an extra guest to impress with her cooking. Hope's face visibly relaxed when she cut into the lasagne, revealing vegetables. "Thank the lord," she whispered and Ana stifled a laugh. "I hope you like veggies okay?" Her brow furrowed and Ana nodded in reassurance.

The Browns were friendly throughout dinner and asked Ana questions about her family and school. Martha beamed at Hope when Ana told her she was helping her with homework, even although it should technically be Hope who was behind.

Edward insisted on giving Ana a lift home after, with Hope asking to come along to keep her company. Hope told Ana to sit in front and her mind drifted as Hope started to tell Edward a detailed story about an ethical dilemma their Social Studies teacher had presented the class with.

"Ah yes, the run-away tram story." Edward nodded. "Let's hear this version then."

Hope went on to explain how it seemed a simple choice at first. The teacher told them they were the driver of the tram with ten passengers on board. There was a car coming through the crossing, with only an old lady behind the wheel. They had a minute to decide; crash into the car, or swerve and take the tram over the side of an embankment? Ten passengers, including them as the driver, or one old lady. Who would they save? As their classmates started to shout out answers, the teacher added in the final dilemma. *The old lady is your mother.*

Ana would save her mum. Time and time again, no question. Some asked how old she was. Was she ill? Was there a baby on board the tram? It didn't change her answer. And she knew it didn't change

Hope's even although they both stayed quiet in class.

"It's a tough one," Edward said, but Ana caught the way he looked at Hope in the rearview mirror and she knew he understood what Hope's choice would be. She had real-life experience of losing her mum so it was understandable.

Ana wondered what it said about her own morals, the fact she didn't even consider the other lives. Of course she would feel guilty, but no matter which way she looked at it, she knew she would always swerve to save her mum.

Ana laughed along with Hope as Edward tried to understand Hope's description of a new reality show they'd started watching. She liked the way Edward showed interest in Hope's life. It made her feel better after hearing some of Hope's story earlier, knowing the Browns cared. She couldn't imagine having no family at such a young age.

They stopped at traffic lights and Ana gazed out the window, startled when a black car pulled up alongside them. Ms Turnberry was in the driving seat, gripping the wheel, her black leather gloves an appropriate accompaniment to her severe expression. Ana's attention was drawn to the man in the back seat who was leaning forward, talking animatedly to Ms Turnberry and her other passenger. He had on a grey bowler hat which cast shadows and obscured the top half of his face, but his neatly trimmed grey beard and curled moustache made him instantly recognisable. *Dr Carmichael.* Ana stared in wonder as the lights flashed green and they sped off before Edward had even hit the clutch.

What on earth was Dr Carmichael doing in Ms Turnberry's car late at night? She wondered how they knew each other. They had looked so grave and serious, like they were up to no good. Ana turned to Hope, wanting to share her thoughts, but it seemed a silly thing to mention. Hope already didn't seem to like Ms Turnberry much, so probably best not to fuel that fire.

When they reached Ana's house, Ana turned and smiled as Hope waved and shouted goodnight out the car window. It felt good to have a proper friend again.

Chapter Six
Hope

Running late this morning!! Don't wait for me. I pressed send as I threw books into my school bag and grabbed my art folder.

The knock at my door made me jump.

"It's eight thirty, Hope."

"I know, Martha." I gritted my teeth, resisting the urge to be sarcastic. "Just coming." I was surprised to see her still standing in the hallway. She smiled, holding out a banana and apple.

"You can eat these on the way."

My exasperation softened as I shoved the fruit in my bag. Week by week, I was becoming more comfortable with the Browns, adapting to my quieter life. I couldn't understand why nightmares had started to plague me.

I glanced at my reflection as I grabbed my coat, balking at the dark circles under my eyes that my rushed make-up application failed to hide. The terror of last night's nightmares still clung to my bones as I hurried down the street. I pulled the zip up on my jacket as far as it would go, shivering as a flock of birds squawked above.

Unwelcome images flooded my brain. Ms Turnberry stabbing a needle into my arm, blood trickling down my fingers, a pool of blood soaking my shoes, making me slide and slip every time I tried to run. Turning to see fire blazing in a window, flames curling up exterior walls of a mansion, hearing shouts from the roof, arms waving in silhouette.

Then Mum appearing at the front door, engulfed in smoke, screaming for me to run, to stay away. The smoke swirled faster, blacker, thicker, and then she was lost.

I wiped at my eyes, realising with embarrassment that I had started to cry. Hands shaking, I dug around in my bag for my compact mirror. My boot caught on litter, and I stumbled, poised to kick it to the side when I noticed the grainy face of a boy gazing up at me. I used the toe of my boot to straighten the paper, revealing a poster.

"Missing. Seb Masterson," I whispered his name, looking into his eyes. He looked very serious. And gorgeous. Elliot's foster brother. I realised with a pang of guilt I'd been so preoccupied with my own life the past few weeks that I'd forgotten about my suggestion to Elliot, that I could ask Ruth about Seb and the other names he'd mentioned.

I tried to read the rest of the poster but it was shredded, letters faded and weather beaten, making them illegible. I slid my phone out of my pocket, snapping a photo of Seb. I could show it to Ruth later, ask her if she recognised him. It wasn't the best photo, even blurrier due to erosion, but enough to make out his face.

By the time I arrived at school first period was nearly over. I hesitated by my locker, deliberating whether to just wait for the next class. My stomach growled and I pulled out the banana, thanking Martha silently for being such a great feeder.

"Hope Devaney?"

I turned in surprise at my name, expecting to be chastised by a teacher for not being in class. Instead I was greeted by a smiling petite brunette, dressed in a smart skirt and blouse, a lanyard slung round her neck.

"I came looking for you in class this morning. My name is Clara Dean. I'm the school nurse."

I swallowed my last mouthful of banana. "I was late this morning." I eyed her suspiciously, wondering how she recognised me when I was sure we'd never met.

As if reading my mind, she gestured to a file in her hand, my photo pinned in the corner. "I printed off some details from your last school. I think it's a while since you had a chat with the school nurse?"

I nodded in surprise, struggling to remember a time when I had *ever* had that kind of chat. I didn't even know schools had nurses on site.

She glanced at her watch. "We still have ten minutes before the change-over of period. How about we head to my office just now?"

I shrugged, following her down the corridor.

"How are you liking Oakridge?" She asked.

"It's okay." I glanced at my file in her hands, wondering what was inside.

We turned a corner and she stopped at an unmarked door, stooping to unlock it with a key attached to her lanyard. I glanced at the photo on her badge, thinking it didn't do her justice.

The room was bright and airy, a large desk in one corner, with a bed and screen in the other. Clara gestured for me to take a seat across from her and I started to feel nervous, always hating visits to the doctors. She took the banana peel from my hand and threw it in the bin under her desk.

"Glad you had some breakfast. Would you like a drink of water?"

I shook my head no, wishing she'd offer me a hot tea instead.

Clara started to explain that she would be asking me a series of questions, just to check I was coping alright with school and my new move, as well as checking my general health was okay. "I'd like to weigh you and take a couple of blood tests if you're okay with that, Hope?"

For the first time I noticed a row of three needles sitting inside plastic bags on the desk, different coloured labels wound round each.

An image of blood dripping down my fingertips swirled in my head and I swallowed, telling myself the nightmare was just a weird coincidence.

"Are you scared of needles?" Clara's voice was soft and reassuring as she looked at the needles, then to me. She tilted her head and smiled. "I have a light touch, I promise."

Needles never bothered me, yet I did feel uneasy. *It's just because of the nightmare*, I told myself. The hairs on my arms stood on end as she asked me to roll up my sleeve.

"Let's get this part over with first."

Something about her manner struck me as false. She was all smiles, with a sing-song voice but the joy didn't reach her eyes. The contrast was unnerving.

"Sorry, why did you say we were having this appointment?"

Clara's smile tightened. "It's part of a welfare initiative. For young people, like yourself, in the care system. We just want to ensure you are being well looked after. The blood tests are to check you're in good health."

I relented and rolled up my shirt sleeve.

Clara chatted about the weather and the school as the needle pierced my skin, pausing to compliment me on my easy to find vein. It seemed a weird thing to be praised for. As she slid one needle out, she handed me a tiny piece of cotton bud to press against the spot of blood and cheerfully bundled it into the bag, sealing it and reaching over to slide out the next.

"What are you testing for?"

"Oh, a couple of things. Like your iron levels. How's your diet? Do you get your five a day?"

"I probably do now," I nodded. "Martha, my foster mum, has started to make me lots of vegetable dishes."

"Very good. And you like those okay?"

I nodded, my eyes drawn to the ruby red blood filling up the vial. "I'm a vegetarian so it's probably the best I've ever eaten."

Clara's eyes flashed and her smile slipped. She was a bit rougher taking out the second needle and I flinched. "Just be careful you do eat enough iron rich foods, Hope. It's important for girls your age as you can become anaemic easily. We'll wait and see what comes back in the results. I could easily prescribe you some supplements."

The bell for next period rang just as I was stepping on the scales. I'd put on a few pounds since I last weighed myself and I realised it was probably because of Martha's great food, but also because I had started to relax. The buzz of adrenaline and stress that had plagued me since I knew I was moving on from Lucy and Andy's had simmered down to a manageable hum.

I slipped my boots back on, hoping I would be allowed to leave. Clara's questions were intrusive and embarrassing, asking me about periods, boyfriends; *Are you sexually active? On the pill?* Should I be? I nearly asked. My face burned at the thought of confessing I'd never even kissed a boy.

Have you ever been depressed? How was I supposed to answer that? I wasn't sure if grief was the same as depression; my doctors hadn't seemed sure either. I'd met with a counsellor, but never needed medication.

"You seem a very strong and resilient girl, Hope. Not many girls in your situation would cope so well. It's difficult, losing someone you love." I noticed a shift in her expression, like she was remembering something painful. Then she blinked and flashed me one of her not-quite sincere smiles.

"Remember to come along to my lunchtime clinic if you ever feel the need."

I slid on my coat, my arm stiff to bend after the needle intrusion. I thanked her and left, relieved to escape the cold, clinical room and return to the noise and chaos of the corridors.

At break Ana was waiting for me outside the canteen.

"Maths was torture without you. Mr Kane kept picking on me, asking me questions I'm pretty sure he knew I would never be able to answer."

"Sorry. The school nurse kidnapped me and stabbed needles in my arm."

Ana looked alarmed. I grinned, to show I was half-joking, and pulled her to a quiet table in the corner. "Apparently ensuring I'm being looked after. Have you ever seen the school nurse?"

Ana looked thoughtful. "Maybe in second year, for some jag."

"She seems to love her jags." I wriggled out of my coat, and slid up my shirt sleeve, a blue and purple bruise already blooming around the edges of the tiny plaster.

"Ouch," Ana grimaced.

"Where's Elliot?" I scanned the crowds of the canteen.

Ana shrugged, her cheeks flushing. "I think he had Tech second period. It's on the other side of school."

I pulled out my phone, scrolling to the photo of Seb. "I tripped over one of the posters of his missing foster brother this morning and took a photo of it. I'm going to show my social worker later today when she visits."

"What's your social worker like?" Ana asked, eyes shining with curiosity.

"Ruth is cool." I could sense Ana wanted to ask me more, but I didn't feel much like explaining my life history just now. I slid my art folder up on to the table, eyes tracing the tarot symbols I'd started to paint.

"Have you ever had your cards read?" I asked.

Ana shook her head, frowning. "Like, tarot?"

I nodded, pulling out my velvet pouch from the folder. "I'll do a quick reading for you just now, if you want?"

Ana watched as I spread the cards on to the table. I could see the doubt in her face. "What if I don't like what you tell me?"

"The focus is on helping you gain insight into problems you might be facing." I quickly added, "Not that I'm saying you have any."

Ana sat forward. "What do I do?"

"I'll do a Past, Present, Future spread for you. Pick three cards that you feel drawn to. Take your time but not too long. Don't overthink it."

Taking a deep breath Ana scanned back and forth along the cards, then pushed three above the spread and I slowly turned them over, observing the images.

The Hermit, a wise looking old man carrying a burning lamp; Queen of Wands, a woman in flowing robes, holding an elaborate wand beneath a flaming gold pillar and Five of Swords; a man carrying blue jewelled swords.

Ana groaned as I picked up The Hermit card.

"I think that's a pretty accurate description of my life the past few months. A loser loner." Ana flushed and I shot her a reassuring smile.

"The Hermit is about growth, taking time to learn who you are and what you believe. Maybe becoming more independent?" I suggested. Ana looked thoughtful but didn't comment.

I gestured to the Queen of Wands. "This is a good card."

"She looks a bit more attractive than the bearded old dude."

We giggled and I traced a finger across the red ruby at the top of the image. "This card represents your Present. This Queen suggests you've got a lot of passion for things, but you've been suppressing that side of your personality. You might be drawn to starting a new project, or helping someone with something important."

"That sounds a bit more exciting," Ana said.

I smiled mischievously. "Elliot seems like he's on a mission just now, to find Seb. Maybe it involves helping him."

Ana shot me a wary look and I turned back to the spread.

"This card," I picked up the Five of Swords, "is quite powerful. It suggests you might have something tough to face, a potential battle." Ana frowned, her expression darkening and I was quick to continue, "But the fact you drew this combination of three tells me that whatever the battle is, you're ready for it, almost like it's something meant for you to tackle, that you have strength to see it through."

Ana didn't look convinced. I gathered up the cards, shuffling them back into the pack. "It's just a bit of fun, really. Will I do my reading now?"

Ana nodded, watching me spread the cards across the table again. As I slid my three forward, I was aware of Ana's attention shifting, a startled expression on her face.

I instinctively placed my hands over the cards, a protective gesture, as I turned my head. My heart sank when I clocked Ms Turnberry striding towards our table, shaking her head disapprovingly.

"Hope Devaney. I hope you're not practicing witchcraft in my school?"

Words popped out before I could process them, "If I was, would you burn me at the stake?"

Ms Turnberry recoiled, as if I had slapped her. She quickly composed herself, face turning pink, blushing into a deeper purple, as she drew her shoulders back. "Ms Devaney," her voice was low and even, "I do not stand for cheek. And I do not stand for this type of nonsense." She flicked a dismissive hand at the cards. "I want you to put these away in your locker out of sight or I will confiscate them."

I glanced at Ana, her eyes wide with fear. Slowly, I gathered up the last of the cards, taking my time sliding them back into the pouch, tying the string into a tight knot. I stood up abruptly, my chair skidding backwards, nearly knocking Ms Turnberry's knees.

I smiled sweetly at her. "No problem, Ms Turnberry." The bell rang, the canteen erupting into elevated noise. Ms Turnberry held my gaze, eyes blazing. I didn't flinch, or look away, holding my breath, waiting for her anger to implode.

A piercing shriek behind us broke the tension, the splat of overturned food pulling Ms Turnberry's attention. She marched off to find the offender and I let out a shaky breath.

Perhaps it was me, not Ana, who would be facing a battle.

*

"Hey, kid."

A warmth spread through my body at the sight of Ruth on the doorstep, a half grin on her face. I leaned forward, squeezing her in a hug, a cloud of recently extinguished nicotine shooting up my nose.

"Any spares?" I whispered in her ear.

She pushed me playfully. "No. And I told you, I'm not allowed to hug you. Get out the way and let me in."

I smiled, shutting the door, watching Ruth take in her surroundings. She turned to me, looking me up and down.

"You're looking good, kid. All going okay?"

I grinned. "Yeah. I like it here."

She winked. "I thought you might."

"Ms McDonald. Good to see you." The kitchen door swung open and Martha appeared in the hall, bringing the scent of freshly baked cake with her.

Ruth shook her hand. "And you, Martha. I was hoping I could have a chat with Hope alone first for ten minutes, then we can talk?"

"Of course. I'll bring you a coffee in. Black, two sugars?"

Ruth nodded. "Great memory."

I pushed the living room door open. "Let's go in here." I took a seat on Edward's armchair, feeling a strange mix of nerves and excitement at seeing Ruth. The last few weeks tumbled out of me, my only pause when Martha brought in the coffee and cake.

"I can see why you like it here so much." Ruth tasted a mouthful of cake, closing her eyes in ecstasy. "She should be on Bake Off."

"I said that." I laughed. "I had to show her an episode on catch up. She looked horrified at the thought."

"School okay?" Ruth asked.

I shrugged. "It's okay. I've made a couple of friends. And had a meeting with the school nurse."

Ruth looked up from her cake in surprise. "What about?"

"She did some blood tests. Asked me a few questions."

Ruth frowned. "Some schools have a welfare initiative, giving support to young people in care. I didn't realise they were so thorough."

Ruth stood up and walked around the room, glancing at the sole photo of Martha and Edward on their wedding day on the mantelpiece. "I think you'll be good for the Browns, Hope. You bring a bit of life to the place."

I hadn't ever thought what I could bring to the Browns. Just what they could provide for me.

Ruth hesitated, as if she wanted to tell me more. "Have they mentioned much about their background?"

I shook my head. "They're both quite…reserved. Though I feel like I'm slowly getting to know them better."

Ruth nodded. "The last boy who was here caused a bit of grief. He was quite violent. I think it shook Martha a bit and they weren't sure if they wanted to foster again. So just give her time to trust." She turned to me, a proud expression on her face. "She told me that she thinks you're a wonderful girl when I visited the other week."

Wonderful? Martha wasn't big on the compliments so for her, that was gushing. I dug my nails into the palm of my hand, feeling tears threaten. Lucy used to say I was wonderful. Beautiful. I swallowed the feeling of affection, reminding myself how quickly that could fade.

Ruth sat down again, opening her bag. "Just take your time settling in, Hope. I know Martha isn't the only one who needs to build up trust."

How did she do that? I watched as Ruth packed her papers away. She always picked up on my emotions. I realised she was taking her time shutting the bag. Her hand grasped a bit of paper, then let it go.

"There's something in here for you, but I'm not sure I should give it to you."

"Is it a jumbo pack of cigs?" I laughed at my joke. Ruth barely cracked a smile. Whatever it was, must be pretty serious.

The paper was now in her hands. I realised it was an envelope. As she slid it across the table towards me the loopy handwriting caused a jolt in my gut.

"Lucy called me. She asked me for your new address, but I explained I couldn't pass that information on, so I agreed to be a go-between. Only because she told me you've ignored all her emails and texts."

That's my right, I wanted to say. *I get to control this part.*

"I'm sorry if I've done the wrong thing, passing the letter on. She sounded desperate. And sad."

I squeezed my eyes shut, a big part of me pleased that Lucy was in pain too. But another part of me was annoyed that she hadn't just let me be. I wondered if this attempt at communication was just a way to ease her guilt.

I slid the letter into my school bag, needing time to decide if I was going to read it. Or bin it. Or burn it.

"Okay, kid. Shall we ask Martha to join us now?"

I jolted back to the here and now. "Before Martha comes in, I wanted to ask you something." I scrambled for my phone, bringing up the photo of Seb. "This is my friend's foster brother, Seb Masterson. Do you recognise the name? Or recognise his face?"

Ruth frowned. "The name does sound a bit familiar." She took the phone from me. "Was this the boy you mentioned in your message?"

I nodded. "He disappeared from his placement about a year ago." I pulled out the other list of names Elliot scribbled down for me at lunch. "And Elliot thinks these kids might be missing too."

Ruth took the list hesitantly. "What do you want me to do?"

I shrugged. "Is there a way you can look up their files on your system? Those two names." I pointed to the list. "Scott and Aidan. They apparently went missing from a Children's House near Edinburgh. Could you even find out if they actually returned?"

Ruth pursed her lips. "I'll see what I can do. It's not information I'll be able to share back though. If I find their files, it's confidential."

"I figured as much." I nodded. "I think Elliot just wanted to feel like he was doing something for Seb, you know. Just in case something happened to him."

"I'm sure the police would have investigated that at the time." Ruth slid the note of names into her pocket. "Sometimes kids unfortunately run away and the system loses track of them. Especially if they move to another council area. But I'll check it out."

Ruth asked me to go and fetch Martha. I hesitated at the door, realising I was lucky to have someone like Ruth on my side. I wanted to thank her for not giving up on me, for always tracking me down when I thought I wanted to run away and disappear.

I realised how easy it could be to disappear and never be found.

Chapter Seven
Ana

"Ana, we've chosen the film. Hurry up." Maisie threw Ana's door open, jumping on to the bed beside her. "What're you looking at?"

Ana tilted the screen of her netbook away from her. Maisie stretched forward, pressing against her shoulder blades, breathing loudly in her ear.

"Memory loss. What are the main causes," Maisie read slowly and loudly.

Ana snapped the lid shut. "Can you ever mind your own business?" She pushed the netbook under her pillow, wriggling away from Maisie.

Maisie stuck her tongue out. "I just have a lot of curiosity." That was her favourite retort when Ana accused her of sticking her nose into everyone's business. A tactfully worded line a teacher had written in one of her school reports that Maisie interpreted as a compliment.

"Come on then." Ana tugged at her dressing gown and Maisie raced ahead, beating her to the best spot on the sofa for Sunday night film time.

"D'you want salted or sweet popcorn?" Dad shouted from the kitchen.

"Sweet," Maisie and Ana called simultaneously as Mum opted for the other.

"I'll do both," Dad said. Ana picked up her empty glass from dinner, using it as an excuse to talk to him in the kitchen. She still hadn't had a chance to quiz her parents about the Carmichaels.

It took Dad a while to place them. As soon as Ana

reminded him about Barbara rifling through their bins he nodded. "Ah yes, that poor woman. I used to meet Dr Carmichael at the swimming sometimes."

"Do you know if they moved away?"

Dad scratched his stubble. "I think so. I'm sure Dr Carmichael moved to work in a private clinic somewhere outside Glasgow. I haven't seen him for a good couple of years."

"What kind of doctor was he?" Ana asked, wondering if maybe he had managed to get his wife some sort of specialist treatment at his private clinic.

"Haematologist, I think. I remember him mentioning having to work with children with leukaemia, sounded awful."

"So is that a cancer doctor then?"

Dad shot her a curious look. "What's with all this interest?"

Ana's face burned. She was a terrible liar. "I'm doing a medical project at the moment in Biology. I was wondering if there was anyone local I could ask about it."

"A haematologist specialises in blood disorders I think." Dad handed her a bowl of popcorn. "All set. Come on, I can hear the opening credits running."

Ana chewed on the popcorn, already planning her next Internet search. If Dr Carmichael's clinic was fairly local he shouldn't be hard to track down.

*

Hope was late for school again the next day. When Ana met her after first period at her locker Hope's eyes were heavy with tiredness.

"You okay?" Ana asked.

Hope made a face. "I keep having weird nightmares. I couldn't get back to sleep for ages last night when one woke me. I get bad insomnia sometimes. Then I sleep through my alarm. And Martha knocking." Hope rolled her eyes. "I thought she was going to have a canary rushing me out the door this morning."

Hope pulled out her art folder and Ana noticed scribblings of tarot cards. She thought back to the reading Hope had done for her. The part about having a lot of passion for things and getting involved in something big. Maybe she should try to help Elliot. She was so deep in thought it took her a few minutes to notice desks had been re-arranged when they arrived at English.

"What's the deal, Mr Darwin?" Hope gestured to the name tags sitting on desks of pairs.

Ana's heart thumped when she noticed she'd been paired with Elliot at the front two desks. She scanned the room looking for Hope's name.

Hope strode to the back, throwing her bag down on the table, picking up her partner's name tag. Ana caught a glimpse: *Gordon*. Jenna was going to be mad.

"We're focusing on Shakespeare plays. I wanted to set you all a task of re-writing a scene in modern day language and I thought it might be fun if you work in pairs, one of you focusing on the male speech, the other focusing on the female."

Ana smiled at Elliot, secretly pleased they'd get the chance to work alone on the task.

When Jenna and her gang arrived it didn't take long for them to protest loudly at their pairings. Jenna strode up to Hope, dumping her bag on the desk.

"I'll swap seats with you."

Mr Darwin motioned for Jenna to move. "No you won't, Miss Blackwood. On you go, back to your own desk please."

Mr Darwin walked around the room, laying down text. Romeo and Juliet was printed along the top, with a couple of scenes in the handout. Their first meeting, the famous balcony scene, and the death scene.

"You can choose one of the scenes, try them all or just use them as your inspiration."

Murmurs of protest circled the room. "This language is ridiculous, sir. How are we supposed to know what it means?" Jenna threw her text down on the desk.

"It's the language of love," Gordon shot Hope a lecherous look. "I understand exactly what it means."

Jenna stared incredulously at Gordon as the room erupted in giggles. She silenced her friends with a death stare.

"I think most of us are familiar with the concept of what's going on in the text, Jenna. I'm not expecting you to translate it per se, word for word. Think of a situation where a girl and a boy might meet in modern day but can't be together." Mr Darwin leaned against his desk. "Maybe they live half-way across the world from one another and can only communicate online."

Ana glanced at Elliot. He was reading through the script, deep in thought.

He turned to her and she averted her eyes, not wanting him to think she was staring.

"Romeo is such a lame character."

She waited for Elliot to explain.

"At the start he's pining for Rosalind, then as soon as he meets Juliet he's instantly in love with her. Then when he thinks she's dead he kills himself. It's all too intense."

She grinned. "When you put it like that he sounds a bit of an idiot. But maybe he was just a hopeless romantic?"

Elliot looked back down at the script, tapping his pen against his chin. "Romeo compares Juliet to the sun, but what if we re-write it and actually she's from the moon, like a lady on the moon, who's come to earth for a limited time and everyone thinks she's weird..."

"...because she actually glows yellow," Ana interjected, as Elliot scribbled notes.

"Yes!" he grinned. "But Romeo is fascinated by her, he kind of likes that she's a bit weird. And he's attracted to her light, like he says in the play."

"And when it comes for the time for her to return to her moon, Romeo kills himself and turns into a star?" she suggested.

Elliot drew a crescent moon, adding a star hanging from the tip. "And they get to hang together forevermore." They laughed.

Gordon's voice boomed from the back of the classroom, distracting them. Realising he had an audience, he stood, addressing his script to Hope.

"Oh Juliet your lips are so fine. Geeze a kiss and I'll show you a good time. I don't care if your Da says you're too young for a lumber, c'mon over to mine for a slumber. There's a wee twinkle in your eye, you cannie deny, that you think I'm a pretty hot guy. I will forever live in HOPE, that you'll allow me a grope..."

The room erupted in laughter and wolf whistles.

"Alright, Gordon. Very amusing." Mr Darwin gestured for him to sit down.

Gordon bowed, attempting to take Hope's hand. She yanked it away, face burning brighter than her hair.

Jenna's face was thunder. Her friends tutted and

shook their heads in solidarity, flashing Hope looks of disdain. Not Gordon of course. It was Hope's fault.

As soon as the class ended Jenna was by Gordon's side, grabbing his arm, pulling him away.

"Parting is such sweet sorrow. Until we meet again." Gordon blew Hope a kiss, and Ana was convinced Jenna might actually self-combust.

Hope rolled her eyes and Ana smiled nervously, wondering if she realised the potential monster she had just unleashed.

Ana waited for Hope to gather her stuff, pleased that Elliot was also hovering by the door.

Mr Darwin nodded to Ana and Elliot. "You two get on to class. I want to have a quick chat with Hope."

They exchanged puzzled looks and Hope waved. "Tell Mr P I've been held up."

Ana nodded and set off with Elliot, noticing Jenna and Gordon arguing further up the corridor, Jenna gesticulating in frustration.

"Do you know how humiliating that was?"

Ana caught snippets of their words as they climbed the stairwell.

"Can't you take a joke? It was just a bit of fun. We're not married for god's sake."

Elliot let out a low whistle. "Looks like Jenna might kill Romeo."

Ana looked down, watching as Jenna unclipped her silver heart necklace, throwing it on the ground.

"We're done. You're welcome to that skank."

Hope didn't appear in any other classes that morning. Ana found Elliot at lunch and they pondered over where she could be.

"Maybe Jenna murdered her." Elliot meant it as a joke, but a part of Ana was worried. Hope hadn't responded to her message either. Elliot nudged her, nodding at the half-eaten onion ring on his plate. "Moon shape."

Ana smiled, hoping that Mr Darwin kept their new seating arrangements in English. For a while at least.

"Miss me?"

She turned in relief as Hope laid a hand on her shoulder.

"Where've you been all morning?" Ana watched as Hope dumped her bag on the table.

"Mr Darwin told me I've to work on extra credits for a while, for assessments I missed. He said he would bring me lunch, to let me continue working, but I was like, no way, see ya later." She craned her neck, glancing up at the food cabinets. "I'm starving. Be right back."

Ana noticed Hope's canteen card lying on the table. She grabbed it, hurrying after her.

"Hope!" Ana called. She turned and then everything slowed down. An arm shot out and icy liquid slammed against Ana's chest, chocolate gunk spattering her face and glasses.

Ana gaped at Hope in shock then turned to see Jenna staring, guilt and regret on her face, and Ana knew from her expression she'd got in the firing line. A crescendo of laughs erupted across the canteen and Ana stared in dismay as thick chocolate milkshake slid down her jumper. *Get out of here. Just run.* A voice was shouting in her head, but all she could do was helplessly look around the room, a crowd of mocking faces, fingers pointing.

"Why did you do that, Jenna?" Hope grabbed napkins from a nearby table, thrusting them at Ana.

"It was meant for you, you cow." Jenna seethed.

"Fight, fight, FIGHT." A chant erupted from a

nearby table of boys, cutlery slamming, echoing across the canteen.

Hope tried to mop down the mess, "It's in your hair, Ana. Let's go to the toilets." She manoeuvred her away from Jenna, holding more napkins against Ana's dripping top.

"Chocolate and strawberry. Mmm." A boy grabbed at Ana's hair on their way past.

Hope slapped his hand away, practically hissing in his face.

"Stop this noise IMMEDIATELY."

They froze at the voice behind them. Ana turned to see Ms Turnberry pointing at the slob of shake smeared across the floor. "Who is responsible for this mess?" An eerie silence swept the room.

Jenna had conveniently snuck away to her table of friends. Ms Turnberry glared at Hope, her eyebrows shooting up at the sight of Ana.

"Ms Gilbert. I think you should go home and change."

"I'll go with her," Hope volunteered quickly.

"No, you will not, Ms Devaney. Ana is a big girl. You can stay behind and explain exactly what happened here."

Hope squeezed Ana's hand. "Walk fast and don't look at anyone on your way out," she whispered.

Ana nodded, practically running back to their table. Elliot handed over her bag and coat. She couldn't even look at him. She grabbed them and ran, praying that the image of her dripping in chocolate milkshake wouldn't linger in his memory.

As soon as she left the school grounds Ana pulled off her jumper, rolling it and stuffing it in her bag. The chocolate had seeped through to her shirt. She slid her arms into her coat, zipping it up. She rooted around for wipes, rubbing at her face and glasses so she didn't get strange looks on her walk home.

As soon as Ana turned on to her street relief flooded through her shaking body. She squeezed her eyes shut, trying to block out the humiliating images of a hall full of pupils laughing and pointing. Please let no one have taken a video. *Oh God.* As soon as the thought flooded her brain she knew someone was bound to have filmed it. She pulled her phone out, checking for notifications, praying nobody would post it. *Bloody Jenna.*

The sight of Mum's car in their drive halted all thoughts. Ana glanced at the time on her phone, just to double check. One thirty. Why would she be home from work already? Heart thumping, she hurried up the stairs, trying the handle. It was open.

"Hello? Mum? Are you home?" Ana shut the door, straining to hear any noise. The ticking of the clock in the hallway echoed in the silence. "Mum?" She called again, dumping her bag in the hall, unzipping her coat. She pushed the kitchen door open, the smell of freshly brewed coffee in the air. A half-eaten sandwich was on the kitchen counter. The door to the conservatory was ajar and Ana walked towards it, realising she was practically on tip toe.

Through the gap she could make out the form of Mum, curled up on a chair watching a video streaming on her netbook. Ana hesitated, wanting to know what she was watching and worried if she made her presence known, she would hide it from her.

Images of brain scans flashed up on the screen, zooming out to reveal a woman talking on a stage, with red letters spelling TED behind her. Mum loved watching TED talks about all kinds of topics. The image changed, with neurons filling the screen.

Words like Synapse and Amyloid Beta flashed up. Ana repeated them over and over in her head, trying to commit them to memory so she could google them later. *Memory*. As she watched Mum reach for a notebook and pen, scribbling frantically, Ana knew she must be watching the video for research purposes. She wanted to know what she had found.

Ana opened the door wider and her mum jumped, sensing the movement. Ana smiled and waved and Mum slammed the lid of her netbook shut.

"Ana, why on earth are you home? Are you okay?" She jumped to her feet, moving towards Ana, her eyes registering the chocolate shake in her hair.

"I'm okay. Someone spilled milkshake on me at lunch. The head teacher told me to come home to change."

Mum's semi-panic visibly melted to relief. She glanced at the netbook and looked poised to explain her own presence. Ana knew she was going to lie.

"Mum," Ana interrupted. "I want to ask you something."

Surprise flashed in her mum's eyes.

"I overheard you and dad talking the other week about an appointment you had. At the memory clinic."

Mum's face paled. She slumped against the arm of the chair, looking down at the closed netbook like it had betrayed her. She nodded, as if making a decision.

"Okay, sit down. I have to be back at work soon so don't have long. Did you have lunch already, you want anything to eat?"

Ana shook her head and folded herself into the sofa across from her mum, wondering if she was really ready to hear the truth.

Mum took a sip from her coffee. "You know everything that happened with your Grandma…"

Ana held her breath, watching as she attempted a reassuring smile.

"I've been having some memory issues lately and finding it quite difficult to focus at work, which can be quite common for women my age. You've heard me grumbling often about my perimenopause. But your dad got a bit concerned about a few things, and there's history with not just Grandma but her older sister, my Aunt Fran, who you never met because she passed when you were very young. She had early-onset dementia; it started in her early fifties, and when the opportunity arose for me to get tested I decided to just go for it as that type can sometimes be hereditary."

Mum was talking fast, which she always did when she was nervous, or upset. Ana hugged the cushion tight.

"I was very fortunate to be sent for one of the newer PET scans. It's a biomarker test where they can detect amyloid protein which is something that builds up in the brain and can be an indicator if there's anything going on. We're still waiting on results, so I don't want you to worry, okay?"

She reached forward and squeezed Ana's hand and Ana squeezed back, not wanting to let go and wanting to ask a million questions, but not knowing where to start.

Mum tapped the lid of her netbook. "There're some good talks by smart people who can explain things a lot better than I can about the science part. Want me to email you the link to the one I was just watching?"

"Sure," Ana attempted to smile. "When will you

get the results?"

"We're not sure. Hopefully it won't be long." Mum held her arms out. "Now come on and give me a hug before we go back to the grind."

Ana clambered over to her mum's sofa and swallowed back the tears threatening, squeezing her extra tight. The worry that had been nagging at Ana the past few weeks started to loop round her head and an overwhelming sensation of wanting things to always stay the same and never change washed over her. Their list of birthday milestone trips and plans now seemed too far in the future.

Ana untangled her limbs from their hug and shot Mum a hopeful look. "How about we just skidge the rest of the day? Hop on a plane to Barcelona?"

Mum chuckled. "Nice try kiddo." She ruffled her hair. "You never explained the milkshake highlights. I'll drop you back at school once you change and you can tell me on the way. And let's watch a film tonight. You get to choose."

The worry dulled to a distant hum as Ana ran upstairs to put on fresh clothes. The test results weren't back yet. There was no point in obsessing over something that wasn't even a certainty.

Chapter Eight
Hope

Jenna and her friends lined up at their lockers, watching my every step, whispers of 'slut' trailing at my heels. Ana didn't leave my side, furious that Ms Turnberry hadn't even given Jenna a warning.

"I'm going to put in a complaint, then."

I shook my head, turning the combination of my locker. "It'll just provoke Jenna more. Let's just ignore her." The part that made me angry was finding out Ms Turnberry had called Martha, making it sound like I had caused an argument with Jenna and she had 'accidentally' spilled her milkshake in the altercation. Martha convinced me she was on my side, but I could tell having Ms Turnberry call her about my behaviour embarrassed her. Like it was a judgement on her ability to take care of me.

I turned my head as Gordon attempted to catch my attention.

"Hey, Hope. Looking forward to English later." He called down the corridor. I ignored him, pulling Ana in the opposite direction. "I'm skipping English today. There's no way I'm going to be part of their drama."

"You shouldn't need to avoid class because of them." Ana frowned.

I shrugged. "You fancy coming to mine for dinner tonight?"

Ana's face brightened. "That would be great." She hesitated, her smile disappearing. "Actually sorry, I forgot, I'm having a film night with my mum. I'd invite you, but there's some stuff going on at home just now. Another time?"

"Sure, no problem. Everything okay?" I was curious. Ana didn't talk much about her family, but I got the impression they were a tight unit.

Ana shook her head. "It's a long story. I'll explain another time."

"Okay." I nodded in the direction of Biology. "I've got higher. Catch you later."

When English arrived I slid into the senior girls' toilets, knowing the door was always unlocked. I was relieved to have the place to myself and hoisted myself up beside the sinks, raking through my bag, searching for my phone. Lucy's letter caught my eye. I still hadn't read it, and still wasn't sure I wanted to. Maybe I should just destroy it. My lighter was poking out of a half-empty cigarette pack I kept for stressful emergencies. I held up the letter, counting to three in my head. My thumb sparked a flame. Images of Lucy, sitting penning words, a concerned frown on her face flashed through my head. I knew the pages would be full of guilt and apologies, but also love and reassurance. A craving hummed inside for her words, her comfort.

I unfolded the letter, hands shaking as I scanned over the words.

Dear Hope,

I don't know how many times I've tried to write this letter and the words are still not enough, I know that. How can I explain how much you were loved by us both, when I know you must feel I abandoned you, and let you down. We tried to figure out a way to keep you with us, but Mum's house is too small and she was too ill to travel up here to be with us. I'm not sure she would have survived the journey. This must all sound like excuses, I'm sorry. We were advised you need stability and routine and we were just unable to offer either anymore.

I hope wherever you moved to that you are happy and that you have a wonderful life. You are such a beautiful, special girl, Hope. So smart and mature. Your life has so many possibilities and I know it must feel like you've had to take a lot of unwelcome turns, but don't give up. I want you to know how much we loved having you, how you brightened up our lives. You have no idea. So please, don't be sad, or angry. Know how loved you were, are. I've put my mum's address at the bottom of the letter. I would love to hear from you. My mother has been making me plan her funeral the past few days. Awful, but so like her. She told me to include this poem for you, that she has insisted I read at her service (replacing the word 'father' with 'mother'). She said it is 'words we should all live by' and that she's sorry she stole me away from you.

Take care, Love Lucy xxx

I refused to let the words penetrate anywhere near my heart, holding my breath, as if that prevented me from absorbing the full impact. I chose to focus on the last lines, the apology from Lucy's mother. She sounded like a woman who took no nonsense and it made me want to read the attached poem: *Do Not Go Gentle into That Good Night* by Dylan Thomas.

I read the poem over and over, trying to memorise the lines, even although I didn't fully understand it. I liked the fierceness behind the idea of 'raging against the night'.

My eyes were drawn back to Lucy's words; *You are such a beautiful, special girl, Hope.*

I shoved the letter back in my bag, blinking back

angry tears, ranting to Lucy in my head: *So special, you abandoned me. You just decided, like the rest of them, what was best, without actually asking me.*

I dug out the cigarettes. The surge of nicotine shot through my body. I closed my eyes, leaning my head back against the mirror, squeezing my eyes shut, trying to stop the tears, trying to block out her words. *'Know how loved you were, are.'* Empty words, easy to write in a letter.

"If you really loved me, Lucy, you would have found a way," I grumbled, between puffs.

My phone vibrated against my thigh, a welcome interruption. Balancing the cigarette between my lips I pulled it out from the zipped front pocket.

A message from Ana flashed up: *Jenna isn't even in class. Bet she didn't want to face Gordon.*

I sighed, debating about heading up late. Then I noticed a text from Ruth, sent earlier: *Been looking into those names. I can't tell you anything but I want to have a chat with your pal, ask him some questions about that boy, Seb.*

No problem. Can arrange for you to meet him anytime or can give you his number. Let me ask him. As I hit send a blaring alarm pierced the air. I jumped down in shock, frantically stubbing out my cigarette, looking at the ceiling for smoke alarms.

I ran the taps, waving my hands around, trying to get rid of the smoke. Sounds of doors slamming, clambering footsteps and excited chatter floated under the door. I realised the alarm was in the distance, not inside the girls' toilets. It couldn't have been me. I deliberated about going out. It was probably just a drill. And then Mr Darwin would question why I hadn't been in English. I paced up and down, the sounds of laughter and chatter rising and falling as crowds passed the doorway. Then eventually, silence, the sound transmitting now in the distance from outside, across the playing fields where classes were gathering and registers would be called.

Mr Darwin would need to raise the alarm that I hadn't been in class and couldn't account for my whereabouts. Then Ms Turnberry might call Martha again. And there was also the possibility the school might actually be on fire. I slung my bag over my shoulder and headed out. The memory of my nightmare from a few nights ago, with Mum surrounded by smoke shouting for me to 'get out' sent a stab of fear shooting up my legs and I picked up pace. As I hurried along the corridor I spotted someone hovering by the lockers. They had a jacket and hood up, so it was hard to make them out.

"Ms Devaney."

I jumped at the voice, turning away from the locker. Ms Turnberry glared down at me.

"Why are you not outside with the others?"

"I was in the toilet," I mumbled.

She sniffed the air. "Why do you smell of cigarettes?"

I was tempted to tell the brazen truth, but the voice warning me to stay under the radar made me hesitate. "Girls must have been smoking in there earlier."

She shot me a withering look, her face inching closer to mine. "Don't ever take me for a fool, Ms Devaney. The other stragglers vape, making your filthy habit all the more noticeable. I know a troublemaker when I see one. Outside this instant."

By the time I made it downstairs and out the fire exit, crowds were dispersing and classes were being herded back in to the school again. I scanned the crowd, clocking Ana. I waved but she nodded at Mr Darwin, shaking her head, motioning for me to go back inside. She made a sick gesture and I gave her the thumbs up, grinning.

The bell for next period rang and I relaxed, realising I had no other classes that day with Jenna or Gordon. As I walked past the lockers I looked for signs of the hooded figure but they had gone, crowds obscuring any possible sighting.

Elliot passed me on the stairs and I caught his attention. "Hey, Elliot. Can I pass your number to my social worker?"

He frowned. "Has she found out something?"

Boys shoved me from behind, asking me to move.

"Maybe. I'll explain later."

In Music I settled into class, enjoying the ritual of Mr Beck playing a relaxing piano piece as we took our seats. I knew it was a tactic to quieten us down and it worked, calming the chat instantly. I closed my eyes, feeling the notes wash over me, my fingers restless, wanting to play. I'd loved Mum's old piano and the music she taught me. Mr Beck started a familiar melody, one of my favourites. I absorbed the music, memories caressing me with a reassuring warmth I wanted to never forget in case I never found that feeling again.

The music stopped abruptly. I opened my eyes, a cold dread extinguishing my calm when I saw Ms Turnberry. She motioned for Mr Beck to get up, talking in hushed tones. He glanced in my direction and my gut tightened. *What now?*

"Ms Devaney. I'd like you to come to my office," Ms Turnberry instructed.

Heads turned, curious eyes watching as I stood. I looked to Mr Beck for answers. He stepped to one side and shot me a reassuring smile but it did nothing to comfort. Ms Turnberry's expression was cold, brimming with menace. As I made a move for my bag she shook her head, "Leave that."

Reluctantly I laid it down and left the room with her.

"What's going on?" I asked, following her down the stairs, wondering if there was CCTV in the girls' toilets and she'd found evidence of me smoking.

As we turned down the last steps into the main corridor Ms Turnberry's continued silence did nothing to reassure me. Her heels clip-clipped in time with my heart. She stopped at her office door, gesturing me inside. A throb of panic pulsated through my veins as I obeyed, even although every part of me wanted to run.

Chapter Nine
Hope

"Sit down," Ms Turnberry instructed.

I took a seat on a green leather chair, my eyes scanning her desk, noting a bulky plastic bag and familiar folder. *My art folder*, I realised with a jolt, tarot card pouch visible through the clear plastic. My eyes returned to the other bag, a sickening feeling creeping up my throat as I registered the coloured pills.

"Do you recognise the items on my desk?" Ms Turnberry asked, her beady eyes fixing on mine.

"I recognise the folder, it's my art folder." I shook my head. "But not the bag. That's not mine."

Ms Turnberry didn't react. She stood up, walking over to a kettle on a tray behind her, flicking the switch and placing a tea bag in a cup. A trail of her perfume circled the air, sickeningly sweet in the enclosed room.

"Would you like a cup of tea, Hope?" She turned her head.

"No." I wanted to tell her to stop playing around, to get to the point. I guessed she was enjoying drawing things out, like she was playing some psychological game. I glanced at the photo sitting on her desk. A pair of Siamese cats, paws intertwined, lying on a chaise lounge, ruby red collars around their necks.

"I received a tip-off this afternoon. Reports that you've been supplying drugs to pupils."

"What?" I spluttered, the sense of dread blooming

into panic.

Ms Turnberry held up her hand. "Let me finish, Hope." She waited for the kettle to boil, stirring in milk and two sugars before sitting back down across from me. "I have to take these allegations very seriously of course. So I asked the janitor to give me access to your locker. Imagine my absolute shock and disappointment to find this *assortment* hidden in the back." She gestured to the pills in disgust.

"That is not my bag. I've never seen it before." I heard the tremble in my voice and I forced myself to breathe, to try to calm the fury and horror rising in my chest. "You must have opened someone else's locker."

Ms Turnberry licked her lips, red lipstick bleeding into the creases. She took a sip of her tea, talon nails curling round the handle. "But you just said this is your art folder. We found them in the same locker."

"Anyone could have put that bag of pills in my locker. In fact I saw someone hanging around there earlier." I sat up, remembering the hooded figure.

"What are you implying, Hope?" Ms Turnberry laid her cup down, the tea slopping over the side. "I had your pastoral care teacher accompany me to your *locked* locker, along with the janitor. As far as we could see there was no sign of forced entry. Your pastoral care teacher is on the phone to the Browns right now."

No. I shook my head. "I want to speak to Martha."

Ms Turnberry tapped my art folder. "I'm hazarding a guess that pouch inside there contains your tarot cards? Can I look?"

I watched as she opened the folder and slid out the pouch, not waiting for permission.

"Do you like having foster carers, Hope?"

If she'd asked me that question when I was staying with the O'Brians then my answer would have been no, I did not enjoy that ugly picture of their 'family' unit, and never felt cared for. Living with Andy and Lucy always felt too good to last. A stab of hurt reminded me I had been right to think that. With the Browns, even with their peculiar old-fashioned manners, came a comfort, and a sense of order.

Before I had a chance to confirm just how much I did like the Browns, Ms Turnberry continued, "Being in the care system can be a lonely and unpredictable life. I've encountered many young people over the years who find it hard to navigate, finding themselves taking the wrong path."

She untied my tarot pouch. "I can see you're a smart girl, Hope. And I'd like to offer you an alternative path today that I think would suit you immensely."

I watched in confusion, wondering if she was going to burn my tarot cards in some sort of sacrifice and bring out a Bible.

"I don't understand what you're saying." I wanted her to hurry up, to let me out of here so I could get home to Martha and tell my side of the story. The end of period bell rang, making me fidget.

Ms Turnberry pursed her lips and set the tarot pouch to one side. "There is an alternative *children's house* available to a hand-chosen few. You would get to stay there, have your own room, meals cooked for you, on-site tutors with other excellent facilities. The other young people there have found it an excellent arrangement."

I shook my head. "I don't want to move to another place. I like the Browns. I'm happy in this school, I've made friends and I'm doing well in class…"

A flicker of irritation crossed Ms Turnberry's face, her mouth straightening into a hard line.

"You *were* getting on well in class," she interrupted, holding up the bag. "I don't think you understand the severity of this situation."

I shut my mouth, waiting for her to lay it out clearly for me.

She dangled the bag between her nails. "I don't tolerate drugs in my school. It's an automatic expulsion. I'm not sure you'd find Brackley High quite so friendly at the other part of town. And of course I should call the police. Dealing to other students takes it to more serious levels. Can you imagine the humiliation Martha Brown would feel if you were to be carted off the school grounds in the back of a police car?"

I watched as she swung the bag closer towards me, taunting me, parading her power. *Look what I can do. Look how I get to control your life, your everything.* That helpless feeling, of being at the mercy of too many adults who didn't want to know me, was a familiar dull ache inside my bones.

"Your foster carers certainly would not tolerate this kind of behaviour."

An image of Martha hovering at my bedroom door, sniffing in disgust at my incense sticks. I could imagine her passing out at the sight of the delights in this bag.

I flinched as Ms Turnberry slid her talons across my tarot pack. I willed her to move her hand away. "And a religious woman like Mrs Brown would certainly not approve of *this* dark hocus pocus either. I hinted of my worries about you when I spoke to Martha yesterday. Why are you using these cards in your art project, Hope?"

A fizz of anger sparked in my throat as I watched her sausage fingers slide the top of the pack open, flicking the tips of the cards. *Tarot is about light and goodness, something you would never understand*, I wanted to shout. But instead I sat watching, gripping the sides of my chair, nails digging indents into the leather arm rests.

"Do you really want the unpredictability of new foster carers? So many variables, aren't there?" She smiled, a horrible knowing smile. "To be honest, with this new development in your behaviour it's very unlikely you'll be placed with another family. I think I would need to have a long chat with your social worker about your re-location. A secure unit could be another option to ensure you don't step out of line again any time soon."

I frowned, detecting grave promises in her tone. How much power exactly *did t*his woman have?

"I'd like to speak to my social worker, actually. Right now." I cursed myself for not demanding that first. I pictured the steely determination of Ruth's eyes, her authoritative clipped tones which told everyone around her she meant business. The thought of her by my side made me sit up straighter and calmed the sense of doom.

A smirk played on Ms Turnberry's lips. "I'm afraid your social worker, Ms McDonald, won't be able to help you. She's been suspended pending an enquiry and all contact with any current caseload is forbidden. I would be happy to call the department to request that Mr Hobbs join us today. When I called the department earlier, Ian explained he has taken you on to his caseload. He's a good friend of mine, worked closely with staff and pupils in our school for many years, a very well-respected man." She paused, her eyes casting an assessing glance across my face. I tried to bury the sense of panic rising above the anger. Ruth couldn't be suspended.

"You're lying. Ruth texted me earlier today." I reached down for my bag, forgetting it was still up in music.

Ms Turnberry looked pointedly at her watch, tapping the glass frame. "I believe Ms McDonald was escorted from her offices at precisely three thirty this afternoon. Coinciding with the exact moment you could have done with her support the most. Isn't that most unfortunate, Ms Devaney?"

Ms Turnberry reached for her cup of tea, hand perfectly steady as she took a slow sip, staining the rim scarlet. Her eyes met mine. "I can see you're upset about Ruth."

Upset was a word that sounded too soft for the rush of dread I felt pumping through my body. The one person who would fight to get me out of this mess, had now been extracted from my life.

Ms Turnberry shook her head. "You have to remember, Hope, that you youngsters are just another statistic in a case file. Your social worker isn't your friend. The sooner you young people understand that, the better for you. It never pays to get attached. Can we move on now?"

Something I'd held tightly wound within me for the past couple of years threatened to snap. *Not here. Not now. Not in front of this woman.* The voice was clear and strong in my head. Often I wondered if it was just a memory of Mum's reassurances to me in life, or if she was actually butting in to be heard above my own inner thoughts. It was totally her style, to butt in and be listened to. Today, I allowed myself to truly believe it was her, and that she was going to be beside me, through this, whatever was next.

I waited for Ms Turnberry to continue, clenching my hands together, trying to control my emotions.

"So let me return to my offer. In this new house, this exclusive place for young people in…*your position*, you will have your own space, you will have the best education. There is an in-house cinema, a library, your own room…"

I watched her face carefully, my disbelief rising as she listed the luxuries, like she was selling a dream holiday. Why had I been chosen for this exclusive place? Why had Ms Turnberry gone to such lengths to set this up? A shiver shuddered through my body.

"I want to stay with the Browns." I tried to keep my voice strong and steady.

Ms Turnberry held my gaze, unable to hide her irritation. "Stay here. Let me check in with how the conversation is going with Martha." She gathered up her keys, closing the door behind her and locking me in. Like she was scared I would do a runner. I folded my arms. Accurate, as that was exactly what I wanted to do. The clock ticked loudly on the wall and with each minute that passed, a sense of dread bloomed deeper in my gut, making me feel nauseous.

The key turned in the door and I held my breath as Ms Turnberry strode back in. I watched the expression on her face carefully, hopefully, praying that Martha was on her way to collect me.

She took her time sitting back down across from me, clearing her throat and patting her hair.

"What did Martha say?" My voice was quieter, and my nerves were betraying me, causing a quiver.

Ms Turnberry's smile was tight and dripping with fake sympathy. "I'm afraid Martha has requested we find alternative accommodation for you."

I stared at her, feeling the room tilt, another part of me cracking inside. Tears burned behind my eyes. Martha was choosing to think the worst of me. Why wouldn't she? She hardly knew me.

I watched as Ms Turnberry ran her hands over my pack of tarot cards. "Martha thinks this new house sounds like a splendid idea. An ideal place to help you get back on track. But of course, if you'd rather we put you back in the other residential house you were previously in, that can also be arranged…"

I held my breath as a couple of the cards started to slide out from the pack. I didn't want her negative energy contaminating my cards. They belonged to me, to my mum, to gran, my family. Seeing her with them felt like she was rifling through my soul.

"Stop." I slammed my hand down on the desk, causing her to nearly jump out of her chair. A rash of red snaked up her neck, her lips trembling in rage at my outburst.

"I'll go to this house, this new place." The words tumbled out in desperation, my heart pounding.

She cleared her throat loudly, no doubt swallowing the tirade of abuse that was cooking in her head.

"Excellent." Her tight smile slithered back into place. "I knew you'd make the right choice. I have a car waiting round the back of the school for you."

A *car*? What kind of creepy operation was this?

"Can I have my cards back?" I held her gaze, determined, defiant.

She sighed, gave a shrug and thrust the pack in my direction.

I gathered them to me in relief, fingers deftly sorting through them as I watched Ms Turnberry rise from her chair. She touched the bag of drugs. "You won't be getting that back of course."

I shot her a withering look.

"I'll arrange for your schoolbooks and study notes to be sent on at a later date."

"I want my phone and purse. They're upstairs in my bag."

"Don't worry about your bag. Someone will have gone to fetch it for you. Your phone will be with your driver and you will get it back on arrival at the house. You will be permitted to send one text message."

"I want to speak to Martha. I want to phone her now." I glanced at the phone lying on Ms Turnberry's desk, trying to remember the Browns' home number. It was important I still had the chance to tell my side of the story.

Ms Turnberry stood, leaning in close across the desk. "If you come now without a fuss, Ms Devaney, I don't need to get the police involved. You can use your message to text Martha from the house."

I faltered. A million questions tumbled through my head. I tried to calm my mind so I could assess my options. If I refused to go and the police did get involved, that could make everything worse. Ruth had warned me that Martha needed time to trust me. Maybe if I went to this house, stayed there for a bit and then spoke to Martha once she'd had time to calm down I would have a better chance of talking her round.

"You said there's other young people in this house? Who runs the place?"

"All will be revealed when you arrive." Ms Turnberry clicked her fingers impatiently, signalling for me to stand. As she turned away from me, I slid out a tarot card from my pack and grabbed a pen lying at the edge of the desk. I suspected the 'one message' from my phone would be monitored. This could be my last chance to attempt to leave another one behind.

As Ms Turnberry fumbled with her keys, I scrawled two words on the card, sliding it up my sleeve. I would need to let it 'drop' somewhere between here and the walk to the car. I slid the rest of the pack in my skirt pocket, imagining a light of protection burning from them, encircling me. Ms Turnberry motioned for me to move faster, locking the door behind us, starting off down the corridor. My boots squeaked against the floors, echoing in the eerie silence of the empty corridors. Everyone had gone home except for any after school clubs. A distant drum beat and piano melody wove down from the stairwell of the Music department as we turned a corner. A strong desire to run up the stairs towards the comforting tune slowed my steps.

Ms Turnberry craned her neck, sensing my hesitation.

"I don't have all day, girl. Come on."

The corner of the tarot card I needed to leave behind prodded at my wrist as I glanced around the corridors, desperate to find a place for it. A janitor carrying a mop nodded at us as he walked past and I realised I couldn't risk just letting it drop to the ground in the hope Elliot or Ana might find it. It was sure to be swept up with all the other litter, or lost in the stampedes between classes in the morning.

As we walked past the lockers I felt light headed, unable to believe it had only been an hour ago I had been blissfully unaware of the fate which awaited me. As I clenched my fist in anger I felt the stones from my thumb ring pierce my skin. I glanced at the trail of stickers curving down the edge of Ana's locker. I slid my ring off, resting it inside the ball of my fist.

"Ms Turnberry?"

"What?" She snapped, turning to me.

I glanced over at the lockers, heart hammering. Mine was still ajar. "Can I get one last thing from my locker?"

Ms Turnberry shook her head. "I told you. I'll arrange for your books to be sent on."

"It's more important than that. It's a ring. I took it off earlier before Art so it didn't get covered in paint…" Ms Turnberry opened her mouth, poised to protest. "Please. It's my mum's. It means a lot to me."

"Hurry up." She waved her hand, turning her head, craning to look further down the corridor as if expecting someone.

I took advantage of her wavering attention, sliding out the tarot card from my sleeve and slipping it through the vent of Ana's locker. I made a show of slamming my locker door shut and sliding my ring back on, this time on my middle finger.

"Open your hands," Ms Turnberry commanded and I slowly turned my palms over, a layer of sweat snaking down my back. She ordered me to hold my arms up and I resisted the urge to recoil as she frisked me, swift and harsh, like an airport security officer. "No more dallying, come on."

I let out a sigh of relief, heart hammering at the thought of Ana opening her locker tomorrow to find my card. It wasn't going to tell her much, just enough for her to know I needed help. I thought of Elliot and his determination to find his foster brother. I hoped they both cared about me enough to have the same desire to search for me.

A swish of cold air hit me like a slap in the face as Ms Turnberry pushed the fire escape door open. A grey car with blacked out windows sat waiting, engine running. My heart was beating so fast a wave of dizziness caused me to falter.

"Hang on," I grabbed Ms Turnberry's arm. "I just have one more question."

"Yes?" she sighed impatiently, shaking off my grip.

"This place you're taking me to, it sounds too good to be true. What's the catch?"

She hesitated, lowering her voice. "It's all true; the luxuries, the comfort." My attention wavered as the back door of the car opened. A petite brunette woman climbed out, walking towards me, a white cloth folded in her hands. Something about her smiley face was familiar.

Ms Turnberry's voice pulled me back to focus on her words, "All they want in return is one little thing. Your blood."

Chapter Ten
Ana

Dark clouds dominated the sky, a damp fog winding around trees, obscuring a clear path, complementing Ana's mood. Her steps felt heavy, like she was walking through a dream.

After her conversation with Mum and watching the TED talk link she'd sent, Ana kept googling like crazy when she couldn't sleep, researching tips for the prevention of Alzheimer's, now understanding her weird new 'diet'. She'd also managed to find out more information about Dr Carmichael's clinic, bookmarking information about groundbreaking blood trials he referenced, originating from America, where scientists believed pure plasma transfusions could boost cell production and possibly eradicate symptoms of early on-set dementia.

Ana pulled out her phone, re-reading the string of messages she'd sent to Hope last night, willing a reply to pop up. Was Hope angry with her because Ana had said no to her dinner invite? The sense of unease heightened when Ana arrived at the school gates, no flash of red hair in sight. The last she'd seen or heard from Hope was yesterday on the playing fields. What if she really had fallen ill? Karma, or what.

"She's not with you, then?"

Ana turned to see Elliot. They waited another few minutes, shivering in the cold.

"She didn't reply to my message last night." Elliot frowned. "Which I thought was weird as she stopped me in the corridor yesterday making it sound like her social worker wanted to talk to me."

"Oh yeah? About your foster brother?"

Elliot shrugged. "I think so."

They checked their phones one last time, exchanging glances as the bell rang.

"She probably slept in again." They said their goodbyes agreeing to meet at interval.

As soon as Ana walked into class the murmurs started, gazes following her to her seat. Ana did a quick scan to make sure she hadn't trailed toilet roll in on her shoe. Maybe someone had uploaded a reel of the milkshake massacre after all. She slumped down in her chair, wishing she could sink through the floor.

Whispers hissed from the desk behind where Jenna and her friends sat. "I heard she's been suspended after her locker raid."

Ana turned her head, straining to hear. Jenna's friend, Kim, talked animatedly. "She was apparently supplying pills to pupils, desperate for cash. She lives with a foster family, right?"

"Shut up." Ana slammed her bag on the table, gaining a glimmer of satisfaction when Jenna jumped, colour draining from her face. "If you spread those stupid rumours I'll…"

"You'll what?" Jenna leaned forward, propping her arms on the back of her chair, eyes challenging.

Ana desperately tried to think of a smart comeback, but could see Jenna's friends watching, smirking.

Jenna moved her face closer to hers. Ana could smell mint chewing gum on her breath as she hissed, "This isn't a stupid rumour, Ana. Go and ask a teacher. Your new pal is probably rotting in a cell somewhere." Jenna's friends giggled and Ana pulled her chair forward, away from their gossip.

Ana pulled out her phone, scrolling to Hope's number and pressed call, ignoring the disapproving glances from the sub teacher. The number connected, rang once and then went to voicemail, Hope's voice in her ear: *If you leave me a message make sure it's interesting.*

*

No teachers were willing to disclose any information, rumours shut down with angry warnings at the start of every new class that day. Jenna and her friends didn't mention their drug theory again, or why they suspected it.

"What if she planted drugs on her?" Ana said to Elliot over lunch. "It's totally Jenna's style. She never got her revenge satisfaction with the milkshake because it hit me."

Elliot frowned. "I dunno. Seems a bit extreme, even for Jenna."

"I think we should go and ask Hope's pastoral care teacher."

Elliot looked reluctant. "There's no way her pastoral care teacher is going to share private information with us."

Ana sighed in frustration, knowing he was right. "Her foster carers will know what happened. How about we go there after school?" She could feel her pulse throbbing in her throat, the panic of the situation making her bold. She would never usually have the guts to ask Elliot to go anywhere with her.

"Let's wait and see if we hear anything later. Maybe Hope will turn up for afternoon classes."

But she didn't. On Ana's way to last period she passed the pastoral care base. She hesitated, turning down the corridor, trying to remember what teacher had been assigned to Hope. The door was ajar as she approached. A few teachers were standing making coffee. She hung back, listening as the school careers adviser read out a list of names to one of them.

"You'd asked me to book in an appointment for the new fifth year, Hope Devaney. Her Maths teacher mentioned to me today that she's left. Has she transferred to another school?"

Ana froze, creeping back from the door, pressing herself against the wall.

"Jean, do you know anything about that girl, Hope?"

"I need to check a few things with Ms Turnberry, but I don't think she'll be back. I think she's gone to England."

England? The thought of Hope leaving, without saying goodbye, was like a kick to Ana's gut. Why would she go to England? Ana's phone sat heavy in her pocket, the unanswered messages feeling like an unfinished conversation. *Where did you go, Hope?*

"Can I help you with something?"

Ana jumped at the familiar voice, heart hammering as Ms Turnberry glared down at her.

"Why are you listening to private conversations?" Ms Turnberry pulled the pastoral care door shut, eyes boring in to her.

Fear stole Ana's voice, a blush of mortification at getting caught snaking up her face. Then she thought back to Hope in the canteen, how she stood up to Ms Turnberry, the way Ms Turnberry blamed Hope for the milkshake incident, refusing to punish Jenna. Ana's anger made her stand taller. "I was looking for Hope Devaney. She hasn't turned up to any of her classes today and I haven't been able to get in touch with her."

Ms Turnberry's glare darkened. The coward in Ana wanted to apologise and slink off. She forced herself to hold Ms Turnberry's gaze.

"You've become quite good friends with Ms Devaney, haven't you Ana?"

Surprised that she even knew her name, Ana nodded dumbly.

Ms Turnberry looked her up and down, "From what I know of you, you're a conscientious student, a polite girl from a nice family. I don't think you like trouble, do you?"

Ana stuttered no, wondering where the conversation was going.

"Ms Devaney, on the other hand, courts trouble, can't resist the allure of deviancy. Not surprising really with what she's been through." Ms Turnberry straightened her box jacket, the buttons straining against her plump midriff. "You don't want to get mixed up in any of her nonsense, Ana. Because I guarantee it will lead you down a very dark path. Do you understand what I'm saying?"

"Not really," she said, wanting Ms Turnberry to tell her more.

Ms Turnberry tutted, "You youngsters never *do* understand. You don't need to worry about Hope. In fact, my advice to you Ana, is to forget you ever met her. Return to class and go back to working hard."

"But," Ana shook her head, not willing to accept such a flimsy explanation. Just forget she ever met Hope? "I want to know what happened."

Ms Turnberry's eyes flashed. "Back to class, Ana. And if I find you sneaking about, listening to private conversations again then you will understand the meaning of trouble."

As soon as last period ended Ana shot out of her seat, messaging Elliot to meet her by the lockers. After Ms Turnberry's weird conversation about deviancy she was convinced Hope must have been caught with drugs, and Jenna had to be the one who engineered it.

Hope's locker door swung open, an empty hole of nothing. No books, no trace of her. Ana ran a hand along the inside, wanting to find a clue. Where had everything gone? When did she leave the school building? She slammed the door shut, resting her head against the cool metal. If only Hope had joined her on the pitch. Ana shouldn't have warned her not to come back to class. If they'd been together, at least Ana could have tried to help.

"Hey." A hand touched her shoulder.

Ana turned to Elliot, concern mirrored in his eyes.

"All of her stuff has gone. Someone must have cleared it out," Ana gestured to the locker. "I overheard a teacher saying she won't be back and I had a weird conversation with Ms Turnberry. She told me to forget I ever met her."

Elliot's face fell, "D'you think if she did have drugs that she was arrested?"

Ana sighed. "I don't know." She opened her locker, trying to remember what else Ms Turnberry had said. ... *can't resist the allure of deviancy. Not surprising really with what she's been through.* What exactly had she been through? Ana realised there was so much she still didn't know about Hope. Maybe she was desperate for money, like Jenna had implied.

As if reading her mind, Elliot said hesitantly, "You don't think the rumours could be true, do you? That she was dealing?"

Hearing Elliot say it out loud sounded ridiculous.

Hope was focused on getting good marks, on settling in to her new home. Ana crammed her Maths textbook into her locker, deciding that talking to the Browns was the only way they could find out the truth.

"You dropped something."

Ana stepped back, watching as Elliot bent to pick up a card, the glowing sun and ruby red symbol catching her attention.

Elliot flipped over the card. "What is this?" he frowned.

Ana grabbed it, an image of a lion and a goddess staring up at her, fire manes blazing, the words FIND ME scrawled in bold below them.

"It's a message from Hope." A chill rippled through Ana's veins. If she needed to be found, it meant whatever had happened, it hadn't been her choice to leave.

Chapter Eleven
Hope

Darkness swirled, pulling at me, consuming me. Every part of my body felt too heavy, eyelids weighted shut. My fingers twitched, brushing against leather. A sharp movement dunted my body forward. The squeak of brakes. My eyes flickered. More darkness swirled, but then colour. Raindrops on a window, the whoosh of traffic as cars rolled past, lights blurring red, amber, green.

"I think she's waking up." A voice beside me, a cold hand on my wrist.

I yanked my arm away, a familiar face forming. Dark hair, a pretty smile. Dead eyes.

"We're not there yet. Put her under again. I don't want any fuss on arrival." A clipped voice from the front. Male. Polite.

"No." I shrank back, shoulder digging against a door handle, seatbelt cutting into my neck. A white cloth folded, hands moving towards my face.

"It's okay. Shh. Go back to sleep. It's okay."

Mum. Help me. I want my mum. Please.

The darkness found me again, cloaking me, pulling me under.

*

The sunlight was warm on my face. I twitched, pulling soft covers up to my chin, head sinking into pillows which smelled of fresh cotton. As I rolled over I pictured Mum downstairs flipping an omelette, sprinkling an extra helping of cheese on top. I jolted awake, heart hammering, eyes darting around an unfamiliar room. My brain caught up, remembering, months, years, of grief turning in my mind, a searing pain that left me breathless.

I rubbed at my eyes, head fuzzy. My lips were dry and cracked, throat parched. A wave of nausea rolled. I sat up, taking in the surroundings. I was in a bed double the size of any I'd ever slept in, an elaborate headboard adding to the grandeur, carvings of roses looping together across the wood. Threads of sun strained through a gap in thick velvet curtains, illuminating a large oak desk and to the left a matching wardrobe with full size mirror standing in the corner, gold leaves twisting around the frame. To the right of the bed, a tightly packed bookcase, rows and rows of books with rainbow-coloured spines.

I threw the covers off, shivering as unfamiliar silk blue pyjamas slid against my body when I moved. Who had dressed me? *Undressed* me? Another wave of nausea rolled. My school uniform was folded on a stool in the corner, boots underneath, toes pointing inwards, as if clicking a wish: *There's no place like home.*

Grabbing for the glass of water sitting on the bedside cabinet, I tried to focus on the events from yesterday? (what day was it?), a film on fast forward, pausing, rewinding. Gulping down the water until the glass lay empty, I looked around for a clock, a watch, anything that would give me a clue to time. Nothing.

The sun dipped, darkness bleeding into the room, the heavy curtains smothering the faded light. I clicked the bedside lamp on and crept out of bed, not wanting to make any noise, not wanting to face anything which might lie beyond this room.

A radiator clicked and fizzed, waking up. I tugged at the velvet curtain, peaking through the gap. The window was adorned with criss-cross black diamond patterns, brass levers either side of the middle divide. I held my breath as I pressed and turned the lever, expecting to be met with resistance. A surge of relief flowed through me as the window sprang open, a fresh breeze fluttering in. I gulped in the air, my eyes trailing across acres of garden, a grassy verge extending miles, down to secluded trees. A winding driveway snaked through the grounds, leading down to iron gates, a metal fence with metal wires and strange discs looping along the top, creating a barrier to the outside. From the height and angle of my view I guessed I might be on the top floor. I opened the window further, sticking my head out, straining to make out more of my surroundings. To the right I could see a windowsill, the brickwork curving underneath like a turret. A wind picked up, rippling my hair, a chill cutting through my flimsy nightwear. Shivering, I pulled the window shut and turned back to survey the room.

Ms Turnberry had been right; if this was 'the house' she spoke of, it was luxurious. I shut my eyes, head throbbing as distorted images of a grey car with blacked out windows flashed through my head, and a smile that shouldn't be trusted. Nurse Clara. The house might be posh, but being drugged and bundled into the back of a car by the school nurse tainted the edges.

Ms Turnberry's parting shot made me sway on my feet: *They just want your blood.* What did that mean? That I'd been taken to some vampire lair?

I strained to hear sounds. Radiator pipes clanged and hissed, and floorboards creaked but I heard no voices, no real sign of life. Walking to the door I turned the handle as quietly as I could, gently pulling.

The door didn't budge. I pulled harder. Locked. Fear hummed in my bones.

Hurrying over to my folded uniform I checked underneath the stool, hoping they'd returned my bag, my phone. I'd been promised a text message. Nothing. Opening the bedside drawers, I found face moisturiser, a brush, comb, toothbrush, face cloth, soap, deodorant, sanitary products, painkillers. Like I was in a well-equipped hotel. Or prison. I wandered back to my uniform, remembering I'd shoved my tarot cards in my skirt pocket. Relief flooded through me as my hand touched the familiar pouch. I slid the cards out, fanning through the familiar images.

What felt like an hour passed. I paced round the room, my tummy growling, bladder heavy. They couldn't just keep me locked in here forever. I doubted anyone wanted to clear up my pee. I eyed the bin in the corner, deciding it would need to do if someone didn't arrive soon.

The creak of pipes, different from the radiator, started clanging, a sound like water running. I hurried to the far wall, pressing my ear against it.

"Hello?" I knocked loudly. "Hello, can someone let me out please?"

No response.

I ran to the door, pounding my fists against the wood. "Let me out. Someone let me out." Blood rushed in my ears as I pressed my cheek against the door, trying to calm my breathing so I could hear properly. Metal scraping in the lock made me jump. I stepped back, shivering as the door swung open.

Nurse Clara smiled. "Good morning, Hope. Did you sleep well?"

I stared at her, incredulous at her casual tone, as if drugging people to sleep was an everyday normal occurrence. Perhaps for her it was. I glanced over her shoulder, a hallway extending to reveal more doors, an ornate banister circling a central balcony.

"I need the toilet," I said.

"Of course. Follow me."

I hesitated, following her along the corridor, the red and gold rug stretched along the hardwood floors prickly underneath my bare feet. She stopped two doors along from mine, pushing it open.

"There you go. I'll wait for you back in your bedroom."

The bathroom shone white, large bath dominating, a rain shower in the corner. As I flushed, I noticed a row of mini candles curving around the edge of the bath. The room smelled of lavender and vanilla. Expensive and clean.

I took my time washing my hands, shuddering at the clown face that stared back at me, eyeliner and mascara smudged halfway down my cheeks. I scrubbed at the stains, washing my face clean. Fear shone in my eyes and I gripped the sink, staring hard, scowling at my reflection.

"Toughen up, you loser," I said to my reflection. I thought back to reading Lucy's letter in the girls' toilet. Fractured words of the poem circled round my head: *Do not go gentle into the night…Rage, rage, against the dying of the light.* I stared and stared until the fear dimmed and a defiance shone. My hands shook, reminding me it wasn't that easy to pretend to be brave.

An impatient knock on the door signalled I'd been too long.

"All okay in there?" Clara's sing-song voice bled through the cracks.

Taking a deep breath I opened the door. Clara

peered over my shoulder, scanning the bathroom, as if checking I hadn't demolished the place. Satisfied nothing was amiss, she summoned me back along the hallway. A movement caught my attention and I looked towards the staircase, heart hammering as a dark-haired boy climbed the stairs, hair obscuring his face. He was dressed all in black. Black jeans, black t-shirt, black trainers. As if sensing my gaze, his head shot up. Our eyes locked. A jolt of recognition made me stare. Curiosity sparked in his eyes.

"Hope." Clara turned, motioning for me to move. Her expression darkened, frowning at the boy. She shook her head, as if signalling for him to stay silent.

An image of a crumpled poster, a faded photograph, formed in my fuzzy brain. "Seb," I whispered.

He looked stunned, like I had slapped him.

Clara grabbed my arm, yanking me back inside my room, slamming the door shut.

Chapter Twelve
Ana

The Browns' curtains were drawn and no one answered when Ana rang the bell. She rapped the letterbox, determined to bring someone to the door.

"I don't think they're home," Elliot glanced at his watch. "It's only four. They'll still be at work."

Ana shook her head. "I don't think Mrs Brown works." She glanced at the window, watching for signs of movement. Sighing, she unzipped her bag, searching for a pen.

"What are you doing?"

"I'm going to post a note through the door with my number."

Elliot stuffed his hands in his pockets, watching her scribble. "We could always swing by before school tomorrow morning, catch them before they go out?"

Ana nodded, sliding the note through the letterbox, hoping she'd hear something before then.

*

Conversation at dinner was a distant hum. Ana was vaguely aware of Maisie swinging her legs beside her, chattering about a gold star she'd received for spelling. Ana jumped when Maisie reached across the table, a floret of broccoli falling in her juice.

"Maisie!" Ana exploded as her sister giggled uncontrollably.

"It sounded like a poop. Plop!" Maisie giggled, hands smashed against her mouth.

Ana pushed her plate of untouched food away,

pulling her phone out.

"No phones at the dinner table." Dad shook his head.

"I'm leaving the table." Ana got up, sliding away from Mum's concerned touch. She noticed the subtle shake of her head in Dad's direction, silencing his protest.

Ana's heart jumped when a message from Elliot popped up on her phone: *Any news?*

Checking her call list for the hundredth time, she messaged back a despondent no. What if the Browns had left too? Maybe that was the real reason Hope had gone. Maybe it was nothing bad, just that they had to go on a trip and they'd taken her with them. Ana had nearly convinced herself when she remembered the tarot card.

Elliot said it felt like when Seb left. He went to school one morning and never returned home, leaving all of his clothes and possessions behind.

"But you did hear from him again?"

Elliot made a face. "Just one text. He texted Mum. Which was weird as he knew she was hopeless with texts. It was a miracle she even noticed it as her phone was always switched off."

"What did it say?"

"That he was sorry, that he wanted to start a new life now he'd turned sixteen. Not to look for him and he thanked us for everything."

Ana turned up the volume on her phone, scared she wouldn't hear a call, or a message.

Pacing her room, she tried to think of anything unusual Hope had said or done the last time she'd seen her. She'd said she hadn't been sleeping well, and had nightmares. Maybe something had been troubling her. Ana scrolled her phone, checking

Hope's one social media account. She had no posts and was only following a few accounts, Ana being one. The rest looked like professional artists and photographers. Ana had thought it was kind of cool that Hope seemed to distance herself from online contact. Now it was frustrating as she had no way of trying to find out anything personal, or trace anyone who might have known her in previous schools.

Lying down on her bed Ana flipped open her netbook typing in Hope's name. It brought up a few images of people who were not Hope. She thought back to the photograph Hope had shown her of her mum. Ana changed the search to Daphne Devaney and old news stories popped up.

Thirty-five-year-old mother collapses at Scottish summer music festival after taking MDMA. An image of Daphne's smiling face appeared below the headline.

Daphne Devaney died after she collapsed at popular music festival Echo in the early hours of Sunday morning. Friends reported the mother, whose twelve-year-old daughter was also at the festival, had purchased ecstasy from an unknown source to help her 'relax' and 'enjoy her last night of dancing'. Tragically, these were prophetic words, as paramedics at the scene failed to resuscitate Daphne.

A sickening feeling washed over Ana as she continued reading. She scrambled for her phone, snapping a photo of the article, sending it to Elliot. *Maybe the drug rumours are true after all?*

A few minutes later Elliot's response beeped. *Doubt she'd want to deal the drugs that killed her mum.*

Ana read back over the line: *twelve-year-old*

daughter was also at the festival. What if Hope found her? She couldn't even imagine. Ana squeezed her eyes shut, tears threatening. Losing her mum, because of one stupid night.

"Ana." There was a quiet knock on her door.

Ana slammed her netbook shut, wiping at her eyes. Mum sat down on the bed beside her, nodding towards the netbook. "What's the homework tonight?"

Ana was tempted to tell her the truth, that she was trying to find out where her friend had gone, then she remembered the research she'd been doing the other night.

"Science." Flipping open the lid, Ana clicked on her bookmarks, calling up Dr Carmichael's clinic. She swivelled the screen round so Mum could see. "Have you ever read about transfusion trials in America, with the theory that pure plasma transfusions might fight off diseases like MS, Parkinsons…and Alzheimer's?"

"No, I have not." Mum scooted closer beside Ana, peering at the screen. "Who's that dapper looking gentleman?"

"That's Dr Carmichael. They used to live on our street. This is the website for a private medical clinic he owns. The clinic seems to focus on a lot of cosmetic procedures but in the part about him, it says he's been doing research into the transfusion theories. It doesn't specify if he's taking part in similar trials himself. There's a contact form on his site. I was thinking about getting in touch."

Mum shot her a hesitant look. "To ask him what?"

Ana shrugged. "I was curious about what he might have found. It ties in with things we're learning about just now in science." Lie. She didn't want Mum to think she was crazy, or deluded, or worried about her potential decline.

Mum laid a hand on hers. "I was hoping our conversation the other day hadn't been playing on your mind. You haven't been worrying too much?"

Ana hesitated, searching her eyes, "Aren't you worried?"

Mum sighed. "Why do you think I'm doing my own research? Watching TED talks about scientific terms I can't even pronounce." She laughed, tilting her head in wonder. "Maybe we should set up a meeting with this Dr Carmichael, as long as he doesn't charge us a fortune in the process."

"Really?" Ana sat up, not thinking for one minute Mum would have been interested. The image of Barbara Carmichael, unrecognisable from the days she'd wandered the streets filled her with excitement. What if her transformation was linked to these plasma trials? Ana didn't want to share that theory yet, until they found out more. It might give her too much hope.

Mum kissed her forehead on her way out and Ana started to type a message on the contact form, shivering in anticipation.

Chapter Thirteen
Hope

The girl looking back at me was all wrong. Too sweet, too *soft*. The clothes Clara laid out for me clung to my frame in unflattering shapes. The capri pants were too baggy at the top, folding like a fancy restaurant napkin when I moved. The beige top sat weird across my shoulders and the non-colour made me look ill. White on white was never a good look. Worst of all was the nakedness of my skin. Clara refused to give me any make-up.

"You don't need it. You're beautiful. I'd kill for those freckles."

I was tempted to ask if she would also kill for my blood. So many questions circled my head I didn't know which one to start with, or if Clara was even the person who could answer them.

I touched the watch at my wrist. At least I could keep track of time now. She assured me some of my clothes and possessions would arrive soon. When I asked about my phone Clara said they had it downstairs and I would be permitted my one text message after breakfast.

Breakfast. Tummy growling, my body reminded me I hadn't eaten for a couple of days. Clara explained they'd let me sleep longer than anticipated so I'd lost a whole day. There was no apology or explanation for the drugging.

With one last glance in the mirror I took a deep breath, my steps awkward in the clothes that didn't belong to me.

The floorboards creaked as I crossed the landing. I hesitated at the banister, peering over the circular balcony to the central hall below. Dark hardwood flooring, a grandfather clock ticking loudly, a bouquet of exotic flowers, blooming red, white and purple, their petals scattering across an ornate table, the air heavy with their perfume.

As I descended the grand staircase, I let my imagination take over. Holding my head high, I visualised myself in a floaty ball gown, descending to take tea in the drawing room. Light caught the stained-glass window above the oak front door, red and gold beams dancing across the ceiling, reminding me of my tarot cards. I pictured Ana opening her locker, finding the card and my message. How was she going to find me when even I didn't know where I was?

Voices echoed across the hallway. I followed the noise and the smells of toast and bacon and eggs. Stopping at a closed door I took a deep breath, heart hammering. It was going to be hard faking confidence when I looked like a pathetic loser. The door swung open to reveal a massive kitchen, as if from a Victorian drama. A wooden table extended across the centre of the room cluttered with plates of food and bowls and a chopping board stacked with vegetables. A shiny row of pans of varying sizes hung on hooks above an old-fashioned black stove and oven.

A plump ruddy faced woman hoisted a bag of potatoes on to the table. She looked up in surprise at my arrival, wiping pink hands on her apron and smiling.

"Well, well, who do we have here?" There was a soft lilt to her voice and I liked her immediately.

"I'm Hope."

"Hope. A fine name. I'm Margaret, the cook. What will you be having for breakfast? Got some fresh bacon sizzling on the stove over there."

I shook my head. "Eggs and toast will do me."

"Alright, lass. Go on into the dining room and I'll bring it out to you. There's hot drinks and juice and cereals all laid out."

I hesitated, looking longingly at the wooden chair set out at the top of the table, wishing I could stay in here.

"It's just through yonder." Margaret gestured towards a door at the other side of the kitchen. "The other kids are looking forward to meeting you."

Other kids. Seb. A sickening realisation hit that he had been here a year, with no proper contact with Elliot. It didn't bode well. I was desperate to quiz him. I wasn't so keen to meet anyone else.

Laughter and screeches rolled towards me as I pushed open the adjoining swing door. I stood observing, taking advantage of their failure to hear my arrival above the noise. Two scruffy looking boys threw rolls across the table at one another, two other boys in grey tracksuits watching and egging them on. An older boy sat alone at the top of the table, munching on what looked like a triple bacon and slice roll, hood up. A girl with masses of spiral brown curls sat cross-legged, sipping on a cup of weird smelling tea. A boy dressed all in black sat beside her. My heart flipped when I realised he was observing me too. The only one to notice my arrival. Seb. His eyebrows twitched hello, lips curling into a half smirk as he gave my outfit the once over.

I folded my arms, walking to the far end of the table, far away from his scrutinising gaze. One by one voices silenced, curious eyes tracking me.

"It's the new girl." The boy at the top of the table pulled down his hood, revealing a deep scar running from ear to lip. I tried not to stare. "What's your name?"

For a moment I was tempted to make it up. To start again and wipe my slate clean. But then it would feel like I might truly disappear. That wasn't the plan. "Hope."

Curly haired girl snorted. "Is that a joke?"

The roll throwing boys sniggered.

"No. It's for real." I sat on my hands, suddenly feeling stupid and out of my depth.

"Well, it's what we need around here that's for sure. Hope." The girl stuffed a shred of croissant in her mouth and I couldn't tell if she was being genuine or taking the piss.

"I'm Aidan." The boy with the scar reached across the table and shook my hand firmly. "That duffus there is my brother, Scott, and that's Jimmy, Dylan, Joe, Seb and this beautiful girl here is…"

"I can introduce myself," the girl cut in. "I'm Phoenix."

I stared at her, wondering if *that* was a joke. She stared back, a challenge in her eyes.

"When did you arrive?" Aidan asked, stuffing the last of the roll in his mouth, chewing loudly.

"A couple of days ago," I answered, just as the door opened and Margaret walked in, plate stacked with toast and three types of egg – scrambled, poached and fried.

"There you go, lass. I forgot to ask how you like your eggs done so I made you a variety. Don't worry if you can't manage it all, the boys will help you." Margaret winked at Scott and swooped back out of the room.

All eyes were on me, watching.

"No bacon?" Aidan surveyed my plate, looking disappointed.

I shook my head. "I'm a vegetarian."

Phoenix snorted. "Good luck with that in here." She frowned at the eggs. "Thought veggies didn't eat eggs or dairy."

I cut into the toast. "Some don't. I do. I just don't eat flesh." I flinched at my choice of words, the unwelcome thoughts about blood creeping back into my head.

I was conscious that Phoenix watched me as I ate. "You won't have met the Carmichaels yet then?" she said.

I shook my head. "Who are they?"

Phoenix exchanged a glance with Aidan. "You'll find out soon enough."

"Where are you from?"

I didn't need to look up to know that question was from Seb. He was attempting to sound casual, but I heard the eager undertones.

"Oakridge. Not originally, but most recently." A spark fired in his eyes. I imagined the questions tumbling through his mind. How had I recognised him? Who had I spoken to?

Phoenix uncrossed her legs, bolting upright. "Another one. They're starting to act stupid, pulling us from the same place."

"Are you from there too?" I frowned.

"Oakridge High, yeah, but I stayed in the Children's House just outside town. Wasn't there long."

I turned to Seb, waiting for him to add his story. He stayed silent. Suddenly I wished everyone else would leave, so I could tell him I knew Elliot.

The chiming of a clock distracted the boys. Aidan stood up, draining his juice.

"Outside time. Let's split."

I watched as they all cleared their plates, dashing out of seats. Scott stuffed a muffin in each pocket.

Seb stayed seated and a rush like electricity wound its way up from my ankles when I realised he was openly staring at me. The room emptied, door banging shut, leaving us in silence, alone.

"What's outside time?" I asked, annoyed that my voice sounded less confident than I wanted to project.

"We get to run round the gardens like dogs on walkies." Seb's voice was thick with contempt. He nodded at my half-full plate. "You should finish that first. Meals are very regimented in here. And don't be thinking breakfast is this amazing every day. We're allowed a treat today because it's Scott's sixteenth birthday and we don't have donations."

A piece of egg stuck in my throat at the word donations. What was he talking about? I gulped down some juice.

"I'll wait on you and we can go together." Seb sat back in his seat, arms folded, eyes never leaving me.

A flush of heat snaked up my neck, making me feel lightheaded. I told myself it was just the hunger or the after effects of whatever drugs I'd been given. Not because he was still looking at me.

I reached across for tea, gulping down a full mug. An amused smile crept up his face. I refused to meet his eye.

I started to speak but he silenced me before I got the words out.

He shook his head. "Let's wait till we're outside."

I instinctively glanced at the ceiling, searching for cameras.

He laughed. "It's okay, we're not being watched."

He paused, leaning forward, closer towards me. "But I'm not convinced they don't listen, maybe bug some of the rooms."

I laid down my knife and fork, no longer hungry.

"Ready?" He stood.

I nodded, not convinced I was.

Chapter Fourteen
Ana

They met early, huddling under Elliot's golf umbrella, walking in silence to the Browns. Ana grabbed Elliot's arm when she spotted Mr Brown's car in the drive, rain battering the bonnet, the noise mirroring the pounding in her chest.

She climbed the stairs to the front door, hand shaking as she rang the bell. They exchanged nervous glances as they waited, listening for signs of life. One minute, two, three. Ana swallowed, pressing harder and longer, the shrill ringing demanding attention. She held her breath, leaning closer towards the door. Elliot tilted the umbrella as he looked up at a window.

"I'm sure I saw a curtain twitch," he whispered.

Ana raised her hand to knock just as a key turned in the lock. She swallowed, resisting the urge to grab Elliot's hand and squeeze tight. They both instinctively took a step back as the door swung open.

Mr Brown surveyed them with an irritated glance. "Yes?"

Ana looked him directly in the eye, knowing he wasn't seeing her properly, that he wasn't interested in the unwelcome interruption to his morning.

"Mr Brown, it's me, Ana."

He blinked, addressing her with a blank stare.

"Hope's friend. Ana Gilbert. I came over for dinner. I left a note."

Mr Brown's face paled, like she had aged him five years. He clung to the doorframe, shoulders visibly slumping.

"Yes, what can I do for you, Ana?" His voice was hesitant.

She glanced at Elliot, not encouraged by Mr Brown's reaction. "I wondered...well, we wondered, if Hope was home? We wanted to talk to her."

Mr Brown looked between them and shook his head. "I'm sorry. Hope doesn't live here anymore." He started to shut the door.

"Wait." Elliot reacted before Ana, surprising her as he blocked the door with his foot. "Please. We need to know where she went."

Mr Brown hesitated, casting a nervous glance over his shoulder. "I don't want to upset Martha."

"We don't want to either, please, we just want to know what happened." Ana stepped forward, hearing the pleading in her voice.

Mr Brown scratched his head, a clear internal debate occurring.

"It's okay, Edward. Invite them in."

The door swung open wide, Mrs Brown meeting Ana's gaze with steely eyes. "You might be able to help us with some answers too. The kettle's just boiled. Come on in out the rain."

Elliot flashed Ana a relieved grin as they hurried inside. He awkwardly folded the umbrella, trying not to drip everywhere.

"Don't worry about that," Mr Brown shook a dismissive hand. "Just prop it open by the door. Let's go into the lounge."

His briefcase and raincoat lay across the sofa and Ana glanced at the clock, realising he was probably about to leave for work.

"Will we make you late?" Ana asked.

Mrs Brown appeared behind them with a tray of drinks. "Never mind that. Take a seat."

Once settled, Mrs Brown started the conversation. "I don't know how much you do and don't know so let me go first and you can fill in any blanks. Before I start though I need to make it clear I wanted Hope to stay here, with us."

"Martha," Edward sat forward in his chair, gripping his mug.

She held up a hand to silence him, shaking her head angrily. "I don't care what you say, Edward. That girl was not trouble. Not like the last boy, not even close."

"Well, I know that," Mr Brown stumbled with his words. "But it would have been upsetting all the same. The police would have been involved. Ms Turnberry explained."

Ana exchanged a worried glance with Elliot. She laid down her tea, too nervous to drink, looking expectantly at Mrs Brown, prompting her to continue.

"I received a phone call two days ago from the school, from Hope's pastoral care teacher explaining she'd found a bag of drugs worth hundreds of pounds in her locker."

Ana felt her body deflate, trying to catch Elliot's eye but he was frowning intently, engrossed in Mrs Brown's words.

"Apparently there had been reports of some younger pupils buying drugs on the premises and it matched the type found. Her teacher said Ms Turnberry was reluctant to involve the police, which was a small mercy, and she would send over social work to have a chat with us." Mrs Brown paused, looking over at Mr Brown, her face suddenly looking drawn and tired. "I wish we'd insisted on going to the school to have a joint meeting with Hope, to bring her home, but it all happened so fast. I hadn't realised it would just be social work coming over, that they wouldn't bring her too. And I was expecting, Ruth, Miss McDonald. But it wasn't Miss McDonald who arrived."

"Why not?" The thought popped out before Ana could censor it. Ana sat back, shaking her head in apology as Mrs Brown gestured with her hand, signalling she would get to that.

"A man arrived, calling himself Ian Hobbs. He said he's taking over as Hope's social worker because Miss McDonald has been suspended."

"What?" Ana shot Elliot a look. His expression darkened but he didn't react.

Mrs Brown's mouth formed a thin line, her lips practically disappearing into her weary face. "He wouldn't disclose any detail, but said she's not allowed to make any contact with her caseload and her work phone and laptop were confiscated whilst the investigation is ongoing. He reassured me that he had spoken to Hope, that she was safe and would be well looked after. They all presumed I, we…," Mrs Brown glanced at her husband, "…that we wouldn't want to keep Hope here, not after what we went through last time with the lad. There was lots of police involvement, court cases and violence."

Mr Brown slid forward, placing his hand on Mrs Brown's, squeezing tight. "It was a difficult time for us."

Mrs Brown looked Ana straight in the eye, serious, defiant. "But this wasn't the same. Hope was not the same. I wanted her home. But they didn't give us a choice. Arrangements had already been made to take her to a secure house where her behaviour could be monitored. Ian explained it meant no police involvement. No record to affect Hope's future. She's a bright girl, isn't she?" Mrs Brown's voice trailed off, a wistful look on her face.

"But did she come home to say goodbye? Did you talk to her?"

The Browns exchanged uneasy glances, Martha's resolve wavering. She shook her head tightly. "They wouldn't allow it. Told us it would be easier for Hope. That she was ashamed and didn't want to face us." Her knuckles whitened as she clenched a fist. "I want to tell that girl she has nothing to be ashamed of. I don't believe for one minute those drugs belonged to her."

"Well, why don't we go to see her in the house? You could tell her." Ana sat forward, getting excited at the prospect of being able to see Hope again. Then she remembered hearing the teachers talking about England and a part of her deflated. "Did they say if the house was in Scotland? Local?"

Mr Brown patted his wife's hand as he turned to me. "They won't give us any specific information, dear. We know that it must still be in the area though, for Ian Hobbs to take her on. They want her to have a clean slate, a fresh start."

But why, Ana wanted to shout. That was ludicrous. Carting her off with no goodbyes. And why did the teachers think she had moved to England?

"So you haven't spoken to her at all?" Elliot asked, drawing their attention.

"No, but," Mrs Brown paused, rising from her chair, knees clicking. She pulled a small phone off the mantelpiece. "I bought this a few days ago. Hope was teasing me for not having one, but I don't have a clue how to use it. Hope set it up for me. I did wonder if she would try that texting thing, but I don't even know how to look for it. It made a funny noise earlier.

Would you have a look, son?"

Elliot took the phone, which looked about twenty years old. It made a beeping noise as Elliot punched the keys. *Beep beep beep.* They all sat watching, waiting. Ana wanted to tell them that Hope hadn't responded to any of her messages. Or Elliot's. So it was unlikely Hope would try to message Mrs Brown, knowing she didn't have a clue how to use her phone.

"Here," Elliot's face lit up in anticipation. "There's a message here."

"Well, read it out," Mrs Brown said.

Ana already knew the message was disappointing before Elliot started to read, seeing the light disappear from his eyes.

"I'm sorry," Elliot spoke hesitantly, "I really did love my time with you and Edward. I'm sorry to have let you down. I want you to know how much I appreciate everything you both did for me. I chose to go to a new place and I'm happy here. I'm sorry I never got to say goodbye but it's for the best. Please don't try to get in touch, it's easier for me this way. Hope."

They sat in silence, Elliot shifting nervously in his chair, blinking at the phone as if wishing he could drop it and run. Mrs Brown held her hand out, gesturing for him to pass it back. He did so, almost guiltily. Ana watched as Mrs Brown sat back in her chair, the phone beep, beep, beeping as she scrolled through the message.

"How do I phone her from this thing?" Mrs Brown asked, her voice wavering, eyes shiny.

Elliot rushed over, taking the phone back, clicking buttons, pressing the call button, holding the phone to her ear. Mrs Brown shook her head after a few minutes.

"It's going to voicemail." She gestured for Elliot to kneel beside her. "Show me how to send a message back, son. I want her to know she can call me."

As Elliot explained and Mrs Brown typed slowly, Ana patted the front of her bag where Hope's tarot card sat. She glanced at Mr Brown, wondering if she should mention it. Then she saw the worry etched across both of their faces and realised it would only torment them further.

"Do you have any idea why Hope's social worker would have been suspended?" Ana asked Mr Brown.

He turned his attention to her, shaking his head. "No idea, love. Mr Hobbs wasn't allowed to give us any information."

"Do you have Mr Hobbs' number?" Ana asked.

Mr Brown kept glancing over at his wife. He nodded distracted. "I think so. He's actually coming over later this morning, to collect some of Hope's belongings."

Elliot turned his head, clearly listening in. He looked at Ana, expectant.

"Would you mind if we stayed, if we could talk to him?" Ana asked.

Mr Brown started to protest, saying they should really be getting to school, that he had work and they should leave Mrs Brown in peace.

"Let them stay, Edward. I'd appreciate the company. And I haven't had the chance to ask any of my questions yet."

Mr Brown let out an inaudible sigh, a simultaneous look of resignation and frustration washing over him, similar to one Ana's dad got whenever Mum disappeared into a shoe shop.

As soon as Mr Brown said his goodbyes, Mrs Brown sat up, turning to them both. "Right, now. I want you to tell me any detail you can think of, anything strange that's happened during your time with Hope these past few weeks. I'm not an idiot and I know someone is trying to pull the wool over my eyes and I've got a feeling you two are thinking the same. So let's crack this together."

Ana smiled in surprise at Elliot. She unzipped her bag, realising she'd underestimated Martha Brown. She laid down Hope's tarot card.

"Let's start with this."

Chapter Fifteen
Hope

Clara intercepted me as I walked out to the garden with Seb, saying she wanted a chat. Seb pointed to a bench under a winding trellis, indicating he'd wait for me.

Clara pulled out my phone from her pocket, halting me as I moved to take it. "Would you like me to read out your message?"

I frowned. "What do you mean?"

She smiled. "The message you are allowed. I sent it to Martha Brown."

I sighed in frustration. "She doesn't know how to use her phone. I want to text my friend." I held out my hand, eyes locking with Clara.

Clara shook her head sharply. "One text. That's the rule, Hope."

"But I didn't get to send it, *you* did."

Clara ignored my protest and switched the phone off, the screen fading to black. "You won't have use for this anymore. I think you'll find it freeing, not living your life inside a box, no longer defined by simulated likes."

I wanted to shout I had never lived my life inside a box, that I couldn't care less about social media 'likes'. But I did mind losing connection to my new friends. I watched helplessly as Clara dropped the phone on the ground, smashing her heel into the screen, her smile widening as it crunched.

I stared at her, seething inside.

She tilted her head towards Seb. "Better not keep

him waiting."

Seb glanced up as I approached, simultaneously pushing buttons on a hand-held game console, an electronic melody of beeps and explosions permeating the air.

"What did Clara want? You look pissed off."

I sat down beside him, trying to calm the anger bubbling inside as I recounted what happened.

Seb sighed. "She's serious by the way. That one text was my last and only contact with the outside world since I've been here."

I curled my arms around my body, trying to calm the dread seeping in. "What exactly is this place? I need you to explain."

Seb laid down his console, shaking hair out of his eyes. As his gaze locked on mine, I noticed how the light changed his eyes from brown to a light green. A jolt wound around my heart, and I tried to ignore it. He eyed me curiously, like he wanted to delve into the inner workings of my brain and I found myself unable to look away.

"You first, how do you know me? Have we met before?"

"I know Elliot, your foster brother."

A smile of realisation. "He talked about me?"

I nodded. "And he puts missing posters with your face plastered on them around the village. He never believed you ran away."

Seb's face brightened into a full smile. It was contagious. I felt my expression mirror his, a light blasting through the simmer of anxiety that had been on a constant loop inside my head since I'd arrived.

"Elliot," he shook his head in admiration. "I hated him thinking I'd just run off with no goodbye. I'm guessing no one else questioned it too much?"

I shrugged. "I think his parents assumed because you'd turned sixteen you decided to start your own life. Elliot didn't tell me much. But he was convinced something was going on and he seemed to think a bunch of kids in care were going missing. He showed me a list of names." I thought back to the names I'd passed to Ruth, and the introductions at breakfast. "In fact, I'm sure Aidan and Scott were names on the list."

Seb frowned. "How on earth did he make that connection?"

"Some newspaper stories. He never got anywhere though. I wish he had and I wish I'd listened to him earlier." I smiled wryly, kicking myself for not texting Ruth any of Elliot's details before we lost contact.

"I'm guessing you have no idea where this place is?" I gestured to the grounds that extended for miles, looking up at the sky. "From the shitty weather I'd say we're probably still in Scotland."

Seb nodded. "We were all drugged on the journey here so no one knows for sure how far out we are but the staff are a big clue. We can't be that far."

He was right. If Clara spent some of her days in Oakridge High we couldn't be far.

"Do we ever get to go outside, like away from the house?" I asked, dreading the answer.

Seb extended his hands, gesturing to the gardens. "This is it. We never get beyond the main gates."

"Have you ever tried to escape?" I looked across the vast grounds, gaze lingering on the wires and discs winding along the tops of the walls and gates.

Seb smiled wryly. "What do you think? Let me save you some bother, in case you get ideas. The wire strung along the gates and walls is electrified. The gates have electronic locks. There's cameras set up at all the potential exits."

I shivered. "What about the blood thing? You said something about donations at breakfast?"

Seb's face darkened. "Our plasma donations? I hope you're not scared of needles."

"So they extract our blood, like a blood test?"

"It's our plasma that's extracted. You're hooked up to a machine. You'll start donating once a week, then as long as you have no weird reactions they'll up it to twice a week, sometimes three depending on the demand. But it's usually just the boys who donate more, because there's less risk of our iron count being affected."

"The demand? What's it for?"

"For rich people to stay young and healthy forever."

"What?" I laughed, wondering if Seb was pulling my leg.

Before I had a chance to ask more, a shadow fell across us and Seb's expression hardened and shut down. I squinted up at a tall older man, dressed in a tweed waistcoat suit, grey hair slicked back, a twirly moustache adding an almost comical element to his steely manner.

"Hope Devaney," he boomed, his voice clipped and posh. A memory swirled, a voice in the dark, *Put her under again*.

"Our new arrival. I'll excuse you for your laziness on your first proper morning with us, but not you, Sebastian. I believe the others are doing laps round the house. You still have half an hour before your medical check." He gestured to the console. "And you know these are forbidden outside. To me." The man snapped his fingers, his eyes speaking a warning.

Seb stood slowly and deliberately, head-to-head with Dr Carmichael, eyes defiant.

He handed the console over, frown lines creasing his brow. The man slid it into the top pocket of his waistcoat, nodding for Seb to get on his way.

Seb shot me a look which promised more conversation later, before turning and breaking into a jog, leaving me alone.

"Dr Carmichael," the man extended his hand. His grip was firm, crushing bones. "Time I gave you a proper welcome. Let me give you the tour. Follow me, please."

The tour started on the ground floor, Dr Carmichael opening a door to a small one-screen cinema, rows of plush red velvet seats curving down five rows. A red and white candy-striped trolley sat outside the door, matching cardboard containers stacked upside down beside a glass cabinet exploding with popcorn, an assortment of multi-coloured sweets in jars lining a shelf above.

"Cinema nights are twice a week. You take it in turns to choose the film, if you enjoy these things." His tone suggested he couldn't understand why anyone would be interested in such nonsense.

Further along the corridor he opened the door to a games room, rows of pinball machines dominating one corner, pool tables in the centre, games stations and large screens in the opposite corner. My eyes were drawn to the table at the back below the window, a wooden chess board set up for a game. Dr Carmichael noted my interest.

"You play?"

Andy tried to teach me. I had only started to grasp the rules before they were taken away from me. I shook my head. "Not really." A row of board games was stacked in shelves lining the walls. Cluedo, Monopoly, Don't Panic.

Don't Panic. The words looped inside my head as we walked further down the corridor, Dr Carmichael's shoes clicking against the polished wood. Stag heads hung on walls, their eyes dark and glassy. An image of them running, being hunted, made me imagine fear in their eyes. I shivered, quickening my steps to keep up.

Dr Carmichael stopped at a stained-glass door with a decorative circular gold handle. As the door swung open a sense of calm folded around me, the familiar scent of books and leather enticing me in. I stared in wonder at the floor to ceiling bookshelves, resisting the urge to run inside, to pull books off the shelves and flick through pages. Large windows circled the room, casting shaded light against polished tables, a mist of dust spiralling up to the wood panelled ceiling.

"You will be tutored in here each afternoon after lunch. A variety of subjects: English Literature, Philosophy, History, Psychology." As if he could detect the hunger in my eyes, he added, "And of course you can spend time in here reading. I believe we house over one thousand books."

I tried to hide my awe and excitement. I was afraid to react to anything, until I had a proper understanding of the rules and expectations.

We turned a corner, taking us back near the entrance door and staircase. We passed a wooden closed door adorned with a NO ENTRY sign.

"That part of the house is off limits. A private annexe," Dr Carmichael said, not elaborating, continuing to lead me down an opposite corridor, passing a gym and another locked door. "The grand ballroom. Only opened for special occasions."

Voices echoed from further down the corridor and I watched expectantly, wondering if 'outside time' had now ended and the others were back inside.

A tall, gangly man wearing a blue uniform came into view, his dark greasy hair sticking up in tufts at the back, as if he had fallen asleep at an awkward angle. He moved with uncoordinated, jaunty steps, his eyes darting around, not quite focusing on anything, an expression of innocent expectation on his face, giving him the appearance of an overgrown boy. He trailed beside a small immaculately dressed woman, her silver hair secured with a butterfly hairclip sparkling under the light as she moved her head to talk. Her suit shimmered blue and green as she took sharp, small steps.

The man noticed me first, a spark of delight animating his eyes as he bundled towards me.

"Pretty colour." Plump fingers reached out to grab a clump of my hair and I recoiled in shock at the unexpected contact.

"Billy," the woman shot forward, pulling him back, eyes darting towards Dr Carmichael who raised a hand as if to strike the man. Billy cowered, bunching fists against his mouth, looking between the two, remorseful and fearful.

Dr Carmichael lowered his hand, curling it into a fist. "You know it's not polite to grab people, Billy. We've had this chat many times before."

Billy pointed at me. "I just wanted to touch the pretty hair."

"It's fine to look." The woman took his arm, pulling him back to her side, her eyes sliding up and down my body, a reproachful and cold look, as if my youth disgusted her. "You must be the new girl,

Hope. I'm Barbara Carmichael."

I nodded, my voice unable to carry the lie that it was nice to meet her. I was relieved she didn't try to shake my hand.

Dr Carmichael continued the tour upstairs, explaining some of the staff slept on the first floor, boys on the second floor, girls on the third, with a shared bathroom on each. I wondered what other staff, besides Margaret, resided here. The Carmichaels were housed in the private annexe, separated from the rest of the house, and were never to be disturbed, unless at their request.

"There's one last place I want to show you before we go back down to my study."

I followed along the third floor, curious as to what would be significant on this level. As we passed the bedrooms, a defiant voice shouted from behind a half-open door. I stared, taken aback by the sight of a large girl waving a finger in the face of an unimpressed woman, who stood listening, arms folded. The woman was tiny, with a mass of blonde curls and vine tattoos snaking up her arm. She didn't look intimidated or bothered by the girl towering over her. The girl wore an ill-fitting vest top, revealing a neon bra, ample cleavage half spilling out the top, cow patterned pyjama bottoms completing the look. Her body jiggled as she yelled.

"You can't just lock me in there. I'm no' a fuckin criminal. It's no' right."

"The more you shout, Stacey, the closer you are to going straight back in again."

"I'm no' going anywhere. You can't make me, you stupid cow."

Dr Carmichael slid past me, slamming the door fully open, the edge smacking against a cabinet, the sound of glass smashing.

The girl's face contorted into rage, her mouth curling into a roar which failed to reach full volume when she registered who had opened the door. She instantly shut her mouth and stepped back, tugging self-consciously at her vest.

"Is there a problem in here?" Dr Carmichael's voice on the surface was polite and calm, but I knew, and it looked like Stacey also understood, that there was a dark fury simmering.

The blonde woman stared at Stacey, nodding at her, encouraging her to respond. Red dots spread up Stacey's chest, mottled on her neck, and blotched across her cheeks.

"Everything is sound." Stacey relented. Disgust puckered her lips as she gave me the once over.

"Excellent. I trust you will be getting dressed now, Stacey? You've missed breakfast but you still have time to run a lap outside before your medical check."

Stacey tutted and Dr Carmichael tensed. "What's that, Stacey?" He cupped his ear, as if he was playing around, but there was nothing jovial in his manner.

Stacey stared at the carpet, burrowing a toe into the plush fibres. "Yes, Dr Carmichael."

"Very good." Dr Carmichael turned away and Stacey's head instantly shot up again, eyes locking with mine in a defiant stare. She made a slit throat gesture, an acrylic pink nail scraping across her skin, eyes never leaving me, until the member of staff pushed the door shut from the inside.

"One of our newer arrivals." Dr Carmichael sniffed as if she emitted a bad odour. "This is precisely why the next room exists."

We stopped in front of a locked gate. Dr

Carmichael reached into his pocket, keys jangling. He spun the keys round, settling on a rusted brown one which slid into the gate, metal hinges squeaking as it swung open. He clicked a light switch, a soft orange fuzz illuminating another metal door, with covered top hatch. He inserted another key and the door swung open to reveal a dark, grey room with exposed bricks for walls. A cot with a thin mattress and flimsy sheet lay against one wall, a small table with jug of water and glass beside it. An open toilet sat in the opposite corner, like in a prison cell. Foul odours hit me in wafts. I held my breath, trying not to gag.

"This is what we call the Bothy. One might argue it's not quite as fun as an actual Bothy but it's sparse and it allows some calm time. That can be a necessity once in a while, as I'm sure you can imagine, when overexcited teenagers spend too much time together."

His tone was conspiratorial, as if he was a guide taking me on a jolly tour. The thought of being locked in there, behind a solid iron door and gate, with no windows, sent tremors of panic shooting up my legs.

Dr Carmichael smiled tightly, hand clamping down on my shoulder. "No need to look so worried, Hope. As long as you follow the rules this will be the first and last time you cast eyes on this room."

I was relieved we didn't linger. The air changed instantly as we stepped back out into the hallway, and I gulped hungrily, as if I had been underwater, drowning.

"Now, time to have a sit down and I can explain our rules. We like to give you a few days to settle in, Hope, before starting your regular routine. I think a bright girl like yourself is going to find our house most agreeable. Do you have any questions?"

I thought back to the library, the silence and calm

of the surroundings and access to thousands of books. My luxurious bedroom and porcelain bathroom. A cook providing meals. An image of my smashed phoned lying under Clara's foot.

"Do we have internet connection in here, or TV?"

Dr Carmichael looked momentarily surprised, as if he hadn't actually expected me to ask any questions. He shook his head firmly. "None of those daily distractions to rot your brain. Think of this place as a digital vacation."

So we were truly cut off from the outside world. No social media or news updates, no messages to anyone anywhere. But the house wasn't exactly lacking in other benefits.

I ran a hand up my bare arm, thinking back to Seb's explanation about the donations. Luxury didn't come free, I was well aware of that. Nothing good did, especially not for me now that I didn't have any family looking out for me. There were much worse payments than blood, or plasma, like Seb had explained. It seemed like a minimal, inconsequential exchange.

This is your life now, I reminded myself. There was always going to be some kind of compromise needed in order to stay safe, looked after and fed, until I was savvy enough to forge out on my own. I flashed a reassuring smile at Dr Carmichael, convincing him I was the girl who always stuck to the rules. I could become that girl. I could become anyone, I realised, if it meant having some good things in return.

Chapter Sixteen
Ana

Ian Hobbs was not a likeable man. He was small, with a slippery insincere smile and piggy eyes and a voice that sounded like it came out of his nose, rather than his mouth. The middle button of his shirt popped open when he lowered into Edwards's chair and Ana averted her gaze, trying to look at anything but his hairy belly.

He slurped his coffee loudly, fat fingers grabbing at the biscuits offered, crumbs trailing down his shirt before he'd even opened his case files.

He looked at Elliot and Ana in disapproval. "These children should really be at school, Mrs Brown."

"They have a free study period. And they're young adults, not children." Martha took a seat across from Mr Hobbs, folding her hands in her lap. "Before we begin, I would like a landline number for Hope so I can make contact. Ms Turnberry assured me at our meeting Hope would have permitted calls."

Mr Hobbs stuffed the remains of a biscuit in his mouth, scratching the bald spot at the top of his head. He shook his head. "No, I'm afraid not. Ms Devaney has requested we don't give out her new number or address. I'm bound by client confidentiality and GDPR. You would need to wait on a call from her or try her mobile."

"But she's not even sixteen. I think it's within her best interests if I can speak to her, reassure her that we're not angry. We don't want her foster placement to end."

"She's a *young adult* and has rights," Mr Hobbs shot Mrs Brown's slight right back at her. He shifted in his chair. "I really don't feel comfortable discussing this in front of other young people."

"Ana and Elliot are Hope's friends. They were very concerned when Hope didn't show up for school."

Mr Hobbs sighed, shuffling his papers. He flashed them a patronising smile. "All I can say, folks, is that Hope is fine. She's happy in her new place and unfortunately this is what happens sometimes with kids in care. They don't always stick around long enough to make proper friends."

Ana and Elliot exchanged looks. Ana could tell Elliot was even less impressed than her. She wanted to shove the tarot card in Mr Hobb's face and demand an explanation. If Hope was so happy to go, then why had she left Ana a message? Martha had warned her not to mention it, saying until they figured out what was going on disclosing anything to the wrong person might make things worse.

"Are you able to tell me why you've taken over as Hope's caseworker? Why Miss McDonald was suspended? She's a lovely young lady. It would reassure me to know she at least will be staying in touch with Hope."

Mr Hobbs shot Ana and Elliot another irritated look and Ana knew Martha was going to find out more without them there. Ana edged forward in her seat.

"Um, would it help, Mr Hobbs, if we gathered Hope's stuff together for you?"

He nodded, clearly relieved to be getting rid of them. "Yes, that would be very helpful." He handed

Ana a carrier bag. "These were books from her locker."

Martha caught Ana's arm on her way past. "I've arranged everything in piles on the bed. Her case is in the wardrobe."

Outside in the hall Elliot made a face at Ana. "What a prat."

Ana shushed him, hovering by the gap in the door, trying to listen.

Mr Hobbs spoke in long stretched out sentences, as if the very act of talking was a big hassle for him. "Miss McDonald's conduct is under question, details of which only my senior managers are privy to. It's unlikely she will be back at work anytime soon until a full investigation has taken place. Let me reassure you, Mrs Brown, that I am a highly experienced social worker and will be keeping a close eye on Hope. You have nothing to worry about."

He sounded like a politician giving the most insincere speech of his life. Ana wondered what could possibly have happened for Miss McDonald to get suspended. She pressed her ear closer to the door, straining to hear the next part of the conversation, only catching the words, 'Concern' and 'Behaviour'.

"I find that very hard to believe, Mr Hobbs. Hope was very focused on her schoolwork. The idea that she was running some kind of drug ring is quite frankly ludicrous. She never asked for much, but we would not see her short of anything. I issued her a weekly allowance as social work know."

"I have no doubt about that, Mrs Brown. It's obvious you and Mr Brown have done a wonderful job of caring for the girl, but I really don't think it's always about the money incentive. It's often about the attention, the need to establish some kind of identity in a new school. I believe she was fighting with a girl in her year too. It's very common they present one version to you at home, and quite the other in school."

Ana wanted to slam the door open, tell the idiot that he knew nothing about Hope. The girl he was describing was a fabricated lie.

"What's going on?" Ana jumped as Elliot breathed in her ear.

"That idiot is making up stories, that's what," she hissed.

Elliot raised his eyebrows in amusement. "Shall we go and pack her stuff?"

Ana nodded, following him upstairs, pausing at the top, trying to remember which room was Hope's. She tentatively pushed the door to the left open, eyes drawn to her desk, a stack of books and pen and notebook laid out, as if Hope had just gone to get a cup of tea and would be back soon. Elliot hovered in the doorway, glancing around, looking hesitant and awkward as if he didn't want to intrude in her private space.

Mrs Brown had placed the clothes in neat piles on top of the bed. Ana laid the carrier bag beside them. She wondered if Mrs Brown had left the books arranged on the desk, unwilling to let go of the possibility that Hope was really gone, never to return. Ana unclipped the photo of Hope's mum from above the dresser mirror, sliding it carefully inside the notebook. Out of everything, she knew Hope would want to be reunited with that the most. Ana wondered where Hope was, what she was doing. She ran a hand down the notebook, a realisation dinging in her head.

Excited, she sat down at the desk, ripping out a page, scrambling for a pen.

"What are you doing?" Elliot asked.

"Writing Hope a letter. We can hide it in one of her pockets."

Hi Hope,

It's Ana. I'm sitting writing this in your bedroom. I found your tarot card in my locker and I know something weird is going on. I'm here with Elliot, we're packing up your stuff and I really hope that slimy toad downstairs passes everything on and that you find this.

The slimy toad I'm referring to btw is your new social worker, Mr Hobbs. I don't know if you know this but Ruth got suspended. Something to do with her conduct. If you can believe that, as Blobby Hobby has just sat and told a pack of lies about you to Martha. Don't worry. Martha knows something's up too and we're all trying to find you. It's hard though as Mr Hobbs said you don't want to be contacted and that you're happy where you are. I know you sent Martha a text saying that too. I really do hope you're happy, wherever you are.

We want you to know that we miss you. Martha didn't want you to go. She's not mad, so if you can, please come home. Try to text us, phone us, email us, send us smoke signals. I've scribbled my address at the top in case you can get a letter to me.

Your friend, Ana Gilbert

Ana folded the note into a small square and rummaged through the bags Elliot had packed, looking for something with pockets. She realised there might be items Hope rarely wore. The jeans she found looked too new, no signs of fading or creasing. She debated about leaving it in the notebook but it might fall out if anyone glanced through it before passing things on. Her eyes were drawn to the cosmetic bags lying at the bottom of the bed. She grabbed one, unzipping it to find little tubs of eyeshadow, eyeliner and mascara. Hope loved her eyeliner. Ana slid the note into the inside pocket, leaving a corner peeking out and placed the cosmetic bag at the top of the case of clothes.

"She's not really got much stuff," Elliot commented as they zipped up her small case.

Ana thought of her loft at home, the boxes overflowing with old school report cards, science projects, badly drawn art homework, childhood toys and books she couldn't bear to say goodbye to. She thought of the photograph of Daphne Devaney tucked inside the pages of Hope's notebook. She guessed Hope had already said goodbye to the most important part of her childhood. Maybe nothing else mattered now, or maybe it was easier travelling light.

"You look really serious." Elliot moved closer beside Ana on the bed. Her heart thumped, every part of her conscious of the heat radiating from him. He was so close she could smell his clothes, freshly laundered with undertones of spicy deodorant and that weird indefinable boy smell.

A shrill ringing from Ana's bag made them both jump, her heart soaring into overdrive.

She scrambled for the phone, her first thought thinking it could be Hope. That she somehow sensed them in her old room, and knew Ana was trying to get a message to her. Ana's heart sank when she saw 'Mum' flashing on the screen.

Before Ana had even said hello Mum's voice blared in her ear.

"Where are you?"

Ana frowned, momentarily confused. Then she remembered a failed sign-in at school generated a text to Mum's phone.

Ana opened her mouth to speak just as her mum interrupted with, "And don't try to tell me you're sick. I know you're not at home."

"How do you know I'm not at home?" Curiosity

got the better of Ana.

"Because I'm here. What's going on?"

Ana glanced at her watch. Ten thirty. *I could ask you the same thing, Mum,* she wanted to say. She wondered if Mum had more medical appointments, like when she'd called in for lunch on her way back to work the other day. But she wouldn't usually do that mid-morning. *What if she got her test results?*

"It's a long story. I'm on my way home now. See you soon." Ana cut the call before she had the chance to ask more. She slung her bag over her shoulder. "I need to go. Your parents will have been sent a text too. You might want to think up some excuse now."

They opened the bedroom door just as Martha and Mr Hobbs appeared at the top of the stairs.

"All packed?" Martha asked.

Ana nodded. "We've left the case by the bed. We have to go now but we'll speak to you later, Martha…Mrs Brown."

"Okay, dear. I'll let you out. The door's locked."

As she walked them down the stairs she whispered to them, "Use the google to try and find Ruth McDonald. She won't be able to talk to me because of her suspension, but she might agree to talk to you. Don't tell her straight off that you know Hope. Make up some story about a Modern Studies project or something where you need information about social services. She's most likely on social media."

Ana smiled, saluting Mrs Brown on her way out the door. Elliot grabbed his umbrella and waited for her to join him underneath. As they walked down the path together Ana visualised the Five of Swords card from Hope's tarot reading.

My sword is drawn, Hope, and I'm ready for battle.

Chapter Seventeen
Hope

"I can't eat half of those meals." I slid the menu cards back across the desk, already knowing I was failing as the girl who followed all the rules. Dr Carmichael met my gaze, moustache twitching in irritation.

"It's non-negotiable, Hope. It's important that we build your haemoglobin levels. Your initial blood test results from Clara's sample indicate you are borderline anaemic. The iron tablets will help of course, but it's important we introduce red meat to your diet. I need to ensure you keep a healthy red blood cell count during donations."

I shook my head, gripping the edge of the desk. "I've not eaten meat since I was ten years old. That's not going to change."

The tips of Dr Carmichael's moustache trembled a warning. He sat forward in his chair, eyes black like thunder, hands flat on the desk. "A lot is going to change, Hope. The quicker you step into line, the easier this whole transition will be."

I sat back, folding my arms, breathing in and out, trying to calm the fire burning inside. It blistered my tongue, enticing me to lash out. I swallowed the rest of my protest, deciding I could try to sweet talk Margaret into cooking me substitute meat.

I listened as Dr Carmichael ran through a list of other dietary instructions printed in the booklet he'd given me. Foods not only high in iron but also protein and calcium. A diet low in fatty foods, restricted caffeine intake, and zero alcohol unless during special occasions. I wanted to ask what kind of special occasions occurred in the house. In the six hours leading up to donations the restrictions tightened and water intake increased. Dr Carmichael explained it was important to be fully hydrated before a plasma donation to ensure no dizziness or other reactions. I flicked through the booklet as he talked, paying attention to diagrams where individuals lay hooked up to specialised plasmapheresis machines. During the procedure blood cells and plasma were separated, with the plasma collected. Dr Carmichael explained during plasmapheresis they used a chemical called citrate, to stop blood clotting, which could also deplete calcium so was another reason to monitor their diet.

"The leftover blood cell components will be returned to your body," Dr Carmichael explained, touching his arm.

So technically they weren't extracting our blood, they were taking our plasma. A translucent component of blood, I read in the information section of the booklet. A straw-coloured liquid, the weak pigment a misleading representation of its potential.

"The proteins and antibodies in plasma are beneficial for a number of conditions. We're just at the start of exploring the benefits. You should be excited to be a part of such groundbreaking medicine." Dr Carmichael sounded like an over-excited salesman.

I wasn't the prime audience here. I was the participant who lay on the stage, the magician's assistant who facilitated the magic. *Who is the audience?* I wanted to ask. *Who receives these gifts?*

And then as if by magic, I got some of my answers. The last pages of the booklet contained case studies, good news stories, detailing how residents' pure plasma donations had provided cures for many 'patients'. Pages full of little miracles. Barbara Carmichael's face smiled out from the last page. The sentence, 'daily transfusions slowed down Alzheimer's deterioration, after a year a reverse in the condition occurred, resulting in a near full recovery,' jumped out at me. I looked up in surprise, watching as a small satisfied smile tugged on Dr Carmichael's lips.

"I can see you're impressed. I hope this gives you some reassurance that we're not monsters here. That we've not imprisoned you in some vampire lair." His laugh was hollow, creepy, a total antithesis to his attempt at putting me at ease.

My eyes trailed to the painting above the desk as Dr Carmichael closed over the booklet and shuffled through the rest of my medical notes. A flock of bats circled a bleeding heart, the ruby red dripping through the black and grey landscape, pooling into ripples of blood. Vampire bats, I realised.

"A talented former resident's idea of a little joke," Dr Carmichael explained, without looking up. I strained to see a signature, thirsty to know who had been here before me, where they had escaped to. Maybe Art school, or Paris, painting landscapes along the riverbanks of the Seine.

Dr Carmichael pushed his reading glasses up, peering at a slip of paper in front of him. "You have a very desirable rare blood type, Hope. AB positive. Only three per cent of the population have this."

I wasn't sure how to respond. It sounded like a compliment, an achievement, like a grade on an exam. AB +

"You may already know this makes you a

universal recipient if you ever needed a transfusion, but it also means you are a universal plasma *donor*. We rarely find plasma donors with this blood type. It's even more important to stick to your diet as we need you to be able to donate your maximum of twice a week, but hope to increase this as time goes on."

Twice a week being hooked up to some machine via a needle for an hour and a half. It didn't sound so bad. Who knew it would be the food thing that was going to be the tough part.

"One last piece of paperwork and then I'll release you so you can have your tea break before meeting with the other staff." He produced an official looking document, slid the crisp white paper towards me.

Confidentiality Clause was printed along the top. I scanned the key points, statements outlining instructions. On my release on my eighteenth birthday I would be presented with twenty thousand pounds, to be paid into an account I would have instant access to. I was forbidden to disclose any aspect of my life inside the house, or its existence, or the money would instantly be revoked, with penalties.

"Where will I say I've been?" I asked aloud, grasping the gold pen Dr Carmichael had slid across the desk.

"Don't worry yourself about that just now. We always help you prepare a story."

"Why the secrecy? If you're doing good things here, why not share it with the world?"

Dr Carmichael adjusted his bowtie in irritation. "A number of reasons, Hope. Medical regulations being the biggest. It's not the norm to allow people under seventeen to donate plasma. And the methods. I don't think many people would get on board with my idea of such a controlled environment, do you?

You're a smart girl, Hope. Don't ask stupid questions."

I shut my mouth, tapping the pen against the dotted line. "What if I don't sign?"

The dark storm swirled in his eyes, moustache twitching. "Then we release you to the police, you get sent to a residential unit, we create a backstory that we found you high on drugs to ensure no one believes stories you might want to tell."

And in that instant the shadow of the man I had seen in the car emerged. The man who extracted kids from school, drugged them and bundled them into the back of a car. I pictured Martha at home, her phone untouched, her head full of lies from Ms Turnberry, Ana waving around my tarot card, shouting into an empty abyss, demanding attention from whom? Who would come looking for the girl who was trouble, who didn't belong to anyone, who could disappear without a trace?

I pressed down hard with the pen. As my fingers looped the letters the irony was not lost on me. Signing my name, *Hope*, like it was a wish, a dream for a better future.

Chapter Eighteen
Ana

Ana found her mum in the kitchen, a cup in her hand, tilted at an angle that suggested she was so engrossed in the paperwork in front of her that she forgot she was holding it.

"Hi," Ana laid her bag down on the floor, bracing herself for a severe telling off.

Mum looked up in surprise, folding over the letter she was reading, coffee dripping on the counter. She cursed, grabbing kitchen roll to mop it up.

Ana's chest tightened when she clocked the puffy red eyes and smudged mascara. She wasn't wearing the work clothes she'd left the house in at breakfast.

"What's wrong, Mum?" Ana could hear the panic in her voice and tried to swallow it.

"It's okay, Ana. I've just been sent home from work, for a while."

"A while?" The panic throbbed in Ana's throat. Mum loved her job in the student support department at a local University.

"When term starts it's always manic. The past month has been difficult." She massaged her brow with finger and thumb.

Ana hadn't given much thought to what Mum's job actually involved. The daily tasks she would need to focus on, the meetings, the information she needed to retain.

"My manager asked me to take a couple of weeks off. I don't want you to worry, okay?" Her eyes pleaded with Ana and she nodded, both of them knowing it wasn't as easy as that. "I only agreed to it because I want to see if having some quiet time helps. It'll allow me to come up with better strategies too, force me to be more methodical in my job. You know me, always diving in with no proper structures to anything."

Ana tried to smile, already picturing her own colour coded study plans and how she could teach Mum to be more organised. She tried to rationalise her break as being a good thing. Maybe stress had been the main culprit really, information overload causing Mum's brain to stop absorbing, to refuse to listen. It was like when Maisie tried to watch television and do her homework and talk to Ana at the same time. She would read the same question over and over, asking Ana to help, saying it was too hard.

"I'm going to call Dad at lunchtime and explain to him. I'll tell Maisie I'm working from home. She's too young to understand and I can't deal with her questions when I don't know the answers."

Ana nodded, grateful that she was trusting her to be able to handle knowing. Her comment also reminded Ana not to ask too many questions, even although her head was exploding with them. When was her next medical appointment? Why hadn't she got her test results yet?

Ana tried to remember Grandma's journey to help her understand what might be happening, but she realised her Alzheimer's had developed long before she was even aware anything was wrong. It was only when things started to get extreme, when Grandma got her mixed up with her younger sister who had died when they were teenagers, that Ana realised the full extent of her decline.

At first it had scared her, but she played along,

pretending to be 'Doris' curious as to what Grandma's sister had been like. Ana let Grandma stroke her hair, and style it, often weaving the strands into plaits, cooing about how pretty Doris would look and maybe Jim and his brother would be at the shops later. Ana wanted to ask who the boys were. Grandma had met Grandpa during her first job as a typist. Her conversation was before Grandpa's time and Ana wanted to know who she'd been then, but only ever got snippets of answers in passing comments and wistful musings. Jim's name came up often and it made Ana wonder what they had been to one another, and what had become of him. Sometimes Grandma would fire demanding questions and Ana was always too scared to try to answer those.

Mum tried to explain to Ana that Grandma's mind had started to rewind, that she was still Grandma, just an earlier version and really it was special, wasn't it, getting to glimpse a part of her they would never have known. Like stepping into a time machine and getting to travel with her to the past.

Ana watched her mum move around the kitchen, picturing the younger versions she'd glimpsed of her in old photo albums and video clips from Dad's computer. Everyone had a Before version. Ana wanted to tell her that she would travel with her to her 'before' if it came to it. If her journey started to rewind, Ana would visit ghosts and places and people she didn't know how to talk to. She would try not to be so scared this time.

"So, enough about my morning." Mum turned to Ana and the present was sharp and clear in her eyes as she waved her phone in the air. "School want to know why you're not there, and I do too. So talk."

*

Elliot was waiting for Ana at the school gates. It was lunchtime and no amount of begging had persuaded her mum to allow Ana the whole day off. Elliot messaged saying he'd texted his mum to tell her a sub teacher had failed to sign him in. Ana cursed herself, wishing she was a better liar. They'd agreed to go back for the afternoon classes together.

Elliot had his camera slung round his neck. He had it focused on his boots. Ana watched as he lifted his foot, stamping in a puddle. *Snap.* What was interesting about that image? Was he seeing patterns and colours only visible to his eye?

He lowered the camera and looked up, waving when he spotted Ana, a thoughtful expression forming on his face, a smile playing on his lips. Ana's stomach flipped over, heat shooting from her toes to her ears. When he raised the camera and pointed it in her direction she looked away, hiding her face with her hands.

"I hate getting my picture taken."

"Please." He moved forward, touching her hand. She was surprised by how comfortable the gesture felt, a warmth spreading up her arm. His eyes were kind, encouraging. Curiosity made her pause. She wanted to know how he saw her.

Ana brushed her fringe back from her eyes and faced him, trying to smile, feeling her jaw tighten and cheeks flush.

"You don't need to pose. Just think of something good, something you love."

An image of Sunday night film time, Mum's head falling on Ana's shoulder as she dozed off, snoring loudly. She grinned at the memory.

Snap. Elliot lowered his camera.

"Will you show me it when you get them

developed?"

"Of course," he nodded.

What if he captured her crooked front tooth and the spots on her face? It didn't look like the kind of camera you could scroll through to check photos and then delete, so she resisted the urge to ask. It definitely didn't have a filter button. Elliot now had a close-up, unedited photograph of her in the autumn light. The thought was simultaneously terrifying and exciting.

A 'ping' sound emitted from his pocket. He pulled out his phone and smiled as he read the screen. For a fleeting second Ana imagined it to be Hope and she tensed in anticipation.

Elliot grabbed her wrist, steering her away from the school gates. "I found Ruth and she wants to meet us. We have to go now, come on."

Ana glanced back at the school building in hesitation, worrying Mum might get another message. Elliot was halfway along the street, marching towards a bus stop, not considering she might protest. She hurried after him, too curious to care if she got in more trouble.

*

The café smelled of stale chips and cheap disinfectant. There were only two people inside. An old man in a raincoat eating eggs and beans, reading his paper, and a slim female sitting in the back corner, scarf wound high around her neck as if she was trying to obscure her face, leg jangling. She was tipping what looked like her third packet of sugar into a large mug.

"That must be her," Elliot said.

Ana's tummy growled as the smells of food swirled in the air reminding her they'd missed lunch.

The bus journey had taken nearly an hour by the time it wound its way round all the streets into town.

Ruth looked up and motioned them over, like she wanted them to sit down quickly and quietly. They both obeyed. Ana slid into the seat directly across from Ruth, taking in her pointed features, her messy brown hair. There was a weariness in her eyes as she smiled a quick hello. She gathered up the discarded sugar packets in her hands, dropping them onto her saucer.

Before they had the chance for introductions a bored looking waitress appeared, notebook in hand.

"What can I get youse?" She didn't bother to look up.

Ana glanced at Elliot, wondering if he was going to be polite. She was relieved when he ordered a cheeseburger and chips. She did the same.

Ruth waited until the waitress had left before she spoke. "I don't have long and I need you both to know how much trouble I would be in if anyone, and I mean *anyone*, finds out I've agreed to meet you today."

Elliot blinked in surprise and Ruth shot him a wry smile.

"I know you don't want to talk to me about a Modern Studies project, son. As soon as I saw your name popping up in my message box I knew. You're Hope's pal, right?"

Ruth looked between them and they both nodded.

"I thought she'd have been here too. She alright?" There was a long pause as they realised Ruth didn't know anything. Ruth frowned, gripping her mug tight. She read their expressions, lowering her voice. "What happened?"

"She's gone," Elliot said, matter of fact.

"Disappeared from school, never returned to her foster carers, just like my brother Seb."

Ruth's face stayed neutral but the tapping of her nails on the mug gave her nerves away. "And Ian Hobbs has taken over as her case worker?"

"Yes," Ana swallowed, wondering how she knew.

"I agreed to meet you, Elliot, because the day I got suspended I tried to access some files on our system. For your foster brother, Seb, and those boys who went missing from a local Children's House. I couldn't find any trace of them. Sometimes that happens if I can't find a date of birth, so I contacted our data services department to see if they could trace any files matching those names. And what do you know, they found Seb's, then the other boys, including someone called Davey, in an archive marked for deletion. All files were last updated by Ian Hobbs. The last recorded notes suggested they'd moved outwith Scotland so it takes them off our caseloads."

"Would that delete the files?" Ana asked, adding, "I overheard teachers in school saying they thought that she'd moved to England, but would need to check with Ms Turnberry."

Ruth frowned, tapping a nail against her cup, as if thinking about what Ana had just said. She shook her head. "Not straight away. Before I could do any more digging, I found myself in my manager's office, being told I was being investigated for misconduct. Apparently one of my young clients accused me of supplying them with cigarettes, alcohol and super strong painkillers." Ruth took a long sip of her coffee.

"What?" Ana blinked in shock and Ruth shot her a withering look which made Ana blush to her toes.

"It's fabricated lies. Problem is, I've been known

to offer a stray fag here and there to some of my kids. It doesn't bode well if my managers start questioning, digging around. I've got no access to my work phone or to the work system. Convenient, eh, when Hope disappears?"

Elliot sat forward. "Did you notice anything else on Seb's file?"

"I didn't have proper time to look. I thought I'd be able to read it later."

They all fell silent as the waitress returned with food. Ana stuffed a couple of chips in her mouth.

"We met Ian Hobbs," Ana said. She wanted to add that she didn't like him.

Ruth looked at her in surprise. "When?"

"This morning. At Martha Brown's. She told us to get in touch with you."

"Did she?" A smile played on Ruth's lips. "I like that woman."

As they ate, Ana and Elliot explained the story, the accusations of Hope selling drugs, the move to a new place, her text message, but also her tarot message. Ruth stayed silent, listening intently, not reacting to anything.

"So what do you think's going on?" Elliot asked, clearly impatient.

"Nothing good." Ruth frowned. She shrugged, like she knew it was a lame answer. She pulled a pen from her top pocket, grabbing Ana's napkin. She wrote Ian Hobbs' name in the middle, extending lines out to Ms Turnberry, Oakridge High and Oakridge Children's House.

"Who's Hope been hanging around with in school?" Ruth asked, tapping her pen against her chin.

"Us," Ana said. She tried to think back to the past

few weeks. "She got in a sort of fight with a girl in our year, Jenna."

Ruth added Jenna's name to the diagram. "Why did they fight? Anyone else involved?"

"Jenna's boyfriend, Gordon. He was flirting with Hope." Ana frowned at Ruth's scribbling, glancing at Elliot. He raised an eyebrow, indicating he wasn't sure what she was doing either.

"Was she ever taken out of class? Did she ever disappear any other time?"

Elliot shook his head as Ana tried to remember. She thought back to the day Hope was late for lunch, when she hadn't replied to her texts and missed some classes. "Yes. She had a blood test."

"A blood test?" Ruth frowned, then a realisation formed on her face. "The school nurse. I remember her mentioning that. What's the nurse's name?"

Ana shrugged. "I don't know."

Ruth added Nurse to the napkin. She folded it over, sliding it into her pocket. "Okay, I have to go now. What I'm going to do is try and speak to the staff at the Children's House. They won't know I've been suspended. I need you both to keep your eyes open in school. Tell me if you see Ms Turnberry meeting with anyone unusual and if you see Ian Hobbs hanging about."

Ana frowned. "Do you think Ms Turnberry has something to do with this?"

Ruth drained the last of her coffee. "I don't know, kid. I'm keeping an open mind." She nodded at Elliot. "Keep in touch via social media. I don't give out my personal number." She stood up, the conversation closed. Ana watched as she strode across the café, hurrying out into the rain. Ana made a face at Elliot.

"Bit of an abrupt goodbye."

Elliot shrugged. "I guess we're lucky she even met us."

Ana thought back to her napkin diagram, the lines connecting names. It surely couldn't be a coincidence the day Hope went missing Ruth got suspended. Ana's phone vibrated in her pocket. Her first thought was Mum, that the school had sent out an afternoon text. She pulled it out, bracing herself. She realised it was an email, not a phone call.

Her heart leapt as she registered the name and email title.

Dr Finlay Carmichael: Re clinic query
Dear Miss Gilbert

I read your message via my website with much interest. Your query in relation to my research into blood trials pleased me. It's highly unusual for me to receive interest in this from those outwith the medical profession.

I would be happy to set up a meeting for you and your mother to visit my clinic. If you would be so kind as to forward on a suitable contact number I will have my assistant, Faye, contact you in due course.

Best Wishes,
Dr Carmichael

An image of Dr Carmichael in his car flashed in Ana's mind. Then another. In the back seat of Ms Turnberry's Porsche. She thought back to Ruth's napkin diagram, to Ruth's request that they pay attention to any unusual meetings Ms Turnberry might have. Ana drew another line of the diagram in her head. That was a connection she wanted to unravel.

Chapter Nineteen
Hope

Margaret read my menu cards and scribbled notes in a book laid open on the wooden table in the kitchen. She wasn't alone today. Pollock, a small bald man with tattoos of pin-up girls curling round his arms, stood by the stove slicing vegetables, his knife making a rhythmic 'thunk' against the wooden chopping board. 'Assistant Cook' was embroidered on his white chef jacket. He was the only member of house staff who stayed silent during my introductions. I didn't take it as rudeness, just that he liked to keep himself to himself and I respected that. Viv, the petite blond I'd seen upstairs with the screaming girl, was the opposite. Talking a mile a minute, her voice sounded like gravel and stale cigarettes, ice blue eyes drawing attention away from her broken teeth. She was the house cleaner and also in charge of our fitness regime.

Then there was Ryan, Margaret's nephew, who supported in the kitchen and did the gardening. And Billy, the 'Security Guard' who patrolled the house and gardens, getting distracted with insects and shiny objects and smiling hellos to all who passed by (so really Mrs Carmichael took the lead on security watches). I wanted to know their stories, what brought them here and what made them stay. Seb said he'd heard stories about their pasts being littered with crime, with the Carmichaels offering a 'safe haven.'

Ryan stood at the stove, stirring the soup Pollock was preparing. He kept turning his head to stare at me, eyes scanning my body. His hair was slicked back with too much gel, his pale face punctuated with spots and freckles. A permanent smirk rested on his lips, as if he was in on a joke I'd never understand. I stared back at him, defiant, hoping I sent him a clear message: I didn't *want* to understand.

Margaret made a clucking noise, laying my cards aside. "Lots of hearty dinners to follow, lass. I think we'll make some Steak Pie for this evening, boys."

I gripped the edge of the table, feeling sick at the thought.

"I was wondering, Margaret, if you might have some kind of meat substitutes that you could use?" I tried to keep my voice low, so that Ryan wouldn't overhear.

Margaret laughed, the red on her cheeks deepening. "Och no, my love. There's no meat substitutes in my kitchen. Why would you suggest such a thing?"

"Because I'm a vegetarian."

Pollock stopped chopping, looking round at Margaret. Ryan halted his stirring, shaking his head and sniggering. Margaret's brow furrowed.

"No, no, no lass. There's none of that in this house. None of that." She bent to pick up a dish from below the table. "It's important you keep up your strength. You need your iron, alright? You'll see."

"I can get iron from vegetables, from pulses, tofu."

"Tofu?" Margaret practically spat.

"There's none of that shite in here, Hope," Ryan piped up from the corner.

"Language, Ryan." Margaret smacked him on the back of the head and he turned back to stirring, the tips of his ears blooming a bright pink.

I sighed. "No one can force me to eat meat."

Margaret leaned across the table and pressed her hands flat, looking at me intently. A warning with a ripple of fear flashed in her eyes. "You do as they say, lass."

I wanted to ask why. What was the worst that would happen if I didn't? I'd get locked up in the cell with no windows?

The door swung open, slamming against a shelf on the wall, Margaret's jars of ingredients rattling.

Margaret clutched a hand to her heart. "Billy, you'll give a woman a heart attack, so you will, clambering around like that."

"Sorry, Magrat, sorry." Billy hopped from one foot to the other, staring at his shoes.

Margaret swooped over beside him, stroking his arm. She pulled out a biscuit from her apron pocket, sliding it into his hand. He grinned and she winked. As he started to chew, Margaret watched him expectantly.

"What can we do for you, Billy?"

He blinked, as if surprised by the question. He swallowed the remains of his treat and stood up straighter, pulling up his trousers. His 'Security' hat slid down to his nose, obscuring his eyebrows, casting a shadow over his eyes.

"Hope's to go to the library. Her tutor's here."

I hopped down from the stool, smiling. "Thanks, Billy. You want to walk me there?"

Billy pushed his hat up. "Yes, yes, I do."

I followed him out the kitchen, the door nearly slamming me on the nose as he forgot to hold it open. He sloped along the hallway, taking big strides, running a hand absently against the gold embossed flowers on the wallpaper.

"How long have you been in the house, Billy?" I moved into step beside him, glancing around, checking no other staff were about.

"A long time. Since I was small."

"Small?" I prompted.

Billy started counting on his fingers. "Since I was fifteen. I'm twenty now."

I observed him with interest. If he arrived when he was fifteen, was he once a donor?

"I'm special. I get to stay. Got a job." He touched his hat.

"Who brought you here to the house, Billy?"

He frowned and didn't say anything as we turned the corner towards the library and I wondered if he wasn't going to answer, or maybe he didn't remember. Then he stopped and looked down at me.

"I came in a car. I didn't like my last family. They were mean. I like Mrs Carmichael. She's nice."

I nodded. He chewed his lip, reaching his hand out, touching my hair tentatively.

"I like the colour of your hair. It's pretty, like a fox."

"Thank you." I tilted my head forward, allowing him to run a hand down the strands, understanding that there was nothing threatening about Billy. He was like a child. Bruises and puncture marks on his skin caught my eye.

I stepped back, touching his arm and he froze.

"Sorry, I didn't mean it, sorry," he panicked.

"Shh, it's okay," I soothed. "I was just looking at your arm. Do you donate?"

Billy ran a hand absently along his skin, nodding. "Billy's blood is special. They need lots."

I wondered if the other staff used to be donors too, then got to stay, offering to help in the house. But that didn't make sense as they were a lot older than Billy and Dr Carmichael had emphasised the use of young blood in the trials.

I started to ask more, when a sharp voice cut into our conversation. I startled when Mrs Carmichael appeared in front of us, coat buttoned up to her pointed chin, clutching a shiny black handbag. She pushed the library door open.

"Your tutor is waiting, Hope. I think you've bothered Billy enough, don't you?" The question was rhetorical. "Billy, come along. Clara is in the car already."

Billy shot me a smile then hurried after Mrs Carmichael. I watched curiously, wondering if Billy got to leave the house. Mrs Carmichael turned her head sharply, as if sensing my gaze. A coldness and outright hostility radiated from every inch of her. I quickly turned away, a shiver trembling through me.

I pushed the library door open, breathing in the reassuring scent of books. As the door clicked shut, I immediately felt soothed by the silence. I glanced around, wondering where my tutor was. The rustle of papers drew my attention to the back of the library under the bay windows. A beam of light stretched through the glass, obscuring my view of the male who sat in shadows at one of the tables.

I walked towards him, attempting to shade my eyes with my hand. As he looked up, his face came in to focus. I stopped dead.

"Hello, Hope." He half rose from his chair, hesitant and awkward.

"Mr Darwin?" I shook my head, baffled. "What are you doing here?"

He gestured for me to sit down. I stared at him as I took my seat, a flutter of relief settling in my gut.

Here was someone from outside. A teacher.
Everything was going to be okay.

Chapter Twenty
Hope

Mr Darwin took his time re-arranging the books on the table, positioning them in a line, sliding a couple of notebooks towards me.

"Your schoolbooks arrived today."

I grabbed the notebooks in delight, flicking through them. Seeing my handwriting looping across the pages felt like being reunited with an old friend. A rainbow coloured one caught my eye. I could picture it on my desk at the Browns. I opened it and Mum's photo fell out. My heart constricted as her face beamed up at me. I traced a finger over her smile.

"Did you collect these from the Browns?" I asked.

Mr Darwin shook his head. "Not me, someone else. Mrs Carmichael brought the books here to the library. I believe the rest of your belongings are upstairs in your bedroom."

I resisted the urge to run up to check all my clothes had arrived. I couldn't wait to get back to being me. My substitute clothes made me feel I'd been erased.

"Why are you here?" I repeated my original question, studying Mr Darwin's face. He wouldn't meet my eye.

"I tutor here two days a week."

"The days you're not at Oakridge." Ana had been right; the cancer rumours weren't true. "Do you know what's going on here? Do you know I was drugged and bundled into the back of a car, taken from school without being allowed to say goodbye to anyone?"

A pulse throbbed in his neck and he still wouldn't meet my eye. "Yes."

"Doesn't that bother you?" I could tell from the expression on his face that it did. But the lack of eye contact signified guilt. Acceptance. Not someone who was here to tell me anything good.

He finally looked up, his voice devoid of any emotion. "They'll take good care of you in here, Hope. There are worse places to be. Shall I talk you through your study plan?"

I slammed my notebook shut and he flinched.

"Why are you being so weird?" I hissed. "This isn't normal. Why are you acting like it is?"

He didn't react and I wanted to shake him.

"I need you to get a message to my foster carers and Ana and Elliot. I want you to explain to them what's happened." I grabbed a pen.

"I can't," he said.

I turned to a fresh page in my notebook. I stabbed the paper with the nib. "Why not?"

"No one knows I do this. I've signed a Confidentiality Clause."

"Oh for god's sake. Do you get a golden cheque too?"

He frowned. "What do you mean?"

"Well, what's in it for you? Why have you agreed to this?"

Mr Darwin shifted in his chair. He unscrewed a tin flask that sat beside his unopened textbook, gulping down the liquid. I smelled the tang of coffee and my lips tingled at the thought of a caffeine hit. I waited for him to explain.

"I had a bad year last year," he hesitated as if he wanted to say more but then changed his mind. His expression closed. "The important thing is I can support you here with your studies. Dr Carmichael wants to keep your minds stimulated."

"So are you all in on this? Ms Turnberry and Clara? Do they get some pay off?"

He sighed, "We really should get started on some work, Hope. Maybe that's enough questions for today?"

"Okay, but this question is important to me. Will you be putting us forward for exams? Will we get qualifications by doing this work?" Getting out of here at eighteen meant I could still pursue opportunities. My future plans didn't have to change.

Mr Darwin hesitated. "I believe Dr Carmichael has some kind of arrangement set up with Ms Turnberry."

I took the textbook Mr Darwin slid across the table, itching to ask more about Ms Turnberry's involvement. I thought back to the day we'd seen her exit her Porsche and Elliot's confusion as to how she could afford such a car.

"Does Dr Carmichael pay Ms Turnberry?" I blurted.

Mr Darwin's head darted up. He cleared his throat, shifting in his chair. "That's none of my business, and it's none of yours. Can we focus now on the work? How about you turn to page fifty?"

Time passed quickly, the familiarity and normality of Mr Darwin and schoolwork offering a welcome reprieve from the unknowns of the house. As Mr Darwin packed away his belongings he issued me with a reading list, encouraging me to make use of the library's Philosophy section, explaining we would get started on that work next time.

The silence of the library folded in around me as the door clicked shut. I wandered between the shelves of books, running my hands over thick leather bindings which smelled of old wisdom I wanted to absorb. A light shone in from the far window and I turned to look out at a paved section of the garden, squinting to make out two figures taking a stroll along a path lined with small spindly trees. The light shifted and I realised it was Dr Carmichael and Phoenix. She looked like she was listening intently to whatever he was saying, nodding occasionally. He placed a hand on the base of her back, an affectionate gesture like he was an adoring grandfather. She turned to smile up at him and I frowned, wondering if I had read him wrong. They disappeared from view and I turned back to the shelves of books.

I carried a couple of Philosophy titles back to my table, starting with an Introduction to Plato, musing over the thought of leaders without greed or a desire for power. Another image of Ms Turnberry in her office, swinging the bag of drugs in my face, entered my thoughts, wondering if her greed and desire for power motivated her involvement with the house. I tried not to think of the rest of our conversation that day, the smug way she announced Martha didn't want me home, with threats of where I might end up. Mr Darwin was right of course, there were worse places to be than this house.

The door slammed open, causing me to jump. I closed the book, heart sinking as Ryan sauntered in, an amused smile playing on his lips. I started to gather up my belongings, skin prickling with unease at the thought of spending any time alone with him.

"Did you enjoy your tutoring session, Hope?" He pressed his hands down on the table in front of me, craning his head to read the titles of the books. "Lots of boring reading there to keep your pretty little head occupied."

I added the Plato book to my pile, heading towards the door, conscious Ryan's gaze followed me.

"It's cute you think any of this will lead you anywhere," Ryan called, amusement in his voice.

My hand gripped the door handle. I knew I should ignore his taunting, but curiosity won over. "What do you mean?" I turned my head.

"No one knows you're here and that's how they like it. Why would they then submit you for exams?" Ryan smirked, his eyes flashing with disdain. "You're nothing more than a donor in here, Hope, so you can stop thinking you're better than the rest of us."

Why would Dr Carmichael go to the bother of employing Mr Darwin if there were no exams to work towards? *What was the point if there was no end result?* Anger scorched my cheeks as Ryan whistled a discordant tune, enjoying my confusion. I wasn't going to give him the satisfaction of reacting. I yanked the door open, striding out into the corridor.

I turned a corner and smacked into a body. "Ow." My books thudded to the ground.

Seb rubbed his chest, an amused look on his face. "What's the hurry?" He bent down to my level, helping me gather up the books. His arm brushed mine and I felt a charge of electricity. He paused, turning a photo over between his fingers. "Who's this?"

Cheeks flaming, I grabbed it from him. "My mum."

He paused, like he wanted to apologise and ask more. I looked away, trying to calm my breathing.

"Are you okay?" He brushed his hair back from his face and I tried not to stare as the lights made his eyes shine green.

I nodded. "I'm fine."

"Good." His lips curled into a mischievous smile. He picked up the library books, taking my free hand. "There's somewhere I want to show you."

Before I could protest, he pulled me along the hall, my body acutely aware of the sensation of his hand wrapped around mine. As we climbed the central staircase I dropped his grip, conscious of the sweat curling in my palm. I gathered my notebooks close, pretending I needed both hands to carry them comfortably. When we reached the second floor he motioned for me to follow him past the boys' bedrooms, stopping at a panelled wall. He flashed me a smile and placed a palm flat against one of the panels, pushing firmly. I watched in amazement as it swung open, a secret doorway. He shoved a hand round to the inner wall, and clicked a switch, an orange glow illuminating a rickety wooden staircase.

"Cool, eh?" He wiggled his eyebrows and I smiled in agreement, hurrying up the stairs after him.

At the top of the stairs, Seb pushed open a wooden door, clicking another switch, bathing the room in yellow light. Wooden slanted beams framed the ceiling, a skylight indicating we were in the attic. Dusty bookcases lined the walls, a battered velvet red chaise longue in the corner with a patchwork blanket draped over the back, a faint musty smell swirling in the air. I stepped into the room, eyes drawn to the old brown piano in the corner.

"This place is amazing." The floorboards creaked and groaned as I walked, making me choose my steps carefully. I laid my notebooks on top of the piano and pulled out the heavy, wooden stool, sinking into the green leather seat. I ran my hands up and down the keys, admiring the intricate rose patterns carved into the wooden façade of the piano. It was old, the keys yellowed and sturdy, a contrast to the ebony keys on Mum's, but it had character. I pressed my feet down against the heavy metal pedals, testing a note.

"You play?" Seb smiled in surprise.

I shook my head, suddenly self-conscious. "Just a little. It's been a while…"

"Would you play something for me? I've been trying to get a tune out of this old thing for months."

I hesitated, fragments of familiar tunes circling my head. I looked up at him. "In a minute. I need to ask you something first."

He laid the Philosophy books on top of my notebooks, glancing at the titles. He raised his eyebrows expectantly.

"I had my first tutoring session with Mr Darwin. You never mentioned he was part of this?"

Seb looked taken aback, like it never entered his head to mention him. "I was hardly at school. Was he your English teacher?"

I nodded. "Why on earth would he get involved in any of this?"

Seb leaned against the table behind us. "Phoenix told me his wife got sick and had to leave work and they got into debt. I think he was gambling or something. He gets paid extra for this gig and his wife gets free infusions." Seb shrugged. "There's always something with the staff. Some kind of pay-off that benefits them."

It made me melancholy, to think how easy it was for Dr Carmichael to enlist people to do his bidding. I thought back to Phoenix walking around the garden with Dr Carmichael. Was she worming her way in, to become a confidante to him too? She was obviously friendly with staff, extracting more information from Mr Darwin than I had managed.

"Mr Darwin told me we got subbed for exams, but then Ryan said we don't..." My voice trailed off. I knew from the expression on Seb's face who had been telling the truth.

"It's part of the façade. Dr Carmichael acts like he's giving us access to something good here. Really, it's just to keep our minds occupied." Seb made a face. "I hated school anyway. Probably had no chance of getting any qualifications."

"I like school," I answered sharply. "And I know I would have got good grades."

There was an uncomfortable silence. Seb placed a hand on my shoulder.

"That sucks. I'm sorry. I bet you could catch up when you leave. Go to college..."

I shrugged, tracing my fingers up and down the piano keys, trying to calm the anger fizzing inside at the thought of my future being taken away from me.

"Will you play for me?" Seb asked again.

"Okay. But don't watch me. It's making me nervous."

"Okay." He backed off, the floorboards squeaking as he crept to the other side of the room.

I pressed down on the notes, cringing at the lack of tuning, and my clumsy fingers. As I relaxed, my hands found the music, and I felt it move through me. I closed my eyes, enjoying the sensation of not having to think, just feeling; *'the flow'* Mum called it. Like getting lost in a daydream.

I ended brashly, an off-key note hanging in the air. Seb clapped loudly. I laughed and turned to him. The admiration was clear on his face and a warm glow spread to my toes.

"That was amazing," he said.

I shook my head, embarrassed by my lack of grace and dud notes. The rendition sounded like a nervous stutter. "I made a lot of mistakes."

"I loved it. I loved that it wasn't perfect." He said it with such sincerity I blushed. I had a sudden overwhelming feeling to let him see all of my flaws and tell him all of my fears and dreams.

His fingers trailed along the notes, shoulder brushing against mine, our hands nearly touching. I held my breath as he pressed down on the minor keys, playing a melancholy tune over and over. He stepped forward, a sunbeam from the skylight lighting his eyes and I felt caught in the glow, my heart catching fire.

We fell into a comfortable rhythm, sitting side by side, our knees touching, the stool barely wide enough to fit us both. I wanted to sit with him forever, playing discordant melodies, feeling like the girl I used to be.

*

Later when I returned to my room, the door was ajar. Slowing my steps I pushed it fully open, watching in disbelief as Stacey raked through my suitcase, pulling out clothes, throwing piles on the floor, others on the bed. She held up a black dress, then walked over to the full-length mirror, pressing the material against her body.

"It won't fit you." I pulled it from her hands. "Get out of my room."

Stacey's lip curled, fake eyelashes flicking as she looked me up and down. "You think you're something special, don't ye? All la-di-da with your fancy clothes."

I grabbed items off the floor, hands shaking.

"I'm talking to you, spoff." She stamped a foot on the top I was trying to lift, the material ripping against her weight. I relented, letting it drop back down and stood to face her.

"What do you want?"

She licked her lips, raking through the clothes on the bed. She unzipped a pocket inside the case and pulled out a glass perfume bottle, misting her wrists with the sweet scent. Clinique Happy. Mum in a bottle. I tried to grab it. She pulled back, shaking her head, smirking.

"I'll be having that." She tucked the bottle into her joggy bottoms, then wound a purple and black scarf around her neck. "Pals share their stuff, don't they?"

I counted to ten in my head to calm my temper. I could take my belongings back by force but Stacey would probably enjoy that, and there was a good chance she'd smash the bottle in my face.

I thought back to the time I'd spent in a residential 'house', before I was placed with Lucy and Andy. There was an underlying sense of dread seeping through the carpets, clinging to the walls. A girl younger than me, with unwashed hair and ripped jeans sat cross-legged at the bottom of my bed. Even although we had our own rooms she said she had night terrors and never slept, often wandering unannounced into my space. She sat up all night staring, eyes burning with rage and defiance, like one wrong word or movement from me would spiral her into attack. I had buried further into the sheets smelling of other people, wishing I hadn't run away from the O'Brians, wondering how long it would take Ruth to find me somewhere else. In the end it hadn't taken long and I vowed to never return to that place.

Now, there was no running away, and no Ruth to

come and collect me.

I pulled out a powder blue hoodie Andy had gifted me last Christmas. It was too big and bulky for my frame. I handed it to Stacey. "You should take this. The colour will suit you."

She snatched it from me, slipping her arms inside, pulling up the hood. Her chin jutted out as she gazed in the mirror, turning from side to side. Satisfied with her haul she headed for the door, flashing me the finger on her way out. "Catch ye."

My body sighed with relief as she disappeared from sight. I shut the door, sliding the bolt from inside. I wondered if Clara would give me a key to lock the door from the outside. Stacey might sneak in any time she wanted and there were limits to what I was prepared to let go of.

I thought back to what Ryan had said, about me being nothing more than a donor. Working towards nothing. I was hurtling towards becoming nothing and no one. I lay back on the bed, closing my eyes, exhaustion washing over me, too tried to even cry. What was the point? Tears never changed my pathetic life.

I reached under my pillow, thankful my tarot pouch was untouched. I slid out the cards, closing my eyes as I spread them across the bed, breathing in and out, trying to empty my head of negative thoughts. *Give me a sign it's all going to be okay. Please.*

I flipped over a card. Two of wands. I heard Mum's voice inside my head: *Let your intuition guide you and have courage to move forward.* I stared at the card, wishing I had a magic wand which could transport me back in time instead. How could I move forward if I was trapped in here and had nowhere to go? I tidied away the cards in frustration, zipping the pouch into the front of my school bag and putting it in the bottom of my wardrobe, hoping Stacey would be put off with the schoolbooks if she happened to find this bag.

I thought about staying in my room, to avoid dinner and film night. Then I pictured Seb and his smile and those eyes. He looked at me like he wanted to know me.

I started to unpack the rest of my case and pulled out my cosmetic purse from the top, relieved to find my make-up all there, already picturing the extra layers of eyeliner I would sculpt. My face was too soft bare. Stacey needed to know I was no push-over.

As I pulled out the contents a square of paper fluttered to the ground. I recognised the handwriting as soon as I unfolded it.

"Ana." A jolt of excitement as I scanned the note, reassuring words jumping out at me: *We're all trying to find you. We miss you. We will find you.* And the line I really needed to read; *Martha didn't want you to go.* I read the lines over and over. Ms Turnberry lied. The note shook in my hands, a mix of emotions charging through me.

Please, Ana. Find me soon.

Chapter Twenty-One
Ana

"I'm not happy about you missing another morning of school." Mum pinned her hair back, then let her brown curls fall loose. She tugged at her blouse.

"Relax, Mum. It's double maths this morning. I wouldn't have understood that anyway. This is a much better use of my time."

"What's a better use of your time?" Maisie clung on to Ana's school bag, sliding her hand into her jacket pocket. Ana extracted her hand, giving it a squeeze. "Nothing, toots."

Maisie folded her arms, exaggerating a frown which she directed first at Ana, then her mum. "You're both acting weird. I know something's going on. I'm six, not stupid."

Mum flashed Ana an amused smile and Ana curled Maisie's ponytail around her finger.

"You're so smart I think you should go to Maths for me and sit my test."

"You have a test? You didn't mention that." Mum hesitated at the door, gripping her car keys.

"I'm just kidding." Ana made a dismissive gesture with her hand, mouthing to Maisie, *'No, I'm not'*, making her giggle. Ana shushed her, widening her eyes. Maisie winked, tapping the side of her nose.

Once they'd dropped Maisie at school Ana typed the address for Dr Carmichael's clinic in to google maps. It was forty minutes away, in a remote area between Glasgow and Edinburgh. Ana stayed quiet, allowing Mum to listen to the robotic voice, holding the phone out for her to see which way the road curved when the instructions became vague. Maisie loved imitating the voice and Ana knew she'd be going crazy right now if she was here, her favourite line, *'Take the route'* repeating over and over.

"I'm taking the bloody route," Mum muttered, doing a U-turn.

Once they were back on track she turned to Ana. "Dad's not sure about us meeting with this Dr Carmichael you know. I told him it was partly for you to ask questions for your science project, but he didn't buy that."

Ana attempted to maintain an innocent expression. "Wasn't he curious, when you told him about the trials?"

"Hmm, he read about ones which took place in America. There were no conclusive results apparently."

So why are so many people in America paying for the pure plasma transfusions? Ana wanted to say. She'd read about a private clinic in California where people were paying $8000 for a two day 'young plasma' treatment. She'd watched TED talks delivered by a neuroscientist at Stanford University, where he talked about ageing mice being injected with young mouse plasma, a term called 'parabiosis' which improved their health and cognitive functions.

The one image she couldn't shake was Barbara Carmichael, sitting coiffed and lucid in the car beside Dr Carmichael. Barb's miraculous transformation had to be the biggest hint that there was something magic at work here.

Her mum turned onto country roads, straining to see signs, looking for the turn-off to the clinic. Ana checked her phone and the dot on the map, the voice telling them, 'Your destination is on the right.'

"I think we might have gone too far," Ana said.

Mum checked her rear-view mirror. "I need to find a place to turn."

The car rocked side to side, as they drove up the gravelly road, fields extending for miles to their left, rows of hedges to their right. The path continued to a smoother winding road, rows of trees lining the way, branches bowing to one another, like they were dancing and forming arches. Black iron gates came into view, spear shaped spikes jutting along the top. A wooden sign to the left announced: PRIVATE GROUNDS DO NOT ENTER. Ana strained to see beyond the gates; it appeared that the path continued, like a long driveway.

The car shuddered into reverse as Mum took advantage of the gap to the left of them, rolling unsteadily on uneven ground, until they pointed back the way they came.

Half-way back up the path she slammed on the breaks, a blue car speeding towards them. The seatbelt cut into Ana's neck. Startled eyes stared: a dark-haired woman and a man with a blue cap, the words 'Security' embroidered in gold. The man smashed his fist to his mouth, his body rocking back and forth. The woman motioned for Ana's mum to drive on, reversing to make room, irritation souring her delicate features. She wound down her window as they levelled with the car, prompting Mum to do the same.

"Are you lost?" The woman asked. Her expression changed when her eyes turned to Ana, a flash of shock and almost panic, which she immediately attempted to hide with a smile. She glanced at her school tie. Ana stared back, confused.

"We're looking for Dr Carmichael's clinic, Oak Spring." Mum craned her neck. "I think we missed the turn off?"

The woman eyed Mum curiously, like she was trying to figure out why they were heading there. "Yes, about fifteen minutes back up the road. It's a sharp right. The sign is half obscured by greenery. Do you have an appointment?"

Mum was clearly taken aback by the question. "Yes, we do."

The woman smiled tightly. "I know he's very popular. Long waiting lists I hear. I wouldn't want you to have a wasted journey." Her window slid up, announcing the end of the conversation.

Ana glanced back, wondering what lay beyond the iron gates. As her mum hit the accelerator, she motioned for Ana to pay attention until she pointed out the sign ahead.

They soon rolled into a modern looking car park, a bungalow style white building with lime green 'Oak Springs' lettering winding above the glass doorway.

"I wonder how he managed to fit us in if he's got such a long waiting list?" Mum murmured as she reached for her handbag.

Ana wondered the same. A feeling of unease started to creep into her gut.

"It looks like a hot tub lodge," Ana whispered as she followed Mum into reception.

Ana's feet sank into the plush carpet as they approached the front desk. A young blonde woman with tight ponytail and flawless skin greeted them with a smile. Her teeth looked too perfect and too white, just like the reception area. A white desk, bright white walls, with cream leather sofas off to the side.

The receptionist's name badge told her this was Faye, the woman she'd spoken to, who set up the appointment. Ana glanced at the posters along the walls as Mum gave their details. Beautiful women with smooth sculpted skin, the words Botox, Lip Fillers, non-surgical enhancements winding above their heads, like cheat sheets revealing their secrets.

Ana followed Mum to the seating area, her body sinking into the soft leather sofa. She adjusted her skirt, feeling nervous and messy in such chic surroundings. Classical music floated from the speakers. She glanced at Mum who was checking her phone, the creased line on her forehead telling Ana she was nervous too. Ana laid her hand on top of her mum's giving a quick squeeze. Mum turned her hand around to squeeze back.

A few minutes later the reception telephone rang and Faye smiled in their direction.

"Dr Carmichael will see you now. Just through the glass doors there, then his office is first on the left."

Mum murmured her thanks. The sofa squeaked when they rose and Ana's toes curled in her shoes. Mum knocked quietly on Dr Carmichael's door and they glanced at one another when he announced, 'Come in.'

He rose from his desk as they entered, revealing a tweed three-piece suit, burgundy bow tie adding to his eccentricity. The curve of his moustache gave a menacing air to his face, the cool steel of his eyes doing nothing to ease Ana's perception. He shook their hands, his grip so crushing Ana expected to hear her knuckles crack.

Once they were seated, Mum started to explain that she'd been doing a lot of reading about experimental trials in America where they were testing the theory that plasma transfusions from 'young blood' could improve brain cognition, along with other health benefits.

Dr Carmichael's gaze fixed on Ana as her mum spoke, a small smile playing on his lips. "And what do you make of these trials, Ana? Do you think there's weight in the theory?"

She stumbled over her words, not expecting to be asked for her opinion. "I think it's all very fascinating. I know there was success in the mouse trials. I'm not so sure the human ones have displayed the same results?"

He laced his fingers in a steeple, his chair squeaking as he sat back. "You're right that the Stanford results only produced marginal improvements. A small percentage of patients with Alzheimer's in the study saw small increases in concentration when performing everyday tasks, but nothing of great significance. It's impossible to know the conditions of the donors used however."

Ana frowned, waiting for him to elaborate.

"For instance, they were using young people, yes, but most were college students, in their early twenties. And we don't know anything about their diets, their lifestyle. One wonders how pure their blood, their plasma, actually was."

Mum glanced at Ana, who could tell from her expression she was already questioning their visit.

Dr Carmichael shifted his attention back to Mum, as if sensing her scepticism. Ana watched her re-arrange her face back into an expression of polite regard.

"Your daughter mentioned that there was a personal reason she was interested in these trials?"

"Ah." Her face reddened and Ana tensed,

wondering if she would be angry with her. Mum clasped her hands. "Perhaps. I've been undergoing some early tests. Nothing conclusive yet. There's a family history…"

Dr Carmichael nodded. "I understand. My wife, Barbara, was diagnosed with dementia years ago."

"Oh, I'm sorry." Mum's brow furrowed. She looked like she'd just remembered something. "My husband mentioned you lived in Oakridge for many years?"

Dr Carmichael looked between them. "Yes. I'm sure we must all have met before."

Ana thought back to the day he nearly ran Maisie over. Something in his expression told her he was remembering that moment too.

"Your wife, I remember, seeing… meeting her," Mum's voice tailed off, her cheeks flushing in embarrassment. Ana wondered if she was picturing Mrs Carmichael searching through their bins.

"Yes, people were most kind. I always knew she would find her way back, when neighbours were looking out for her." Dr Carmichael cleared his throat. He stood up and Ana thought that was the conversation over, and he'd ask them to leave. But then he turned to the metal cabinet behind him, rifling through papers. He pulled out a booklet and laid it down on the desk in front of them. He explained there was scientific information throughout that Ana might find helpful for her science project.

"I think you might find the last few pages particularly interesting, Mrs Gilbert, the case studies," he turned to her mum. "I've been running my own trials, in a very controlled environment, and I think you'll agree my results are quite conclusive. That this can work."

Ana held her breath, watching as Mum flicked through the pages, stopping at a 'Before' and 'After' picture of Barbara Carmichael, with a transcript underneath detailing her monthly progress.

"This is amazing," Mum breathed, reading through the report. A shiver of excitement laced up Ana's back, as she read the evidence in black and white. Batty Barb's transformation was real. This plasma thing worked.

"Where do your donations come from?" Mum barely looked up from the booklet, flicking forward to other stories of success. A man whose symptoms of Parkinson's lessened, a woman with chronic fatigue syndrome completing her bucket list of Munros.

Dr Carmichael smiled tightly. "I'm afraid I'm unable to disclose that piece of information. It's all very top secret, tightly controlled. We're at the edge of some groundbreaking science here. I don't usually disclose this much, not to the general public."

The way he emphasised 'general', made Ana wonder what members of the public he *did* usually talk to. How did his patients sign up for treatment?

As if reading her mind Dr Carmichael slid another small booklet towards Ana's mum, the words 'Treatment Plan' embossed in gold on the cover. Mum took it hesitantly, flicking through the pages, stopping at one headed 'Cost.' Ana craned to see, a part of her deflating when she read the figure; £8,000 per transfusion. There was no way her parents would be able to afford this. Ana instantly felt sick, realising she'd just given her mum a massive beacon of hope that she would never be able to take advantage of.

Mum pursed her lips and shut the booklets, sliding them back across the table towards Dr Carmichael. "This is all very interesting, Dr Carmichael. You're doing excellent work here, and I hope one day it will be recognised by the NHS."

Dr Carmichael sat observing them, twirling the end of his moustache between his fingers. "Plasma is of course already being used in medicine. It's often used to help those with autoimmune conditions. But my trials are different. We're trailblazing, looking at cures for a wider range of disorders. It has a hefty price tag, I know, but it's the only way to ensure a truly controlled environment with specialist equipment and premium plasma."

"I understand." Ana's mum smiled tightly, rising from her seat.

"If you ever want to sign up, Mrs Gilbert, you know where I am. It was a pleasure to meet you both." Dr Carmichael rose from his seat, stretching across to shake their hands again. Ana flinched at his touch. He held on to her hand a little too long. "Such an inquisitive child, Ana. Be sure to take these booklets for your project."

Ana nodded a thanks, gathering them up, shoving them in her bag. Mum strode out the room and Ana could tell she couldn't get out fast enough, as she walked ahead, not speaking, not even saying goodbye when Faye called out on their way past reception. Guilt gnawed inside Ana as she climbed back into the car. Mum had the engine started and the car in gear before she'd even put her seatbelt on.

"I'm sorry," Ana whispered.

Mum shook her head and Ana felt a stab in her gut when she noticed her eyes were brimming with tears.

"It's okay," Mum whispered back. "It's going to be okay."

Chapter Twenty-Two
Hope

Ryan laid the steaming plate of food down in front of me. "An extra big portion of steak and sausage pie for you, Hope. Dr Carmichael asked me to report back that plates are cleared so be sure to enjoy every last bite."

I glared at him, the smell of meat turning my stomach.

He hovered at my shoulder, bending to whisper in my ear, "You look very sexy tonight by the way."

The seat beside me jolted backwards, nearly knocking Ryan over. Seb forced him to step back as he sat down.

"Alright, Sebastian. Don't get your knickers in a twist." Ryan slammed Seb's plate on the table, gravy slopping over the edge.

The door flew open and Stacey swaggered in, walking to the top of the table, taking a seat by herself. Phoenix watched her, turning to whisper to Aidan.

Stacey's face contorted in disgust as Ryan unloaded her plate from his trolley.

"I don't want that shite. I want a burger. And where's the ginger?"

Ryan returned her look of disgust. "Ginger?"

Stacey gestured to the jugs of water and orange juice on the table. "The fizzy stuff, posh boy. Where's the Irn Bru?"

Ryan's face was in hers, tone threatening. "Don't talk to me like that."

"I can talk to you how I want, pizza face."

We all paused, watching as Ryan flamed beetroot. He grabbed her plate, placing it back on the trolley.

"Hey, you can't take my food."

"I can do whatever I want." The trolley squeaked as he wheeled it away, door slamming shut behind him.

Stacey muttered to herself, swearing under her breath. I cut the crust off my pie and slopped the sausage and steak on to my side plate.

Seb watched me, curious. "What are you doing?"

"I can't eat meat," I whispered. I carried the plate over to Stacey. "Here."

She viewed me with suspicion, then grabbed the plate, stabbing at the steak with her fork. It was easy if I was able to offload my meat to the others.

When I returned to my seat my plate was piled with extra veg and mash. Seb winked and I tucked in hungrily.

Phoenix shook her head at us and I wondered what her problem was. The boys were all talking loudly with their mouths full but she sat quietly, by Aidan's side. Every once in a while, he moved his hand to touch hers, her fingers curling underneath.

"Phoenix doesn't look happy this evening," I whispered to Seb.

Seb looked up briefly, his gaze flicking towards Aidan. "It's Aidan's birthday soon."

I frowned. "So? Isn't that cause for celebration?"

"He turns eighteen."

"Oh." She would be losing him. I glanced at Seb. How long until his escape? The thought of being in here without him made me uneasy.

Dessert was rice pudding with raspberries. I was so hungry I wolfed mine down. Stacey slopped hers around with a spoon, spilling half of it on the table as she spat it out in disgust. I thought back to the argument she'd had with Viv, her protest at being 'locked up.' I shivered, the memory of the windowless 'Bothy' like a flashback to a scene in a vivid nightmare.

Seb leaned in towards me, lips brushing against my hair. "Let's get out of here. We can get a good seat in the cinema." His scent, fresh soap with a musky undertone, wrapped around me, pulling me in. When I stood, my head spun, from standing too fast, or his close proximity, I couldn't be sure.

As we walked along the hallways, we passed the door with the red 'No Entry' sign. I slowed, running my hand over the wooden panel.

"What do you think is behind here?"

"It's the annexe, where the Carmichaels live."

My curiosity spiked, remembering Dr Carmichael telling me on the 'tour' that they lived in a separate part of the house we were forbidden to enter. I pressed my ear against the door, straining to hear sounds. My heart jumped as Seb grabbed my arm.

"Come on, I need some popcorn to take away the taste of that foul pudding."

I relented, then froze when I heard shuffling and a cry. I pressed my cheek against the door.

"What are you doing?" Seb looked at me like I'd gone mad.

I shushed him, holding my breath as a wailing started. "I want out, I want out, let me out."

I jumped back in horror as the handle rattled from the other side.

"Who's in there?" I hissed.

Seb shook his head, bemused. We stood waiting, watching the door. A part of me wanted it to swing open to reveal the woman. A bigger part was terrified at the prospect.

The rattling of the handle stopped. A lower, gruffer voice muttered in soothing, repetitive tones, "It's alright, darling. It's okay."

"Children."

I jumped as a hand clamped down on my shoulder, nail digging in. I turned to see Mrs Carmichael, mouth puckered as if she'd sucked a sour lemon.

"I presume you're on your way to film night? The cinema is *that* way." She pointed down the hall, manoeuvring us away from the door. "If I find you hanging about this area again it will be straight to the Bothy."

The dungeon, I shivered at the thought. I hurried after Seb, wondering who and what we had just heard. As I glanced back, Mrs Carmichael's eyes blazed a warning.

The popcorn cart outside the cinema spun sweet flavours in the air, yellow and pink fairy lights strung along the top shelf.

Billy stepped forward, transformed from his navy security uniform into a white suit, red candy-striped apron and hat matching the pattern on the cart.

"Hello, Sebastan. Hello, Hope. You look pretty tonight."

"Why thank you, Billy," Seb cracked a smile and I nudged him.

Billy shook his head. "Not you. Hope." I laughed at his bluntness and Seb pretended to be offended.

"Popcorn?" Billy shovelled a scoop into the machine, the golden nuggets tumbling inside the glass, the sweet scent making my mouth water. "Just caramel tonight. No butter."

Containers full, we entered the cinema. We followed blinking cat eye lights down to the middle row, behind Phoenix and Aidan.

"This had better be a good one, Phoenix," Seb said, stretching his feet up against the seat in front.

Phoenix turned to him. "It's an old Kaufman. Probably too complex for you."

Seb rolled his eyes at me. "That's code for pretentious bull. Why do you always choose crappy ancient films, Phoenix?"

The screen fizzed with static and I dug into the popcorn, wondering what the others were doing. Probably in the games room, too hyper to sit through a film. I snuck a side long glance at Seb, wondering if he usually came along to film night, or if he was making a special effort for me. I sank lower in my chair, enjoying the close proximity of his arm beside mine.

Billy hurried down the aisle, throwing his hat on a chair. "It's time for the film to start," he announced, disappearing behind the screen. The lights in the aisle dimmed further and the room fell into darkness, the hum of the screen pronounced as we waited for something to happen. The screen blinked black then blurry circular lights and the words 'Focus Features' filled the screen. As the opening scene played, I relaxed back in my chair, remembering rainy Sunday afternoon cinema trips with Mum to a small art house cinema she loved. My favourite films were the French productions, mesmerised by the lilt of passionate foreign words, convincing myself I was fluent in their language by the closing credits, forgetting I'd been reading subtitles. Mum promised she would take me to Paris when I was older, when I could truly appreciate its complex beauty. Waiting was a word that no longer held anticipation. I wished we'd talked less about the future and just lived it instead.

Phoenix's choice of film was weird and surreal, but the concept, that partners could erase each other from their memories fascinated and depressed me in equal measure.

Sometimes I wanted to forget the life I had before, to turn off the pain. Then I could never miss it, or Mum; the hollow ache like I had lost a part of me could be sealed up and I could be stitched back together again. Other times I panicked when I couldn't picture her face, or remember her voice. It was a juxtaposition of wanting to forget, but needing to remember. And so many parts of her were intertwined within me, it was important not to forget.

As the film progressed, I realised the procedure could never actually erase the fact the characters once had a connection. It extracted memories, but I liked the suggestion that even if memories of your experiences with a loved one were taken away, they would always be familiar to you, known to you. The procedure erased memories but not feelings. At the core of their memories was love, and love was a feeling that permeated so many parts of us it was hard to destroy.

At the closing scene I turned to speak to Seb. He was fast asleep, mouth wide open, eyes shut. I had a sudden desire to curl up beside him and rest my head on his shoulder. A longing throbbed through my body for love, for comfort, to fill the hollow ache of loneliness.

Phoenix and Aidan watched the end credits roll, their heads tilted together, his hand on her knee. I looked back at Seb. My heart couldn't cope with another loss, another goodbye. I slipped away while he slept, realising I was trying to erase our memories before they had even formed.

I hesitated at the bottom of the main staircase, feeling a sadness tug, knowing if I went to bed unwelcome thoughts would intrude in the darkness. I headed for the library, craving the solace of escaping into another world. A lamp had been left on in the corner by the windows and I headed over to the bookcase nearest, choosing a fantasy book and settling into one of the large armchairs. When the door opened a few minutes later I startled, snapping the book shut.

"Hope," Aidan hesitated, looking surprised to see me. "Enjoy the film?"

I shrugged. "It was okay." I eyed him curiously as he approached the shelves. He was the last person I expected to see in the library.

"This is one of my favourite rooms in the house," he said, as if reading my thoughts. He pulled out a thick book, dragons and fire adorning the cover. "It reminds me of the one decent part of my childhood where I'd go to the local library, hiding out every Saturday. We never had any books in my house. Did you?"

"Yes. My mum loved reading."

"Was she good to you?"

"Very," I nodded, feeling the sadness grip tighter.

"My mum tried her best, but she had bad taste in men." Aidan touched the scar running down his face. "I tried to protect her from them, but they didn't like that much. You might have noticed my brother, Scott, doesn't talk much. He carried the emotional scars, I carried the physical."

I inhaled sharply, not knowing what to say.

He settled into the chair across from me. "This is

also a good place to hang out when the sleep demons haunt you." He gave me a knowing look and I felt a sense of comfort, knowing I wasn't alone with my troubled thoughts. "You settling in okay, Hope?"

The genuine concern in his voice took me by surprise and tears prickled behind my eyes. I frantically blinked them away, not wanting to cry in front of him. "I guess so." I hesitated, trying to find the right words to express how I really felt. "But I don't know if I can ever feel settled in a place like this."

Aidan shrugged, "It's best not to overthink things. That's my motto in life. Go with the flow." He sat back, like he was relaxing on a beach lounger. "And when it all goes to shit, get lost in a book."

"Seb said it's your eighteenth birthday coming up soon. Are you looking forward to leaving?" *Escaping* was what I really wanted to say.

Aidan pondered the question. I saw a flicker of fear in his eyes which his smile only partly masked. "As I said. Best not to overthink things. Hopefully I can build a decent life for myself. And for Phoenix and Scott, when they get out. I don't like leaving them behind. So watch out for them, would you?"

"Of course."

He opened his book, and we settled into a companiable silence. The sadness in my gut dulled to a hum, and for tonight at least, I was grateful to be in the house.

Chapter Twenty-Three
Ana

The atmosphere in English was flat, an undercurrent of tension rippling through the classroom. Even although they were free to move desks back to their original places Ana stayed at the front beside Elliot, Hope's absence hanging in the air. Gordon and Jenna sat at opposite ends of the classroom, Jenna keeping her head bowed as her friends whispered and texted on their phones. Usually, Mr Darwin would have confiscated the phones by now but he seemed preoccupied. He told them to quietly read through their work, remaining at his desk, hunched over papers.

Ana stared out the window, watching orange and red leaves tumbling in the wind, wondering what Hope was doing right now. She and Elliot had dropped in on Martha on the way home yesterday, updating her on their meeting with Ruth. Martha seemed satisfied that Ruth was going to try her best to find more information. Ana didn't mention any time she'd tried to call Hope's phone it now sounded disconnected. Maybe Hope really did want to just move on, forget and start over. Then an image of the fiery manes on Hope's tarot card flashed into Ana's mind and she could hear her voice clear and urgent, FIND ME.

The shrill beep of the bell jolted Ana from her thoughts. Elliot grabbed his bag, saying he'd see her at lunch. Ana took her time, stopping at her locker, dreading Maths without Hope beside her to help. It took her a few minutes to register someone hovering behind. She startled when she realised it was Jenna.

"Hi, Ana."

"Hi." Ana slammed the door shut, hoping Jenna sensed her hostility.

"Have you heard from Hope?" Jenna asked.

Ana frowned. "Why do you care?"

Jenna shrugged, attempting to look nonchalant. "I just wondered where she'd gone. If she, got into, you know, lots of trouble?" Ana saw a flash of guilt in her eyes.

"Did you plant those drugs in her locker?" Ana hissed, surprising herself with her directness.

Jenna stepped back. "No." She shook her head vehemently, looking over her shoulder as if worried someone was listening. "Did the police get involved?"

Ana shook her head. "All I know is she's gone somewhere new and we can't get in touch."

"I'm sorry I was such a cow to her. I didn't know that she'd lost her mum. I didn't realise she was in care, what it meant." Jenna's cheeks flamed and Ana stared at her, baffled. Jenna hesitated, as if she wanted to say more.

"Do you know something?" Ana moved closer. Jenna opened her mouth and Ana waited, knowing she wanted to say something. Then Jenna smiled tightly.

"I was just curious, that's all. I'd better get to class." Ana watched as Jenna disappeared round a corner, a feeling of unease weighing down on her.

The corridors were emptying fast and the thought of Maths did nothing to calm Ana. She decided to go the long way, forming an excuse in her head for her lateness. As she turned a corner she saw a petite dark-haired woman walking in the direction of Ms Turnberry's office. The woman turned her head to smile at a teacher and a jolt of recognition shot through Ana. The woman from the car on the country road. Her head spun, remembering the woman's strange expression when she clocked Ana's school tie. Was she a teacher here?

Heart thumping, Ana waited until the woman had gone through the swing doors and then followed, careful to pull them shut so they didn't slam. Ana pressed up against the wall beside Ms Turnberry's door, praying no teachers would walk past. The woman had left the door ajar and Ana strained to hear them talking.

"Slight teething problems but she's settling in. We always knew she'd rebel against some rules, but as you know we have ways of making them co-operate. It's always worth a bit of extra effort for the universal donors."

What on earth was a universal donor? Ana held her breath when she heard Ms Turnberry's commanding tone.

"You mentioned you had some other concerns. Connected to a pupil here?"

"Yes," the woman paused. "Ana Gilbert."

Ana's heart leapt. She edged away from the door, scared the woman had somehow sensed her outside.

"Ah, yes, Ms Gilbert. She was quite friendly with Hope."

"I take it no one else is aware of this connection?"

"Why do you ask?" Ms Turnberry sounded wary.

"Apparently Ana and her mother visited the clinic to discuss the groundbreaking plasma trials."

A pause. "They what?"

The woman continued, "And they got lost on the

way. I discovered them far too close to the house. I'm sure they got as far as the initial gates."

"I presume you mentioned this to Finlay?"

"Yes. He found it amusing. You know how arrogant he can be. And he never listens to me."

Ms Turnberry cleared her throat. "I'll have a word with him. That girl has too many questions as it is, not helped by the fact she socialises with that Elliot boy."

"The one who pins up the missing posters?"

"Hmm."

"You don't think they've figured it out?" The woman sounded nervous.

A pulse throbbed in Ana's throat, her mind spinning, desperately trying to make connections. What house? She thought back to the iron gates, the sign: Private Grounds No Entry.

Ms Turnberry tutted. "Don't be ridiculous. Finlay must have his reasons for talking to them about the trials. He won't have disclosed anything about the house. You know he would never do that."

Why were they so concerned about keeping the house secret? Ana thought back to the conversation Ian Hobbs had with Martha, talking about how Hope was happy in her new place. Excitement tingled up Ana's spine. Maybe she was there, beyond those gates. Not so far away after all.

"We need to start broadening our area. When we take them from such a small radius, people start to notice."

"You know it was because we found out she's a universal donor. It's rare and can't be ignored, not with the higher demands now from the members." Ms Turnberry's voice had a familiar condescending tone.

"The higher the demands, the darker this all gets.

It's not something I'm on board with. And what happens when Ruth McDonald returns to work? I doubt she's going to drop this now."

Ana's excitement dissolved, a feeling of dread washing over her. So it hadn't been a coincidence. It was all connected, they were all connected. She thought back to Ruth's diagram, the lines all joining. And what did universal donor mean?

"Don't you worry your pretty little head, Clara. You know the benefits and Finlay has it all under control. Ruth won't be returning to work anytime soon. An important senior figure in the social work department just signed up to the gold membership."

Panic washed over Ana. She pushed the doors, legs shaking as she hurried along the corridor, scrambling for her phone. She tried to steady her hands as she typed Elliot a frantic message. *Ms Turnberry is in on it. I think I might know where Hope is.* She was just about to hit send when she slammed into someone, her phone falling and sliding along the ground.

"Ana." Mr Darwin grabbed her arm. "What are you doing?"

Ana shook her head, glancing at the phone, wanting to snatch it. She saw the concern in Mr Darwin's eyes and for a second considered telling him, asking for his help. Then she heard a clip of heels behind. She broke free from his grasp, diving for her phone.

"Are you okay, Ana?" He called after her and Ana waved a hand, trying to reassure him, hoping the woman didn't see her.

She ran round the corner, up the stairwell, taking the stairs two at a time, only stopping to catch her breath once at the top.

She closed her eyes, trying to calm her breathing, trying to process what she'd just heard. She hit 'send' on the message, anxious to speak to Elliot.

Chapter Twenty-Four
Hope

The heat soothed my bones as I lowered my body into the bubbles, a knot of tension unfurling all the way to my toes. I lay back, inhaling the sweet lavender scent, wishing I'd thought of this before bed last night. Even with the relaxing hour in the library reading, nightmares had invaded my fractured sleep and when another jolted me awake at six the appeal of a couple of hours silence before breakfast tempted me out of bed.

My mind wandered, nerves shaking my calm at the thought of the day ahead. After breakfast we would be expected on our morning run round the garden, then it would be my first visit to the plasma donation centre. A shiver convulsed through my body at the thought of seeing the machines, having a needle stuck inside me.

The door handle rattled, making me bolt upright. I watched as it turned, straining against the pressure of the lock.

"I'm in here," I shouted as a fist pounded the door.

"I need to pee, let me in."

I rolled my eyes at the sound of Stacey's gruff voice. I was tempted to tell her to use another toilet on the floor below, but knew what her response would be. Hoisting myself out of the bath I pulled the plug and grabbed the fluffy towel from the rail, wrapping it round me.

The door swung open as soon as I undid the bolt,

Stacey pushing forward. She scowled when she saw me in my towel.

"Might have known," she grumbled, shoving past me. I barely had time to step into the hall before she slammed the door in my face.

"You're up early."

I jumped at the voice. I turned to see Phoenix dressed in leggings and over-sized hoodie which I guessed belonged to Aidan, her curls piled on her head in a messy bun.

"So is everyone else," I said dryly.

Phoenix shot me a half smile, and I knew she'd heard Stacey's shouts. She gestured to a blue doorway at the end of our hall.

"I'm heading up to the roof. There's a staircase that leads you there through the door. You should come and join me once you're ready."

"Okay." I realised I hadn't properly explored the house yet. I hurried to my room, burrowing through the collection of clothes I'd stuffed in drawers, deciding on casual wear, like Phoenix, realising it was standard during the day here and comfortable for a morning run. I opened the wardrobe, pushing aside my collection of near identical black boots to find the one and only pair of trainers I owned. They were faded and scruffy but at least they still fit and had comfortable soles.

As I pulled them out, the lace caught on the zip of my school bag. As I untangled the trainer the bag opened and my eyes were drawn to a white envelope. Lucy's letter. Since coming here, the life I'd had with her and Andy seemed even more like a dream, like it had happened to a girl I used to know, who no longer existed. I zipped the bag shut, closing out thoughts of the lives I had wanted which were taken from me, one by one.

The hallway was eerily quiet as I exited my room. I was relieved to see the bathroom door was still shut, meaning Stacey wouldn't try to follow me. I broke into a run, just in case. Cold air blasted as I opened the blue door. The steps narrowed nearer the top and I gingerly felt my way out onto the opening. The sky was a dull blue grey, not quite dark, not quite light. The moon was a faded white haze in the cloudless sky. I looked to the left, where Phoenix sat on flat concrete, a rail running around the parameter. I hoisted myself up, scooting along beside her, bunching my knees up to my chin.

Phoenix sat cross legged, hands resting on her thighs. She had her eyes shut and for a moment I wondered if she was meditating. I studied her face, the sprinkle of dark freckles dotted down her nose and across her cheeks, stark against her light brown skin. Her eyelashes were long and lush, cheekbones cut like razors, full lips set in a scowl. A fascinating mix of toughness and vulnerability. She opened one eye, as if conscious of my scrutiny. I quickly looked away, turning my attention to the view.

The gardens stretched for acres, the concrete paths winding in circular patterns, at parts twisting like knots on a Celtic cross. My eyes were drawn to the row of thin electric wires strung above the perimeter of the walls, black discs secured on a pole, each disc adjacent to a wire. It reminded me of guitar strings. But then I remembered Seb's warning about them being electrified; the current they emitted was a song of death.

Beyond the main black gates a tree-lined drive extended for miles, surrounded by countryside, acres of green, dense fields, leading to nowhere. The remoteness filled me with a sense of dread. The further away we were from civilisation, the less likely we would be found.

"You can see a bit further in summertime, or on a clear day, but there's nothing revealing," Phoenix followed my gaze. "I've stopped wondering where we are and if I can escape. I don't want to escape anymore. This place is like a sanctuary."

"Is it?" I wanted her to persuade me.

Phoenix turned to face me. "It is if you learn to follow the rules." She shot me a look which made me feel uncomfortable, and I thought back to the way she shook her head in disapproval when I passed my meat to Stacey and Seb. "You don't have to like it. But if you play along you can make it a much more comfortable experience."

I thought back to when I saw her walking with Dr Carmichael in the gardens. Was that what she was doing? Playing along so that he treated her well?

She tilted her head as if trying to figure me out. "You don't look convinced. All I know is it was a relief to say goodbye to that stupid angry girl with no friends whose clothes smelled."

I studied her face, confused, taking a few minutes to realise she meant herself.

Phoenix continued, pulling her knees up to her chin. "She was too thick to read or write. In here, the words make sense. Mr Darwin taught me to rearrange the jumble in my head. You think this place is bad? School for me was like a jungle. Humiliation in class when I didn't understand the questions, never mind know the answers."

I didn't know how to respond. That might have been her life, but it wasn't mine.

"So what's your damage, then? On a scale of one

to ten how fucked up were your parents?"

Before I had a chance to answer, she pulled down the neck of her hoodie, revealing a faded silvery curve along her throat. "I'll go first. My mum tried to kill me. More than once but this one was too difficult to explain away. I was ten."

I swallowed, feeling sick at the thought. The horror of her mum only reminded me of the warmth and kindness of mine. A sadness swept over me, for the love she never got, and the love I lost.

"I got moved around foster carers a bit. Most of them didn't know how to deal with my temper. One sleaze got a bit handsy and I hit him over the head with a vase. I'd just turned thirteen and never got placed again because it was me who was trouble of course, not him. I stayed in units, in a house. There were different versions of Stacey in those houses. There was too much noise, fights and anxiety. No sense of order, even although the staff in the house tried to give us a routine."

Phoenix stretched her arms out, turning her face up to the sky. "This space, this silence, you don't need to worry about anything in the outside world, like school. You can just live and forget yourself. It's bliss. I've been here a year now and I don't miss my old life. Not one bit."

I shivered, pulling my hoodie sleeves over my hands. *But what about our freedom?* I wanted to ask, thinking of the electrified fences keeping us trapped. *And our rights.* I thought back to the revelation that we wouldn't get any qualifications. Maybe Phoenix hadn't figured that one out, or like Seb, she didn't care.

Phoenix folded her arms, her eyes questioning. "So, tell me your story."

I hesitated, considering lying, wondering if I should make myself appear tougher than I was. Match her horrors to establish some common ground and quicken a friendship. Something about her manner told me she wouldn't appreciate bull and would probably detect it a mile off.

"My mum died when I was twelve. I don't have any other family, so," I shrugged, mortified when a surge of grief swept away the rest of my words.

Phoenix didn't say anything. We sat in silence and I was grateful she allowed me time to compose myself, without making a big deal about it.

"I'm guessing your mum was pretty decent?" She didn't look at me.

"The best."

"That sucks. At least I have no one to miss." She made a face, tugging absentmindedly on the frayed edges of the hoodie. "Not yet anyway."

Aidan. He was written all over her face.

"How old are you?" I asked.

"Sixteen."

I blinked in surprise. She smiled wryly, "I know, everyone always thinks I'm older. Aidan says I'm an old soul."

The unspoken thought hung in the air. It would be two more years before she was allowed to leave.

"He'll wait for you," I said.

Phoenix snorted. "This isn't a feckin Hollywood romance. I'm not stupid. He's turning eighteen and is horny as hell." She giggled and it was contagious. We laughed, our breath smoking the air. Phoenix shook out her curls and glanced at her watch. "Come on, let's go down for breakfast. It's donation day which means porridge. Yummy."

As I followed her down the staircase, I thought

back to her comment about the house being a sanctuary. Maybe she was right. Listening to her alternative life this was like paradise in comparison. But what about the others? Elliot said Seb was happy with his family. I'd been happy with the Browns and settled in school, with friends and a potential future.

We shut the door behind us, walking along the hall.

"Mandy, Hope. There you are." Clara intercepted us in the hallway. I frowned in confusion, looking to Phoenix.

Phoenix sighed in irritation. "That's not my name, Clara."

Clara smiled dismissively. "We need you down on the staff floor. A clothes delivery has arrived and Viv wants to check your outfits fit."

I shot Phoenix a questioning glance. "Outfits?" I whispered.

She shook her head, as if indicating she'd tell me later. We followed Clara to the first floor, an identical row of doors lining the hallway, but with subtle differences in decoration. The ornate paintings hanging on the walls and tables lined with exotic flowers branding this corridor as having more importance than ours. Clara stopped at a half-open door, knocking.

"Come in," Viv's crackly voice called out.

I startled when Clara pushed the door open to reveal Seb standing in the middle of the plush bedroom, dressed in a tux, black hair slicked back. His eyes met mine, a mischievous glint in his eye, and a surge of heat scorched my cheeks. I looked away, painfully conscious that he didn't.

"Doesn't he look handsome?" Viv smiled approvingly, pushing him forward like he was a dog on show.

"Wonderful. I think we made a good decision ditching the kilts." Clara squeezed her hands together and I wondered what they were talking about.

I glanced over at the four-poster bed, eyes drawn to beaded dresses laid out across the silk duvet, deep hues of jade and purple sparkling under the light. Matching sandals sat on the carpet underneath, diamante studs sprinkled across the toe straps.

"Take your mask, Seb, and go and hang your tux up in your wardrobe to keep it good. No flinging it on the floor, like you do with your other clothes." Viv handed Seb a black jewelled masquerade mask and he pressed it against his eyes, walking close to me on his way past.

"Where did you disappear to last night?" he asked, sounding wounded.

My heart jumped, the mask giving him a darker edge. "I was tired," I mumbled, the excuse sounding lame even to me.

"Hope, come here and try on your dress." Clara grabbed my arm, pulling me away from Seb. She turned to him, smiling wryly as he lowered his mask, eyebrows raised. "That's your cue to leave, Seb."

He grinned cheekily and mouthed, "Catch you later."

Clara lifted the emerald dress and held it against my body. "We weren't sure of your exact measurements but Viv took a note of your clothes size when your case arrived." She gestured for me to remove my clothes and I blushed, realising Phoenix already stood in her underwear. I averted my eyes from the pink raised scar across her midriff which glowed against her skin. It looked like a horse-shoe shaped burn. I shivered at the realisation these were probably more wounds from her past.

I turned my back on them all, sliding out of my trainers and stripping off my clothes, cringing at the thought of exposing my pale mismatched underwear. Clara handed me the dress, which was surprisingly heavy. The beads scratched my legs as I slid it up over my hips, the lining tightening against my bust as I pulled my arms through the short-capped sleeves. Clara pulled up the zip at the back, the fabric moulding against my waist and bum, the hem sitting high. Turning to the full-length mirror I did a double take, unused to seeing my body exposed in such a tight-fitting outfit. I tugged at the sweetheart neckline, not sure I liked the way it exposed my cleavage.

Clara pulled the band from my hair, my auburn waves tumbling loose over my shoulders.

"Beautiful." She smiled at my reflection in approval.

I glanced beyond my reflection at Phoenix, her lean legs seeming to extend for miles, the purple of the dress adding a regal air. She could easily be a model, I thought, watching as she stepped into her strappy shoes, adding unnecessary inches to her height. As she turned away from the mirror my eyes were drawn to the tattoo peeking out of her backless dress, flames fanning across her shoulder blade from the wings of an orange and gold bird. A Phoenix I realised, smiling.

Viv appeared at my side, handing me a black mask, the green encrusted jewels sparkling under the light. She followed my gaze. "I can do one for you too if you want. Quite a talented artist, so I am, and good with that kind of needle."

Her gruff laugh made me nervous. I held up the mask. "Are we having some sort of ball?"

"The Carmichaels are hosting the gold members at the weekend and they want you to waitress."

I glanced at Phoenix. "I don't understand. What's a gold member?" It sounded almost comical.

Viv and Clara exchanged looks, and I realised they presumed I'd already been briefed.

Phoenix stepped forward to explain. "The gold members pay premium prices for more regular transfusions and they have access to the Gold Bar which is a party room adjacent to the Club House. The Carmichaels host events when new members sign up."

I shivered at the thought of coming in to contact with the people paying for our plasma, turning the mask over in my hand. Would they realise our real purpose in the house?

Phoenix touched my hand, lowering her voice. "It will be good to have you there this time. We can stick together."

Her words had the opposite effect of reassuring me. The dress felt too tight, constricting my breathing. A snake of sweat curled down my back at the thought of having to parade in front of a group of rich people, serving them, tantalising them? I swallowed, realising I'd never considered the possibility that our payment didn't stop at plasma.

Chapter Twenty-Five
Hope

Seb fell into step beside me on our group walk through the gardens to the 'blood house', the nickname they all used for the donation clinic. He'd kept his hair slicked back and it made him look older and more serious. *And good looking*, that annoying little voice taunted in my head.

"How did your dress fit?" he asked casually, a hint of a smile playing on his lips.

"Fine," I answered, trying to ignore the tingling feeling as his arm brushed against mine.

Two figures walking across the grassy verge in the distance caught my eye. I knew immediately from the gait of the taller figure that it was Billy. The smaller figure, with her careful steps and frail frame had to be Barbara. I slowed my steps, watching as they headed down to what looked like a car park, Barbara leading the way to a grey car.

"What's the deal with Billy? How come he's allowed to leave the house?" I turned to Seb and he shrugged.

"I guess they know there's no threat of exposure."

"What do you mean?"

"He won't spill their secrets. He's obedient and submissive. Plus he likes it here so wouldn't try to do a runner."

"Barbara seems quite protective of him." I thought back to the bruises on his arm. "He said he still donates?"

Seb nodded. "He's a universal donor. His plasma

is in demand." He smiled wryly.

I hesitated, thinking about telling him I was also a universal donor but my attention was drawn to the Blood House, a small grey brick building with sloping red tiled roof. Clara stopped at the grey metal doorway, punching in a code. I tried to pay attention to the keypad but her movement was too swift to register any numbers.

I watched as Scott and Dylan walked on ahead, talking to each other about some new Xbox game they'd played last night. Phoenix and Aidan walked hand in hand laughing together. No one seemed nervous or bothered. I guessed it had become such a regular occurrence it was no big deal to them.

As Seb explained that the plasmapheresis machines were set up beside beds, meaning we were able to lie side by side and talk throughout the procedure, I vaguely wondered where Stacey was. She had been missing from breakfast which was a relief. Her behaviour was so unpredictable I always felt on edge in her company.

Clara led us along a corridor smelling of disinfectant, harsh fluorescent lights and white walls assaulting my senses. Our trainers squeaked against the polished vinyl flooring, conversation ceasing as Clara stopped at another grey door, swiping a card against a black pad, a red light flashing green. The door buzzed as she pushed it open, revealing a large room, as stark and white as the corridor, the hum of machines doing little to ease my nerves. My eyes were drawn to the reclining beds, burnt orange leather padding projecting an attempt at comfort. A white machine like a photocopier sat between beds, with circular discs down the front, which from where I stood reminded me of mini smoke alarms. Clear plastic bags were attached to the front, one at the top, the other lower down. A blonde woman in a white coat walked between the machines, pushing buttons, checking their electronic screens.

A wave of panic washed over me at the sight of the machines, the mechanical sounds, the hospital smell. It was a danger signal imprinted on my brain, my only memory of a hospital synonymous with death and devastation. I watched as everyone hoisted themselves up on the beds and laid their bare arms out to the side, the blonde nurse walking between them, cuffing the top of their arm then inserting a needle carefully into a vein. Seb gestured to the bed beside him. The nurse had already hooked him up and images of Mum lying in the ambulance, wires around her body, flashed in my head.

"I reserved this one for you," he joked.

As I hoisted myself up onto the bed I watched as Seb picked up a red ball from the table beside him, squeezing it in his hand.

"Is that a stress ball?" I asked curiously, trying to get comfortable on the bed, the leather feeling too cold beneath me.

"We need to squeeze every few seconds to help keep the flow of blood going."

Clara arrived by my side, telling the nurse she would help me get started. "How are you feeling?" she asked.

I shrugged, trying to hide my nerves. The cuff felt tight around my arm, like my muscles were inflating. I tried not to flinch as Clara slid the needle in. She handed me a cup of water. "It's important to keep hydrated. You might feel a little dizzy and sick, just call me if you do."

Oh goody, I wanted to say.

"What do you think of the centre?" She asked with a swoop of her arm, like she was showing off a fancy spa.

I gulped the water down. "It all looks quite hi-tech."

"It's all very controlled and efficient. You're in good hands here." She took the empty cup from me. "How is your eating plan going?"

I hesitated, thinking of the extra food I'd given to Seb and Stacey. I smiled tightly. "Fine."

Clara raised an eyebrow. "The meat isn't bothering you?"

I was aware Seb was staring, waiting to see how I would respond. "It does bother me," I said, deciding I didn't have to tell an outright lie.

"Keep taking your iron tablets too. Your last results showed your levels are still quite low."

I nodded, trying not to laugh as Seb wagged his finger at me behind Clara's back.

Clara handed me my own red squishy ball. I took it gratefully, happy to have something to distract me. Clara glanced at her watch, announcing she'd return in an hour and a half.

I started to squeeze the ball hard, conscious Seb was lying back like he didn't have a care in the world.

I watched as one of the black discs on the machine spun, red lights flashing. Yellow liquid trickled into the clear bag at the bottom of Seb's machine and my tummy churned.

Seb glanced at the bag, then at my face and grinned. "It's pretty gross, like pee."

"Is that the plasma?"

He nodded, pointing to another bag at the top, filling with red liquid. "That's the blood components coming out there. The black spinning disc is basically signalling the separation of the plasma from the blood. Halfway through, the blood will start to come back into the body. Pretty cool, huh?"

I tried to smile, thinking it was yucky. Maybe by the hundredth time I'd done it I would be as relaxed as Seb.

Across the room Phoenix and Aidan lay on beds side by side, ear buds stretching from a shared iPod, one in each of their ears. They had their eyes closed, Phoenix's feet twitching to the music and I pictured them dancing in a dream together.

"I can't decide if that's cute or sickening." Seb interrupted my thoughts.

"It's cute. Phoenix is going to miss him."

Seb nodded. He shot me a curious look, "Who do you miss from outside?"

I thought about my brief time at Oakridge. I told him about the Browns and Ana and Elliot, and how it had started to feel like a place I could call home. "But…" I started, and Seb finished my sentence for me.

"It could never truly feel like home?" His eyes were searching and I nodded, wanting him to understand. He lay back against his pillow, looking up at the ceiling. I had to strain to hear him above the whirring of the machines.

"My mum killed herself when I was twelve."

I squeezed the ball harder, holding my breath as Seb continued his story.

"I never knew my dad. He left when I was a baby, moved back to Australia or something. My mum always said she didn't blame him for leaving, that her dark moods drove him away. I stayed with my grandparents until I was fourteen, they got ill and couldn't cope." He smiled wryly. "I was a bit of a nightmare, climbing out of windows in the middle of the night and getting brought home from the pub by the police. I got placed with foster carers but hated them all, until I went to live with Elliot and his family. His mum was a bit intense, overprotective, but I kind of liked having someone who cared that much, you know? Elliot mentioned his older brother had a major bust up with his parents before he left for university and didn't talk to them much so I think I filled a gap."

I was grateful for his honesty. I wanted to hug him, to tell him I understood. Instead I told him my story, the life I'd had with Mum 'before'.

"She sounds like an amazing mum." He grinned and I swallowed, wishing she could meet him.

The machine whirred and I closed my eyes, feeling a wave of nausea and dizziness.

"You okay?" Seb's voice sounded far away.

I made an a-ok sign with my fingers, sinking further into the pillow, waiting for the sensation to pass. A dull ache throbbed in my arm and I wondered if the blood was passing back in to me.

Clara appeared by my side. "Everything okay?"

"Fine," I said weakly.

"Not long now," she said, tapping her watch.

The last half an hour felt like an eternity. Seb gave up talking, my one-word answers making it hard to continue the conversation. I felt guilty, hoping he realised it was because I felt sick and not because he was boring me. As soon as Clara unhooked me I relaxed, desperate to escape outside. To my dismay, she asked me to stay behind, to have a chat. Seb smiled and waved, telling me he'd save me a seat at lunch.

Clara took me to the far end of the room and sat

me at a desk. She pulled out a carton of orange juice from a mini fridge beside her desk, along with a chocolate bar. "It'll help get your blood sugar levels up." I munched on the chocolate gratefully, enjoying the sugar hit.

Clara pulled out a clipboard asking me a series of questions about how I was feeling, and medical questions relating to my sleep, periods and moods. There was no genuine concern in her tone and I wondered if she thought of us as anonymous patients, part of an experiment.

"Anything concerning you?" she asked.

I was tempted to answer with a sarcastic, *Where do I start*? But something was bothering me and although Clara wasn't exactly the warm confidante I craved, she understood the rules of the house and I knew she'd be honest with me.

"What exactly is the...expectation...at this gold member night?" I wasn't sure I wanted to hear the answer.

Clara laid down her pen, giving me her full attention. "You waitress, you make the guests feel welcome. Sometimes wealthy males think they're entitled to whatever they want. Pander to them, but be rest assured they only get to look, not touch. We don't run that kind of establishment here." She stood up, indicating the conversation was over. "You can leave through the fire exit there. You should have a rest before lunch."

My body sighed with relief, another layer of anxiety unfurling at the confirmation nothing darker was going on. I watched as Clara walked back towards the machines, wondering what her story was. There was a hint of disdain when she referenced 'wealthy males'. I wondered if she was in a similar situation to Mr Darwin, that there had been a bargaining pull to bring her here, into this world.

I pushed the fire door open, following a path winding round the back of the clinic. As I walked along the paving stones, I noticed a small brick building sitting apart from the clinic, the surrounding garden an explosion of autumn colours; red and gold trees and bushes obscuring my view. Curious, I ventured towards the building, unlit red and white lanterns lining the path towards glass French doors. Bold gold letters spelled out 'Club House' on a sign hanging above the door. Walking up the burnt orange stone steps I stopped at the doorway, straining to see inside, a beam of sunlight reflecting my own face back at me. I blinked at my reflection, feeling an out of body sensation, like I wasn't really here.

A scuff of shoes on gravel made me jump. I turned to see Billy walking clumsily towards me, carrying a large box which obscured his view. I hesitated, waiting to see if he was alone. Satisfied he was, I called out hello so he wouldn't get a fright when he lowered the box.

He stumbled and I rushed forward, helping him steady the box. He laid it down on the step, objects clinking inside. He took off his hat, breathing heavily, trailing a hand across his sweaty forehead.

"Hello, Hope." He smiled, staring at my hair, waving a hand in front of the light, his lips forming an 'O'. "There's gold in your hair."

I smiled, tilting my head more towards the light. "It's nice to see the sun shining isn't it?"

He nodded. He looked down at the box. "I've to put these inside."

"D'you want some help?"

He nodded, pulling out keys and unlocking the

doors. "There's lots of decorations in there. We got them from the fancy shop."

"Where's the shop?" I asked, stretching to help him lift the box.

"In the town. Beside the big clock tower."

"What colour is the tower?" I asked, heart hammering.

"Orange and it's got a big blue face and gold numbers."

"In Glasgow?" I glanced towards the trees, checking no one was coming.

"Not supposed to tell you." Billy shook his head, grabbing the box from me, knocking me off balance.

"Sorry. I didn't mean to be nosy." I stepped back, head whirring. "Do you have time to sit with me in the sunshine, and have a chat? It would be nice to be friends."

Billy looked at the box, then at the Club House, then back at me. I sat down on the steps, smiling up at him. He hesitated, then laid down the box and plonked himself beside me, his legs stretching out in front, feet nearly double the size of mine. He picked at a loose thread on his trousers.

"It's been a while since I've been to Glasgow. You're lucky getting to go trips in the car," I said.

Billy looked at me out the corner of his eye, lips twitching. He nodded his head. "I like going in the car. I wasn't always allowed."

"I used to like going on trips into Glasgow with my mum. She used to take me to art galleries to see paintings. Sometimes she'd take me for ice cream after."

Billy's face brightened. He laughed, as if remembering something good.

"Do you like ice cream?" I asked.

He nodded. "And sweets. If I'm good Mrs Carmichael buys me sweets when we go out."

"Mrs Carmichael is nice to you isn't she?"

Billy's smile widened. "She lets me call her Mum. I never had a mum and she told me she never had a baby. So it's nice we have each other, isn't it? I had an uncle but he was a bad man, used to hurt me and said I was stupid. Mrs Carmichael saved me. I like her, she's my friend."

I thought back to Phoenix's comment about the house being a sanctuary. Maybe the Carmichaels were in their own way doing good here. Billy seemed happy, and Mrs Carmichael was protective of him, even if it was a bit weird that she seemed to treat him like a son.

"What's your favourite sweets?" I asked, trying to tread carefully, silently screaming, *Where do you go? Where does she take you?*

"Lolly pops. Or the green plums from the glass jars."

I thought back to his description of the clock tower, tried to think of old-style sweet shops. My heart lurched. "Glasgow has some of the best sweet shops. My mum used to take me to the one beside the old Panopticon Theatre."

Billy nodded excitedly. "Mrs Mitchells. That's where I get lolly pops." He stared at me in panic, jumping up and grabbing the box, shaking his head.

"It's okay, Billy." I rose to my feet, trying to pat him reassuringly on the arm.

He scrambled inside the Club House, slamming the door behind him. He stood looking at me through the glass, holding a finger against his lips in a 'shh' motion, eyes wide with fear. "Dr Carmichael will be angry. I can't tell. He won't like it. He'll punish me."

"It's okay, Billy," I said again, pressing my hand to the glass. "You didn't do anything wrong."

"Leave me alone," he shouted. "You have to go away now."

I hesitated, keeping my hand pressed against the glass. "I promise I won't tell. I'm your friend, okay?" I waited, smiling at him.

He laid the box down at his feet, keeping his eyes on me. He smiled, pressing his hand against the glass on the other side. "Friends."

My heart soared as I ran back to the house. Glasgow. We were near Glasgow. Which meant we were also near Oakridge. Seb had been right, with Mr Darwin on site half the week, and the other half at school, it wouldn't have been possible to be too far from Oakridge High.

Just hearing it, and knowing Billy was allowed to walk freely around town gave me hope. Maybe if I got him to trust me he could get a message to Ana, post a response to her letter. It would just take patience, and some planning. I had plenty of time for both in here.

Chapter Twenty-Six
Ana

Ana watched as Elliot typed Ruth's names into various social media channels bringing up the wrong results. Her profiles had vanished, meaning they no longer had a way to contact her. Ana couldn't understand why Ruth hadn't messaged Elliot first, to let him know if she had found something. But what if she had uncovered something big, and people weren't happy? Ana shivered at the thought of Ruth needing to go into hiding, or worse, being made to.

Elliot paced up and down the small strip of corridor in the cloakroom, the only quiet place they could find to talk. He didn't seem surprised when Ana had revealed Ms Turnberry's involvement. She told Elliot about seeing Dr Carmichael in the car with Ms Turnberry one night, about Ana's visit to the Dr's clinic, missing out the part about Mum and her true motivations for meeting with him. Elliot was momentarily baffled by Ana's fascination with the science. But he took Physics so had no clue as to what she actually studied in Biology or Chemistry.

They speculated about Ms Turnberry visiting Dr Carmichael's clinic for cosmetic surgery.

"She looks younger, like she's had some serious Botox," Ana said.

Elliot didn't agree or disagree, just voiced that it would cost money, and he muttered about the fact she was driving around in a Porsche.

"She must be getting some kind of pay-off for helping them disappear," he said.

Ana looked at him questioningly. But *why* were they being taken? For what? She tried to silence the dark thoughts circling her head. She remembered Ms Turnberry's mention of universal donors; could it have something to do with the trials? She thought back to the articles she'd read, about billionaires in America paying good money for 'young blood' transfusions. Then recent topics they'd covered in Modern Studies class popped into Ana's head. Trafficking. A wave of dizziness caught her off balance and she sat down, looking at her shoes. That was too awful to comprehend.

"We have to go to the police," Ana said.

Elliot didn't react and at first she thought he hadn't heard. Then he stopped pacing, his voice weary. "And say what? I used to demand answers from them all the time. They weren't interested."

"But we can tell them we think Ruth's gone missing now. I could explain what I heard."

"We need proper evidence." Elliot sat down beside Ana on the bench, unzipping his bag, rummaging before pulling out his notebook and pen. "Call up google maps on your phone and type in the address for that doctor's clinic."

Ana did as he said and he took the phone from her as the clinic flashed up on the screen. He clicked on the photographic Street View image, directing the cursor to 'walk' them along the path back out on to the country road. Ana balanced the phone as he took notes, instructing her to navigate the map in the direction of the gates she and her mum had diverted to by accident. Straining to see the road Ana clicked and clicked but the cursor refused to turn in the direction she wanted.

Elliot sighed in frustration. "It must have gone off

grid for Street View. We could look on the satellite view but we need a bigger screen for that." He glanced at his watch. "We've still got ten minutes before lunch ends. Let's go to the library."

They hurried upstairs and Ana let Elliot take control of the computer, watching as he turned the view into satellite buildings. She scanned the image trying to make out the country road. Elliot pointed to a small building. "I reckon that's the clinic." He traced a finger out onto a road. "Left or right?" The bell rang and the library exploded into noise as a group of seniors packed up their bags and books, laughing together. Ana glanced nervously at the librarian who shot her a look, pointing at the clock.

Ana turned back to the screen. "Left. Along that path." Elliot trailed the cursor along the screen, on and on, until he reached a large building with surrounding grounds. "This must be the house."

Ana sat forward in her seat, trying to make out the surroundings, trying to make sense of the shape.

"That bell ringing signifies the end of lunch."

Elliot and Ana both jumped at the voice. Heart hammering Ana looked into the dead eyes of Ms Turnberry, her mouth pursed into such a tight scowl her lips sank into her face. Ana tilted her body towards Elliot, desperately trying to hide the image on the screen, which only made Ms Turnberry more determined to see.

"The two of you are skating on thin ice." Ms Turnberry lowered her voice, her attention focusing on Ana. "Especially you, Ms Gilbert. Your teachers tell me you've missed a few classes recently."

Ana swallowed, feeling heat shoot up her face. "My mum's not been well," she said meekly.

Ms Turnberry sniffed. "That might be so, but you

can't just come and go as you please. Get off now, both of you." She waved her hand and they grabbed their bags, practically running out the library.

"It's like she's got a radar," Ana hissed in Elliot's ear as they hurried up the corridor.

"Like an insect with a tracker."

Ana shuddered at the image. They agreed to meet at the end of the day, Elliot suggesting they stop by Martha's.

"We need to update her about Ruth," Ana agreed.

"I think we should ask if they would drive us to the house at the weekend. It's the quickest way to find out if Hope's there."

A shiver of excitement mixed with fear shot up Ana's spine at the thought of breaking into the house and finding Hope. Somehow she doubted it would be that easy, just turning up and sneaking in. The gates looked secured.

Ana turned the corner and her stomach dropped as she watched Mr Darwin disappear into his classroom with the mystery brunette, the door shutting behind them. Surely Mr Darwin couldn't be involved too? She had nearly confided in him earlier. How was she supposed to know who to trust?

*

As Ana stood waiting on Elliot at the gates she flicked through her phone, googling Dr Carmichael, trying to find out more information about his blood trials. It led her to more articles about Alzheimer's. She zipped up her coat, shivering against the cold as she scanned the symptoms and the suggestions for support. She clicked on to a carer's story, a son talking about how he had created a 'memory book' for his mum, containing cuttings and photos from her past, as well as people from her daily life to help her remember key family members and significant events.

Goosebumps shot up Ana's arm as she realised this was something she could do right now, with Mum's support; start a story of her life. Maisie and Dad could help. Maisie would enjoy including her own pictures and stories and Dad would have unique memories only he and Mum shared. They'd met young, only nineteen. Ana jumped in fright as Dad's name popped up on her phone, nearly dropping it.

"Hello?" She frowned at the strangeness of Dad calling just as she was thinking about him

"Ana, are you home yet?"

She gripped the phone tighter, hearing the stress in his voice.

"No, why? What's wrong?"

"Everything's okay. Your mum just forgot to pick Maisie up from school. I'm stuck in meetings. Would you be able to do us a favour, love, and go to her school now?"

Ana mumbled an 'okay' at the same time wondering why Mum wouldn't just drive there now. "Is Mum at home?"

A long pause. "No. She's out."

"Where is she?"

Another pause.

"She's on the bus. She'll be home soon."

Ana blinked at the phone, wondering what on earth Mum was doing on a bus. She could sense Dad wasn't able to talk properly. She disconnected the call, promising to fetch Maisie and take her home, distracted by the sight of Elliot walking through the playground towards her. Her heart sank at the thought of having to abandon their plans. A part of her wondered if they could take Maisie to the Browns with them, but she knew Maisie would be a nightmare, asking too many questions, no doubt embarrassing Ana in front of Elliot.

And a bigger part of Ana wanted to rush home, to wait for Mum, wondering why she'd disappeared on a bus when she was supposed to be collecting Maisie.

Chapter Twenty-Seven
Hope

White lanterns flickered in the darkness, the orange glow illuminating the path to the Club House. Fairy lights blinked in the trees, and around the doorway, creating an illusion of beauty and magic. A string symphony melody vibrated in the air and shivers of fear and excitement washed over me as we climbed the steps.

Phoenix turned her head, checking I was close behind. She pulled her mask down over her eyes and I followed her lead, securing mine as we approached the glass doorway. I tugged at my dress, beads and sequins scratching against my wrist. The gloss Phoenix had applied earlier was sweet, like bubble gum, on my tongue, as I nervously licked my lips.

I felt detached from the girl staring back at me through the darkened glass. Our dresses and sandals were too flash and formal, as if we were playing dress-up. Phoenix could pass for at least twenty and I suddenly realised why Mum used to despair when I experimented with her make-up. I'd give anything to return to a life where I got to curl up on a sofa beside Mum in my PJs and watch daft films. I didn't want to enter this adult world.

A blast of noise and heat hit as Phoenix opened the doors. I blinked, adjusting to the dim lighting. Tables were furnished with white tablecloths and tall candelabra centrepieces, candlelight casting shadows across the faces of the seated diners, creating ghoulish distortions.

None of the guests wore masks, although they too had dressed for the occasion, the room a sea of colourful dresses and monochrome tuxedos. Conversation buzzed in the air, accompanied by a chorus of clinking glasses and the pop and fizz of champagne bottles opening and pouring.

Sensing my hesitation, Phoenix curled her fingers around my arm, pulling me gently towards the back of the room, smells of rich food wafting towards me. I tried to avoid catching anyone's eye, my body tensing at the scrutinising glances from the women and penetrating stares from the men. Heart thumping in my throat I kept focused on the make-shift kitchen up ahead. Margaret stood in her whites, directing Pollock and Ryan towards rows of metal chafing dishes, waving a spoon, her face scarlet with the heat.

Ryan noticed us first, a smile creeping up his face as he looked me up and down, his gaze like blisters on my skin. I instinctively tugged at my dress, trying to cover flesh. He smiled wider. I glowered behind my mask, hoping he could sense the revulsion radiating from me.

"You're late," a voice hissed in my ear. I turned, taking a moment to register Clara beneath her turquoise and lilac mask, the colours intensifying the blue of her eyes. I was already in trouble; the blood analysis from my plasma donation indicating little improvement in my haemoglobin levels. I balked at the memory of the new personalised meal plan Clara had given Margaret, liver at the top of the list. I'd have a hard time convincing anyone to take that off my hands.

As Viv barked a quick run-over of the courses and serving order I sensed a presence behind me. Without turning my head, I knew it was Seb. It was as if my body had a 'Seb sensor' - a surge of heat wound round my waist, zigzagging up my spine. He stepped forward, his gaze having the opposite effect of Ryan's.

Viv motioned for me to step towards the food table. Margaret beamed at me, complimenting my dress and hair, like a proud gran waving me off to prom. Pollock looked bored as he handed me three small plates, fresh salmon curled on top of cream cheese and oatcakes, green sprigs and lemon slices garnishing the dish. I tried to focus as Viv and Clara told me which tables I would be serving, drawing my attention to numbers pinned on black metal spiral stands that stood beside the candelabras, red carnations threaded through the gaps.

"Lucky number seven," I muttered under my breath, forcing a smile as I approached the guests at the circular table, trying to balance the plates so the food didn't slide off. The table consisted of three sets of couples, two elderly, and one younger, perhaps in their thirties. I was careful to serve the ladies first, remembering the brief training session Viv led after breakfast. The older women barely glanced in my direction, too engrossed in excited chatter.

When I laid the plate down in front of the younger woman she smiled kindly. "I love your dress." Her skin was translucent, delicate blue veins accentuating the dark circles under her eyes, creeping towards her cheek bones. I smiled a thank you, trying not to stare at her arms which were so thin the bones jutted at the elbows.

When I returned with the rest of the plates the older males raised their glasses in approval. "A fine young specimen indeed," one of them laughed jovially, stroking his beard as he eyed my dress, his cheeks pink from alcohol. None of the males looked at my face. I watched as the bearded man stabbed the salmon with a fork, swallowing it whole. I shuddered, winding my way back to the food table.

Ryan handed me new plates. "Looking sexy as always."

Before I had a chance to respond, Seb appeared by my side. "Alright, Ryan. And you're looking as slippery as that salmon."

Ryan sneered, handing Seb a plate. "Run along, servant boy, your guests are waiting."

Seb caught my eye as we turned together. "You do look good."

I smiled, a thrill darting through me. He stayed close behind, whispering comments about an eccentric man at his next table, making me laugh.

The laugh died in my throat as I approached my new table and spotted a familiar plump face and coiffed hair. Ms Turnberry. My hand shook as a tremor of anger and disbelief rumbled through me, memories of our last encounter flashing through my head. *You set me up*, I wanted to scream. *You made me think Martha didn't want me*. I served the two ladies either side first, then slammed Ms Turnberry's plate down, causing her to startle. Her eyes darted up, lips parted, poised to react. Then recognition dawned and her mouth clamped shut. I held her gaze, bending close to her ear. "I hope you choke on that, Ms Turnberry." Before she had an opportunity to retort I backed away, intercepting Phoenix.

"I need you to take table eight. I can't handle serving that woman. I think I might do something stupid."

Phoenix hesitated, then took one look at my face. "Okay. You take table thirteen. This is the last of their first course." She handed me plates and I thanked her, trying to calm my breathing.

Once the first courses were served Clara instructed us to keep an eye on our tables, watching for empty wine and champagne bottles, as well as refilling the water jugs. I was surprised to see her and Viv and the blonde doctor, Faye, from the Blood House all waitressing too. I hovered by the serving area, gulping down a glass of water. Seb appeared beside me.

"Why don't the others have to do this?" I asked him.

He made a face. "Can you imagine Stacey here?"

I smiled in acknowledgement. "Okay, I get that. What about Aidan, Dylan, Scott, Joe?"

"Aidan spilled dinner over someone important last time and the other boys have no sophistication."

"And you do?" A teasing smile played on my lips and Seb placed a hand against his heart, mock offended.

His expression darkened. "I've overheard the Carmichaels telling the guests at nights like this that they're getting to 'view' the premium plasma on offer. Like we're on show for them, giving them a glimpse of the youthfulness they're all chasing."

I tugged at the hem of my dress self-consciously, not wanting to be on show for anyone.

Seb scanned the room and tilted his head closer to mine. I gripped my glass tighter, palms sweating at his close proximity.

"Don't you think it's weird that we get to see their faces?" Seb said. I followed his gaze around the room.

"What do you mean?" I frowned.

"Well, I'm going to be out of here in a couple of

months. That guy over there is a Z-list Scottish celeb. He hosts some cheesy quiz show. I doubt he'd want the public knowing he's a part of this."

I tried to push the 'out of here in a couple of months' comment to the back of my head, the thought causing a stabbing pain in my chest.

Seb continued, "According to Ryan that guy beside the Carmichaels is high up in the police and his wife works for social work. No one here would want their names linked to a house like this. So why take the risk? Why are *we* the ones wearing the masks?"

I looked to the centre table where the Carmichaels laughed alongside a well-dressed couple.

Seb's words bothered me. He was right. It should be their anonymity that was protected, not ours. I thought back to the confidentiality clause I signed in Dr Carmichael's office. "I guess they would take our money back though, sue us or something if we tried to leak any of this information."

"Think of the money we could get if we sold our story to the press, contacted television channels," Seb said. "It was something Davey talked about." Noting my confused expression Seb explained that Davey had left the house before I arrived. That they'd been good friends. "I warned him not to do anything to muck up his chances of a good life but I'm surprised he's not tried to come back for me and bring help. I know he wanted to expose this place and didn't care if it meant losing his money."

I looked back at the plump man beside Dr Carmichael. "If that guy is high up in the police what if he has the power to shut down any attempts at investigations?"

Seb shrugged. "Maybe. I just get a bad feeling

about it all."

Before he had a chance to explain further, Viv appeared by our side, scolding us for loitering, telling us to tend to our tables. As I turned, I realised Ryan had been watching us, a calculating smile on his face.

The main courses consisted of chicken stuffed with haggis, with an accompaniment of leek mash and asparagus wrapped in ham. The creamy smell of the mash made my tummy grumble.

"You're doing a fine job, lass," Margaret winked as she loaded up more plates. I tried to ignore the sweat pooling at the base of my back, the steam from the serving area adding to my discomfort. I hadn't been able to shake a headache after my initial donations and it was making my temple throb. Viv touched my arm on her way past, muttering instructions to charm the old men at table ten as they were new members. My skin crawled at the thought of flirting with them. The balls of my feet stung as I circled the tables, re-filling glasses and clearing dirty plates. One of the older men pressed a twenty-pound note into my hand, his palm sticky and hot. I wanted to ask him where he thought I could spend it.

As the last of the dessert bowls were scraped clean, the music stopped and Dr Carmichael stood, tapping a fork against his wine glass. Barbara dabbed a napkin against her cerise lips, smiling up at her husband.

"I'd like to thank you all for joining us tonight, and express a warm welcome to our new gold members."

An approving murmur circled the room as Dr Carmichael talked about the importance of the blood trials, explaining how their money contributed to advancing research and equipment, as well as allowing the maintenance of a top-class control group. I listened as he talked about the strict health plan 'his young people' followed, ensuring the highest quality plasma was extracted and donated. Seb caught my eye during the speech, his expression hard to read. My mind wandered as I studied the crowd, wondering if they were hoping to reverse ageing or cure ailments. The younger woman I'd served looked deathly ill. I balked at the thought of Dr Carmichael taking payments from her at a time she probably needed money to sustain a comfortable life.

Doors opened at the back as the guests vacated tables and I realised I'd missed Dr Carmichael's closing remarks. I breathed a sigh of relief, hoping this was our cue to leave. Viv and Clara motioned for us to follow the guests and I fell into step beside Phoenix and Seb, watching as the back doors opened out into a smaller, more modern looking room.

The lighting dimmed as we entered, low ceilings creating an intimacy, with circular strip lights emitting a muted blood-orange glow. A gold bar curved along each side, small tables and booths dotted around the centre. Each table had a weird elevated centrepiece, like a metal candlestick with a miniature red hose wrapped around it.

"What are those?" I nudged Seb, nodding towards the table closest to us.

"The Carmichaels' version of a Hookah Shisha," he said. "Instead of a pipe there's a cannula inside the hose, connected to an IV, so it's not tobacco they get a hit of. It's called Blood Rushing."

I watched in horror as guests took their seats, Clara and the nurse circling.

"But how does it work?" I asked. "Where's the

blood?"

Seb nodded to the metal sculpture twisting above the Hookah. "My guess is the bag of blood is hidden inside that. And there must be a filter connecting to the IV to remove any clots inside the bag."

I shot him a puzzled look, not expecting him to know quite so much.

He grinned. "I don't follow the subscribed reading lists. The library has a whole medical section which I figured might give me some answers about what's going on. Look up James Blundell. He performed the first human to human transfusions in 1818. Phoenix filled in the rest of the blanks. Dr Carmichael likes the fact she shows an interest in what goes on here."

I turned back to watch the procedure. "So with this process, it's actually blood, not plasma?"

Seb nodded. "Yup."

I watched as Clara smiled at the ill-looking young woman I'd served earlier, chatting as she stretched up to the elevated platform above the table, unwinding the hose and straightening the woman's arm as she pierced her skin.

"It's an 'exclusive' feature of the gold membership. The blood bags are small samples from us. When you start going for your regular health checks you'll donate blood. Clara will say it's for regular screening checks, but really it's to collect samples for this. Couples share the same Hookah and they're labelled so they keep them personalised with no risk of contamination. It's elevated so the gravity helps run the blood through the patient," Seb explained. He smiled wryly. "Welcome to the Gold Bar."

Dr Carmichael's obsession with my iron levels made sense now, if they were also going to start taking blood. I watched as the woman smiled keenly, a desperation shining in her eyes. She closed her eyes as Clara completed the insertion and I wondered whose blood was entering her veins. Would our plasma and blood really bring them health benefits? I thought back to the case studies in the manual, the 'before' and 'after' photograph of Barbara Carmichael a compelling testimony. But her 'before' photograph might be fake. All of this could be a lie, with Dr Carmichael the illusionist at the centre of an elaborate façade.

Phoenix snapped her fingers in front of my face making me jump. She balanced a tray of drinks in her other hand. "Get moving. Ryan is loading up drinks for you." She nodded towards the bar and I followed Seb, my heart sinking at the thought of more hours on my feet.

Ryan handed me a tray of glasses half-filled with gold liquid. From the small measure and woody scent I guessed it was whisky. He pointed towards a secluded booth to the side of the bar, where a group of older men laughed and roared, their fat fingers pulling cigars from a silver tin. Ryan smiled. "Those gentlemen requested a young female server. Play nice."

As I approached the table a puff of smoke circled the air, shooting up my nostrils. I coughed, the tray wavering, glasses knocking against each other.

"Steady, sweetheart," one of the men touched the base of my back, his fingers creeping down over my bum. He squeezed and I slammed the tray down on the table, yanking my body away, a shot of fear and anger bolting through me.

A couple of the men whooped loudly, chuckling as my assaulter took a slow drag of his cigar, this time purposely blowing smoke in my face. He smacked my behind eliciting an amused roar from the table. Fat fingers crept up my thigh, squeezing at my flesh. *Please stop, please stop.* The noise of their laughter rose in waves around me and through me, elevating my anger, up and up, bubbling...

"This one's a right firecracker." The man pulled me down onto his knee and I wriggled, clawing at his arm which was a wrench around my waist, keeping me pinned. He grinned, cigar clamped between yellow teeth. "You're new here, aren't you? Lovely, fresh blood."

"Let me go," I yelled, my cries only making them all roar louder. Tears stung my eyes as I struggled and kicked, his grip tightening, constricting my breathing.

"Relax," he growled in my ear, using his free hand to tuck a strand of hair behind my mask. "I'm just playing. You're supposed to be making sure we have a good time here." He turned to his friends. "Wonder when it'll be her grand finale on the throne? I'm salivating at the thought. Though I think there would be more valuable uses for this one." He pretended to snap his fingers at an imaginary waiter, "Sir, I'm putting my orders in for an exclusive bid."

I stared at their laughing faces, not understanding, wanting them to stop.

As he traced a finger along my collar bone I flinched, a thrum of panic tightening in my throat. I thought back to Clara's reassurance that they could look, but not touch. They were not entitled. Straining against his weight I reached forward towards the table, grabbing a glass and threw the liquid in his face. He recoiled in shock and I wriggled free, taking advantage of his loosened grip.

His face contorted with rage as he dabbed at his

eyes with a napkin, spluttering, the cigar falling from his mouth into the puddle of liquid on the table.

My heart thumped through every inch of my body as an eruption of belittling obscenities rippled around the table. The man stood, towering over me, eyes bulging. He raised a hand and I froze, cowering.

"Stop!" A voice yelled above the din. Seb jumped in front of me, catching the man's arm as he swung, holding firm.

A shudder of relief trembled through my bones as I stumbled backwards.

Seb's grip on the man didn't waver, his eyes burning with rage behind his jewelled mask.

The man relented, yanking his arm back from Seb, smoothing his shirt, adjusting his bow tie. He looked between the two of us.

"You've caused me to have a very unpleasant evening." He sat back down on his seat, his friends glaring at us in disapproval. The man looked beyond us, clicking his fingers, gesturing for assistance.

I squeezed my eyes shut, allowing Seb to pull me in close against his chest, his heart thundering against my ear.

Shouts of apologies and outrage circled as the Carmichaels rushed over. Dr Carmichael pulled me from Seb, flinging me towards Barbara as if I was a rag doll. He grabbed Seb by the arm, pulling him across the room.

"No," I shouted, watching helplessly as Dr Carmichael shoved Seb back into the dining area, slamming the doors shut behind them. I turned to Barbara, pleading with her. "He was just trying to protect me."

Barbara's grip tightened round my wrist, her nails piercing my skin. "Walk with me and stop making a scene," she hissed, smiling politely as we passed Ms Turnberry, who averted her eyes, like she was too ashamed to watch. "You've both let us down tonight. For that, you need to be punished."

Images of the Bothy filled my head and I struggled against her grip, explaining it wasn't my fault, the men had broken the rules, that they'd touched me.

"Silly girl," Barbara shook her head, motioning for Clara. "These people don't need to follow rules." Clara pulled me towards her, a needle stabbing my arm. I tasted tears as she walked me out of the room, a rush of darkness pumping through my body, my muscles loosening and melting.

"They are not entitled," I murmured, and she caught me as I fell.

Chapter Twenty-Eight
Ana

Ana stood at the window, watching as her parents climbed into Dad's car, Mum's face pale and drawn. The memory of the muffled tears in the early hours of the morning shook Ana to her bones, the realisation her mum was not invincible, that things might be spiralling out of control.

Maisie nudged Ana's hip, sliding her body in front, her breath steaming the glass. Maisie pressed her nose to the window and Ana laid her hands on her shoulders, comforted by her sister's warmth.

"Why can't we go with them?" Maisie whined.

Ana tugged at her ponytail. "Dad wants to take Mum on a date to their favourite café."

Maisie's head darted round, her nose screwed tight. "But they're married, they don't go on *dates*. Dad had better bring me home a cupcake."

As the car disappeared down the drive Ana turned away and sprawled across the sofa, flicking through Maisie's streaming channel, thinking she should indulge her today after the trauma of being forgotten.

It had taken Mum another hour before she returned home on the bus yesterday and she looked crestfallen when Maisie refused to speak to her. Ana didn't mention Maisie had cried all the way home, upset she had to sit in her classroom alone, waiting for one of them to arrive. Thankfully Ana had met Maisie's teacher before so there was no awkward moment of disallowing Maisie to go home with a pink-haired teenager.

Once Maisie was settled in bed, Mum had a proper chat with Ana explaining the trip had been a silly impulsive decision and she had wanted to reconnect with one of grandma's old friends. She got on the wrong bus home, ending up at the opposite end of Glasgow. Ana tried to tell her it wasn't a big deal, that she hated buses too, and who didn't get lost when there was no way of knowing what stop you were at in an unfamiliar area. Mum said she'd been distracted, with too much on her mind, dropping the bombshell Ana had been dreading.

"I had a medical appointment this morning. My test results came back."

A wave of dizziness washed over Ana, giving her an odd out of body feeling. "What did they find?"

"Biomarker tests found I'm showing signs of Prodromal Alzheimer's. It means I'm in the very early stages. It's a good thing that I was given the opportunity to have these tests, as we can now explore potential medications. Don't look so worried, love."

Ana had tried to stay positive for her mum's sake. But hearing her crying last night left a heavy feeling in the pit of her stomach.

Ana turned to Maisie, shaking off the worry as she watched her sister wind herself up in the curtains. "What should we watch, toots?"

"Beauty and the Beast." Maisie grinned and Ana made a face.

"Are you sure? Haven't you watched that a lot lately?" Ana counted at least four watches during Sunday night film night.

"Just five times," Maisie beamed. "Once more. Please, please, please."

Ana relented, scrolling along to the film.

"Oh, look who it is." The curtains dropped as Maisie jumped back to the window, pressing her hands against the glass. She giggled and waved.

"Who?" Ana frowned, wondering if Maisie had spotted the old man along the road.

"It's that boy. The one with the funny hair."

"What?" Ana threw the remote down, alarmed. Maisie giggled, enjoying her panicked reaction as Ana glanced down at her scruffy jeans and t-shirt. She hadn't even brushed her hair yet.

The bell rang and Ana jumped, swearing under her breath. She glanced at her phone, realising she'd forgotten to reply to Elliot's message yesterday to confirm their trip to the house.

"There's old people in a car waiting on him. Is that his parents? Are his whole family here?" Maisie squealed in delight and realisation dawned. The Browns.

Grabbing Maisie's pink comb from the table Ana frantically ran it through her hair as she walked along the hall. She threw it into a shoe as she unlocked the door.

A rush of heat scalded Ana's cheeks as she greeted Elliot. He was dressed in scuffed boots and blue jeans, camera slung over his neck. He looked different out of school uniform, older and less familiar. He gave her a once over too. Mercifully his gaze didn't linger on the throbbing spot on her chin. "What are you doing here?" Ana glanced at the envelope he clutched in his hands, wondering if he'd found something.

He gestured to the Browns. "We're going to the house. I thought you wanted to come?"

"What house?" Maisie appeared, pulling the door open wider and Ana cringed.

Elliot raised his eyebrows as Maisie stuck her hand out.

"I'm Maisie, Ana's little sister. I'm six. What's your name?"

He smiled and shook her hand. "I'm Elliot. I'm sixteen."

Maisie flashed him a delighted smile. "Are you Ana's boyfriend?"

Elliot looked at Ana in alarm and Ana grabbed Maisie, shooting her death glares. "Maisie, I thought you were going to put on the film?"

Maisie made a face then tilted her head, scrutinising Elliot. "You could come in and watch it too if you want?"

"No. Elliot doesn't want." Ana flashed him an apologetic smile, nudging Maisie. "Go, Maisie."

Maisie let out an exaggerated sigh and stomped back through to the living room.

"Sorry." Ana smiled weakly. "My parents had to go out unexpectedly today and I have to look after the little monster. I should have messaged you back but things got a bit crazy here."

Elliot's face deflated and Ana chewed her lip.

"Well, she could come?" Elliot's voice trailed at the end and Ana knew he realised it was a bad idea as soon as he suggested it.

Ana smiled wryly. "Thanks, but I don't want Maisie knowing anything about this. Plus she wouldn't give us a minute's peace."

He shrugged. "Fair enough. Sorry you can't make it. We'll still go and I'll message you later?"

Ana nodded. "I hope you find something." She stepped forward to wave at the Browns. Martha frowned, clearly wondering why she wasn't coming. Her car door opened and she stepped out. Ana moved to meet her half-way on the drive, ignoring the damp earth seeping into her socks.

"What's wrong, dear?" Martha asked.

"I'm sorry. I have to look after my sister today."

Martha's mouth formed a disappointed 'Oh.' She patted Ana on the hand. "Well, how's about we all agree to meet at ours tomorrow? You can both come for lunch." She nodded at Elliot. "Means we can give you a proper update, Ana."

"Okay," Ana smiled. "That would be nice, thanks."

Martha waved and walked back to the car.

"I'll still message you tonight," Elliot said. He hesitated, shoving the envelope in Ana's hand. "This is for you. See ya."

Ana watched as he climbed into the Browns' car, the thought of them finding Hope making her shiver with excitement. She tried to bury the disappointment that she had been the one to stumble across the potential house but wouldn't get to investigate.

Maisie shouted from the living room and Ana rolled her eyes, resigning herself to a day of Disney.

"Just a minute," Ana called, turning the envelope over in her hands. It was sturdy, like there was a cardboard inlay inside. Baffled, she slid the seal open, pulling out a photograph. She did a double take, realisation dawning that this was *her*, from the time they'd stood outside school and Elliot insisted on taking her photograph. A mixture of happiness and shyness shone from her eyes and smile, the muted sun casting a flattering glow against her skin, the gold flecks around her irises catching fire behind her glasses. Elliot had managed to capture something deeper than a surface smile. A warmth spread to Ana's toes. He made her look beautiful, suspended in light. She slid the photograph back in the envelope, zipping it inside her bag. She wanted to treasure it and keep it private, like a secret conversation between them.

*

A damp fog spread through the streets, spindly tree branches piercing the mist, like gnarled fingers reaching out to Ana. She shivered, pulling the collar of her coat up, wishing she'd remembered her hat. Her bag was weighed down with biscuits, Mum insisting she take them as a gift to the Browns. Mum was still distracted, presuming Hope was still with them, but her smile had returned and it filled Ana with relief.

Ana's phone beeped in her pocket. She glanced at the message from Elliot: *Running late. Be there soon.*

Ana sighed, still deflated by his report last night. They had been unable to make it past the gates. When they pressed the buzzer a female responded, instructing them to leave as they were trespassing on private land, claiming no one called Hope stayed there. Elliot said the path beyond the gates was too long and dense with trees to see anything in the distance. They'd stopped in at Dr Carmichael's clinic on the way home, hoping to speak with him but the receptionist said he was unavailable all weekend. Going to the police was now looking like their best option.

The rev of an engine interrupted Ana's thoughts. Fog obscured the road, swallowing any signs of life. She quickened her steps, the quiet of Sunday adding another layer of eeriness to the surrounds.

The sound of tyres rolling against gravel alerted her to the approach of a car. A flash of grey metal and blacked out windows appeared through the mist. The passenger window slid down. Ana didn't need to see the face of the driver to know who would speak.

"Good afternoon, Ms Gilbert."

Dr Carmichael flashed her a smile, the curve of his moustache conjuring up images of the Cheshire Cat. The passenger seat lay empty.

"I was hoping we could have a chat, Ms Gilbert," he continued.

Ana slid her hands up inside her coat sleeves, shivering against the cold. "I'm on my way to visit friends."

He made a dismissive noise, drumming his fingers against the steering wheel. "I think you might want to cancel. I have an offer to make you and I'd like to get things moving along as quickly as possible."

She thought back to the booklet he'd given her, the blood trials and the costs. She shook her head. "I'm not interested."

He smiled, amused. "But you don't even know what's on offer. It's bitter out here. Jump in and I'll explain everything."

Ana stepped back. "I can't. I'll be late for lunch."

"I think you'll find this is far more important than lunch," Dr Carmichael sighed, reaching to press a button. "If you don't trust me, then perhaps this gentleman might convince you."

The back window slid down and Ana startled when Mr Darwin smiled sheepishly. "Hello, Ana."

"What's going on?" Ana looked between them.

"Dr Carmichael wants to help you and your family," Mr Darwin said. He nodded to the empty passenger seat. "We know you've got questions about Hope, so let us help you understand."

At the mention of Hope, Ana's heart jolted. "You know where she is?" Ana hesitated. "Will you take me to her?"

Dr Carmichael sighed impatiently. "Get in the car, girl. One question at a time."

Ana opened the passenger door, every part of her logical brain screaming at her not to get in. She thought about Hope, about the unsuccessful mission yesterday, about Elliot's desperation to find Seb. And most of all, Mr Darwin's words that they wanted to help her family. Mum. Ana climbed in, a shiver of fear shooting up her spine as the locks clicked and Dr Carmichael hit the accelerator.

Chapter Twenty-Nine
Hope

Pain shot up my side as I turned, springs digging into my spine. Opening one eye, I squinted, trying to make sense of where I was. Darkness surrounded me and my heart hammered in panic. My head spun as I bolted upright. I grabbed the sides of the bed, trying to quell the dizziness.

Smells of unwashed toilets permeated the air and I balked, stuffing a fist against my nose and mouth. Tentatively I reached out into the darkness, fingertips grazing a cold brick wall to my left. I turned to my right, stretching my hand up, then down, knuckles hitting solid wood. Lowering my body from the bed I half crouched, hands feeling along the edge of a table. My knuckles knocked against a solid object, and I jumped at the sound of shattering glass on the ground, liquid dripping. I cursed, slowing my movements, fingers tracing the curve of metal, a stand of some sort, the base narrowing as I slid my hand up, thumb finding a switch. I clicked and recoiled as light accosted my eyes.

A blast of ice shot through me as I slumped on the floor, concrete cold and hard. I registered the bare brick walls, the high circular ceiling with no light, the iron door with no handle. Anger coursed through me and I balled my fists, encouraging the rage, to keep fear and panic from consuming me.

The cold air stung my cheeks. I pulled my knees up to my chest, hugging my legs, trying to stop the uncontrollable shivers. At least in a real Bothy there would be a fireplace and freedom to collect firewood. I folded my hands inside the sleeves of the unfamiliar baggy grey hoodie, grateful that someone had at least dressed me in warm clothing. The tracksuit bottoms were loose around my waist and I pulled the drawstring, toes curling in the thick socks. I stretched towards the table, pain shooting through my shoulder. My whole body ached of tension and cold after a night spent on a hard thin mattress.

I reached for the jug of water, grateful I'd only smashed the drinking glass. I tipped it towards my chafed lips, trying not to dribble down my chin, guzzling thirstily. The balls of my feet still ached from the waitressing and I sat down on the bed, pulling the flimsy pillow towards me, hugging it against my chest, rocking back and forward. Images from the bar flooded my brain, Seb being dragged through doors by Dr Carmichael. I squeezed the pillow tighter. Where was Seb? If I was here, what was his punishment?

A sob caught in my throat and tears exploded, loud messy cries I hadn't allowed myself give in to since I'd arrived at the house tumbled out of me, wracking my body, echoing against the walls. Thoughts I had tried to suppress flooded my brain. I was going to be stuck here, in this house for another two years. With no freedom and the constant threat of this windowless prison. *No one is going to save you. No one cares about you.* I tried to catch my breath, body shuddering as my tears refused to stop.

The emotion was too close to what I felt during the first year of losing Mum. An overwhelming sense of fear and loneliness and lack of control. The realisation adults wanted to decide the life I should lead, giving me little say in the process.

"Why did you leave me?" I shouted up at the ceiling, as if Mum had flown to heaven and I could command her to answer my cries.

The squeak of a door caused me to pause, tears catching in the back of my throat.

A key turned, bolts slid. I sat up straight, wiping at my eyes and nose with the sleeve of the hoodie, a thrum of relief singing through me. Maybe I was being released.

The door opened slowly, tentatively.

"Hello?" I called, standing.

Billy's face popped round the door, cheeks flushed.

"Billy!" I rushed towards him, throwing my arms around his waist. "I'm so glad to see you."

He patted my head like I was a dog. He stepped inside, closing the door quietly behind him. He put a finger against his lips. "Shhh. I'm not supposed to be here." He pulled a bag of sweets from his pocket. "I heard you crying. I brought you a present."

I smiled and sniffed, taking the bag from him. "Thank you, Billy."

"We're friends," he said.

I nodded. "We are. Thank you for sharing your sweets." He watched me expectantly. I opened the bag and pulled out a pink bon bon, the toffee sticking to my teeth as I bit through the sweet powder coating. I offered him one and he pulled out two, stuffing them in his mouth.

"Why are you crying?" He asked, in between chews.

"I'm scared," I said. "I don't like being locked in here."

He looked around the room, then back at me. "You must have been bad."

"No, Billy." I shook my head firmly, waiting until he met my eye. "The Carmichaels are the bad ones for locking me in."

Billy's lip trembled. He scratched his head. "Mrs Carmichael is nice. She's like my mum."

I took a deep breath. "Can you let me out of here, Billy?"

He backed away, fear in his eyes. "No. Not allowed. Shouldn't be here. I need to go now."

"Wait." I followed him to the door. "What time is it?"

Billy looked at his watch, studying the face. "Lunchtime. Ryan is bringing your food. Got to go."

"Okay." I was tempted to grab his arm and not let go. "Come and visit again?" I asked hopefully.

He hesitated, then nodded.

A part of me died when I watched him leave and heard the locks turn, bolting me in.

*

It felt like hours passed before I heard the squeak and swing of the exterior gate, then a key in the lock and bolts sliding. Even the prospect of seeing Ryan was a welcome distraction to the stark silence and never-ending thoughts tumbling through my head.

The door swung open and Ryan wheeled in a food tray, a smug smile on his face.

"Well, how the mighty have fallen," he said, looking me up and down. "Not looking so hot right now, Hope."

All feelings of warmth faded with his sneer. I sat on the bed, folding my arms.

"You thought you could get away with whatever you wanted in here, didn't you?" He pulled off a lid from the silver serving dish, sniffing the plate of steaming food theatrically. "I've got a lovely dish here. Sausage and liver casserole. Yumm-ee."

I balked, turning away from the smell.

Ryan lifted a set of cutlery from the tray and walked towards me with the plate. He sat down on the bed, stabbing a piece of liver with a fork.

"Do you think we're stupid, Hope?" He moved his face closer to mine, his breath stinking of stale cigarettes and coffee. "Slipping your food to Stacey and Seb. Stacey isn't your friend. She tells me everything that goes on in this house. She's figured out I'll sneak her treats if she sneaks on you." He pressed the fork to my closed mouth, the liver slithering against my lips.

I recoiled, turning away from him.

"Where's Seb?" I asked, trying to distract him.

Ryan paused, smiling lazily. "You like him, don't you?"

I ignored his question. "Did Dr Carmichael hurt him?"

Ryan shrugged. "We're keeping him busy. He's down for triple donations and he's helping us prepare for Aidan's leaving party, which you'll miss. Boo-hoo."

The thought of being kept in here, trapped, made my stomach churn.

"Seb's real punishment of course is knowing you're locked up. And that I'm your sole visitor."

Would Seb try to break me out? If he did, we'd probably both end up back in here.

"Eat." Ryan grabbed my face, squeezing my cheeks with his thumb and finger, forcing my mouth open. "If you don't eat, you don't get out of here."

I tried to pull back as he slid the meat in.

"There's a good girl." He clamped my jaw shut and I grimaced, swallowing whole, gagging.

I shoved his hand away. "I need a drink." I retched at the aftertaste.

He looked to the bedside table, his gaze falling to the broken glass sprinkled across the floor. "Clumsy, aren't you?" He walked to the trolley and picked up a glass of orange juice. I stared at the back of his greasy head, fantasising about hitting him over the head with my plate. Even if I managed to get out of the room, where could I run to? A part of me was tempted to try. His head snapped round as if sensing my thoughts.

As I took the juice from him he stood and watched me drink, arms folded. "You remind me a bit of Phoenix when she first arrived. Full of big ideas and bravado. She soon learned."

I turned to the plate, balancing it on my knee, cutting into the casserole with my knife and fork. I took a huge mouthful, eyes never leaving him. I tried to imagine it was tofu, hardly chewing, not wanting to taste. Ryan stood watching until I had swallowed my last bite.

He lifted my plate and squeezed my knee. "That wasn't so bad, was it?"

Bile rose in my throat but I smiled tightly, glaring at him, defiant. "Nothing I can't handle."

"Of course, the mighty Hope." Ryan shot me a look of disdain. "There were lots of girls like you at my college, thinking they were above me, looking at me like I was a weirdo. One had a very protective boyfriend. Guess what happened to him?"

I tensed, wishing he would just leave.

Ryan pulled a lighter from his pocket, sparking a flame. "He burned. In his bed one night. Handy with a lighter, so I am." He smiled smugly. "And thanks to my Aunty Margaret I never got caught. She used to be the Carmichael's cleaner and helped cook meals. They did her a nice deal when they heard the rumours about me, the troubled nephew she'd taken in. They brought us here when the police started knocking on our door, with the understanding Aunty would be lead Cook, with me assisting and doing other chores. Not a bad deal, eh?"

I watched in horror as Ryan strode towards me.

He bent down to whisper in my ear. "I'll be back to bring you dinner. And then maybe I'll tuck you up in bed and read you a story." He ran a finger lightly down my cheek, then across my lips, his pupils dilating.

A tremor of fear gripped, the feeling of helplessness threatening to pull me under. I watched him load the dishes back on to the tray, my body relaxing when the door shut, blocking him out.

I ran over to the shards of glass on the ground that he hadn't bothered to take away, slipping two large pieces under my pillow.

If there was one thing I had learned over the past couple of years, it was how to survive.

A cretin like Ryan was not going to break me.

Chapter Thirty
Ana

The car rolled to a stop at the gates and Dr Carmichael gestured for Ana's phone.

"I can't risk any exposure. We'll return it to you on departure. You messaged your friend to explain your absence?"

Ana nodded, a flicker of panic firing in her gut as she watched Dr Carmichael press the off switch, her phone disappearing into his top pocket. He picked up a black fob from the dashboard, pointing it out of his open window towards the gates, jabbing a triangular shaped button. A green light flashed on a keypad to the left of the rails and the gates parted slowly, the clunk and squeak of metal permeating the silence.

Dr Carmichael hit the accelerator and the car rolled forward, the tarmac a smooth contrast to the bumpy country roads. Ana stared out the window, trying to memorise every inch of scenery. Trees lined the drive either side and the road ahead curved too high to see over the bow.

She wondered what this meant, being taken to the house. Why was Dr Carmichael trusting her with this information? Maybe they'd got it wrong and Hope wasn't there, that the house was just an extension of Dr Carmichael's medical clinic.

"I believe your friends attempted a visit yesterday," Dr Carmichael said casually, eyes not leaving the road.

His candidness shook Ana off balance. Excuses jumbled in her head, but none of them sounded plausible. "I wasn't with them." At least that much was true.

"No. Why was that?" Dr Carmichael asked.

"I was babysitting."

Dr Carmichael smiled. "Oh yes, your charming young sister. I nearly ran her over the first time we met." He laughed heartily, glancing at Mr Darwin in the rear-view mirror as if relaying a funny after dinner story.

Ana balled her fists in her lap, trying to calm her breathing. What was Mr Darwin's involvement in this? She kept her gaze focused ahead and another set of gates came into view, this time they extended wider and higher, solid grey panels, with no gaps in between to reveal what lay beyond. Her eyes were drawn to the metal wires and discs strung along the top perimeter. She shivered, recalling images of American high security prisons she'd seen on TV.

"Was there a reason your friends wanted to visit?" Dr Carmichael asked.

"We just wondered what was here."

"All will be revealed." Dr Carmichael's window slid down again as he directed the fob towards the gates, a green light flashing in time with a shrill beep as the panels parted and swung open. A castle-style mansion loomed on the horizon, threads of mist shrouding turreted slate roofs. Red leaves crawled up the walls of the circular pillars, like bleeding ivy, a vibrant contrast to the grey stone exterior.

Dr Carmichael's car rolled up the drive, winding through lush gardens, the autumnal orange and brown landscape muted beneath the grey sky. As they neared the entrance to the mansion Ana looked up to the windows, lights flickering behind glass, heavy curtains drawn in the upper floors sparking her curiosity further. *What was this place?*

The car rolled to a stop outside the main entrance, stone steps winding up to a porch with pillars which led to a burnt-orange wooden door, black metal spirals curving around metal bolts. Dr Carmichael turned to Ana as he unclipped his seatbelt.

"You must understand, Ana, that what I am about to reveal must stay between us. The safety of your friends depends on it. Alright?"

Ana nodded, not understanding one bit. She couldn't tell if Dr Carmichael had just issued a threat, or a friendly warning. As he exited the car with Mr Darwin she paused, her eyes drawn to the black fob on the dashboard. Eyes never leaving the retreating backs of Mr Darwin and the doctor, Ana considered swiping it. But then what would happen when Dr Carmichael needed to open the gates on the way out? She rummaged around in the storage box beside the handbrake, hoping to find a spare one, but instead found loose change and mints.

Mr Darwin turned to look for her and she opened her door, pretending to struggle with her bag. A chill seeped into her bones as she climbed out the car into the damp air. The crunch of the gravel beneath her feet did nothing to drown out the sound of her heart thundering in her ears.

Dr Carmichael unlocked the front door and she tried to catch Mr Darwin's eye but he kept his head bowed, his body language tense and closed.

As they entered the main hall Ana stared in wonder at the grand staircase winding up to high balconies, the plush red carpets, the stained-glass windows and ornate furniture.

"Do you live here?" Ana turned to Dr Carmichael, unable to keep the awe from her voice.

He chuckled. "Yes, but I share the place with others."

She wondered what he meant by 'others.' The house was silent, apart from the pronounced ticking of a grandfather clock to the left of an oak desk, a glass lamp glowing orange, bathing the hall in warmth.

"Before I give you a tour, let's get you something to eat and drink in the kitchen. I believe Margaret has her wonderful ham and lentil soup cooking on the stove."

Ana's tummy growled, part from hunger, part from fear, as she followed him along the hall towards oak panelled doors. The smell of soup and fresh bread circled the air as he pushed open a swing door, the warmth and noise hitting Ana instantly as they stepped inside a massive kitchen. A young man standing at the stove turned his head as they entered. His hair was thick with gel, beady eyes sinking in to pale mottled skin. Ana blushed and averted her eyes from his scrutinising stare.

A plump rosy cheeked woman waved her in, ushering Ana towards the table which was set with a pot of tea and one cup. She laid down a breadbasket beside a butter tray, a curved silver knife glinting under the lights. "You must be, Ana. Take a seat, lass. We've been expecting you."

*

Dr Carmichael returned to fetch Ana after half an hour. Ana kept one eye on the clock the whole time she ate at the kitchen table, nerves churning the food in her belly as she convinced herself it could be spiked with drugs, or worse – poison. Margaret had been evasive when Ana asked which part of the house Hope was in, claiming to have limited contact with 'the youngsters' but added a reassuring, 'She's eating well and looks settled.'

Satisfied she could still walk with no ill effects Ana left the warmth of the kitchen and Margaret's conversation to follow Dr Carmichael further along the hall. He pointed in through open doors, naming each room. "That's the library, the games room, the ballroom. And this," he pushed open a door, "is my study."

Ana paused, surprised to find two young people sitting behind the desk. The girl had a mass of spiral curls, eyes large and inquisitive, glittering with defiance. Ana tried not to stare at the scar curving down the boy's face, the red gash angry against his pale skin.

Dr Carmichael sat across from them, gesturing for Ana to join him at the vacant seat by his side.

As Ana slid into the plush leather chair the girl observed her with a look of puzzled recognition. Ana returned the gaze, trying to place her face. Then a flash of memory hit her. The mass of curls, the smirk as the girl stuck out a leg and Ana skidded along the Music corridor on her knees. The girl's eyes widened as if she realised at the same moment and she grinned, like it was a funny memory. Ana glowered at her. Mandy. The girl who set fire to Elliot's shirt.

"Aidan and Phoenix, I'd like you to meet Ana Gilbert. Hope's friend."

Ana frowned at the girl. *Phoenix?*

Aidan smiled. "Alright, Ana."

Ana shifted in her chair, desperate to ask where Hope was, but realising she would need to be patient.

"I thought instead of trying to explain what goes on here, I'd get two of my favourite youngsters tell you a bit about their experience, and why this place saved them really. Aidan would you like to start? Perhaps you'd like to tell Ms Gilbert a bit about your background first?"

The boy nodded and sat forward in his chair, cracking his knuckles. He didn't meet Ana's eye for the first part of the conversation, his voice monotonous and low as he told her where he came from. She listened as he told his story, taken from his mother who kept returning to an abusive relationship and spiralled into addiction. She couldn't sustain work or stay lucid.

"She had four of us, my brother Scott stayed with me. My half-sisters Cadence and Jayden were babies. They went to different families."

Ana listened as he told her how he was taken to a panel meeting at the age of eleven, sitting in front of a row of adults.

"I felt like I was on trial. That they were trying to decide what was best for me without actually involving me properly in the conversation. I didn't know how to ask the right questions. No one explained anything to me, or if they did, I was too distracted to understand. They all talked at me. I just wanted to go home, to make my mum better, to help her."

He was fostered six times, the first two times without his brother Scott. "I caused trouble until they listened. I was happy again when I was with Scott. It felt like a piece of home. But then I started getting bullied at school." He talked about the endless taunts, the names, Edward Scissorhands. The realisation he didn't live with parents ramping up the abuse at school, rumours spreading that he'd been chucked out his house because he was trouble, that he'd killed a cat that scratched his face in defence. "They made fun of me on social media. Posted photos of Edward Scissorhands and tagged me." Aidan shrugged, his jaw clenching. "I tried to ignore it. I started causing trouble and me and Scott moved to a residential house. But then a kid there was from my school and got others to join in with the taunts. I think they were scared of being the next target so they made sure I stayed the joke." The girl placed her hand on top of his and she squeezed, a reassuring gesture.

Aidan gestured to Dr Carmichael, his face unreadable. "When the Carmichaels brought me here, it felt like a new start. It was a relief to escape it all. And Scott got to come with me."

Phoenix nodded at his words, "We get looked after here. And we get to do something good. Our plasma donations help people."

A bolt of understanding shot through Ana. She stared at Dr Carmichael, a smile creeping up his face.

"Is Hope here?" Ana asked.

Dr Carmichael hesitated. "She is. But it's still very early days, Ana. It takes months, even longer, for young people to adjust to life in here. And to fully understand how good they have it."

"Why hasn't she called us? Why can't we visit?" Ana demanded.

"You're visiting right now." Dr Carmichael said.

Ana clenched her jaw. "You know what I mean. I want to talk to Hope."

He shook his head. "That's not going to be possible, I'm afraid." He nodded at the girl. "Phoenix can vouch for her. You've become friends, haven't you?"

Phoenix held Ana's gaze. "She's safe here and we're well looked after. Outside, it's unpredictable, without a proper family. You wouldn't understand."

Ana's face flamed, the girl's words making her irrationally ashamed for having a family she could return home to. Ana turned to Dr Carmichael. "I don't understand the secrecy."

"For the blood trials to truly work at optimum levels, for me to be able to control every single step of the procedures and the results, this is the way we need to operate. The young people are rewarded for their time but I can't have outside interference. This is why it is most important you keep this secret. I'm trusting you, Ana." He looked to Aidan and Phoenix. "We all are."

Ana stared at Aidan and Phoenix, trying to detect signs of distress, of being forced to lie. They looked calm and composed. She turned back to Dr Carmichael. "Is Seb here too? If I can't talk to Hope because of whatever adjustment time you think she needs, I want to talk to him." She folded her arms. Dr Carmichael's moustache twitched. Ana looked to Aidan and Phoenix, not missing the nervous glance they exchanged.

Dr Carmichael straightened his bow tie. "Sebastian was with us but I'm afraid he left a few months back."

Phoenix and Aidan didn't react. Ana's heart sank, thinking of Elliot, wondering how she was going to tell him. Dr Carmichael stood up and Ana watched as he walked to a cabinet at the back of the room, shuffling through papers. Ana leaned forward, catching Phoenix's eye, "Is Hope really alright?"

Phoenix nodded, her fingers lacing through Aidan's. Her eyes held a warning as if to silence Ana. Ana sat back again as Dr Carmichael turned to them, sliding a document and pen towards her. Ana read the words: 'Confidentiality Agreement.' She turned the page, reading the heading, 'Contract.'

"What's this?" Ana scanned the page, eyes focusing on the opening paragraph. *The Carmichael trial will offer unlimited plasma transfusions to Pamela Gilbert waiving all fees, with the understanding that participation will require the agreement of 100% confidentiality from all involved. Full terms and conditions are outlined hereafter, with penalties laid out if the contract is in any way broken.* She turned to Dr Carmichael. "I don't understand. Why are you offering free transfusions to my mum?"

"Because you want her to get well, do you not?"

"Of course." Ana nodded, trying to digest the meaning in the jargon dominating the written terms.

"This trial is very important to me and to lots of others within these walls. We cannot risk exposure. I need you to work with us, Ana, to stop your friends probing any further. Do you understand?"

Ana understood clearly. He wanted to buy her silence by bribing her. She stood up, closing the papers. "I want to leave now."

Phoenix and Aidan looked at her in surprise. Dr Carmichael raised an eyebrow. "Don't dismiss this opportunity, Ana. Do you realise what you are being offered here?"

Ana stalled, thinking back to her mum's results, the strained looks on her parents' faces when they returned from their 'date.' She desperately wanted Mum to get better, but was she willing to bargain with this creepy doctor man, and accept everything he told her? "I want to see more evidence and results. There's no way Mum is going to agree to this either without them."

He hesitated. "Very well. I'll take you to the donation centre to meet Clara. And we'll stop to talk to Barbara and Billy on the way. Come along."

Ana grabbed her bag, following Dr Carmichael to the door. Phoenix came up behind her.

"Don't ruin this for us. We're happy here. We don't need rescued."

Ana wanted to believe Phoenix. If Hope was happy and safe, then she could properly consider Dr Carmichael's proposal, without the guilt. She also knew deep down if it came to it, she would always choose Mum.

Chapter Thirty-One
Hope

Nightmares threaded through fractured sleep. A fire blazed through the house, Mum's face appearing at an outside window shouting for me to run but the windows were sealed shut and the door handles melted, leaving me locked inside.

Disorientation accompanied my waking moments. It didn't take long to register the stone walls and crippling cold, followed by the realisation my reality wasn't much better than the nightmares. I rolled over on my side, pulling my knees up into a foetal position, attempting to tuck the flimsy blanket around my shivering body to create warmth. A metallic taste swirled in my mouth, the stodgy meat dishes sitting heavy in my tummy. I squeezed my eyes shut, trying to block out the memory of Ryan's slippery touch as he ran his hand up my back, kissing me clumsily on the lips. I knew it wouldn't be long before he demanded more. He was revelling in his power, taunting me. The shard of glass stayed hidden below the pillow, reserved for when I really needed it.

The sound of keys in the lock made me bolt upright, fumbling for the lamp switch. I wrapped the blanket around my shoulders, waiting for the main door to swing open. Tears of relief stung my eyes when Billy clambered in, rolling a breakfast trolley towards me.

"Good morning, Hope."

"Good morning, Billy." I jumped up, hugging him tight. He tensed, then I felt his body relax and his arms folded around me, a warmth spreading to my toes as he stroked my hair. Tears choked in my throat and I burrowed my face into his shoulder. He smelled of washing powder and soap. Wholesome and warm.

"Please help me, Billy." I pulled back, squeezing his hand. "I can't stand it in here."

His bottom lip trembled as he tried to catch the tears sliding down my cheek.

He shook his head. "Can't. I'd get in trouble." He pulled away from me, turning to the breakfast trolley, taking off the silver lid from the large serving dish to reveal a full cooked breakfast, black pudding and all. I balked at the smell of it. "I've got nice food for you this morning."

I sighed, sitting on the bed, pulling the blanket back over my shoulders. "It's so cold in here."

He nodded. "It's because there's no heater or fire." He looked at my blanket. "I'll bring you a warm sleeping bag later."

I smiled. "Thank you, Billy." I hoped he was going to be bringing me all my meals too. "Where's Ryan today?"

"Helping Magrat with the party food."

Aidan's party. I thought of Phoenix and how she must be feeling. Knowing she was going to have to say goodbye. I asked Billy to sit with me as I ate breakfast, encouraging him to have the sausages and bacon which he did without much hesitation.

"What's happening in the house?" I asked, gulping down orange juice, trying to disguise the taste of the black pudding.

He told me in great detail about his chores and that he had made friends with a squirrel in the garden. "Pollock calls him chunky because he's a bit fat. Like me." He poked his tummy and laughed and I laughed along with him, feeling my anxiety unfurl. I moved in closer, comforted by his warmth. "Have you seen Seb much?" I asked, trying to sound casual, anxiety knotting in my gut.

Billy shrugged. "Sometimes. He helps with my chores. He cleans the toilets. He got locked in his room."

I laid down my plate. "Every day?"

"Maybe. Definitely when the girl was here."

I frowned. "What girl?"

Billy stared down at my plate, stealing another bit of bacon. "I don't know." He scratched his head. "Think it's a secret."

I reached for his hand, squeezing gently. "We're friends aren't we Billy?"

He nodded enthusiastically. "You're my only friend, 'part from Mrs Carmichael."

"You're my best friend in here," I said, keeping a hold of his hand.

He smiled shyly. "I've never had a best friend before."

"Best friends share secrets. You want to know one of mine?"

"Yes." His face brightened.

"I'm scared of the dark. It's why I hate it so much in here."

"Oh." His brow creased in a frown. He dropped my hand and stood up, fumbling in his pocket. He pulled out a set of keys and for one heart stopping moment I thought he was going to give me the set, allowing me to escape. Then I watched as he unwound a small pen. He clicked the top, shining a light at my face. "It's a torch. You take it. Click it when you get scared."

I took it gratefully. "The girl you mentioned, is

she living in the house now?"

Billy shook his head. "No, just visited. Dr Carmichael did a tour. I liked her hair, it was pink like the bon-bon sweets."

I stared at him. "Was she my age?"

"Probly." He got up, loading my plate on the trolley. "Saw her before. Clara nearly crashed into her car."

My heart sank. "She drove here?"

"Noo," Billy said impatiently. "Was in a car with another lady last time. This time Dr Carmichael drove her. Mrs Carmichael told me to be a good boy, to tell her it's nice here. It is nice here, so I didn't tell a lie."

"Who else did she talk to?" I sat forward.

"Don't know."

"What was her name?"

He placed the lid back over the serving dish, his face contorting in concentration. "Ana."

I jumped up. "Billy. That's my friend from school." I grabbed his arm, laughing. "She found me. She found us!"

Billy pulled his arm away and stepped back, looking confused. He started to wheel the trolley towards the door.

I followed after him, needing to hear more. "What happened when she was here? Is she still here?"

"Don't know." He fumbled with the keys.

"Billy," I pulled at his shirt, forcing him to turn round. "I need you to do me a big favour. Just our secret, okay?"

He looked at me hesitantly. "Will this get me in trouble?"

"No," I said quickly. "Not if you keep it a secret. If you see Ana again I need you to tell her that I'm in here, that I've been locked in and that I need her help.

Could you do that? Even if you can't speak to her, try and give her a note."

I saw the fear and uncertainty in Billy's eyes. I tried to focus my thoughts. "Imagine I got taken away Billy and you never saw me again. Would you be sad?"

"Yes," he answered straight away.

"I'd be sad too, if that happened to you. When I got taken here I never got to say goodbye to Ana. I think that made her sad."

"Oh." Billy nodded, like he understood. "So I tell her you're okay? It'll make her less sad."

I tried to be patient. "What I'd really like you to tell her is I'm locked in so that's why I haven't been in touch and that I need her help. Can you say that to her?"

"I will, Hope. If I see her I'll tell her."

"Okay. Thank you." I twirled the pen torch between my fingers, remembering that Billy sometimes got to leave the house. "Wait, let me write down the school she goes to. Just in case you get the chance to find her there."

Billy hopped from foot to foot, resisting then relenting as I took his hand and scribbled Oakridge on his wrist. I smiled, putting my finger to my lips. "Our secret."

He nodded solemnly.

As the door slammed shut I bounced up and down on the bed, laughing manically. "You did it, Ana. You found us. Come and get me."

*

The hours dragged. I paced the room, unable to sit still, pressing my ear against the walls closest to the door, straining to hear sounds. Thoughts in my head jumbled as I tried to figure out how Ana found herself inside the house. Billy's comment about Seb being locked in his room during her visit nagged at me. With both of us locked away how would she know we were here? I chewed on my nails, not wanting to believe she could get so close without realising the truth.

I kicked the wall in frustration, recoiling in pain. As I hobbled around in agony a thought circled my head. If I were to injure myself badly would they let me out and move me to the donation centre? Maybe, maybe not. There was a chance they would treat me in here. Or worse, leave me to rot.

I walked over to the bed and pulled back the pillow, the shard of glass glinting at me. It was sharp enough to cause real damage. Pain. I closed my eyes, balking at the thought. I picked it up, turning it gently in my hand. What if Ryan came back and found me injured, and didn't tell anyone? Just kept me here, vulnerable, like an injured animal. The thought made me panic. I shivered and shoved the glass back under the pillow, gritting my teeth in frustration.

I pulled out the pen key ring Billy had given me from my pocket, clicking the torch on and off, trying to calm the anxiety shooting through my body. I pictured the *Strength* tarot card I'd left behind in my locker for Ana to find, turning my hand over, drawing a lion's mane on my palm, transforming the hair into flames. "You have more strength than you know," I whispered, trying to convince myself it was true.

Words from the poem in Lucy's letter circled my head. I pushed my sleeve back, the pen pulling at my skin as I inked words up my arm.

Rage, rage against the dying of the light.

The turn of a key echoed in the silence. I dropped the pen in anticipation, thoughts of escape circling my head. *"Please, please, please,"* I realised I was whispering the plea out loud and didn't stop as I watched the iron door swing open.

Clara appeared in the doorway, a flicker of surprise at the sight of me standing like a praying nun. Her nose wrinkled and I realised I'd become accustomed to the stench of an open toilet.

I let my hands fall to my sides, waiting to hear the reason for her visit. I glanced behind her, realising I was disappointed not to see Ana, and in the same thought, how stupid I'd been to even think that could be a possibility.

Clara pursed her lips, gesturing for me to move forward. "It's time for your donation. You can have a shower first."

I practically ran out the open door, scared she would change her mind. As soon as my feet touched the rug out in the hall I had to resist the urge to run. If I ran where could I go? Instead, I threw myself against the wall, running my hands down the wallpaper, breathing in the fresh air, unable to stop tears of relief bubble from me.

"Hush," Clara patted me awkwardly on the back. "You're okay. Don't get hysterical."

"Please, don't put me back in there." I turned and grabbed her arm.

She pursed her lips in a warning and I dropped my grip. She looked me in the eye and for the first time I saw a glimmer of humanity, a softening. "That's your time in the Bothy over. I'm sure you've learned your lesson, yes?" I knew it wasn't up for debate, that from now on I had to play by the rules.

I nodded, wiping at my eyes, exhaustion washing over me.

"Good. Come along then."

I followed Clara along the corridor, my legs wobbly and weak. The sweet scent of her perfume was overwhelming after the stale air of the Bothy. Soon the sour odour from my body overpowered any other smell, and I balked, desperate to wash away the dirt and soothe my bones in hot water.

As Clara led the way I trailed behind, glancing over the balcony, hoping to catch sight of someone. *Not just someone. Seb. Or Ana.*

Sensing my hesitation Clara turned to me, "Everyone's in the donation centre. The staff are in the kitchen preparing food for later."

A wave of dizziness made me waver and I grabbed the balcony rail to steady myself. If I didn't feel so weak I would be tempted to run down to the kitchen and slap Ryan hard across the face. I stared at Clara's back as I followed her to my room. I was angry with her too. Her words of reassurance before the party had meant nothing. Everyone *was* entitled apart from us, the trial 'subjects.' An image of white mice running around a maze, clawing at walls flashed in my head and I realised it was another scene from my recurring nightmare.

I was relieved to see Clara unlock my door. It meant Stacey wouldn't have been able to raid my stuff. When Clara clicked on the light I had to restrain myself from running and throwing myself down on the bed. It had never looked so soft and welcoming. My eyes trailed to the bottles of water and basket of fruit laid out on the table by the window.

"To get your strength up before your donation," Clara explained. She glanced at her watch. "I'll come back for you in half an hour. Your bath towel is on the bed."

An irrational part of me wanted to turn and hug

her, confused by the conflicting emotion when a few minutes ago I wanted to grab and shake her in a rage.

"Why are you here?" The words tumbled from me before I had time to think. Her hand froze on the door handle.

"What do you mean?" Her smile was tight, but I saw a waver underneath the steely mask.

"Why do you allow this?" I rolled up the sleeve of my sweatshirt, to let her see the bruise blooming from the needle punctures. "You took my new life from me. When so much has already been taken from me."

For a moment I thought she was going to leave without saying anything. Then she shook her head, her voice so quiet I had to strain to hear the words. "Because I thought my father was doing good, that we were on the cusp of a groundbreaking scientific development that would save lives."

I stared at her. "Father?" The realisation of what she was saying hit me like a slap in the face.

She met my gaze. "All I know is we're all in too deep now. And life will be better for you if you play along. Remember that."

The door slammed shut behind her and I slumped on the bed, head spinning.

Chapter Thirty-Two
Hope

The 'Blood House' was empty when Clara hooked me up to a machine. I couldn't stop staring as she fastened the cuff, searching her face for traces of resemblance to the Carmichaels. Her steely eyes matched the doctor's and I realised her chin curved to a point, just like Mrs Carmichael. I couldn't believe I hadn't made the connection before. I glanced at her wedding ring and wondered if her husband knew about any of this, what he would think.

As she slid the needle in, the beeping and whirring of the machines matched the sensation inside my body. I pressed my head against the bed, squeezing hard on the red ball. Waves of nausea overwhelmed me and I grimaced.

"Everything okay?" Clara paused.

I shook my head. "Just feeling a bit sick."

"I'll fetch you some water. I knew we should have waited until tomorrow for this but what the doctor wants, the doctor gets."

She did nothing to hide the resentment in her tone. I sat up, watching as she headed towards the fridge at her desk. Her hand shook as she opened a bottle and poured water into a plastic cup. I held her gaze as she walked back towards me, thanking her. As she turned to go, I asked if she'd sit with me for a while.

Her face told me sitting with me was the last place she wanted to be but then she relented and reached for a chair, the metal legs scraping against the floor as she dragged it to the side of my bed. We sat in silence and I wondered how to start the conversation, to get her to tell me the things I wanted to know.

"Go ahead, ask your questions," Clara said. Her directness was encouraging, but it also made me nervous.

"Have you always worked with your dad?"

"Only when the trials started. Suddenly my nursing qualification wasn't so insignificant after all."

I frowned, wondering what she meant. I didn't need to wait for her to explain.

"I've always been a disappointment, you see. Firstly, that I was a girl, secondly that I didn't get good enough grades to study medicine. But then my job as a community nurse became very important for my father's little operation here. As soon as he heard I had access to young people in the care system he started talking to me like an equal."

I thought back to our first meeting in her office. The blood test, the questions. "You interview us and test us. To see if we're suitable?" I said it without accusation, wanting Clara to keep talking.

She nodded. "You were high risk. Ms Turnberry didn't like the fact you'd settled so well. As soon as you make connections…friends…you're missed. They don't like complications." Clara made a face. "But then your bloods came back. A universal plasma donor. Suddenly you were gold." She made a chi-ching sound and I glared.

She shook her head dismissively. "I don't mean to sound crass. But it is crass, isn't it?"

I squeezed the ball harder, wondering why she was so dismissive of a practice she was clearly such a big part of. I didn't react, waiting for her to continue.

"I only got involved because of my mother. Her mental capacity deteriorated at such a rapid rate I needed to know if this could work. I didn't care at what cost. That's the simple truth. I wanted my mum back. When I lost someone else dear to me it only strengthened that desire." She twisted the gold ring on her finger, and I realised she must mean her husband.

You got your mum back. It was all I could do to stop spitting the words in her face. But then I considered. If someone were to tell me I could get my mum back, even for one day, what would I be prepared to do? Maybe anything.

"But nothing is simple, really. Not when you do a deal with the devil."

Who was the devil? Dr Carmichael?

"This whole thing," she made a swooping gesture with her arm. "It's much bigger than this now. I'd like it to stop but too many powerful people want it to continue. They've become seduced by the idea of being part of some elite 'Forever Young' club. They've got the money and they're prepared to pay for the purest of plasma transfusions in the hope they can live longer, healthier lives. But those men, the way they were with you. I worry I've been naïve."

I was taken aback by her honesty. A sense of dread weighed at me, wondering if she meant she was naïve to think the demands would stop at our plasma. I wanted to ask more, but I could hear the subtle change in the whir of the machine indicating my blood was returning to my body and Clara stood, taking my cup from me.

"I'll get you some chocolate. Lie back and relax, you might feel a bit faint."

As I listened to the sound of Clara's steps retreating something niggled. I thought back to the conversation I'd had with Billy about Mrs Carmichael: *She never had a baby.* Maybe he'd got confused, perhaps Mrs Carmichael meant she'd never had a boy. Clara said the fact she'd been a girl was a disappointment. The few times I'd seen them together they never appeared close, which also didn't make sense when Clara sounded so desperate to help her get better.

But there would be no reason for Clara to lie about being the Carmichaels' daughter. I rubbed at my eyes. My head was too foggy to focus on any complex thoughts.

Clara re-appeared with my chocolate and juice. She glanced at the clock on the wall. "There's a special dinner tonight before Aidan's party. You've to report to the ballroom in a couple of hours. Viv will have left your dress in your room."

I blinked in surprise, presuming I would have already missed his party. Images of handsy old men flashed through my head, the chocolate sticking in the back of my throat.

"Don't worry," she smiled tightly. "No outside guests for this party."

I breathed a sigh of relief, relaxing back against the chair. A tingling wound up my spine at the thought of being reunited with Seb.

*

The dress was black as midnight, tiny satin red roses sewn into spirals on the corseted bodice and woven through the full skirt which flounced when I moved. My body looked and felt like it had shrunk, more bones than flesh. I tied the ribbons tighter at the back.

It felt safer to be sharp than soft. I imagined stamping on Ryan's toes. My feet played out the action, the stiletto heel of my shoe grinding deep into the carpet. Light reflected against the red satin, making them look slippery like blood.

I selected a dark burgundy lipstick from my make-up bag, watching the effect it had on my face as I layered it on, my eyes glowing greener, my skin shining whiter. I would be obedient, but I wasn't going to look like a push-over. My long-sleeved bolero lay abandoned on the bed. I wanted to flaunt my damage and allow everyone to see the bruises and indents running up and down my arms.

As I descended the staircase music floated up from the ground floor and a mixture of intoxicating food aromas circled the air. I took the steps slowly, holding my skirt so as not to trip. A gust of wind and slam of the main door caused me to pause on the final step. A dark figure strode across the entrance hallway and my heart thudded.

Seb stopped abruptly, staring up at me. He too was more bones than flesh, his cheekbones and eyes hollow under the lights. But still handsome. Now, hauntingly so.

"Hope." My name sounded like a sigh of relief on his lips.

Tears stung my throat and I swallowed them away, running to him.

He caught me in a hug and I held on tight, burrowing my face in his neck, breathing in his scent.

"I was so worried," his voice cracked as he grabbed me tighter, squeezing as if to check I was really there.

"Me too," I whispered in his ear.

"Are you okay?" He held me at arm's length, his eyes a mixture of concern and anger. "I wanted to get you out the Bothy but they kept me locked in my room when I wasn't being their slave."

I nodded. "That night…I never got to thank you."

His eyes flashed. "I won't let them hurt you."

"Well, isn't this sweet. Hope and Seb the reunion."

My body tensed as I registered the voice. Seb turned and pulled a protective arm around my waist.

Ryan rolled a trolley full of food along the hall, his eyes scanning my body. "It won't be long before you're back in there, Hope. I know you're disappointed we didn't get to seal the deal."

I tightened my grip on Seb as he made a move towards Ryan, holding him close until Ryan disappeared from view.

"What does he mean?" Seb said through gritted teeth.

Don't make me explain, I wanted to beg him.

"Did he hurt you?"

It depends on your definition of hurt.

Seb pulled back, his eyes serious as he looked down at me. "You're never going back in there, okay? We have to make a plan to get out of here."

A bolt of excitement shot through me, quickly followed by doubt. I started to ask him how and he shook his head.

"Let's talk about it later. They'll be waiting for us."

We entered the ballroom hand-in-hand. Viv and Clara exchanged an eyebrow raise, but we didn't drop our grip. It felt like we'd made a silent agreement that from now on we were a partnership. Us against them. It made me feel stronger.

The room was illuminated with candles and fairy lights, the log fire roaring at the back of the room adding to the warmth and beauty. A long oak table was set for dinner, curving into a U-shape, laid with silver cutlery and intricate centrepieces composed of artificial red roses and green foliage. To one side of the room Margaret and Ryan piled plates with party finger food and Pollock uncovered silver serving dishes filled with roast meats and vegetables. Stacey and a couple of the boys were already seated at the table. Stacey fidgeted, pulling at her silk pink dress, which clung to her body. Her hair was scraped back, make-up brash and smudged. Her plate was piled with food and she nibbled impatiently on mini pizzas, a scowl on her flushed face. There was no sign of Phoenix or Aidan or the Carmichaels.

As Seb and I took our seats Viv and Clara circled with wine and beer.

"A one-off treat tonight," Viv winked as she filled my glass with red liquid.

"Your favourite, Seb." She poured a dark beer into his glass, the woody smell bringing back memories of Friday nights at the O'Brians.

As they moved round the table, Seb leaned in close. "Don't drink the alcohol."

"Why not?" I frowned.

"Every time they have one of these leaving parties, I never remember how I've got to bed and wake up from a dreamless sleep. I always thought it was low tolerance to alcohol but I'm not so sure. I want to stay fully alert tonight and I want you to stay with me."

My heart jolted at the last part. His face flushed and he laughed nervously.

"I mean, I want you to stay alert with me."

The doors swung open and Phoenix and Aidan walked in, arm in arm. Phoenix looked stunning in a jewel green strapless ball gown, her curls pinned half-up, secured with peacock feather clips. She laughed as Aidan leaned in to whisper something in her ear. He looked handsome and older than his eighteen years, dressed in a dark navy suit.

The Carmichaels followed behind, Mrs Carmichael dressed in a flowing red dress which complimented Dr Carmichael's red bow tie and ruby coloured waistcoat.

As Phoenix took her seat beside me she grinned. "I'm glad you're back."

"Me too." I was confused at her exuberance. I'd expected her to be inconsolable, having to say goodbye to Aidan.

Aidan squeezed my shoulder before taking his place at Phoenix's other side. "Glad to have you back, Hope. Don't let them grind you down."

Margaret hovered by our seats, encouraging us to take our plates to the food table to help ourselves. She avoided eye contact, wringing her hands and darting back to pour drinks. Perhaps she felt bad about me being locked in the Bothy. She'd feel even worse if I told her what a creep her nephew was.

At the food table Phoenix and Aidan laughed and joked with Ryan and Pollock. I glared at Ryan any time he glanced my way, fantasising about pouring hot soup over his head. I waited until Phoenix had finished her conversation then walked her back to the table.

"What's going on? Why are you and Aidan so happy?" I asked.

She hesitated, then leaned in closer to whisper, "I wasn't supposed to say anything until the announcement later. I'm pregnant so the Carmichaels are letting me leave tonight with Aidan so we can be together."

I tried to process her words. Pregnant. Leaving. *Pregnant.* I had to stop myself from blurting out, *But you're only sixteen.* I stared at her, not knowing what to say. She hurried back to the table, taking her seat by Aidan's side, their heads tilted close as they talked about their future.

As I took my own seat Seb shot me a curious look and I wondered if I looked as sick as I felt. I watched as the Carmichaels took their seats at the head of the table and a shiver shot up my spine. I wanted to believe Phoenix was heading towards her happy ending but it all seemed too easy.

Chapter Thirty-Three
Ana

The contract shook in Ana's hands as she climbed the stairs to her room. The words jumbled on the page as she tried to remember everything Dr Carmichael had said; images of scientific graphs and reports still flashing through her head. And the house. A luxurious mansion. Who wouldn't want to live in a house like that? Hope would never find that kind of life, here in Oakridge.

Ana's phone beeped. A taunting reminder of the first part of her deception.

She held her breath, heart thumping as she read Elliot's message:

Ana, you can't message something like that and not answer your phone! I'm coming over.

She swore. She should have known Elliot wouldn't leave it at that. Ana sighed, hitting call. He answered on the first ring.

"What happened?" His voice was frantic.

She paused, trying to get the lie straight in her head. "Hope called me when I was on the way to the Browns. I...got to see her new place. She's happy there, Elliot."

She could hear a million questions in his silence. "I don't understand. Did she say why she ignored us? It's been ages. Why is she suddenly calling you?"

"She said she missed us. That she was sorry but she's okay. She was embarrassed about the drug thing."

"She admitted to it?" Elliot sounded incredulous.

A stab of shame flushed through Ana's body. "I guess we didn't know her as well as we thought."

Elliot's breathing was loud in her ear. "It doesn't make sense. What was her new place like?"

A door slammed and Maisie called her name.

Ana squeezed her eyes shut, picturing the hurt and confusion on Elliot's face. "It seemed nice. It's like a home. There's other kids there our age."

"You need to tell the Browns."

Ana's door burst open and Maisie ran in, flinging herself on the bed. Ana turned away, gripping the phone closer to her ear.

"I will. I'll go to theirs later. I need to go just now. My sister is here." She disconnected the call, silencing Elliot's protest.

Maisie tugged at the papers on the bed. Ana slammed her hand down on them, shooting her sister a warning glare.

"Those are private."

Maisie made a face, rolling her eyes. "EVERYTHING in here is private. Was that your boyfriend?" She flipped her ponytail forward. "With the hair."

Ana stood up, ignoring her question. "Where's Mum and Dad?"

"Mum's having a nap. Dad's going to take us to the cinema. He told me to get you."

"I can't go."

"Anaaaa," Maisie whined, tugging on her jumper. Ana pushed her hands away.

There was a knock on Ana's door and Dad popped his head round. "You two ready?"

"Ana's not coming," Maisie sulked, folding her arms. "I don't want to go now."

Dad frowned. "Come on, Ana. Don't be a

spoilsport."

She shook her head. "I've got too much homework."

He searched her face. "Alright, I suppose you were already out at your friends for lunch. But don't disturb Mum. She needs her rest. Come on, toots. I'll get you that horrible blue slush you love."

Maisie relented immediately, a grin spreading across her face. She jumped off the bed, sticking her tongue out at Ana. "Later, loser."

Dad hesitated in the doorway and Ana waited expectantly. He ran a hand through his hair.

"I know Mum spoke to you about the test results," he started.

She nodded, body tensing.

"We've got an appointment booked to talk about medication your mum can start taking. It's good we have these options to explore."

As Dad continued talking it was if his words slowed and warped, the names of the medication sounding like a foreign language. Dr Carmichael's contract burned between Ana's fingers. *This is the medication she needs*, she wanted to say.

"Are you okay, Ana?" Dad looked her straight in the eye.

Ana nodded, trying to smile. "I'm glad they can give her stuff to help."

Dad kissed her on the forehead. "We don't want you to worry. I hope we've made the right decision sharing this with you." He squeezed her in a hug and pictures of Mrs Carmichael's before and after pictures flashed through Ana's mind.

"Mum can have another chat with you after her nap. There's some pizza in the freezer. Maybe wait a bit, then put some on for you both?"

The thought of food made her tummy churn. She managed to convince Dad she would survive and was relieved when Maisie ran back in, tugging him out the door.

The house fell silent and Ana pulled out the contract again, reading through the words, trying to put the thought of Elliot's call and the Browns out of her head as she waited for Mum to wake up, practising what she would say.

*

Mum read the contract in silence, every once in a while chewing on a slice of pizza and pushing her glasses up. Ana tried to read her expression, desperate to ask what she thought but she knew she had to give her time to absorb the information. Mum read it over again, spending longer on the case studies within the final pages.

"It's impressive," Mum took off her glasses. "But I still don't understand. Why does Dr Carmichael want to offer this to me free of charge? You should have woken me up when he came to the door."

Ana shifted uncomfortably at that lie, figuring Mum's nap gave her the perfect excuse to explain he had brought it here. She thought back to Dr Carmichael's coaching. It was crucial Ana made this part sound convincing or Mum and Dad would never get on board.

"He realised after we'd spoken that he didn't have anyone as young as you receiving transfusions for the purposes of helping Alzheimer's. He said you would give his trials another layer, that if you react positively to the transfusions then it gives his theories much more clout when he eventually presents this to the medical world."

Mum nodded slowly. "I suppose that makes sense.

I did start reading up on all of this you know, after that visit."

Ana brightened. "You did?"

"And to be honest after my results I think I'd like to try anything that might help. I'm curious though, who donates for him?"

How many lies are you capable of telling? Ana didn't look her in the eye as she parroted another part of Dr Carmichael's speech. Young students, keen to be involved in scientific developments and contribute to a humanitarian cause. She pictured Phoenix, the look of defiance on her face as she told Ana not to ruin this for them. Ana tried not to think of Hope, to block out what she would think if she could hear her lies. How she would feel, knowing Ana had left without a fight, without properly checking on her.

Ana's phone flashed, indicating a message from Elliot. She turned the phone over, trying to ignore the stab of hurt at the thought of betraying him too.

She watched as a smile played on Mum's lips when she re-read the case studies.

We're doing good things here. Dr Carmichael's voice boomed clear in her head. *You're a smart girl, Ana. I know you'll make the right choice.*

Chapter Thirty-Four
Hope

The music throbbed through my body, as Seb took my hand and led me onto the dance floor, the past few days melting into oblivion. I laughed as he bowed, his eyes shining with mischief and humour. For now, it was just us, on the dance floor, bathed in light. I let him lead me and spin me, enjoying the feeling of falling against him, of being held. It had been so long since someone pulled me close, with real affection. Apart from Billy's clumsy cuddle, I couldn't remember the last time someone held me in their arms.

"What are you thinking?" He murmured in my ear, his lips electricity against my skin.

That I want to stay in your arms forever, but I'm scared. Because I like it too much. And you're going to leave me soon. "Phoenix told me she's pregnant," I blurted.

Seb pulled back in shock.

"Keep dancing," I whispered in his ear. "Apparently the Carmichaels are letting her leave tonight, with Aidan." I could feel the tension radiating through his body, and instantly regretted ruining our carefree moment.

As Seb spun me further around the floor his attention diverted to Phoenix. "She's still got ages before she turns eighteen. Maybe they don't want the complication of a baby? Or does it affect her plasma? I think it stops the antibodies." He seemed to be talking to himself, rather than me.

"You'll be leaving soon, too," I murmured. *I don't want you to leave without me.*

He squeezed my shoulder. "Not without you. I won't leave you behind." His eyes flashed with determination.

I thought back to what he'd said earlier about making a plan to get out of here. I held on to his hand tighter, wanting to believe it could be possible. I watched as Aidan held Phoenix close, her head resting on his shoulder. He kissed her tenderly on the forehead and a jolt of something like envy shot through me. They were breaking free together and he looked so protective of Phoenix. *Maybe*...I ran a hand down my stomach. If it was the only way to ensure I could leave, could I? Would Seb support me?

A hand clamped down on my shoulder, crushing bones. I flinched as Barbara Carmichael smiled in my face, revealing cerise lipstick stains on her teeth. She handed me a glass of ruby red wine. "Drink up, young lady. This is a party."

I took the glass, glancing at Seb and he nodded swiftly. The liquid was warm and burned my throat as I took a gulp. Barbara raised her chin, eyes flashing in satisfaction. "There's a good girl. It's not so hard, doing what you're told, is it?" She touched Seb on the back. "You make a fine couple."

Seb's frown mirrored my own confusion.

"She seems chirpy this evening," I commented, staring down at the remains of wine in my glass. "This tastes weird."

"Let's get more food." Seb pulled me towards the table at the back of the room and took my glass from me. Checking no one was watching he poured the remaining liquid into a discarded plate of casserole.

Phoenix appeared at our side, piling her plate with

mini pizzas. "Won't be long before your leaving party, Seb."

The smile froze on my lips. Seb shrugged. "I still have a few weeks. Hope told me your news."

Phoenix smiled, laying a hand on her stomach. "Gives me an excuse to eat like a pig." She turned to observe the dance floor. "I'm actually going to miss this place."

Seb scoffed, "You're kidding?"

The smile disappeared from Phoenix's face. "I feel safe here. There's a lot, out there, that could go wrong." She shook her head, brow furrowing. "I don't want to muck up my kid's life, you know?" Her hand trembled as she laid down her plate. "I don't want to end up like my mum."

Seb squeezed her shoulder. "You'll be an amazing mother. And Aidan will be with you. He'll look after you." Seb glanced at her stomach. "Both of you."

Phoenix didn't look convinced. She nodded towards the dance floor where Aidan contorted his body in a break-dancing routine with his brother. "He's going to miss, Scott. You'd better look out for him."

"Scott can look after himself, but I'll make sure he's okay."

The music stopped and the doors opened to reveal Margaret wheeling in a large cake, candles dancing around the perimeter. Aidan whooped. "Chocolate, my favourite. You're a legend, Mags!"

Aidan nearly knocked Margaret off her feet, pulling her into an awkward bear hug. She batted him away, lifting the cake onto the dining table as the room erupted into an out of tune rendition of happy birthday.

Phoenix didn't sing, her expression hard to read as

she watched Aidan blow out the candles into smoke. Her green dress flowed out behind her, a majestic bird in flight as she ran across the floor, grabbing Aidan's hands, pulling him to dance.

I watched as Margaret handed a knife to Dr Carmichael, her face sickly pale under the lights. She edged away, slumping into a seat, gulping down a glass of wine and wiping a hand across her brow. Ryan took a seat next to her and she squeezed his hand, the only outward sign of affection I had ever seen her display towards her nephew. Ryan sat rigid, observing the scene with a serious look on his face. A cold dread washed over me as I looked to the other staff – Clara and Viv and Pollock. None of them smiled, their dinner lay untouched. Clara stood beside the fire, arms folded, watching the younger boys downing bottles of beer. The Carmichaels raised a toast to Aidan and Phoenix and none of the staff joined in.

"Something isn't right." I grabbed Seb's hand. "I have a bad feeling." My chest constricted, as if saying it out loud gave my body permission to panic.

Seb laced his fingers through mine. "Just act normal," he whispered as Viv approached with two bottles of beer.

"To toast your friends."

Seb raised the bottle and nodded, flashing her a grin. As soon as she turned her back, he poured the contents into a bowl of soup. He swapped the empty bottle with my full one, and told me to look like I was drinking.

Dr Carmichael cut into the cake, the silver blade flashing under the crystal lights of the chandelier. He laid portions on plates, Mrs Carmichael passing them down the table. Stacey wavered in her seat, fingers stabbing at the cake, frosting smearing across her hand. Her head lulled forward, then jolted up, eyes blinking. She turned to Scott, mouth slack, body falling against him. He shrugged her off, then laughed as her cheek smacked down on the table, arms flopping like a rag doll. Clara rushed over, catching her from behind, signalling to Viv. They pulled Stacey upright and Viv slung Stacey's arm over her shoulder. They dragged her from the table, her shoes sliding off her feet as they hauled her across the room. Scott was still laughing with Joe, then his head drooped and he fell against him. Joe shoved Scott causing him to slam forward, forehead smacking against the table. This time Pollock rushed over, pulling Scott from his seat, cutlery clattering as Scott's hand dragged along the table.

I was only aware I'd started to edge forwards when I felt Seb tug from behind.

"Act like you've not noticed," he hissed in my ear. "Give it a few minutes then slump against me. We'll wait until all of the staff are preoccupied."

It was like watching a contagious sleeping disease spread across the room, limbs loosening, heads bowing. Dr Carmichael presented Aidan and Phoenix with a white envelope, arms slung across their shoulders, directing them towards the double doors at the back of the room, holding them captive with his words, preventing them from witnessing the scene.

I staggered and slumped against Seb, allowing him to half-drag me across the room, closing my eyes for added effect, fighting against my instinct to keep watching, to stay alert. I trusted Seb to lead us. The pulse in my neck throbbed as his steps quickened, his grip tightening as he pulled me to him, holding me close.

I felt him kick a door open and cool air fanned against my face, the music fading behind us.

"We're about to go up the staircase. Let me carry you," he whispered.

I positioned myself so he could easily hook his arms under me, my head lolling against his shoulder as we swayed onto the first step. His breathing was shaky and strained as he began the ascent. I felt his body jolt, the pounding of his heart more pronounced against my ear. I tensed in anticipation, my eyelids fluttering, knowing someone was there.

"Hope?"

It was Billy. His voice tentative, worried, above us.

"It's okay, Billy. I'm taking Hope to her room. We're both very sleepy."

Silence. A shuffle of feet. "You all need to be in bed."

"Yes, that's where we're going."

"I need to be in bed too. Mrs Carmichael told me I can have extra cookies if I go now."

"Lucky you. You'd better hurry."

A clamber of feet, a hesitation, a sweaty hand against my cheek. "Night night, Hope."

I held my breath until I heard him clump down the remainder of the stairs.

"Not far," Seb whispered, shifting the weight of me. I felt the muscles contract in his arms and his steps quickened as we hit level ground. He lowered me gently, my feet touching onto the landing. "Get in, quick." He opened my bedroom door, half shoving me inside as we heard Clara and Viv's voices along the corridor. He left the door ajar, pulling me down onto the bed.

"Lie flat, look dead to the world. We have to let

them see us."

I wanted to laugh at the absurdity of it but did as he said, acutely aware of his fingers brushing against mine as my back sank down against the duvet. My heart hammered as Clara and Viv's voices got louder.

"They'll be arriving in half an hour. Enough time…" Clara halted mid-sentence. My door squeaked as she pushed it open. A pause. "Hope? Seb?" Another pause.

A trembling shot up my legs and I tensed, willing my body to stay still. My heart was thumping so hard I was sure they would hear. I held my breath when I sensed her walking towards the bed. She lifted my arm, the unexpected contact nearly making my heart jump out of my chest. Her hand drew back fast and I let my arm drop.

"I was worried they hadn't drunk enough," Clara said. The heavy sweetness of her perfume shot up my nose as she hovered over me.

"I gave them more beer. Come on, we'd better get ready."

Every inch of my body ached as I tried to lie as still as possible. I didn't move until I heard the door shut, their voices fading. Seb sprang up beside me as a key turned in the door.

"Shit." He slammed a hand down on the duvet. "I didn't think they'd lock us in."

I sat up, my head spinning from the strain of pretending to be unconscious. "We never got to say goodbye to Aidan and Phoenix."

Seb shot me a look that said, *That's what you're most concerned about*? He slid off the bed and I wanted to grab his arm, to bring back the warmth and comfort of his body beside me. He crept towards the door, trying the handle, then peered through the keyhole. "At least they've not left the key in the door. Have you got anything small and sharp?"

I pointed to the dressing table. "There's some Kirby grips there." As Seb attempted to jigger the lock I wandered over to the window, squinting through the glass as I realised the main gates to the grounds were beeping open. I hurried over to the bedside table, flicking off the lamp.

"Hey," Seb called.

"Sorry. I want to see." I watched as a row of cars rolled into the grounds, winding round to the parking bay. "People are arriving."

Seb stumbled through the darkness towards me. "Maybe it's a car arriving to take Aidan and Phoenix away?"

I shook my head. "I don't think so. There's like, four, five cars." I squinted, straining to see as doors swung open. My eyes scanned the parking bay, holding my breath at the thought of Ana, coming back and bringing help. My heart sank when my eyes fell upon a black Porsche. A shiver ran down my spine. "I know that car."

"Why are more people arriving?" Seb's breath steamed up the glass.

I opened the window a crack, a buzz of laughter and greetings echoing across the grounds. The air fizzed with excitement and anticipation. We stood side by side, watching as the party snaked along the grounds, Dr Carmichael walking down to greet them with a commanding wave, gesturing them forwards.

Seb clicked the lamp back on, rushing back to the door, jiggling the lock again. "Get changed into something warm and black, something that will make you blend in to the darkness. If you've got a hoodie I can borrow, get that out too."

I did as he said, raking through my wardrobe, hands shaking as I tried to find something suitable. I tried to process what was going on. The door clicked and I turned to see Seb flash me a victory thumbs up as he tried the handle. I threw an assortment of clothes on the bed, hesitating as I untied the bodice of my dress. Our eyes locked, a frisson passing between us. Seb turned away first, his back to me as he pulled off his shirt, my eyes trailing his body, heart jolting when I saw a familiar horseshoe shaped burn, remembering Phoenix's scarred skin. But this was fresh, red welts indenting up and down his spine. Instinctively I rushed towards him, fingers tracing the scars.

His body tensed at my touch, eyes flashing a kaleidoscope of emotions as he turned to grab my hand; fear, pain, something else... His grip loosened and he pressed my hand against his heartbeat, the pulse throbbing through my fingertips.

"Who did that?" I asked. "The horseshoe burn. Phoenix has one too...did they do that, *in here*?"

He didn't answer, his eyes darkening. His gaze lingered on my lips and suddenly all I could think about was the sensation of my fingers against his skin. My heart exploded as he pulled me closer, my skin electrified as he cupped my cheek. His lips touched mine and the room spun into oblivion. His lips were warm and soft as he kissed me slowly, tentatively. He tasted of beer and something delicious. I wanted to lose myself inside him, to feel every part of him.

"No." I surprised us both as I pulled back, shoving at his chest.

He looked shocked, wounded.

"I mean..." I tried to grab his hand, his fingers

slipping through mine as he jerked away. "Not right now." *Not when I might lose you.*

He was already pulling one of my baggy t-shirts over his head, grabbing a hoodie, turning his back on me.

"Seb," I tried to coax him to turn around.

His expression was closed, defensive. "You should get dressed."

I swallowed the regret seeping through me. Didn't he understand? I pulled a jumper over my head, tugging the dress to the floor, stepping into a pair of black jeans. The images of the red welts flashed in my head and I realised he had evaded my question. I'd presumed Phoenix's horseshoe shaped burn was from before, from her other life. I wanted to ask who had done this, and why. Were the fresh wounds because of the Gold night? Suddenly the Bothy didn't seem so bad.

"Ready?" Seb opened the door a crack and I stood, legs wobbly at the prospect of what might lie ahead. But a spark of anger flamed at the thought of someone harming Seb, of making him suffer.

I tied my hair up, tightening the knot. "Let's go."

Chapter Thirty-Five
Hope

The house was silent as we edged our way down the staircase, eyes scanning the vast entrance hallway. A single orange lamp glowed below, our shadows dancing down the walls. I stared at the main door, wondering what we would do if the group of guests flooded in.

The ticking of the grandfather clock was pronounced as we crept along the polished floors, bodies tense, poised for confrontation or a fast getaway. I wanted to ask Seb if he had a plan. He motioned for me to come closer as we approached the entrance to the ballroom. The oak doors were closed, music silenced, the party over. Seb pressed his ear to the wooden panels, shaking his head to indicate no noise. A crash echoed down the hallway and we both jumped, my nails digging into Seb's arm as I grabbed him in fright.

"Ow," he whispered, rubbing his arm.

"Sorry." I loosened my grip but didn't let go, straining to see or hear clues as to where the noise originated.

A clatter of pans and a familiar lilt pierced the silence. The kitchen.

"Probably clearing up," I murmured. Seb tugged me forward. I resisted, flashing him a questioning stare. "We can't let Margaret see us."

"She won't." He shrugged me off and I hung back, debating about following. After a few minutes, curiosity got the better of me and I joined him at the door, straining to hear the sounds inside. Lots of clattering of dishes, water running.

"I'll do the last of the dishes. You get down to the furnace."

"Plenty of time, Aunty. They'll be another hour at least."

"Not tonight. They want this one to be quick. The girl's already in the annexe."

"You always do that."

I could picture Ryan's smirk. Margaret's response was clipped, impatient. "Do what?"

"Stop calling them by their names. On their last night."

"It's not her last night," Margaret's voice was cold, devoid of her cheery sing-song tones.

"May as well be. She's not important anymore."

Seb and I exchanged looks. Who were they talking about?

"Get on your way, boy. You know it's not a good night to get complacent. Any wrong moves…"

"Alright, Aunty. You know how I like to burn things."

My body tensed at Ryan's guffaw, the image of his beady eyes flashing in my head, cold lips slobbering across my skin. I shuddered and Seb touched my hand in reassurance, misinterpreting my reaction as fear. He nodded to indicate that we needed to keep moving along the corridor.

Margaret and Ryan's conversation circled my head as Seb led us further towards the back of the house. If the girl was Phoenix why would she have been taken to the annexe? And why was Ryan to start a furnace?

Goose bumps bloomed along my arms as Seb stopped at a rusted door I'd never noticed before, hiding down a narrow corridor off the library. He cranked it open, a musty smell like old carpets seeping out of the darkness.

"It leads to the basement that runs under this floor," Seb explained. "There's a small window we can climb out to get to the gardens. Just to warn you, there's lots of spiders down there, sometimes rats. You're not scared are you?"

I shot him a look that told him not to patronise me and he rewarded me with a lopsided smile.

"I think we should check the Club House first?"

I nodded, thinking the same; the well-dressed guests had to be Gold members. But tonight was clearly a private party they didn't want us to be part of.

To hide my fear I stepped in front, leading us into the darkness.

The flickering lanterns lighting the path indicated our hunch had been right. Low lighting glowed inside the Club House but there was no music and the doors at the main entrance were closed, curtains drawn, offering no clue as to what lay within.

We hurried around the side of the building, foliage scraping my hands, plants stabbing my face as we squeezed through a gap that led to the back of the house, the Gold bar. I traced a finger along a cut on my cheek, flinching at the nip. There was no glass at this section, a wall of red bricks providing us no viewpoint. We followed the curve of the building to a fire exit at the back, a yellow light buzzing above the door.

Seb turned to me, his face pale beneath the artificial glow. "I reckon this door will lead to the corridor winding back from the main bar. It's got a release handle from this side. I'm hoping it just turns and doesn't have a lock."

"It might be alarmed though." A shiver convulsed through my body, a part of me wishing I'd just downed the alcohol laced with sleep inducing drugs. Obliviousness held an attraction right now. Whatever was going on here, did we really need to know?

Seb's expression was determined and defiant. I knew I would never be able to persuade him to turn back. He'd been here longer than me, had more time to wonder and had experienced the memory blanks from previous farewell parties.

I relented, nodding, and he stepped forward. The handle turned freely, followed by a click which released the door. We paused, one beat, two. No shrill cries. Seb had been right, as we made our way inside. Symbols on the doors indicated we were at the toilets, set back from the bar. We crept towards a metal door leading into the main section of the bar. Seb motioned for me to crouch behind him, as he peered through the glass panel which stretched down the middle of the door. My cheek rested against his shoulder, body pressed against his back as I craned to see.

Red lights glowed from the ceilings, burning down on a group of people standing in a circle. The bar was cleared of tables, creating an open space for them to congregate. Something in the middle of the circle held their attention, but the backs of the people closest to the door obscured our view. I held my breath as Seb cracked the door open a slither, allowing us to hear.

The low boom of Dr Carmichael's voice echoed around the room, mutters of appreciation falling and rising in time with his measured speech.

"And tonight let us all drink to the promise that I offer you. Of cures from ailments, of the youth that we all chase. Let us give thanks. Let us appreciate the life this boy will sacrifice to bring us this good fortune."

I gripped Seb's arm as the group dispersed, heads tilting towards the ceiling. Music rumbled from the speakers, a melody of string instruments and piano staccato in a minor key quickening and heightening. The lights dimmed and I whispered in Seb's ear.

"What is this, some kind of weird church meeting?"

Before Seb had the chance to answer, spotlights clicked on one by one along the central section of the ceiling, illuminating a large throne sized chair on a raised platform, gold vines twisting along the back, red jewels set into the metalwork, winking under the lights. There was a break in the music and panicked shouts pierced through my heart.

Two masked women in white medical uniforms gripped the chair, one reaching over to straighten wires which extended from the side. I strained to make them out, wondering if Clara hid behind one of the masks. I grabbed Seb's arm at the cries for help, recognising the voice instantly.

The music rose to a crescendo and the chair spun to face us, revealing a pale boy, naked apart from white shorts, a familiar scar even more pronounced against his sickening pallor. His face contorted in terror as he blinked at the audience in front of him. His legs flailed helplessly against the metal chains which secured his ankles to the chair. His arms rested each side of the throne, wrists secured in metal casings, palms facing up, wires winding along his skin.

"You bastard. You promised me freedom. You promised us freedom." Aidan strained against the restraints, staring down at the wires. "What the hell are you doing? You bunch of psychos."

Not wires... it hit me like a thump in my chest. Tubes, cannulas. Spiralling into bags of blood, hanging in rows along a silver pole, connecting to elevated Hookah type instruments like the ones used on the Gold night. One of the masked medical staff motioned for a member of the audience to come forward. I watched as a familiar plump figure strode towards the throne, a silk purple dress moulded around her frame, hair piled high in a bun. She had dressed for the occasion. As Ms Turnberry held out her arm, she tilted her head, smiling as she connected with the Hookah. I wanted to run and rip her arm free and wipe the smug smile from her face along with it.

A strangled yelp gurgled low in my throat. Seb pulled me close against him, clamping a hand over my mouth, our heartbeats thrumming in unison.

Dr Carmichael stepped into the middle of the circle, raising a glass. "Let us drink the eternal youth, let us feast together on this blessed night."

Bile rose in my throat as I watched Aidan twist on the throne, yelling in protest.

"Where did you take her? Where did you take Phoenix?" His voice was hoarse with tears.

I watched the crowd, willing them to react, to do something. A couple took a step back but they made no move to intervene. All stood watching, a hunger in their expressions.

I tried to free myself from Seb's grip but he was too strong. He held me fast.

"We have to help him," I hissed, tears stinging my eyes.

Seb shook his head, his tone defeated. "There's too many of them. We wouldn't stand a chance."

The roar of twisted celebration rang in my ears as Dr Carmichael turned to smile at his audience. "Let us drink his blood dry."

"They're going to kill him." I jumped up. "We can't just watch him die."

A hand grabbed the back of my hair, halting me and I yelped, shouting for Seb to let go. Then confusion as the hand yanked harder, pulling me backwards away from Seb. The fear in his eyes filled me with dread.

Nails dug into my neck and I spun to face Mrs Carmichael, her mouth set in a haggard smile, Pollock by her side. He rushed for Seb, stopping him intervening.

Mrs Carmichael hissed in my ear, "Don't worry, girl. You'll both be joining him, soon enough. But not yet. I think you've had enough excitement for one night." She clicked her fingers and Clara emerged from the shadows, a trace of apology in her eyes.

"Do you enjoy this?" The strength in my voice surprised me as Clara lifted a cloth towards my face. I glared at her. "Drugging me, time and time again. Your mum must be *so* proud."

Clara's face blurred, her eyes melting into her mouth, a drooping sadness, her words falling into my ear as I stumbled.

"That's not my mother. Mum would never want this for me."

Her words fell with me, into my heart.

My mum would never want this for me.

No. No. No.

Chapter Thirty-Six
Ana

The girl at the desk today wore too much make up, her lips an over-inflated pout. Her pink nails clicked against the keyboard as she typed; a rhythmic sound which did nothing to ease Ana's nerves. She wondered where Faye was, and why Dr Carmichael was late. Mum shifted beside her, gripping the magazine she was pretending to read, her knuckles whitening. Ana followed her gaze to the clock; quarter past ten. Her stomach clenched at the thought of the appointment following this; a visit to the Browns. She'd managed to evade their phone calls and invitations, citing family issues, which was strictly true. It was Elliot who had insisted on the meeting. Fed up with Ana's evasiveness at school, he probably hoped Martha would be able to get more out of her.

The phone at the desk rang, causing both Ana and her mum to jump. Ana listened as the girl made some noises along the lines of, "Uh, huh. Okay. Yes, no problem. Okay, see you soon." The girl stood, the wheels on her chair rolling loudly against the laminated section of floor under her desk. She stepped forward, her stiletto heels sinking into the carpet as she walked towards them. Her teeth were unnaturally white and straight as she smiled. "Dr Carmichael will be another ten minutes. He has asked me to take you along to the transfusion room to get you ready, Mrs Gilbert."

Mum blinked in surprise, placing her magazine

aside. She glanced at Ana. "Can my daughter come too?"

The girl tilted her head, eyeing Ana with a condescending stare. "If it's alright I think you should stay here, sweetie. I'll make you a hot chocolate if you want while you wait on your mum."

Ana nodded reluctantly, feeling about six years old. She shot Mum an apologetic smile, wondering if Dad would have been allowed in with her. Ana had asked to come and they hadn't put up much of an argument, deciding it would be easier if Dad took Maisie to her Saturday morning ballet class. Dad had been surprisingly upbeat about Dr Carmichael's offer of free transfusions, deciding it was exciting to be part of new trials, even if he was forbidden to tell a soul about them. Ana found it difficult to join in their enthusiasm, guilt gnawing at her.

"What about her note, on the tarot card?" Elliot had cornered Ana in the library at school. "She asked us to find her. Why would she do that if she was happy to go?"

Ana shrugged, pretending to be engrossed in the textbooks arranged on the table in front of her. "She wouldn't have understood where she was being taken at that point. Trust me, the house she's in, it's amazing."

"So why didn't Seb stay? And why didn't he get in touch when he left?" Elliot shut her textbook over, surprising her with his stubbornness. "You're hiding something."

The door slammed as Mum disappeared through to the clinic with the receptionist, interrupting Ana's thoughts. She glanced at the clock, wishing she'd brought a book to read. She scrolled through social media, absentmindedly clicking on Hope's one profile. Her account was private and she only had a small number of followers, mostly artists and creative companies and Ana and Elliot. Ana scrolled through her photos and a wash of guilt consumed her as she stopped at one of the two of them, not their faces, just their feet side by side, Ana's scuffed pink Converse, Hope's black Doc boots. Hope had written a message alongside it: My favourite friend, my favourite shoes #itsthelittlethingsinlifethatmatter.

Ana's hand shook as she read the words, over and over, her mind replacing the word 'favourite' with *'selfish, bad, loser, fake.'* She glanced at the closed door to the clinic. She hoped this was worth it.

*

Elliot was already on his second can of Coke by the time Ana arrived at the Browns, his leg jangling underneath the dining table, causing the cutlery to rattle. Martha offered her a sandwich and Ana took it to be polite, nerves stealing her appetite. She was relieved that Edward appeared to be out. Martha waited until Ana was settled with a drink until she launched into questions.

"Who's in charge of the house? What were the other young people like? How did Hope appear, is she okay? Do you think she'd agree to see us?"

Ana coughed as part of the sandwich stuck in her throat. She had let them believe she'd actually spoken to Hope, in a roundabout way, but now she was going to have to tell a direct lie. "She looked good. Happy." She gulped down the orange juice. "I think it's like a newer style residential house. Didn't Mr Hobbs explain that part?" Dr Carmichael had given Ana strict instructions to leave the detail of the house to Ian Hobbs. No big surprise that he was in on it. Dr Carmichael had been evasive when Ana asked about

Ruth, if she'd return to work.

Martha pursed her lips. "Yes, but I don't like that man. I don't trust him."

Ana caught Elliot staring. He was scrutinising her with a look that told her he didn't believe a word and it was unsettling. "I saw you and your mum coming out of Dr Carmichael's clinic this morning."

What? Ana stumbled over her words, thoughts whirring. "We...I...Why were *you* there?"

He folded his arms. "I cycled to the gates of the house. I tried the intercom again and asked to speak to Hope. But the woman who answered told me she had no idea who I was talking about. I saw you on my way back."

Martha laid down her napkin, curious eyes on Ana. Ana faltered, panic rising. It would have taken ages for him to cycle to the house. He clearly was not going to drop this.

"My mum had an appointment with him. I was there to keep her company."

"What kind of appointment?" Elliot's voice was flat and cold. It made her feel sick, the way he looked at her. Like she was a stranger to him.

"It's...private." Ana's face flamed and Martha obviously interpreted it as embarrassment.

"That's your mother's business, dear. I used to be friends with the Carmichaels, well Barbara really. I hear Finlay Carmichael is quite the successful doctor these days."

Ana looked at her in surprise.

"Why do you think the woman on the intercom claimed not to know who Hope was?" Elliot pressed, changing tact.

Ana shook her head, trying to think fast. "I don't know. I think they have really tight security; they like to keep the kids safe. She wouldn't want to disclose anything to a stranger."

"So how exactly did you get inside then? And it's not *that* far out of town so why can't Hope still attend our school?" Elliot was beginning to irritate Ana. Martha shot him a warning look, sensing the tension brewing between them.

"I already told you. Hope invited me. And they have private tuition on-site," Ana said through gritted teeth.

She turned her attention to Martha. "I'm sorry I can't tell you more. And I'm sorry she wouldn't give me a number. She said she needs time." Ana curled her fist into a ball, hating the sound of her voice, hating the sound of her lies. She poured herself more juice, hoping they didn't notice the tremble in her hand. "How do you know Barbara Carmichael?"

"Knew. I've not seen her in years. I believe she's in a home now," Martha's brow furrowed. "We used to go to school together. Got called the terrible twins which really riled her actual twin." She smiled, as if remembering.

"She has a twin?" Ana was careful to keep her emotions in check, conscious Elliot was still watching her every move. "An identical twin?"

"Yes, a sister, Patricia McLellan. Nothing like each other otherwise. Barbara was full of mischief, Pat was always so serious. She used to belittle poor Barb all the time. And liked to think of herself as the prettier sister. Barb has that heterochromia – one blue eye, one brown. She hated it, got quite self-conscious."

Ana thought back to her visit to the house, when Dr Carmichael introduced her to Barbara. Her cold steely blue eyes. Definitely blue, vivid like the blouse she'd worn. Maybe she hadn't noticed the brown?

"Does Patricia live local?" Ana asked.

Martha shook her head. "Last I heard she had some highfaluting career in Edinburgh managing a string of boutique shops. She always fancied herself as posh, even although the family were as common as mud really."

A coldness swept over Ana as she remembered 'Barbara's' clipped tones, her posh Edinburgh accent, like Aunt Bessie. She pictured the case study files in the book from the clinic, lying in a drawer in her room. A before and after photograph of Barbara.

Ana's chair scraped against the floor as she jumped up. "I have to go. Sorry."

Martha stood slowly, reaching out her hand towards her. "Are you alright, dear? You've gone awfully pale."

Ana ignored Elliot's calls, and ran out of the house, not bothering to wait for a bus, feet pounding the pavement until her lungs were on fire.

Chapter Thirty-Seven
Hope

Curtains scraped open, light burning behind my eyes. A shuffle of feet, then clearing of a throat announced someone was impatient for me to wake up.

I squinted through the haze, head foggy, trying to process where I was.

A girl stood beside my bed, head tilted, eyes curious. Her hair was long and golden brown. She wore a yellow jumper and faded jeans, the jumper drowning her slight frame. She looked about ten.

"Who are you?" I kicked the sheets back, looking round the unfamiliar room, registering the single bed in the corner, an upturned book and bear sitting on the quilt.

"I'm Flora," said the girl. "Who are you?"

"Hope." I looked down at my black jeans and t-shirt from last night. Last night. The images swirled in my head, fragments like blurs of a nightmare.

I walked to the window, disappointed that the view backed on to a wall sprawling with ivy. A glimmer of sky, visible above. It bled orange and red, the sun glowing on the horizon, rising above the clouds. *Red sky in the morning, shepherds warning.*

"Are you new?" The girl sat on my bed, legs swinging. "I was surprised to find you here when I woke up. But I'm glad. I was getting lonely. And the other girl isn't much fun. I don't think she likes me much."

I squeezed my eyes shut, trying to block out images of Aidan, struggling against restraints.

"Where are we?" I asked the girl, eyeing my jumper folded on a chair in the corner.

The girl smiled, as if she thought I was being funny. "We're in the castle of course. But not the main part. We're in the annexe."

My head spun and I steadied myself against the windowsill, trying to focus. Castle? Did she mean the house? Depending how much she had seen, the outside turrets did give it a castle type appearance.

"How long have you been here?" I swallowed, trying to calm the churn of nausea swirling in my tummy. Seb. Where was Seb?

"Hmm, that's quite a difficult question. Maybe a week. It's hard to keep track of time in here."

"Where did you come from?" I turned, sensing a change of mood in the girl. Her head bowed, and she pulled at a hole in her jeans.

"My dad…got put away. I was staying with Granny but she got sick. I think it was the worry. About my dad and then about me. She always said she was sick with worry."

My heart constricted. I walked towards the girl.

"The worker, Ian, told me I was going to a family. Then I was brought here. It's a funny kind of family." The girl shrugged.

A flare of anger and fear rose up inside me. "How old are you, Flora?"

"Nine." She smiled. "How old are you? You've got really pretty hair by the way."

I touched my hair involuntarily, staring at Flora. At her pale face, her skinny frame.

There was a knock on the door and Flora sighed. "That'll be time for breakfast, then. They keep feeding me tonnes here. I think they want to make me fat."

I strode to the door, yanking it open. Phoenix stared at me in shock, fist still curled. I stared back.

"What happened?" I stepped forward. "Are you alright?"

Phoenix jerked back, her expression hardening, the light in her eyes shutting down. "Breakfast is served." I watched her back retreat down the narrow corridor, disappearing through a door to the left.

Flora ducked under my arm, grinning. "Come on. I think I can smell pancakes."

I followed Flora along the corridor, head buzzing with confusion. Why had they brought me here? And not the Bothy?

We entered a small dining room, grandfather clock ticking in the corner, a cabinet in the other corner stacked with China plates and teapots. An old lady with hair in rollers sat at the head of the table, stacking her plate high with food. She muttered to herself, shaking her head at the empty chair to her left. Phoenix laid a cup of tea to her right, placing a hand on hers. "It's okay, Barb. Take your time."

"Hi Barb." Flora waved as she took a seat further down the table, whispering to me. "If you sit too close she gets angry. The seats beside her are for her friends."

Barb raised her head to glance at us. "Ah, glad you could make it, Matilda. Have you been on holiday?"

I hesitated, wondering if she was addressing me. Phoenix met my eye and nodded, encouraging me to answer.

"Eh, yes…Barb. I just got back last night."

"Ah, lovely. Weather alright? Ted does like the seaside. Did you collect shells?"

I glanced at Flora who was stifling a giggle. Then

returned my focus to Barb, studying her face, a recognition dawning. "Yes, lots of shells. Pretty ones." I frowned at Phoenix, eyes flashing questions. She turned away, not willing to answer. She tucked a napkin in to the collar of Barb's dress and the lady smiled at her, a girlish smile, which created a weird juxtapose of a face which was very old, yet very young all rolled in to one.

My hand shook as I picked up a pot of tea. "Did Seb arrive with me?" I addressed the question to Phoenix, who took a seat at the middle of the table. She didn't look up.

"Who's Seb?" Flora asked through a mouthful of pancake.

I shook my head, indicating it didn't matter. But it did. Where was Seb? Where had they taken him?

I watched as Phoenix sipped her tea, acting as if everything was normal. As if this was an ordinary day, and we were an ordinary group sitting at breakfast. I watched as Barb dribbled syrup over her pancakes, taking in her dishevelled appearance, familiar features but blurred and messy, like a rubbed-out version of Mrs Carmichael.

The grandfather clock ticked in the corner. Tick, tick, tick. A knot of anxiety wound its way around my throat, sliding down inside my chest, until I felt as if I couldn't breathe, as if my ribcage might crack against the strain of every emotion wound inside of me.

I jumped up, teacup rattling as I ran for the door.

"Where are you going?" Flora called.

I ran along the corridor, eyes frantically searching for an exit. I ran towards a wooden door at the far end, rattling the handle which didn't budge, banging on the panels. I turned to a staircase to the right, half-running, half-tripping up the stairs, feet sinking into the plush red carpet. A figure loomed at the top and I recoiled, nearly losing my balance.

"Careful." Dr Carmichael stepped into the light, an amused smile playing on his lips. "Where are you going, Hope?" He stepped forward, forcing me to walk backwards. My hand found the banister, gripping tight.

"Where am I?"

"You are in our annexe. A very privileged place to be. After your adventure last night we thought it was best we keep a closer eye on you. Until it's your time."

"My time for what? To be murdered?" I hissed.

Dr Carmichael chuckled, knocking past me, smoothing his hair. "So dramatic, girl."

"I saw you. All of you. Draining his blood." My voice wavered and cracked and I clenched my fists in frustration, wanting him to hear my anger, not my fear. I followed him back down the stairs, into the hall.

"What you saw, was an important part of medical history. Young blood feeding new life into the old. Such a gift all of you have to give." He placed a hand on my shoulder.

"So you kill us all on our eighteenth birthday? To take all our blood?"

Dr Carmichael smiled, a deranged, satisfied smile. "Pure, young blood, rushed from the beating heart is worth more than any vitamins or anti-ageing nonsense out there. The weak feeding the strong, it's part of evolution. The ultimate Parabiosis. I can give you some interesting articles to read to help you understand." His smile widened as he looked beyond me.

I turned to see Phoenix, hands twisting a dish

towel. "What does she mean, draining his blood? Killing us on our eighteenth birthdays?"

"Phoenix, my love." Dr Carmichael strode towards her, placing a hand on her expanding belly. "How is the little one today?"

Phoenix didn't react, eyes on me, lips trembling. "Do you mean Aidan?"

I hesitated. How could I tell her?

Dr Carmichael made soothing noises, attempting to steer Phoenix back down the hall. She pulled back from him. "You told me you'd taken him to get set up at work…"

Dr Carmichael put an arm around her. "Don't fret, my dear. You know how Hope gets. You're smarter than this. You can see the bigger picture. Haven't we given you so much already?"

"What did you do to him?" Phoenix demanded, struggling against Dr Carmichael's grip. He grabbed her under the chin, forcing her to look directly at him. My heart thudded in my ears. I swallowed, edging closer towards them.

"Do you think he would give you a better life?" Dr Carmichael challenged. He gestured to her belly. "Eighteen-year-old boys don't want babies. They want parties and fun and no drama. I am protecting you. I have always been protecting you. And now we will protect your baby. Never forget that, girl. I am giving you the golden ticket. Only the best get the golden ticket. I am welcoming you into the family." He dropped his hold and straightened his bow tie. "Now enough of this nonsense. Finish your breakfast, both of you. Donations are in one hour, Hope."

I watched as he unhooked a key from his waistcoat and exited through the wood panelled door, locking us in. I turned to Phoenix, watching as she swallowed back tears.

"Phoenix, we need to get out of here…"

She shook her head, jaw set. "You heard what he said. He's protecting me."

"What? But last night, they…I saw them, with Aidan…" The words burned my throat, as I tried to describe to her, to make her see.

"Stop." She held up her hand, eyes closed. She patted her tummy. "You're upsetting me. Mrs Carm…Patricia… said it's important I don't get upset as it hurts the baby. I need to look after my baby. That's all that matters now." She stroked her expanding belly, whispering soothing sounds, a private lullaby to her unborn child.

I recoiled, watching in bemusement as she walked back into the breakfast room, leaving me standing alone.

Chapter Thirty-Eight
Ana

Ana's hands shook as she rummaged through the drawers, pausing to kick her door closed, shutting out the noise of Maisie's music from across the hall as she re-enacted her ballet recital for Mum who lay on her small single bed, wrapped in a blanket, laughing in delight.

Smoothing the booklet open at the last pages she clicked on the lamp at her desk, shining the light directly on Barbara's face. Vivid blue eyes shone back, but how accurate could a photo really be? Ana glanced at the 'before' picture. A bedraggled looking Barbara, eyes still blue. Crazy hair. Make-up free. It would be so easy to stage.

Ana grabbed her netbook, typing Patricia McLellan into the search engine, scanning for stories. The first page of hits was unrelated, bringing up women from other countries, other professions. She adjusted the search, adding in Boutique shop owner Edinburgh. A story popped up from a business pages site from a few years ago. She scanned the headline, *Local business woman sells high-end fashion chain Bonnie Threads*, eyes resting on the accompanying photograph. Patricia McLellan standing beside a rail of colourful clothing, tight smile on her face, cold eyes. An expression which mirrored the woman in the car the first day she saw the Carmichaels. A chill shot down Ana's legs as she observed her clothing, silk turquoise blouse, silver hair wound into a bun secured with a silver butterfly clip. Also matching the woman she'd met in the house. Not Batty Barbs after all. Patricia.

Ana grabbed the clinic booklet again, flicking through the other case studies, the 'success stories.' Were they all lies? She started to type in other names then hesitated.

She'd done her own research, had read about the trials in America. There had to be *something* in it all. She changed the name search to 'benefits of plasma donation', focusing in on the section, 'Higher levels of oxytocin in young blood'. It was nothing new she was reading – she'd seen this before: healing damage, repairing cells, oxytocin could stimulate cells to start dividing again and the plasma was the important part as that contained proteins and hormones.

There was a lot of debate about whether the cells were actually rejuvenated. Indicators to small improvements, Alzheimer's patients performing better in daily tasks. Scientists were also claiming plasma transfusions could have a key role in curing other illness, through building antibodies if new diseases developed and spread across the world.

Ana looked back at the immaculate photograph of 'Barbara' in the case studies. But the transfusions were not a miracle. She threw the leaflet across the room, listening to Mum's applause as Maisie squealed her thank yous.

Maybe having Mum believe would be enough. Weren't there studies about the placebo effect? And what if the studies just hadn't run long enough. Surely cells needed a lot of time to fully regenerate and heal. And she was in the early stages. Barbara's had probably progressed too far to ever have any hope for regeneration of cells.

Ana stretched to pick up the booklet and opened

the drawer, burrowing it deep inside.

Maisie's music started up again, louder, faster. Tip toeing in and holding up a finger to her lips to silence Mum, Ana grabbed Maisie in a spin, eliciting shrieks and giggles. Ana held tight, laughing along, wishing she could capture all of these moments, like a photograph in her mind, and hold on to the detail forever.

*

On the way to school Ana scrolled through the messages Elliot sent last night, her footsteps weighed down in guilt. Part of her was tempted to tell him the truth. But then he'd go to the police. Would that really be so bad? Dr Carmichael hadn't exactly said what he was doing was illegal, and if Ian Hobbs from social work knew about it, and Mr Darwin, then it must be okay. But Dr Carmichael had stressed the importance of confidentiality. And Ana had signed a contractual agreement. Mum had too. There would be financial implications and Mum still wasn't back at work. She couldn't take the risk. What if he tried to sue them?

As school came into view a part of Ana was tempted to run in the opposite direction, the thought of anywhere else more appealing. Then she noticed another message hidden in amongst Elliot's. From Jenna. She stopped in her tracks, wondering why on earth Jenna would be messaging. *I need to talk to you. Meet me in the canteen first thing tomorrow.* Ana was so busy puzzling over Jenna's cryptic request she nearly didn't see the man blocking her path at the gates. She startled and he stepped back in fright. He wore a blue suit, like a security outfit, his cap sliding down over his eyes. Was the school employing guards now?

"Pink hair girl!"

Ana bowed her head, unable to cope with a resurgence of the 'bubble gum' taunts.

"Ana. Ana."

She looked up in surprise, wondering how the man knew her name. He hopped from one foot to the other and a spark of recognition dawned as he pushed his cap up. She remembered him, from her visit to the house.

"Hope's friend?" He rushed towards Ana, nervous eyes looking over her shoulder, making Ana turn to check if they were being watched. "I'm Billy. Hope said if she ever went away without saying goodbye to find you."

"Went away?" Ana frowned. "You mean from the house?"

The man nodded. "I've not seen her the past few days. She not been in dinner. She's not in the Bothy. Seb is in the Bothy."

"The Bothy?" Ana tried to understand.

"It's the bad place. They get locked in there when they're bad. But I've not seen Hope. She never said goodbye."

A flash of dread hit Ana. So Seb *was* there, but locked in a Bothy? The man pulled keys from his pocket. "Here. Billy loses keys all the time so I'll just say I lost them. I put the thingy on it that you need to get in the main gate. I stole that from Mrs Carmichael. I hope she won't be mad at me."

He started to walk away then turned back, grabbing Ana's arm. "Hope said you're her friend. She told me you would help her."

Ana stared at him. "But how did you know I was here? How did you get here?"

"Billy memorised the school Hope wrote on me. I

ran away from the sweet shop and used my money to get a bus. I had to ask for help. I'll be in trouble now but Hope's my friend. Have to go. Bye."

Ana watched as he hurried away, the keys heavy in her hand. She pictured Dr Carmichael, smiling in his office, his reassuring words. That day at the house she'd chosen to believe him, without even demanding to see Hope. She had ignored the feeling, a niggling deep down. For her own selfish reasons.

Her phone beeped as the bell rang.

Waited for you outside the canteen. Where are you?

She ignored the message from Jenna and phoned Elliot. He answered straight away.

"Meet me outside at the gates. I need to tell you something." Ana ended the call, hopping from one foot to the other, staring at the doors to reception, willing Elliot to hurry.

"Miss Gilbert."

Ana jumped at the sound of her name, dread seeping through her as she turned to face familiar dead eyes.

"It would appear that trouble has found you after all."

Chapter Thirty-Nine
Hope

Life in the annexe kept me separated from the rest of the house. Anxiety at not being able to communicate with Seb dulled the relief of avoiding the Bothy and the lecherous gropes of Ryan.

Phoenix refused to engage in chat during mealtimes together and she never accompanied me to donations. Due to being pregnant she was now exempt from that duty. Something in her had shut down. Sometimes Dr Carmichael joined us at mealtimes; usually the days Barbs was most lucid, often in the morning. He sat close by his wife, a reassuring hand resting on hers. His real wife. Now everything Clara said made sense. But if she knew transfusions had failed her own mother, why continue with the macabre façade? Clara no longer oversaw my donations so I was unable to question her. The blonde, Faye, never engaged in conversation. I kept my eyes shut during the sessions, picturing Seb, the ache of wondering where he was and what they had done with him, greater than the nip of a needle.

Today Phoenix sat on Dr Carmichael's other side, laughing politely at his jokes, smiling as he complimented her beautiful dress. I watched in disbelief, wanting to scream at her to wake up, to understand. To help me formulate a plan.

Flora asked questions Dr Carmichael only half-answered. I had plenty of questions I wanted to ask him too. Like why he was now capturing nine-year-old girls. Flora was yet to give a donation but I figured it was only a matter of time. He always insisted she eat seconds and I knew she had been right. They were fattening her up.

I blinked, suddenly aware of the silence. Dr Carmichael cleared his throat, expectant eyes on me. "I was suggesting Phoenix might want to help you select a dress for the party tonight."

"Party?" I looked at him blankly.

His smile curled in amusement. "An early celebration for Sebastian."

A flash of relief at his name spoken in the present tense was quickly followed by a rush of coldness at the thought of how their parties ended.

"And also for you, dear girl," Dr Carmichael raised a glass of juice, as if in a toast.

"Will there be sandwiches at the party?" Barb leaned towards her husband.

"Yes, darling. Plenty of sandwiches." He patted her hand, his eyes never leaving me. "Only the best for two of our brightest. It will be with a heavy heart I bid you goodbye, girl. I had hoped for a different outcome with you, to keep you here with us." He shook his head.

"Am I invited to the party?" Flora sat forward in her chair, grinning. She looked up at me. "Is it your birthday?"

Dr Carmichael laughed heartily and Barb giggled beside him. "I think I'll have some jelly and ice cream."

"Oooh, yes please!" Flora clapped her hands in excitement.

I pushed my plate to one side. "Why don't you tell them how your parties end, *Finlay*?" His name was dirt on my lips, every letter spat in disgust.

He ignored me, addressing Flora's question.

"There will be plenty of parties to look forward to, darling. This one is a bit past your bedtime."

Flora slumped back in her chair. "I never have any fun here."

Dr Carmichael cocked his head to one side. "We are rather boring old farts here, aren't we? Don't worry there will be friends arriving very soon. And Phoenix will keep you company this evening, maybe do your hair?"

Phoenix smiled, no light in her eyes. She started to clear the plates, taking on the role of housekeeper. I stood, helping.

Dr Carmichael shook his head at me. "Leave that for Phoenix. Go and get ready please. You have a donation in an hour. Now, Flora, how about I read you a story in the lounge? Go and choose a book and I'll be right there."

Flora ran excitedly from the table and my heart followed her, wanting to encase her, protect her.

I stood, eyes locking with Dr Carmichael. I waited until Phoenix left the room then walked towards him slowly, deliberately, enjoying the discomfort wavering in his smile.

In a flash I had his fork, and stabbed the spikes into the table, an inch from his hand. He recoiled and the glimmer of fear spurred me on.

"I'm not going down without a fight. So I think it's you who needs to get ready, old man."

*

Phoenix entered mine and Flora's room without knocking, laying a black dress on my bed. "He'll want you to wear this today."

"Phoenix, why are you letting him control you?"

She threw a pair of sandals below my bed.

"That pissed you off." I smiled. "Come on, I know

you're in there somewhere." I waved a hand in front of her face. "Hello? Where is my friend, Phoenix?"

She grabbed my wrist, startling me. "You think you're so smart, don't you? If you were, I wouldn't be dressing you for your funeral."

Our eyes met. A chill ran down my spine as a realisation hit me. "You knew didn't you? That there was no real escape?"

Her silence extended in front of us, an invitation for me to continue.

"The baby...was it was planned? As a bargaining tool?" I looked down at the bump forming beneath her dress.

Phoenix stepped closer, her face so close to mine, her breath was hot on my cheek. "Not so dumb after all." She continued, "Ms McLellan, Patricia, the sister, has always wanted a baby. Why do you think she dotes on Billy so much? She's protective of the vulnerable ones. I knew she'd make sure we were looked after. And I knew the doctor wanted to go younger with the donations."

I balked. "Surely you can't get a plasma donation from a baby?"

She made a face. "Of course not. But they'll grow up here. Pure, perfect blood." She laid a hand on her tummy. "And I'll be promoted to staff."

"But Aidan..." I thought about the days they spent together, arm in arm. "I thought you loved him."

Her mouth set in a line. "I do, did. I thought they would set him up in a job outside, one they would control of course. But I knew, deep down, there was probably no escape." Her voice wavered.

I caught my reflection in the wardrobe mirror, my skin white under the dim light, like I was already a ghost of myself. "We could all try to escape. Get out of here."

Phoenix laughed bitterly. "And go where? Do you know how many powerful people are part of this? Even if you get out of here, you're never going to escape."

It wasn't true. There were people out there who cared. Ruth. The Browns. Ana. Elliot. People who would make sure we could be safe.

I grabbed Phoenix's arm. "I know people who will help, who will listen. What about your baby? Do you really want this for them? You could give them a better life, Phoenix. You're so strong and smart. We can do this together."

The grandfather clock chimed from the dining room. Phoenix shook off my grip. She stepped back and I caught the shimmer of tears in her eyes. "You'd better not be late for donations."

She avoided eye contact as I slid on my boots. When I looked up to say goodbye she had already gone.

*

Faye led me down the hall of the annexe, opening the wooden door into the main house. The entrance hall was silent, the only sound a howl from the wind rattling the door. She gestured for me to keep walking and I cast an anxious eye to the staircase, willing Seb to appear.

As we approached the kitchen I slowed my steps. The door was open a crack and I heard voices from within; Margaret and Ryan. "Two tonight, Aunty. Can't say I'll be sad to see him go, but her, she's a little firecracker." He laughed, as if he was proud of a joke. "Firecracker. She should burn bright."

I recoiled at the sound of a slap.

"Shut your mouth, you little devil. You've never

been right in the head, but don't you dare make light of this horror."

Their voices faded as we continued along to the back of the house, Faye unlocking a side door leading us outside, the wind swirling my hair around my face, like wings of death carrying me through the storm. What did Ryan mean, *burn*? I thought back to his story about being good with a lighter, shuddering. Images of my nightmares flashed through my head, Mum standing in a doorway, flames curling, her mouth forming the word *RUN*.

Clara stood at the entrance to the donation centre, holding the door open for us, face expressionless as she gestured me inside.

"I've to collect them in three hours. Make sure you take as much plasma as you can. The boy, is he still lucid?"

Clara nodded. "Barely."

"Excellent. There should be no fuss from him." Faye smiled and pushed me inside, pulling the door shut from the outside, the clang of metal echoing along the sterile corridor.

Clara paused, then shook her head, as if she wanted to ask a question then thought better of it. I followed her to the donation room in silence, pulse throbbing in my neck at the hope 'the boy' might be Seb.

He lay on a bed in the middle of the machines, motionless and pale, arm dangling over the side, stress ball rolling along the floor, a flash of red on white. Clara hurried to his side, cupping a hand to his face.

"Sebastian. Seb! Wake up, can you hear me?"

I crept towards him, staring at the needle marks and bruises running up and down his arms, the gauntness of his face. "Is he dead?" My breathing was too fast and too shallow, hurting my chest. I grabbed the edge of the bed, finding it difficult to stand up straight. I jumped as one of his legs kicked out. Clara made soothing noises, smoothing his hair back from his forehead.

"You're okay." She helped him sit up, placing a plastic cup to his lips, tilting it slowly. Seb gulped thirstily then gagged and pushed her hand away, wiping at his mouth.

"I feel sick."

"It's alright." She grabbed a cardboard bowl from the chair by his bed and I turned my head as he retched, thinking how I would hate him to see me throwing up.

My legs shook as I waited for the gagging to subside. I turned around slowly at the sound of Clara's footsteps as she carried the bowl away. Seb's eyes were still closed but my body started to relax, knowing he wasn't dead.

"This isn't exactly how I pictured our reunion." A smile twitched on his lips and he opened one eye.

I smiled, feeling a light switch on, resisting the urge to run to him. "I'd ask how you are, but…"

"Ghastly." He struggled to sit up. "But you, on the other hand, look like a beautiful dark angel. I'd ask you to take me away to hell, but I think we're already here."

Heat spread up my neck, warming my cheeks.

"Won't you take a seat," he gestured to the bed beside him and I hoisted myself up.

Seb turned his head so he faced me. I wanted to ask where he had been, what they had done to him but I was too scared to hear his answers.

"I was afraid I'd never see you again, that they

had taken you away forever." He let his hand dangle over the side, his fingers stretching towards me. I let one of my hands drop too, my fingers reaching out to him.

"They took me to the annexe. Phoenix is there and they've got a younger girl. And Mrs Carmichael, the one we see, isn't the real Mrs Carmichael at all."

"What?" Seb lifted his head and grimaced at the effort.

A door swung open at the back of the room as Clara returned, Viv and Pollock following behind. I wondered if they were all here, ensuring we didn't try to make a run for it. Not that Seb looked in any state.

"We have to try to escape."

Seb laughed bitterly. "I can barely walk. They've been draining me dry of plasma. Did you know medically we're supposed to only donate every couple of weeks to allow our nutrients to replenish? They've been hooking me up twice a day this week and Ryan has been conveniently forgetting to bring me breakfast."

"Have they kept you in the Bothy?"

He nodded. "I've been sleeping most of the day so it wasn't too bad. I think they've given my room to a new arrival."

I thought of Mum's photo sitting in the bag in the bottom of my wardrobe, along with Lucy's letter and my tarot cards. If they were moving in new arrivals, I'd never see my belongings again. Clara approached my bed and I lifted my arm, as if I was an obedient servant ready to do her bidding. To them, my possessions were nothing, garbage, just like me. They'd hook me up one last time and then move on to the next round of donors.

"Will there be music and lights for us later,

Clara?" She refused to look me in the eye.

She handed me a cup of water. "You'll be doing a double donation today, so drink up. It's important to keep hydrated."

I grabbed it from her, gulping it down in one go, squashing the plastic. She flinched at the crunch. "It's important to stay hydrated for what? So I don't fall asleep during my final moments? Do you enjoy hearing the screams?"

She moved closer to the bed, lowering her voice. "Lie back and relax. You need to keep your wits about you later."

I resisted the urge to laugh in her face. Was that an attempt at a subtle warning to be aware of the dangers that lay ahead? I handed her my ruined cup. "Do you know they've brought in a nine-year-old girl? Where does this stop?"

Her eyes flashed with shock, then something else, a glimmer of defiance, one I had seen before, when she spoke about Dr Carmichael and males who were 'not entitled.' I sat up, wanting to ask her if it could stop, if she could help. I detected a subtle shake of her head and she pressed a hand on mine. "Not yet."

I wanted to ask her what she meant. *Was* she on our side?

Seb called to Viv, "Bring us the iPod will you and push our beds closer together."

Clara raised an eyebrow.

"Come on. Prisoners on death row are granted their last meal. This is my last request." His eyes met mine, no trace of fear, just a sad resignation.

There are so many things I want to tell you, want to ask you, want to feel.

But instead, I got to hold his hand as we lay side by side, one bud in his ear, one in mine and I closed my eyes and let the music wash over me, then into me. He squeezed my hand and I squeezed back, and I imagined us somewhere good, anywhere but here.

Our grip tightened. *Don't leave me.*

Chapter Forty
Ana

"She can't force us to stay here all day," Jenna's voice was on the verge of hysteria as she paced up and down, rattling the door handle for what felt like the hundredth time.

"She can. Because she locked the door." Elliot emphasised the last four words with a sigh, exchanging a look with Ana that sparked a glimmer of hope that he could forgive her, even when she confessed to her part in all of this.

Ana glanced around the room, eyeing the windows. The handles were attached to the small panes of glass along the top. There was no way any of them could squeeze through that gap, not even Jenna with her skinny frame. Ana's eyes fell to the cats again. The creepiest photo she'd possibly seen of someone's pets. There was something sinister about them, even the way they appeared to be holding hands, or paws. She slammed the photo face down on Ms Turnberry's desk, suppressing a smile when Jenna jumped. Jenna shot Ana a look of disgust, her hand fluttering to her chest.

"Don't do that! I think I'm about to have a panic attack."

Ana rolled her eyes at Elliot. Jenna and her friends between them must have had about twenty 'panic attacks' this term. Mostly in the period before Physical Education, or during.

Elliot stood up and Ana watched as he peered under Ms Turnberry's desk, running a hand along the wall.

"What are you doing, Elliot?" Jenna spun round, arms folded. His voice was muffled from below. She turned to Ana, wide eyed. "What's he doing?"

Ana shrugged. "Jenna, why don't you come and sit down." Jenna's pacing was making her nervous. "You still haven't explained what you wanted to talk to me about."

"Oh god, oh god." Jenna paced some more, pressing a hand against her forehead. "This is all getting too much. We could be in serious shit here. What did Ms Turnberry mean when she said you've gone too far?"

Ana watched her curiously, realising that getting caught ditching first period with Elliot and being locked in Ms Turnberry's office was not the only thing that was sparking Jenna's distress. "It's a long story. I want to hear what you've got to say first."

Jenna sighed dramatically. "Okay, okay. So, you know the day of the locker raid?"

Elliot's head popped up from underneath the desk and Ana shot him a curious look, but he was too busy listening to Jenna.

"Ms Turnberry told me to set off the fire alarm."

"I knew it," Ana folded her arms. "You planted those drugs in Hope's locker."

"No." Jenna looked insulted. "Like where would I even get access to that kind of stuff? I didn't know what was going to happen. Just that it was important there was a distraction. I had to because Ms Turnberry was mad at me for…other things…not going to plan."

"What other things?" Elliot was fully standing now, wiping dust off his trousers.

"I was supposed to befriend Hope. Help her settle.

Then ditch her." Jenna shot Ana a look. "But then she chose to sit with the losers instead."

"Hey," Ana exclaimed.

"Sorry." Jenna waved a hand. "I didn't get why Ms Turnberry was being so weird but she's not exactly someone I'd question. She's really pally with my parents so it made me feel awkward."

"Did something else happen?" Ana shifted in her seat, getting impatient.

"The other night, Ms Turnberry came over for bible study."

"What?" Elliot snorted.

Jenna's eyes were like daggers. "My dad is religious, okay?"

"Okay." Elliot held his hands up to calm her. "Ms Turnberry just doesn't strike me as the holy type."

"None of them are. Trust me." Jenna made a face. "Anyway, I was supposed to be at a party but Gordon was there and it was way too awkward, so I came home early and Ms Turnberry had stayed after the class. They didn't hear me come in and I overheard her asking my uncle if he'd managed to make her file disappear."

"What do you mean?"

Jenna hesitated, eyeing Ana like she was weighing up whether she could trust her. "You have to promise you're not going to spread this round?" She looked to Elliot, seeking his reassurance.

They gave their word.

"My uncle's in the police. High up. I don't even know what his title is. It sounded like someone had tried to report Hope's disappearance. A Rhona McDonald?"

"Ruth," Ana blurted.

"Right," Jenna nodded then paused, frowning.

"Wait, how do you know that?"

Ana shook her head, indicating for Jenna to continue her story first.

"So anyway, he reassures Ms Turnberry it's all taken care of. No trace will be found, no tracks. My uncle is a total creep, by the way, not a nice guy." Ana blinked in surprise. Jenna shuddered. "I don't even know why I'm telling you this bit." She hesitated, taking in a shaky breath. "I needed to tell someone. And she's your friend, so I figured..."

"What?" Ana's pulse throbbed in her throat.

"It sounds like they're kidnapping kids. My parents met with some foster services woman. We were supposed to take in a girl, Flora. I thought my parents had lost their minds, but Dad gets carried away with his do-gooding at the church. Mum told me it had all fallen through, that she'd gone abroad to her grandparents or something. But then I heard Dad asking Ms Turnberry if Flora's bloods had matched okay. What the hell does that even mean?" Jenna's words were all running together, her voice high pitched. "Then Ms Turnberry started saying things like she'll make an excellent replacement for some boy. That her blood will be even purer because she's so young."

Listening to the tremble in Jenna's voice shook Ana. *This should have been your reaction, Ana.* And how young was she talking? An image of Maisie, so sweet and innocent, flashed in Ana's head and she started to tremble.

Elliot stared at Jenna, then at Ana. "What on earth are you talking about?"

Jenna sat down in the chair across from them. "Something else they said. It made me sick."

"What?" Ana's heart was beating so fast she felt

dizzy, like her head was floating away from her body.

"Ms Turnberry said Hope was an example of why they needed to go younger. She was too much of a liability. That they all get restless and ask too many questions the older they get. And they weren't going to wait until her eighteenth to get rid of her."

"We need to get out of here," Ana jumped up, feeling sick. "Elliot, I've got a key to the house. We need to get Hope out. Dr Carmichael has been using them for plasma donations."

"For what?" Elliot's confusion turned to anger. "Why didn't you tell me? Is Seb there?"

Ana shook her head miserably. "They told me he'd left. I swear, I didn't see him. But I think he might be." She didn't bother to admit that she hadn't actually seen Hope either.

"Who's Seb?" Jenna asked. She frowned at Elliot. "What were you doing under the desk anyway?"

"Looking for a landline connection. There's one there. Now we need to find a phone. She must have disconnected it." He started to open and shut desk drawers. "Help me look."

Ana started rummaging through cupboards, hands shaking. Elliot's fury made her burn with shame.

"There's one over there, on the windowsill." Jenna pointed lazily and Elliot rushed over, retrieving a vintage style red phone. He ducked back under the desk, plugging it in.

"Who are you going to phone?" Jenna said. "Do you actually know anyone's number?"

They all looked at one another, the realisation that all of their numbers were stored in their phones, which Ms Turnberry had taken, deflating them.

"I think I know my mum's but she'll have her phone switched off," Elliot shook his head. "She's not allowed to use it at work in the nursery."

"Let's call the police." Ana picked up the receiver, starting to dial.

Jenna grabbed the phone from her. "Let's not. That's a hotline to my uncle and he'll tell my parents and they'll kill me."

Ana shot her a withering look. "From what you just said Hope is literally going to die. I think this is a bit more serious."

"Wait," Elliot grabbed Ana's wrist and she jumped at the contact.

He looked thoughtful. "If the police are in on this we need to be careful who we speak to. I say we call Martha. We can trust her and she'll understand."

"Martha?" Ana pictured Mrs Brown in her little terraced house baking muffins and pouring tea.

Elliot hurried over to a timetable pinned to a board beside Ms Turnberry's desk. He ran a finger down the list of numbers, tapping against the pastoral care teachers' direct lines.

He turned to them. "One of you has to pretend to be Ms Turnberry. You need to call a pastoral care teacher. Choose Ms Docherty. Hazel Docherty. She's a soft touch. Tell her your system is down and you need a number urgently for Martha Brown."

"Are you insane?" Ana stared at him. "There is no way I can impersonate Ms Turnberry. And what if she's there, in the office with her or something?"

"I'll do it." Jenna pushed Elliot aside, grabbing the receiver. "Get me a pen and paper." She snapped a finger and punched in a number. Ana tensed, watching, waiting. Jenna's eyes widened signalling the phone had been picked up. Her knuckles whitened then she launched into a performance worthy of Oscar season. Elliot stared at Ana in amazement, their stifled laughs breaking the tension.

"Yes, Hazel. I realise that Hope Devaney is no longer with us but this is a police matter." Jenna started to scribble down digits, her mention of police obviously speeding up the process. "Uh, huh. Okay. Thank you." Jenna slammed the phone down, erupting into a fit of giggles. She waved the number in front of Elliot. "How was that then?"

"Amazing," Elliot grinned, grabbing the paper and punching in the number.

Ana nodded in approval. "You were great, Jenna."

Jenna did a little courtesy. Elliot slammed the phone down. "It's not working?"

Jenna glanced at the numbers on the wall. "It says dial nine for an outside line."

Elliot's face flushed and he keyed in the number again. Ana glanced at the clock. Nearly lunchtime. She squeezed her eyes shut saying a silent prayer that Martha would be home.

And then Elliot was saying her name. Trying to explain they'd been locked in Ms Turnberry's office. That she needed to come right now. That Hope was in danger.

He slammed the phone down, collapsing into a chair. "She's on her way."

Five minutes later there was a rattle of keys in the door. They exchanged panicked glances. It was too soon for Martha.

The door swung open and Ana's heart sank when Mr Darwin walked in. He shot her a pointed glare. Jenna rushed towards him before Ana could warn her. "Thank god, Mr Darwin. You need to let us out of here."

Jenna tried to squeeze past him, one foot out the door.

Mr Darwin blocked her way, forcing her back into the room. "Not so fast. Hazel mentioned she took a call from Ms Turnberry. From this office."

"She left." Elliot stood up, a determined frown on his face. "You need to let us out of here. There's an emergency."

"Really?" Mr Darwin looked at all three of them in turn, his gaze fixing on Ana. "Why would Ms Turnberry request a number for a Martha Brown?"

"We need to rescue Hope Devaney," Jenna announced and Ana glared at her, mouthing for her to be quiet.

The smile disappeared from Mr Darwin's face. "Is that right?" He directed the question at Ana, his expression darkening. He clicked the door shut. "And what makes you think she needs rescued?"

A tremble of panic rumbled deep inside as Ana tried to catch Elliot's eye.

"We think she's in danger. Well, we know actually." Jenna started to blurt out her story and Ana gritted her teeth.

Mr Darwin leaned back against the door, allowing Jenna to babble on. Ana glanced at the clock. *Hurry up, Martha. Hurry up.*

He made no sign of moving as Jenna emphasised the need to get to Hope, fast. Jenna huffed with impatience. "Mr Darwin, you need to let us out."

He caught Ana glancing out the window, towards the car park. "Martha Brown isn't coming, Ana. I called her from the pastoral care office, telling her there was no need for concern. That there has been a misunderstanding." Mr Darwin shook his head in disappointment. "I really thought Dr Carmichael and I could trust you to hold up your end of your deal. He won't be happy."

Elliot and Jenna spun round to look at Ana.

"What deal?" Elliot stared at Ana, doubt in his eyes.

Ana swallowed, face flushing her guilt.

"Ana, what does he mean?" Elliot pressed.

Mr Darwin smiled. "You'll have plenty of time to tell them about your mum's transfusions later. You all need to come with me."

Mr Darwin grabbed Jenna's arm and she started to protest, struggling. Ana avoided Elliot's gaze, his eyes a fire of rage and disappointment.

"Where are you taking us?" Jenna demanded to know.

They jumped as the door slammed open from the other side. Mr Darwin stepped back in shock as Martha Brown stormed in, eyes blazing.

"Let her go." Martha prodded Mr Darwin with her umbrella. "The only place these kids are going is home with me."

Chapter Forty-One
Hope

Seb's hand twitched in mine and I shot up, a siren penetrating the calming melody dancing in my ear. We pulled the buds out, wincing at the din. A red light flashed at the back of the room, pulsating in time with the beeps of the machines. Clara exchanged worried glances with Viv. She motioned for her to help as they moved to unhook us.

"What's going on?" I shouted, wriggling my arm free as soon as Clara released the needle. I turned to Seb, trying not to panic at the grey pallor of his skin. He looked like he might pass out.

"I don't know." Clara shook her head. Pollock appeared at their sides. "We should get out of here. You know what that alarm means."

Clara shot him a piercing look. "We wait for instructions. Start emptying the freezers just in case. There are medical bags in the cupboards by the sink. Line them with ice packs."

Pollock hesitated, eyes flashing with defiance.

"Just do it." Clara turned her back on him, unhooking the plasma-filled bags from our machines.

The side door opened and Faye marched in. She threw a set of keys towards Pollock. "Get the new kids rounded up. There's a black van outside the main doors waiting for you. The address is programmed into the sat nav. We'll meet you there later tonight or tomorrow. Provisions will be there."

"I'll go with him," Viv stepped forward.

Faye held up a hand. "Not yet. You need to help

with the older kids. Clear their rooms and burn their belongings in the incinerator. Ryan is down there getting things prepared."

Viv glanced at Pollock.

"Move," Faye yelled, prompting them both to scurry to the door. She turned to Clara. "Your father said you need to bring them to the kitchen."

"Ten minutes. We need to gather the plasma." Clara started to walk away.

Faye grabbed her arm, "There's no time. We can start again, when we're settled."

Clara shrugged off her grip. She held up the bags of plasma. "This is rare AB positive. Do you know how difficult it is to find this kind of donor? My father would want to ensure I gather these donations to take with us."

Faye relented. "Fine. I'll get Finlay to call you when we're settled in the new place to give you details."

"Where are we going?" I hissed at Clara as Faye motioned for Seb to stand. "What's happening?"

"The house has been compromised. They need to destroy all evidence." Clara leaned in close. "Delay as long as you can in the kitchen. Talk to Margaret, keep her chatting if she's there. I won't be long."

"Why are we going to the kitchen?" I shrugged off Faye's hand as she steered me away from Clara.

"Move," she instructed and I relented, noticing the slump in Seb's shoulders. I put an arm around his waist, helping him walk. "Are you alright?"

His smile was lopsided. "Maybe they're putting on a three-course lunch for us."

The wind howled as if in answer to the wail of the siren, Faye struggling to push the back door open. She motioned for us to hurry, her heels sinking into mud as she clumsily led the way to the back entrance of the house. Seb slumped against me, the storm battering against us, rain seeping through my dress, chilling my bones. Faye stopped at a metal door with creeping ivy curling along the handle, spreading up the façade of the house. She hammered three times, the noise muffled by the pounding rain ricocheting off an upturned watering can, orange rust bleeding down the sides.

The door creaked open and my stomach lurched at the sight of Ryan. Faye pushed past him, hurrying us inside. His eyes met mine, and he grabbed my hand on my way past.

"Aren't you a sight for sore eyes."

I yanked my hand away and blinked as my eyes adjusted to the dim lighting. With the door shut, a different kind of roar rose from within. As we walked along a stone corridor a warmth radiated from a doorway to the left. I hesitated at the entrance, the blast of hot air soothing my nipping face and hands. Flames danced behind metal grates at the top of two big silver doors.

Seb turned his head towards mine, the fire reflecting in his eyes. "Those are pretty big ovens."

"All the more to cook you nice and crisp." Ryan wiggled his eyebrows at us, his laugh hollow.

Faye shot him a warning look and pushed us forward, my ankle turning clumsily as we started up stone steps. I glanced back over my shoulder and noticed Viv hauling bags across the floor towards the incinerator ovens. She hooked a wooden pole through the handle of one of the silver doors, swinging it open. Flames raged, fingers of fire stretching out.

"Wait," I spotted a familiar bag.

"Keep moving." Faye prodded my back.

"No, Viv," I shouted through the doorway and her head snapped up in shock. "Please, there's a photograph and letter in there. I really need them." I pointed to the bag and she looked to Faye.

"There's no point," Faye started to protest.

Viv slid the bag towards me and I unzipped the front pocket, rummaging around. I found the photo of Mum and grabbed that, then the letter and my tarot pouch.

"Enough. Move on." Faye grabbed the bag from me and threw it back in to the room.

I folded Mum's photograph inside the letter and slid them into the pocket of my dress, stuffing the tarot pouch in the other.

Seb led the way and as we reached the last step, the clattering sounds of pots and pans and the familiar smell of Margaret's soup soothed me. We stumbled into the kitchen. Stacey, Scott and Joe sat side by side at the long wooden table, fighting over the last bit of bread.

Margaret turned to us, but there was no cheery greeting. She handed me a bowl of soup and motioned for me to sit.

"Right, Stacey, boys. You're up. Follow me downstairs." Ryan looked bored as he issued the order.

Stacey shot him a scathing look. "Aye nae bother, wee man." She turned back to her soup, slurping it down.

Seb and I exchanged nervous glances. Downstairs?

Ryan strode up to the table and with one swoop knocked Stacey's soup flying across the room, the bowl shattering against the brick wall.

Stacey recoiled in shock. She slammed her spoon

down. "What are you doing, ya wee psycho?"

"Up." Ryan hauled her to her feet. He motioned to Scott and Joe. "Get moving."

Faye ensured they complied, accompanying them to the stairwell.

"Mercy me," Margaret muttered under her breath, crossing her chest as she turned her back to us, clattering the lid off the soup, stirring it frantically.

I looked at Scott and saw the confusion on his face. I thought back to my conversation with Aidan in the library, how protective he was of his brother. I stood up, drawing Ryan's attention. "Where are you taking them?"

Ryan laughed. "You'll see, soon enough." He shoved them forward and Margaret shook her head, telling me not to intervene. I sat back down.

I remembered what Clara said. Keep Margaret talking. Seb laid down his spoon, his face paling.

"Do you think?" He couldn't bring himself to say the words. We both looked to the doorway Ryan had just walked out of, the staircase leading downstairs to the ovens. I nodded, realising our belongings weren't the main evidence they wanted to burn. If Clara wanted me to keep Margaret talking, maybe she had a plan to save us. Margaret dabbed a cloth to her forehead and I called out to her. She jumped.

"Come and sit with us, Margaret."

"Oh no, no, lass. I have far too much to be getting on with."

I swung my legs over the bench and Seb laid a hand on mine. "What are you doing?" I looked pointedly at the door which led out to the hall, signalling for him to check things out. I poured half of my soup into an empty bowl which lay in the centre of the table then walked towards the stove.

"Your soup is so delicious today, Margaret. I was hoping for some more." I held the bowl out to her and she jumped in surprise.

She muttered under her breath, then lifted the lid of the soup, the steam winding around us. "You got through that fast, lassie, didn't you."

I watched over her shoulder as Seb crept towards the door.

"What do you put in this soup? I can taste something spicy." My pulse throbbed in my throat as I kept one eye on Seb.

Margaret ladled some into the bowl, listing off the ingredients, telling me her secret was cinnamon, that it gave it a real warmth. My whole body tensed as the door squeaked. Margaret slammed the bowl down and grabbed me, her grip so tight it knocked the wind out of me.

"Don't be going any further, Sebastian." Her voice shook, but her grip was strong. She reached over to the knife rack, sliding out a large cleaver, the blade glimmering under the light as she held it to my throat.

Seb froze, his back rigid as if he knew he was going to see something bad. He turned slowly, eyes flashing with fear as he took in the cleaver.

"I don't want to hurt anyone. But I can't let you go out there, Seb. So you'd be leaving me no choice. Do you understand, boy? You both have to sit nicely, okay?"

Seb held up his hand in surrender, walking back to the table. "Okay, Margaret. It's cool. I just wanted to see what was happening." He sat down and picked up his spoon, the tremor in his hand giving away his nerves.

Margaret relaxed her grip. She slid the cleaver

into the front pocket of her apron, sharp end up. She picked up the bowl of soup and handed it to me, as if the last five seconds didn't happen. "Alright, lassie. Eat up."

My legs wobbled as I made my way back to the table, sliding in close to Seb, pressing against his warmth to stop from trembling. Margaret's behaviour shook me. It was clear where her loyalties lay. Was I being naïve, thinking Clara would be any different?

Seb laid a hand on mine. "You're okay. We're going to be okay."

Then the screams echoed up the stairwell from the incinerators and there were no words that could reassure me. I choked back tears and Seb hugged me, cradling my head against his chest and I knew he was trying to shield me from the horror downstairs.

But the sound of death kept calling to us, chilling us to our core.

Chapter Forty-Two
Ana

Ana's knee slammed into the back of the seat as Martha careened round a corner.

Jenna shot Ana a look of terror as her nails left indents in the hand rest between them.

"I didn't know you could drive…this fast, Martha," Elliot laughed nervously from the passenger seat.

Martha kept her eyes on the road, teeth clenched. "Usually I let Edward do the driving. But needs must. I got my old girl out of the garage. Where now, boy?"

"Just up the track, straight line from here."

The car rocked from side to side as they started up the bumpy track. Ana had detached the fob from the set of keys Billy had given her. She gripped it nervously, praying it would work and they could get past the gates.

"I really think we should call the police now, for back up. The evidence is all going to be here for them to see. My uncle won't be able to cover it up." Jenna picked up Martha's handbag. "Is your phone in here, Martha?"

Elliot shook his head. "We don't need the police announcing their arrival with blaring sirens. We need to scope the place and take them by surprise."

Martha adjusted her rear-view mirror. "We're being followed."

Ana turned to see a familiar black car snaking up the path behind them.

"It's Ms Turnberry. Is that Mr Darwin with her?"

Elliot gestured to Martha. "You need to speed up."

Jenna shook her head. "I think you're going quite fast…" Her last word was swallowed by the rev of the engine as they hurtled towards the iron gates.

"Give me the fob, Ana." Elliot wound down his window and she passed him the fob. He positioned it and pressed the triangular button frantically. They held their breath as the gates swung open. Ana shot a triumphant smile out the back window imagining Ms Turnberry's shock. As they sailed through the gates Martha slammed on the brakes throwing them all forward.

"What the?" Jenna squealed. "What are you doing you crazy old lady? Are you INSANE?"

Martha turned to watch the gates swing shut. "You all need to get out and run to the house. I'll back the car up as close to the gates as I can to try and block them. And Jenna's right. Now's time for me to call for back-up. I suspect our friends there will have already raised the alarm inside." She rummaged around in her handbag. "Elliot, son. Dial the number for me will you?" Elliot fumbled with the phone then passed it back.

"Let's go," he shouted and Jenna hesitated.

"I might just stay with Martha? Ms Turnberry likes me. I can try to help keep her chill."

"Whatever." Elliot shrugged. He nodded to Ana, "Come on, Ana."

"Be careful," Martha shouted, her voice lost in the wind as they clambered out of the car.

Ana's lungs burned as they ran and ran, the driveway a lot longer than she remembered. The rain pounded in time with her heart, ice dripping down the back of her neck. As they approached the final set of gates Elliot positioned the fob. Ana doubled over, panting, blinking rain out of her eyes. What would they do when they got inside? They had no weapons, nothing. And even if they did, she would have no clue how to use them.

The gates swung open and a siren blared. Elliot grabbed her hand and pulled her through as the doors juddered and started to retract, as if in response to the alarm. A sinking feeling of dread washed over Ana as she watched the gates slam shut, sealing them in.

"Come on, we're nearly there," Elliot shouted, like this was a good thing and they were running to victory.

The house loomed on the horizon, a grey mist from the rain circling the turrets. The alarm still blared, like a warning shout inside Ana's head, *Stop, go back, get out*.

Then she thought of Hope, of what she owed her and she ran faster, ignoring the burn in her chest, focusing on her breathing.

As they approached the main grounds they stalled to a walk. Ana grabbed Elliot's arm, pausing to let a stitch in her side fade. He pointed up ahead.

"There's a black van parked at the entrance."

Ana squinted up ahead, the blacked-out windows reminding her of Dr Carmichael's car. Elliot motioned for her to follow him and they hurried through the gardens, the muddy grass sucking at their shoes. They sheltered under a tree and watched as a bald man with tattoos led a parade of kids out of the house. He slid the side door of the van open and motioned them inside. Elliot craned to see and Ana knew he was scanning their faces, expecting to see Hope and maybe Seb.

"Those kids are young," Ana said. "I never saw them, when I was here."

"Do you think Hope and Seb will be in the van?"

Ana thought back to the conversation with Billy at the school gates. "Billy said Seb was locked up somewhere, he called it a Bothy. And Hope left without saying goodbye. She might be locked up too?"

"Let's see if there's a back entrance." Elliot set off in a sprint, zigzagging his way through the grounds, across the gravelled driveway, keeping a big enough distance from the van so as not to draw attention.

They crouched low as they crept past windows, circling round to the side of the house. The rain subsided, making it easier to see their path ahead. As they turned a corner round to the back, they jumped, coming face to face with a woman. She had dark hair and familiar piercing blue eyes. She was dressed in a white nurse uniform, clutching a black leather bag, like an old-fashioned doctor's bag.

The woman stared at them both, recognition dawning on her face when she glanced at Ana's tie, at the same time Ana remembered.

Elliot opened his mouth to speak.

The woman held a finger to her lips to shush him, "You'd better come inside."

Chapter Forty-Three
Hope

"Let us go together, please." Desperation made my voice shrill. I dug my nails in to Ryan's arm and he twisted my wrist, the burn a fraction of what I knew awaited me below.

Margaret placed a firm hand on Seb's shoulder keeping him seated as Ryan dragged me towards the stairwell. She kept her eyes averted, as if ashamed.

Seb strained against her grip, pain etched across his face. The light faded from his eyes, helpless defeat turning down the corners of his mouth. "I'm sorry," he cried and I wanted to tell him I was sorry too.

I kicked out as Ryan pulled me down the stairs, slamming my foot against his shin. He yelped, grabbing a handful of my hair, yanking my head up to look at him.

"If you struggle, I'll fetch Aunty's cleaver. Don't think I won't." The glint in his eye told me he would enjoy it too.

The heat curled up the stairs towards us, a suffocation already crushing hard against my chest. I tried to calm my breathing but my body was pulsating with panic and anger and fear.

Ryan yanked me down the last step, his face in mine.

"Usually at this stage your blood has been drained and this part is like your funeral, your cremation." He ran a hand down my cheek. "I feel quite privileged to hear your last words. Your final screams."

I snapped at his hand, biting hard.

He squealed in pain and slammed me against the wall, knocking the wind from me.

"Do you want this to be slow and painful? Because that, I am happy to accommodate." He pressed a hand against my throat, laughing as I choked. I grabbed at his hands, flailing, trying to beg him to stop.

"That's enough." A figure stepped out from the shadows at the bottom of the stairs.

"Clara." Ryan dropped his grip and I gasped in air, coughing. "What are you doing here?"

Clara smiled sweetly. "I thought Viv might need a hand burning the evidence. Perhaps you do too?"

Ryan puffed his chest. "Not at all. You know this is my area of expertise."

"Yes." I caught the scorn in Clara's voice and slipped away from Ryan, taking advantage of his loosened grip.

"Why don't you stock up the incinerator, Ryan? Open the door and get it ready?"

Ryan snatched the wooden pole from Clara's grip, irritated with her orders. As he stepped towards the silver doorway, unhooking the latch, Clara swooped towards him, stabbing his neck with a needle. He roared in anger, stumbling towards the open door, the wooden pole tilting, catching a flame.

"Get back," Clara motioned for me to move and I jumped backwards, out in to the passageway, screaming when a hand clamped down on my shoulder.

"It's okay. It's me, Ana."

I stared. "Ana? You're here." My legs buckled, and Ana grabbed me, holding me tight.

"It's okay, I've got you."

I clung on, sobs rising. "I can't believe you're here. You found us."

"We're going to get you out." Another voice appeared out of the darkness.

"Elliot." I cried harder. I shook my head. "Clara, she won't let us."

"She's helping us. It's okay." Ana's voice was soothing, reassuring.

Uncontrollable tremors shot through my body. "I thought I was going to die. They wanted to burn us." I started to babble. "Seb's upstairs. We have to get him."

Tears streamed down Ana's face as she hugged me. "I'm sorry, Hope. I'm so sorry." I hugged back tightly, my mind not able to process she was actually real.

Elliot moved towards the staircase and I detangled from Ana, brain kicking into gear, frantic to get to Seb.

Clara ran out of the incinerator room, a blaze of fire roaring across the floor, flames igniting bags Viv had failed to dispose of.

"We need to leave now. Viv is waiting outside with a car. We'll take you somewhere safe." Clara's voice was frantic. I stared at Ryan, collapsed unconscious on the floor, flames rushing towards him. I blocked out the image, instead focusing on Clara.

"Seb's in the kitchen with Margaret. We can't leave without him."

Clara shook her head, exasperated. "Fine. Hurry." We clambered up the stairs, coughing as the smoke trailed up behind us.

The kitchen lay empty, a fire alarm beeping as if in mockery.

"Where is he?" Elliot turned to me and I shook my head in panic, slamming through the door out to the main foyer.

"Seb," I shouted his name, again and again. Elliot followed, our voices echoing across the foyer.

An engine roared outside and we ran to the front door. Elliot spun the handle, tugging and kicking. "It's locked."

Ana ran forward, jangling keys. "Try these."

Elliot inserted the biggest first, nothing. He spun to the next, rattling the handle in frustration. A door squeaked open to the right, leading from the annexe.

Dr Carmichael stepped out, with Phoenix and Barb.

"Well, well. What an interesting group we have here." Dr Carmichael's eyes flicked towards Ana. "I should have known not to trust a child."

I shot Ana a curious look. She bowed her head, cheeks blooming pink. She released her hand from mine and I felt uneasy.

Elliot swore under his breath, hands shaking as he spun another key to try in the lock.

Clara stepped forward. "Mum, are you okay?" Barb smiled at her, no trace of recognition in her eyes.

"Of course she is." Dr Carmichael looped his arm through Barb's, pulling her in closer by his side. "We have to be leaving now, Clara." He sniffed the air, smoke and chemical smells burling under the kitchen door. "I believe there was a commotion downstairs. It won't be long until the whole place is ablaze."

He strode towards Elliot and pushed him aside. "Allow me." He stuck a key in the lock and the door clicked open.

"Where's Seb?" I grabbed at Dr Carmichael's

jacket. He brushed me off and nodded outside towards a black van, the engine rolling. "We're taking him with us." He turned to Phoenix, swinging his suitcase "Come along now, Phoenix. It's going to be a bumpy ride along the back fields. You might want to sit up front with Pollock and Billy."

"Where are you going?" Clara stepped forward, shaking her head. "It's over, Dad."

Dr Carmichael turned to his daughter. "No it is not, you stupid girl. We are moving far from here and we will start again like we talked about. I have plenty of friends in high places to make us disappear."

"Just leave Seb behind. Please," I pleaded. "You don't need to take him with you."

Dr Carmichael shot me a look of disdain. "He'll be easier to manage now that he thinks you're dead. I've decided he's too valuable to waste."

Clara stepped in front of him, blocking his path. "The only stupid thing I've done was helping you."

Dr Carmichael sighed impatiently. "Clara, we do not have time for your hysterics. It's time to go. Come on." He grabbed her arm.

"No." Clara pushed back. "I'm done with your bidding."

"If you get caught, you'll go to jail," he snarled in her face.

"It will be worth it if you come with me." She shot back, eyes burning. Her hand was swift, the needle plunging deep as she pierced her father's neck.

Phoenix cried out, rushing forward.

Barb wrung her hands, shaking her head. "Not a silly girl. She's not a silly girl."

Dr Carmichael stumbled, pressing a hand against the glass door. "My own daughter…"

Clara shot him a look of disgust. "I'm ashamed to

be your daughter."

She took her mum's hand, smiling reassuringly. "You're okay, Mum. It's all going to be okay."

Phoenix reached out to Dr Carmichael. "What did she do? What did she do?" She looked round at all of us, eyes brimming with tears as she clung on to Dr Carmichael. She stumbled forward, swinging the front door open, eyes on the black van. "Billy," Phoenix shouted above the roar of the engine. "Come and help, Billy."

"No," I rushed forward, hurrying after her. "Phoenix, wait. You don't have to go."

She turned to me, shaking off my grip. "This is the life I want, why don't you get that? I can't go back. Not now." She touched her bump. "Finlay and Patricia will look after me."

Billy jumped down from the van, smiling in delight when he saw me. "Hope! You're okay. Hello, Hope."

Phoenix grabbed Billy's arm, motioning to the doctor. "I need you to help me, Billy. We need to get Dr Carmichael in the van." Billy slung Dr Carmichael's arm over his shoulder, half-dragging him along the gravel.

I ran forward, Elliot and Ana following. "Seb." His name was raw in my throat as I shouted again and again, willing him to appear. We followed Billy round to the other side of the van as he slid the door open. He turned to me. "Are you coming with us, Hope?"

"No. She's not." Phoenix jumped in behind them, pulling the door shut before we could stop her.

"No! Wait. Seb!" I banged the side of the van, nails scratching the paint as they lurched forward.

My heart dropped as Pollock crunched the gears.

Elliot ran round to the front of the van, throwing himself on the bonnet. Pollock hit the accelerator, the engine revving as the van surged forward, throwing Elliot to the ground. Elliot swore, clutching his knee.

"Seb!" I screamed, running after the van, dust and stones swirling. Ana caught up beside me, the two of us slowing to a halt, watching helplessly as the van sped through the gates, veering right, rolling across the fields.

"What just happened?" She stared at me in shock, out of breath.

I shook my head, tears choking my words. He was gone.

Chapter Forty-Four
Hope

"But I don't understand." Elliot paced up and down beside Martha's car. "Where did the van go? I thought that dirt road was the only road in and out of here?"

Police cars, fire engines and ambulances with the lights spinning blue were parked along the gravel. A woman tucked a silver blanket over my shoulders and handed me hot liquid which tasted of nothing. Someone told me I was safe now, that everything was going to be okay. But it wasn't. Not without him. They led me to the back of an ambulance and suggested I lie down. Ana hovered and asked if she could come and they let her sit beside me. I closed my eyes so I didn't need to listen to her apologies. She kept saying she wished she'd found me the first time she was here, that she should never have left without me.

It doesn't matter, I wanted to say. *Nothing matters. Seb is gone.*

Over the sound of Ana's apologies, I heard a familiar voice which cut through me to the bone. I jolted up, shrugging off the concerned hand of a paramedic as I jumped down from the ambulance, walking towards the angry shouts.

She stood tall and broad, her arms waving from beneath a wool cape, her hair coiffed. Her stance was aggressive, her face too close to Martha.

"Don't be ridiculous, officer. Who would you believe, the words of this senile housewife, or a respected head teacher?"

"Step back from me, you vile woman." There was anger burning in Martha's eyes and a roar to her voice that sparked a fire inside of me.

The police officer secured cuffs around Ms Turnberry's wrists, but still it didn't feel enough. Mr Darwin was already sitting in the back of a police car, head bowed, refusing to make eye contact with anyone.

I walked towards Ms Turnberry, my body shaking with the anger of everything I wanted to say. But I could only manage one word, "Why?"

She sneered at me. "I don't need to answer your questions."

I stepped closer, the police officer holding a hand up. I ignored him, needing to say something. "I hope every night when you go to sleep in your cell you remember me, you remember what you've done, you remember the lives that were lost because you wanted our blood, for what? For youth? Beauty?"

Ms Turnberry shook her head. "You were all contributing to something bigger than you can imagine. To maintain *the elite's* youth and health. It's called evolution." Her lips curled into a smile.

I snorted. "You're an ugly old cretin, rotten to your soul and nothing could ever change that."

Ms Turnberry's eyes flashed, her jowls trembling. The police officer motioned for me to step back as he walked Ms Turnberry to one of the waiting cars. I hoped she could feel my gaze burning indents into her back. *Rage, rage...Do not go gentle into that good night.*

Martha slid her hand into mine, her grip firm as she squeezed. She led me back to the ambulance, telling the other police officers I would give my statement later, after my health had been checked over.

I would make sure they listened carefully. I wanted them to hear my story and understand it all. I imagined Ms Turnberry in a cell, my words knocking her down, making her shrink, making her power disappear.

In the ambulance, I flinched when a paramedic secured something around my arm. I shivered under the blanket and someone squeezed my knee in reassurance. Maybe it was the paramedic, maybe it was Ana, who had insisted on coming along for the ride while Martha and Elliot followed in her car.

I kept my eyes shut, thinking that the gesture held no real warmth. A tear rolled down my cheek as the song Seb and I listened to played in my head on a loop.

Don't leave me.

*

I lay in the half-light of my hospital bed, staring at the ceiling, heavy medication making it easy for me to detach my brain and keep my emotions numb. They'd decided to keep me in longer than expected due to severe hydration, and to monitor 'my mood'. Martha smiled wryly when I voiced my theory that 'professionals' would be paranoid about how high-profile the scandal was and everyone was terrified they would become part of it, if they didn't ensure I receive top care.

I listened to the quiet chatter of the women in the beds across from me, unsure what brought them here. Tomorrow my child protection officer would take me home to the Browns. A lot of people didn't think it was a good idea for me to go back to where 'it all went wrong' but I was adamant that it was at the

Browns, actually, that things started to go right. I needed the support the Browns were willing to offer, to help me get through the next few months, when I was going to have to testify against a string of angry people that had been left to face the music. Even with the unravelling of the powerful ring of police chiefs, social workers, teachers, even a couple of politicians, there was still no lead on where the black van had gone. Viv and Clara claimed to know nothing. I didn't want to think about the day I'd have to face Clara in court. I hoped her mum was being well-looked after now, in a proper home.

No one voiced to me what I knew must be true: all of it continued, somewhere else.

A whole new group of kids out there. Seb still out there. Lost.

I squeezed my eyes shut, tasting the salt of my tears. I grabbed the dressing gown Martha left last night, pulling it tight around me, sliding my feet into the furry slippers, the warmth spreading through my toes. Simple gifts that made me feel safe and cared for. The dressing gown hugged my body as I padded out into the corridor, the fluorescent lights an assault against my tired eyes. I walked slowly, the hum of the vending machine luring me towards sugary snacks. I smiled as I emptied some change from the dressing gown pocket. *Still a feeder, Martha.*

I typed in numbers, watching as a bar of chocolate fell and thudded into the drawer at the bottom.

"I could kill for a Mars Bar."

The voice was an electric shock down my spine. I stared, unable to find words, blinking in confusion. I reached out instinctively to touch the cast on his arm. I shook my head, unable to process that he was here. Standing in front of me. Alive. Free.

Seb stared back. "Is it really you? Or am I hallucinating? The drugs in here are pretty amazing. Please tell me you're really here."

I grabbed his hand and saw the relief and terror and exhaustion I had been feeling the past week reflecting back at me in his eyes. A million questions were on my lips. "How did you get here? I thought you were…What happened to your arm?"

"Don't cry." Seb ran his thumb down my cheek, catching tears I couldn't hold back.

Attempting an awkward hug, I slid my arms around his waist, trying to avoid knocking his cast. He held me tight with his good arm.

"I managed to jump out the van when we were on a quiet road. Then I kept running. And eventually found a petrol station and passed out. They called an ambulance and the police."

I jerked back. "Did they catch them?"

Seb shook his head. "I don't think so. I've been here for days and it's the first thing I asked the nurses, today."

Days. I traced my fingers over the plaster cast. "Why did no one tell me you were here?"

"This is the first day I've been properly awake." He flashed me his lopsided smile, holding up his arm. "I had to get surgery. I still feel woozy."

He glanced over his shoulder, as if expecting someone to drag him back to his room. "Technically I should still be in bed, but I'm starving."

I turned back to the vending machine, jangling the change in my pocket. "What would sir like?"

Seb grabbed my hand, smiling, his eyes changing colour in the light. "Right now, all I want is you."

Warmth spread down to my toes as I tilted my head up towards him, my lips finding his, an ache deep inside me filling with light and love.

It felt like home.

*

Back at the Browns I pulled out Lucy's letter, allowing myself to absorb her words properly. I tried to read with a fresh perspective, wanting to understand her reasons, telling myself she had been trying to do the right thing.

My eyes fell to the lines, *Please don't be sad, or angry.* But I was, many times a day. And that was okay. Because a lot of the time I allowed myself to be happy too.

A soft knock on the door caused me to turn.

"Come in," I called, folding the letter away into the top drawer of my dresser, beside my tarot pouch.

I turned to see Martha carrying a steaming mug of tea and plate of muffins. She laid them down on the dresser, squeezing my shoulder. "Fresh out of the oven. Blueberry as requested."

The sweetness spread through my body as I took a bite. She glanced at my open drawer, and held up a finger, as if remembering something. I watched curiously as she walked towards my bedside table, opening the unused bottom drawer.

My heart leapt as she pulled out a tarot card. She came towards me, tracing a finger over the goddess with the fiery hair. "Edward managed to clean it up for you. I suspected this one might be your favourite."

"I thought it was lost."

Martha placed the card in my hand, holding her own over the top. "I kept it safe for you." She smiled, her eyes full of apologies and affection. "Until you came home."

I stood, pulling her into a hug. "Thank you."

She held me tight.

Chapter Forty-Five
Ana

Maisie squirted the glue too hard and a blob landed on Ana's knuckle. Maisie giggled and stuck a star on top.

"Just be careful." Ana narrowed her eyes in a mock stern look. She pressed another photo into place, admiring their month's efforts. Mum enjoyed looking through the albums they created, snapshots of family activity they thought might help her process short term memories. The medication seemed to be keeping everything stable for now but they were all conscious that could change. The albums were fun activities that might become more important as time went on.

Mum popped her head round the conservatory door. "I printed off some of that poem Hope emailed you. How about we paste it in at the start?" She scooted in beside them, taking the book in her hands, placing a neat square of white paper inside the cover. "Hand me the glue, Maisie."

Maisie leaned forward, reading slowly. "Do not go gentle into that good night."

"Rage, rage against the dying of the light." Ana read the words in time with Mum's voice which was loud and determined as she recited the last lines. Ana knew she wanted to try anything that could help and it made her feel better, to know they were all in this together.

Ana's phone beeped and she sat up when she saw Elliot's name:

Hope and I are on your street. Come out for a walk?

Maisie strained to read her screen. "Is that your boyfriend?"

"No." Ana slid her phone in her pocket, relief washing over her that they had started to include her again. That Elliot's anger had subsided. Hope reassured her she understood how persuasive Dr Carmichael could be, and the desperation Ana must have felt to try anything to help her mum. But it didn't stop Ana feeling guilty every time she thought about what could have happened, her gut twisting at the realisation she had abandoned Hope when she needed her most. Ana vowed to spend every day from now on making up for it.

Hope told her that she'd tracked down the home Barbara Carmichael was in and she asked Ana if she'd go with her to visit sometime to make sure she was okay. Ana didn't fully understand why Hope wanted anything to do with the old woman. Hope tried to explain it was her way of thanking Clara for what she did in the end, that her involvement had started with good intentions. Hope said she needed to find positive ways of processing what had happened. That was something her own mum taught her, she said, to never let the bad feelings smother the good. Ana vowed to try to live by that too.

*

The frost sparkled under the streetlights as they walked side by side, Hope in the middle, a spark returning to her eyes, her voice more animated, as she told them about Ruth's new puppy. After Ruth testified against her managers, she turned down the offer to return to her social work role, choosing to move far away and start her own business. Hope didn't know where she'd gone, just that she was happy. Ana smiled at the photo Ruth messaged, a selfie lying in the grass with her cute Labrador puppy on one side, grinning girlfriend on the other.

Hope had a child protection officer who visited her regularly at the Browns and Hope said the woman was puzzled as to why she would want to return to her old placement and old high school. All the people who thought they knew what was best really didn't have a clue.

As they turned the corner a door opened and a girl stretched down to pick up a cat meowing at her door.

"Jenna!" Hope called, rushing forward.

Jenna turned, expression wary until she noticed the smiles and her shoulders visibly relaxed. The town hadn't been kind to Jenna and her family. Jenna had to testify against her dad and uncle and the thought of that made Ana feel ill, for both her and her mum. Ana noted the For Sale board secured to the lamppost beside their front lawn.

"Hey," Jenna waved, then turned to go back inside.

"Wait." Hope rushed to her gate. "I haven't seen you in school so I didn't get the chance to thank you. Thank you so much. For everything. For being so brave."

Jenna shrugged. "Yeah, well. I figured I probably owed you one." She smiled awkwardly. Ana felt a prickle of shame, at the fact it had taken Jenna of all people to make her finally help Hope too.

They resumed walking and Elliot pointed up at the sky. "Look, a crescent moon." He caught Ana's eye and smiled, and she knew he was remembering their story in English, and it filled her with a warm glow, knowing he didn't hate her.

Hope tilted her palms up. "Hey, look, it's snowing." She spun on her toe, pirouetting off the pavement. Brakes screeched and Ana grabbed her arm, heart thundering as a BMX bike skidded to a halt. A shiver ran down Ana's spine as she pulled Hope back, remembering her first encounter with Dr Carmichael on this street.

Hope wriggled free from Ana's grip, rushing towards the boy on the bike.

Seb hauled the BMX up on to the pavement, flashing them all a grin. "What's happening?" Even although Seb had chosen to apply for his own accommodation, he was only a train ride away and visited Oakridge often.

Ana caught the look that passed between Hope and Seb, the happiness radiating from their smiles. Hope didn't talk much about her experience inside the house, but any time she did, she told Ana she would never have held it together without Seb. He was the one good thing to come out of this nightmare.

Seb grabbed Hope around the waist, whooping with laughter as they whirled, blurs of colour spinning with the snow.

Like a little bit of magic in the dark.

EPILOGUE

As midnight struck, a melody of cries echoed through the house. Phoenix shouted for a mother she never wanted to resemble, as her daughter squirmed and screamed into the world. Faye cut the cord and Phoenix cried with relief and joy. Phoenix pulled her baby close, marvelling at her perfect rose bud lips, stroking her delicate skin.

"Hello beautiful," she whispered, her heart exploding with love. She stared in wonder as her daughter calmed, her cries subsiding into small hiccups. Phoenix rocked her gently, a bundle of pure perfection. She whispered softly, vowing to keep her daughter safe and to love her with every inch of her being.

Phoenix closed her eyes, an overwhelming mix of adrenaline and exhaustion pumping through her veins as Faye helped her lie back in her own freshly made bed, the delivery trolley wheeled to one side.

Her eyes flew open at the sensation of a gentle tug, her grip tightening around her baby as Patricia smiled down at them.

"There, there, Phoenix. We need to take the little one to get her checked and cleaned up. You lie back and rest."

Phoenix hesitated, mesmerised by her daughter's chubby cheeks. She never wanted to let her go.

Faye placed a hand on Phoenix's shoulder, encouraging her to relent. She felt a tug in her heart as Patricia rocked the babe in her arms, cooing and smiling as if doting on a treasured granddaughter.

Phoenix startled when Dr Carmichael entered the room, holding out his arms, nodding in impatience at Patricia, not even glancing in her direction to check she had survived the long and gruelling labour. A flash of hunger and calculation shone in his eyes as he took her daughter in his arms, her wails of protest cutting through Phoenix's soul.

A chill shuddered through her as the doctor and Patricia exited the room, taking her joy with them.

A cry from an older girl seeped through the walls, in alternative waves to the fading echo of her baby. *A symphony of sorrow*, Phoenix thought, anxiety prickling her skin. Her heart pounded at the thought of her baby becoming a part of any of this.

"Rest now, Phoenix. Your daughter is in good hands." Faye smiled, no reassurance in her tone. "I'll look in on you in a few hours. Get some sleep."

Phoenix waited until the clip of Faye's footsteps faded into nothing. She had to be quick, before exhaustion swallowed her resolve. She reached into the top drawer of her bedside table, flinching at the effort of pulling the tape off, releasing the phone from the top panel so that it dropped into her hand.

She pressed the power button, screen glowing blue in the dark, relief flooding through her.

Clara's parting gift the day the old house had been compromised. *"Don't limit yourself to a life with them."*

Phoenix had ensured she hid both the phone and charger from sight, pinning them both to the top of her drawer, charging it late at night. Just in case.

She pictured her daughter in Dr Carmichael's arms. The fear and surge of protection she felt made her understand what she had to do.

It was time. She was ready.

Phoenix punched in three digits she knew would bring help. That would end all of this for good.

"Hello." Her voice shook as the call connected. "I need to report a crime."

THE END

Author Note

My initial idea for *Young Blood* stemmed from an article I read about an American start-up company 'Ambrosia', founded by a medical school graduate in 2016 which sold 'young blood transfusions' (from young people into older people). Charging a large sum of money for these transfusions, they claimed a range of health benefits such as offering treatment for Alzheimer's.

This sparked off the idea of having a powerful doctor set up a premium club for wealthy individuals to access pure plasma transfusions at a premium price. Capturing vulnerable young people from the care system to 'feed' the club members struck me as a depressingly plausible scenario.

In my day job I work with vulnerable teenagers on a daily basis. Often young people in the care system can encounter instability and inconsistent homes throughout their lives. Within my family I have also seen the challenging effects of Alzheimer's. The scenarios within *Young Blood* are fictional, but the topics are very much close to my heart.

When I write YA fiction I am always driven by a desire to give young people a voice, to see them overcome some kind of injustice, and to explore the dynamics of family relationships.

In *Young Blood* I wanted to leave at the heart of the story a sense of love overcoming adversity.

Acknowledgements

Thank you for the unfaltering support throughout the writing of this book from my writer Mum Rosemary and my husband Chris who both offered invaluable advice and encouragement. Meticulous editorial and technical support from Rosemary made it possible for *Young Blood* to launch into the world.

Special thanks to Elaine who offered insightful feedback and structural editorial support which helped me refine and add layers to the story.

Thank you to Rebecca aka Dainty Dora for the technical design support and helping me fine tune my cover design, transforming it into a fabulous cover.

Thank you to writers Elizabeth, Dawn and Sandra for hosting a truly inspirational Chasing Time Writing Retreat back in 2018 which allowed me to extract the first scenes and an outline of *Young Blood* out of my head and down on paper.

The Gothic house setting couldn't have been more perfect and many descriptions of the house in this book are taken from the corridors of Rosely House Hotel!

Thank you to my writing pal Leona who helped me understand some welfare technicalities during our chats at the retreat.

Thank you to the young person who emailed me an honest and emotional account of their time within the care system. It helped me understand the challenges encountered from a young person's perspective.

And thank YOU, reader, for reading my book. Until you start turning the pages my stories can never truly be told.

Acknowledgements

Thank you for the unfaltering support throughout the writing of this book from my writer Mum Rosemary and my husband Chris who both offered invaluable advice and encouragement. Meticulous editorial and technical support from Rosemary made it possible for *Young Blood* to launch into the world.

Special thanks to Elaine who offered insightful feedback and structural editorial support which helped me refine and add layers to the story.

Thank you to Rebecca aka Dainty Dora for the technical design support and helping me fine tune my cover design, transforming it into a fabulous cover.

Thank you to writers Elizabeth, Dawn and Sandra for hosting a truly inspirational Chasing Time Writing Retreat back in 2018 which allowed me to extract the first scenes and an outline of *Young Blood* out of my head and down on paper.

The Gothic house setting couldn't have been more perfect and many descriptions of the house in this book are taken from the corridors of Rosely House Hotel!

Thank you to my writing pal Leona who helped me understand some welfare technicalities during our chats at the retreat.

Thank you to the young person who emailed me an honest and emotional account of their time within the care system. It helped me understand the challenges encountered from a young person's perspective.

And thank YOU, reader, for reading my book. Until you start turning the pages my stories can never truly be told.

Printed in Great Britain
by Amazon